A Summer Promise

Katie Flynn has lived for many years in the north-west. A compulsive writer, she started with short stories and articles and many of her early stories were broadcast on Radio Merseyside. She decided to write her Liverpool series after hearing the reminiscences of family members about life in the city in the early years of the twentieth century. For many years she has had to cope with ME, but has continued to write. She also writes as Judith Saxton.

Katie Flynn

A Summer Promise

arrow books

3 5 7 9 10 8 6 4 2

Arrow Books
20 Vauxhall Bridge Road
London SW1V 2SA

Arrow Books is part of the Penguin Random House group of companies
whose addresses can be found at global.penguinrandomhouse.com.

Penguin
Random House
UK

First published in UK by Century in 2015
First published in paperback by Arrow Books in 2015

www.randomhouse.co.uk

A CIP catalogue record for this book is available from the British Library.

Typeset in Palatino by Palimpsest Book Production Limited,
Falkirk, Stirlingshire

Penguin Random House is committed to a sustainable future for
our business, our readers and our planet. This book is made from
Forest Stewardship Council® certified paper.

MIX
Paper from
responsible sources
FSC® C018179

Printed and bound in Great Britain by Clays Ltd, St Ives plc

For Ken Mack who helps others without thought for himself and always has a cheerful smile.

Acknowledgements

Once more I should like to thank Jean Hughes for helping me to get a picture of life in the ATS; how those girls stuck the conditions and the work I shall never know, but I take off my hat to them. Thanks also to Carol Hainstock for telling me about the Ripon Hornblower and the limestone caves as well as some of the beauty spots (which I could reach) for which the Yorkshire Dales are famous.

Dear Reader,

I started writing this particular book when I decided to have a bit of a break. My friend Carol highly recommended the Yorkshire Dales, so Brian and I set off to have a look at a part of the country we seem to have missed, and were immediately enchanted. Not only is it beautiful and magical but, as I soon discovered, it is believed to be the setting for a book I have always loved; *The Water Babies* by the Reverend Charles Kingsley. I immediately got out my illustrated version of the story and began to research, which was a joy. Just find yourself a beck in the Dales, and there are a great many to choose from, and look into the depths of the water, and if you have a good imagination you will immediately begin to see tiny figures going about their business. When Tom became a water baby he was four inches high, so when Maddy begins her search and embroils her friends in that same search she is looking for a tiny boy quite easily mistaken for a flickering trout or some other denizen of the not-so-deep waters.

From then on my characters began to make

themselves felt. I saw with awe the Malham Cove cliffs down which the little climbing boy was thought to have descended and I, who have no head for heights, did not wonder that he came 'all over queer' in the cottage of the kind old lady.

But I digress; my characters were growing up and leading their own lives, very different lives from those conjured up by the Reverend Kingsley. There was Maddy looking after her cross-grained old gran and the neighbours and friends who take over her care as Maddy, now an adult, joins the ATS as a 'girl gunner' and moves away from her beloved Dales.

So in this book, you can get to relive your childhood and learn about the far from glamorous life of women in the Second World War.

I do hope you enjoy reading it as much as I enjoyed writing it!

All best wishes

Katie Flynn

Prologue

Madeleine Hebditch, secure in her little truckle bed in the room at the farm which had been hers all the time she had lived here, was fast asleep and dreaming. It was a familiar one – the dream of the dresses – and sometimes she thought it was more like memories than a dream, so real was it and so happy at first, and then spiked with such a cruel sense of loss.

The dream always started logically, with little Madeleine no more than three or four years old, certainly too young to have started school, and dressed in a wonderful pink frock with a wreath of tiny roses on her straight and shining hair. Her mother was trying to pin the wreath securely, but the roses did not wish to remain upon her daughter's small head, and every time she stood back exclaiming 'That's fixed it!' Maddy would move, the wreath would slide off and the two of them would collapse into giggles.

Later in the dream she was in a church and knew that she was at a wedding and must behave with decorum, for she and another girl of about her own age were both bridesmaids and train bearers. Solemn as judges, they dared not even smile until the ceremony was over and they were being led by their mothers out of the churchyard and into the hall where the wedding breakfast was already spread out on long trestle tables.

Then the dream changed, and for a moment the scene was obscured by mist. The pink dress had disappeared and Maddy was wearing school uniform, a gingham dress in a rather dowdy shade of brown, and when she put her hand to her head there was no wreath of roses but only two tortoiseshell hair slides to keep stray ends of hair off her face. Her mother, wonderfully pretty in a pale green silk dress, had hold of her hand and was murmuring that everyone had to go to school, that she was going to the very best school in Southampton and she must try to be happy there. 'We could have sent you to a boarding school, but Daddy and I could not bear to part with you for a whole term at a time, so you're going to be a day girl. You'll come home every afternoon to our dear little house by the docks, and when Daddy gets shore leave he'll join us the minute he can,' she told her daughter. 'And every night when I put you to bed I'll tell you another episode of the story you love the most.'

Maddy had been sucking her thumb as she always did when relaxing, but now she removed her thumb with a plop and spoke for the first time. 'You mean the one about Tom, the poor little chimney sweep, who became a water baby?' she said hopefully. 'That's my favourite of all your stories. And don't forget,

Mummy, you promised that when Daddy next had leave you would take me to water baby country so I might see little Tom for myself.'

Click. The scene changed again. Now they were in Daddy's new car. She was in the back with the beautiful picnic basket whilst Mummy sat in the passenger seat and Daddy drove. They were on their way to visit Maddy's grandma who lived on a farm in the Yorkshire Dales and would show Maddy the animals and birds she kept, and perhaps they might even see a water baby! And Maddy had leaned forward and tugged Daddy's shoulder, asking him if they were nearly there, and the car had swerved and crashed into a wall and no matter how often she dreamed the dream she never expected the terrible crash or the screams. Terror had gripped her, but when her mother shouted at her to run as far from the car as she could she had scrambled out of the wreck and tried to pull her parents free, but she was only five, and before either could be moved there was a belch of flame and a great deal of screaming and Maddy felt herself lifted bodily and carried away from the car though she fought to get free, to return to her parents. But she remained cradled in a strange person's arms and bidden not to look. Only she had, of course. Had seen the flames higher than a house, had heard someone saying it was the petrol and adding that no one could survive such a conflagration. She had continued to fight her captor, screaming: 'Mummy! Daddy!' But the arms only held her tighter.

'It's too late, sweetheart,' her rescuer had said gently. 'They've gone; be thankful that you, at least, are still alive.'

But she had not been thankful. Her parents were her raison d'être and without them life held no charm, and the pain of her loss was so great that she could not face it. She knew that her happy life was over and that what was to come was now her responsibility and hers alone. As the woman bore her away she knew there would be no one now to tell her bedtime stories, to tuck her up, to walk through the quiet streets of Southampton to deliver her safely to school.

Click. The scene changed again; this time she was wearing a drooping black dress, far too large for her, and the quiet select streets of Southampton loomed out of the mist and became the farmyard at Crowdale where an old woman waited by the kitchen door to take her in. 'I can't promise her much except food, clothing and an education at the village school,' the old woman said. 'And in return she can give me a hand about the farm.' She scarcely so much as glanced at Maddy. 'Now that her parents are dead I reckon I'm her only living relative. I'm not fond of children, but you needn't worry – I'll do right by her, see she's brought up to be of some use in this world.' She had turned to Maddy. 'Is that all you've got? One tiddy little suitcase? Ah well . . .' she had looked disparagingly over Maddy's clothing and buttoned shoes, 'I expect the rest of your gear will be sent on

4

later. Have you got any clothes suitable for farm work? You don't want to muck up your Sunday best.'

'No,' Maddy said in a tiny voice. She plucked the black dress. 'They gave me this to wear at the funeral. My aunt Jerusha says it's good stout material . . .'

Her grandmother interrupted without apology. 'Aunt she calls herself, does she? Well aunt or no aunt, she was asked if she would take you on and she said she couldn't, so you'll have to make do with me.' She had given Maddy a tight little smile. 'Come along in, girl. I'll show you your bedroom.'

And then there was a sense of terrible sadness and Maddy awoke to find tears running down her cheeks.

Lying in her small bed, as she had so many times in the past, Maddy tried to recall the dear little house by the docks, and the school she had attended for so short a time, but without success. She knew, of course, that there had been a car crash, but her knowledge ended there; she could remember nothing prior to being plucked from the burning wreckage, save that they had been on their way to visit her gran.

She had asked Gran, of course, told her she had nightmares, but Gran had merely shrugged. 'You'll outgrow 'em,' she had said placidly. 'Don't worry your head about it. Now let's get on with our chores or we shall be behind all day.'

Chapter One

1938

Maddy came out of the old farmhouse at a stealthy trot. She had no wish to alert Gran to the fact that she had left the house a great deal earlier than usual, but if there was one thing at which Gran excelled it was sleeping. In fact, when Maddy had tiptoed past the door of her room, the only sound from within had been that of resounding snores, interspersed with the little mumblings and chokings which escape from someone deep asleep and probably dreaming.

Maddy smiled to herself; she could not help it. So much for getting up early and traversing the stairs as if each one were booby-trapped. She might have worn climbing boots and stamped loudly on every step as she landed on it, and Gran would have continued to snore.

She had wondered whether to draw back the faded red gingham curtains at the small windows in the kitchen, but decided against it. Why should she warn Gran that she was up and doing, for goodness' sake? And to be fair to Gran, she was unlikely to ask any questions. That was not her way. Maddy understood that her relative was a little embarrassed by the fact that it took her a long time nowadays to perform even the simplest task, for when Maddy had arrived at the farm Gran had been brisk and capable. Now, seven years later, she needed time to dress, longer to wash, and positively ages to sort out the necessary things to make herself and her granddaughter a fairly sustaining breakfast. So the fact that Maddy had got up early might be construed as criticism, and that was the last thing either of them wanted.

Ever since Gran had begun to slow down more tasks had fallen on Maddy, and though she had sometimes sighed impatiently when catching Gran half in and half out of her big, hand-knitted cardigan and waiting for someone – who else was there but Maddy? – to tug it up over her rounded, forward-stooping shoulders, she had had to learn tact. Gran did her best, but at times her own incapacity irked her and if Maddy was unkind enough to comment she would bring her black walking cane whistling round to land a blow on Maddy's bare legs or arms. Maddy would suck in her breath and mimic twice as much pain as she felt, and Gran would tell her that it served her right, that she must learn to respect her elders and not to give what Gran described as 'sauce'.

But today, she reflected as she slid quietly out of the back door and set out across the farmyard, she was so early that the sun was still below the horizon. Pale mist swirled across the meadows, and the fleeces of the sheep grazing on the sweet upland grass – not theirs, alas, but the flock belonging to Farmer Sutherland – steamed gently in the dawn, adding their own contribution to the pearly white and gold of the haze.

Maddy glanced to one side and saw that Snoops, the sheepdog, had raised his head to give her a doggy smile, his shaggy shoulders emerging from his kennel as he did so. Maddy shook her head at him, but his face was so full of hope that she relented, going over to the kennel and releasing his chain so that he came fully into the open, shaking himself vigorously, and then turning to look at her with that beaming smile, though of course it wasn't really a smile, Maddy reminded herself, rubbing the large, pricked ears. But it was a sign of pleasure, which was just as good, and anyway, who was she to cavil at the friendly greeting, she who got few such? True, Gran sometimes congratulated her on her work, but much less frequently than Maddy thought she might when you considered how hard she had to work now that Gran was not able to do as much as she had once done. But Gran was old; very, very old, Maddy reminded herself, and when people became very old then younger ones had to look out for them. Maddy did not think she could ever have *loved* Gran, but she respected her and took a certain amount of pride in looking after her, even when it interfered with her own life.

For Maddy was a dreamer, and her chief pleasure

was inventing stories in which she was usually the heroine and as such undertook Quests, Adventures or even Rescues, depending on what book she was engrossed in at any one moment. But Gran, who watched her with what Maddy could only conclude was a jealous eye, knew nothing of Maddy's secret imaginary life and would think it simply a waste of time when compared with digging the vegetable garden, weeding and feeding it, and finding the hens' cunningly hidden nests for the eggs which were a major part of their diet. There were even days when Maddy suspected that Gran begrudged the time she spent at school.

Maddy liked school, and she liked her teacher, Miss Parrott. A 'plain, desiccated old spinster' a school governor had once called her in Maddy's hearing, but she was loved by most of her pupils and, more to the point, she understood and sympathised with them. She knew Maddy was a dreamer and encouraged her to give her imagination full rein – though not during arithmetic lessons – and though she had never, she assured them, been good at games herself, she could appreciate the attraction which such sports as football and cricket held for a goodly number of her class. It was unfortunate that her nose was enormous, like the prow of a ship, and sometimes the boys called her 'Old Beaky' and worse, but it was never cruelly meant. Maddy suspected that she knew all about the nicknames, but what did it matter? The important thing was the affection with which all the children regarded her.

Maddy reached the rough track which, if she had followed it, would have taken her down into the village. Today, however, she turned on to a different path, the one that led to Windhover Hall, the largest and most imposing house in the neighbourhood, which also happened to be the home of Maddy's best friend, Alice Thwaite.

Taking this path meant that Maddy had to walk alongside the beck, and she usually stopped to paddle where the water was calmest, but today she was impatient to reach her friend. The previous day Alice had met Maddy out of school and had whispered, as she and Maddy turned away from the village, that if Maddy could get away early in the morning and come to the summer house – their usual meeting place – she had a surprise for her, something her friend would love. She would not say what it was, merely smiling mysteriously, but Maddy hoped it would be a book.

The school did not possess such a thing as a library, only a shelf of well-thumbed volumes of fairy stories, schoolgirl adventures and Blackie's annuals, alongside improving books with a religious bent. But Miss Parrott did her best to offer those of her pupils who enjoyed reading more choice by bringing her own books to class and lending them out as though she herself were a tiny public library. This was sufficient for most of the class, but not for Maddy. She could not remember a time when she had been unable to read, and as soon as Miss Parrott realised that little Madeleine Hebditch could do so better than some pupils twice her age she made it her special task to provide the child with reading matter.

At first Maddy had been happy enough with the books Miss Parrott provided, but then one day, about a year ago, Alice Thwaite had come into her ken. Alice did not go to the village school but had a governess, and in the normal course of things the two girls would not have crossed one another's paths, but it had been a Saturday morning and Maddy had gone down to the village with a basket of eggs and cress to sell at the market. Alice had been given her pocket money and had decided to spend it on some of the home-made sweets which Mrs Foulks from the post office sold on the front of her stall while her husband looked after the shop.

Maddy had eyed the other girl with considerable interest. Alice wore a silky pinafore dress fine enough for a party, Maddy thought, and she had rich dark curls tied back from her rosy face with a blue hair ribbon. She had large blue eyes framed by curling dark lashes, and she always seemed to be smiling. She was both taller and considerably plumper than Maddy, who had watched as Alice chose her sweets and handed over more money than Maddy earned in a whole day helping on Mr Sutherland's farm. As Alice had turned away from the stall Maddy must have caught her eye, for the other girl held out the little white bag, her eyes sparkling. 'Have one; go on, help yourself,' she commanded. 'Everyone likes sweeties, don't they?' And then, as Maddy still hesitated, she had seized her hand and tipped a chunk of toffee into Maddy's palm.

Maddy knew about sweets, of course she did, but she had not then been in the happy position of tasting such things since her parents' death. She had eyed the giver, then the chunk of toffee, then popped it into her mouth. 'Thanks,' she said as soon as she could speak, for the chunk had been a generous one. 'Only I can't give you anything except a bunch of watercress.'

The other girl had laughed; a gay tinkle of amusement. 'That doesn't matter. Too many sweets are bad for one,' she had said. 'What's your name? I'm Alice Thwaite from Windhover Hall. My governess usually comes to the market with me but the poor thing has a shocking headache today so she's kept to her room. You?'

'I'm Madeleine Hebditch – everyone calls me Maddy – and I live with my gran at Larkspur Farm.'

'Larkspur; what a pretty name. It's that tall blue spike of flower, isn't it?'

'Yes, it is.' Curiosity got the better of her. 'You've not been at Windhover long, have you? Otherwise you'd know every farm and cottage in the neighbourhood. When did you come?'

She had been looking into Alice's face as they talked

and had seen a shadow of pain cross it, wiping out the happiness for a moment. 'After my mother died,' she said quietly. 'My father owns a company in Bombay and couldn't return to England, so at first I was sent to a boarding school down south.' She had hesitated, looking searchingly at Maddy. 'But I . . . I was very unhappy and my uncle decided that I should come and live with him since he has no children of his own. And then my aunt said that I was not to go to the village school but to have a governess, so they engaged Miss Spender.'

'I see,' Maddy had said doubtfully, for the truth was she had not seen at all. Surely this pretty, self-confident girl should not be shut away with only adults for company? Hesitantly, she had put her thoughts into words. 'A governess is fine, I'm sure, but how do you meet other children? If you came to the village school you'd have plenty of friends.'

'Yes, Miss Spender said the same,' Alice had said gloomily. 'The truth is, Maddy – is it all right to call you Maddy? – that when my uncle suggested the village school my aunt thought I'd have difficulties. You see, I struggle when it comes to reading. I can manage little words, but I soon get lost.'

'Gosh,' Maddy had said, sounding as horrified as she felt. 'If I couldn't read I'd – I'd die.' Such had been her horror that she forgot her awe of this beautifully dressed and superior child. 'I read lots and lots, only there are no books at Larkspur and I've already read

14

all the ones Miss Parrott, my teacher, lends us.' She had looked hopefully at her companion. 'Do you have books of your own? If you do, I could read them to you. I'd like that.'

She had spoken tentatively, fearing to be thought a show-off, but when she looked at her companion the other girl's face was wreathed in smiles. '*You'd* like it? How do you think I'd feel?' Alice had said joyfully. 'Oh, Maddy, it would be wonderful! You see, Miss Spender understands but I'm afraid Aunt Ruby thinks I'm just lazy. She tests me by making me read out of the Bible to her every night before I go to bed. Or rather she did, before she got bored . . . now she just lets me read a paragraph or two of anything I like. But even when I get it right – the reading, I mean – she's very critical, so if you could help me to memorise some paragraphs it would be wonderful. I'm a quick learner if someone will just read something out to me . . .'

As they talked the girls had been walking slowly away from the market, and at this point Maddy had uttered an exclamation of dismay and clutched her companion's arm. 'Oh, Alice, I'm so sorry! I must go back.' She indicated the basket on her arm. 'I've got eggs and watercress for Mrs Grundy to sell for me. I mustn't be late or I'll lose sales and my gran will be cross.' She had seen the look of puzzlement on her new friend's face and hastily began to explain as they turned back towards the market. 'We've a big flock of geese, a few ducks and some hens, so even though we eat a lot of eggs ourselves we've usually got quite a few to sell as well.' For some reason she felt better, as though the Hebditches' struggle to make ends meet and Alice's struggle to read put them at a similar disadvantage. She had been about to put her thoughts into words when she realised, with a stab of pure pleasure, that the other girl understood. Relieved, they had smiled at one another and begun to make plans for their next meeting.

But now, the sight of Windhover Hall and the small flying figure of Alice as she ran through the formal gardens which surrounded her home brought Maddy back to the present with a jolt. Ever since that first fateful day – which she called 'toffee share' in her mind – Maddy had had an excellent source of books in Alice, for there was a large library at Windhover which Maddy now frequented on a regular basis. The vast majority of children's books in that wonderful room were rather old-fashioned, having belonged to previous generations of the Thwaite family, but this did not put either girl off. Masses of reading matter was what Maddy desired more than anything else, and Alice simply wanted a friend of her own age, particularly someone who was more than willing to read to her from the volumes now at her command. Alice's uncle John had no idea that his niece was getting reading lessons both from Miss Spender and from a ragged little village girl, but he had not failed to notice the improvement and no longer talked of sending her back to boarding school.

Right now Maddy was afire with curiosity, for never before had Alice suggested they should meet as early as possible, seeming to assume that the surprise, whatever it might be, would need time to be enjoyed. She was advancing at a smart trot when, just as she reached the corner of the shrubbery, the sun inched over the horizon, a scarlet ball of flame, sending its long golden rays all across the Hall's formal gardens and creating a picture so beautiful that Maddy stopped dead in spite of herself. The shadows stretched long and blue in a way she had never seen, for she had never before come anywhere near the Hall's glorious gardens at this time of day.

Maddy had always been told that Crowdale village was the most beautiful in all the dales and for a moment she simply stood where she was and drank in the view. The fells rose vivid green against the blue of the sky and the beck babbled through the valley, chattering busily and glinting in the rays of the sun. My father was right, she told herself, and so was Gran, for both of them had said many times over that Yorkshire was the most beautiful county in England and Crowdale the most beautiful village. And if Crowdale is the most beautiful village, then Larkspur is the most loveliest farm and I really am as lucky as Gran tells me I am.

But she wasn't given long to admire the view.

Alice had already reached the summer house and was beckoning urgently, and as she obeyed the silent summons Maddy remembered that though Alice's aunt and uncle would still be tucked up in their beds the servants would be about their tasks and might easily stop to glance out of the long gleaming windows and note that Miss Alice and that little pal of hers from the village were up to some mischief. Accordingly she dodged from one patch of cover to another, then dived breathlessly into the summer house and sank on to the rustic bench within.

'Morning, Alice. Isn't it a grand one?' she said, staring pointedly at the bulge in the pocket of Alice's pale green cotton smock. 'Come on, show me the surprise! I came as quickly as I could but I can't stay long.'

Alice withdrew from her pocket a large, fawn-coloured volume, laying it tenderly upon the rustic bench and keeping her hand spread over what looked like an illustration on the cover.

'Ooh, there's a picture!' Maddy said. She tried to pull her friend's hand away, but Alice, giggling, resisted.

'Let me show you; you're going to be ever so surprised,' she said. 'And I mean to read to you for a change. The book is *The Water Babies* by somebody called Charles Kingsley. Uncle John found it for me and oh, Maddy, it's the illustrated version . . .'

Maddy squeaked; she could not help it. She had

always assumed her mother had made the water babies up but it was clearly not so. Someone had written the little chimney sweep's story down and she was about to see the very book! Her heart beat faster and her breath became short, but Alice, all unknowing, was still speaking.

'. . . and there are forty-eight colour pictures in the book so that even if you can't read . . . oh, you bad girl!'

For at that point Maddy's patience wore out and she tried to snatch the volume whilst Alice, still giggling, defended her property. 'Uncle John says I must take great care of the book because it's a first edition, whatever that may mean. Aunt Ruby said he wasn't to let me touch it with my grimy fingers but that was just her being careful; Uncle John knows I keep my hands spotless.' She cast a critical eye at Maddy but was able to give a nod of approval. Maddy would not have dreamed of so much as touching a book without first making sure her hands, too, were spotless. But the book must be very special indeed for Alice to have gone to such trouble, so she put them behind her back.

'You show me,' she demanded. 'You know my hands are always clean when we meet for a reading session. Miss Parrott says one should show respect for books and I'm sure we both do that.' She examined the cover illustration. 'Oh, Alice, isn't that the most beautiful picture in the whole world? And since your uncle gave you the book to read it must be a true story. Oh, I can't wait to read it and to look at all the pictures. Are we going to keep it in our hidey-hole?' The girls had discovered a loose floorboard underneath the rustic bench, and when they lifted it up they had realised that the cavity thus revealed would be ideal as a hiding place, not just for any book they wanted to keep hidden but for other things as well. Sometimes Alice snitched a bottle of Cook's home-made lemonade from the kitchen, and Maddy, not to be outdone, had brought apples and plums from the farm's ancient but still productive orchard. 'We could ration ourselves to one new picture every time we meet, then it would last us ages and ages.'

Alice, however, disagreed. 'Uncle John would want to know what I'd done with it,' she objected. 'Remember, he doesn't know you've been teaching me to read; he brought the book out from wherever he's been keeping it as a sort of reward for what he called "dear Alice's hard work". You see, he can't read print without his spectacles and when he's finished his dinner and Miss Spender sends me off to the drawing room to bid him and my aunt goodnight he sometimes gets me to read him the headlines in his newspaper or even, lately, to have a go at reading the whole of any article which interests him. I think he really lent me this wonderful book because – I don't know if you've noticed – each illustration has a few lines of writing telling the reader which part of the book the artist had in mind when he painted the picture. Uncle John thought I could enjoy the story just by looking at the pictures and reading what each one says underneath.'

'Yes, your uncle is a nice man,' Maddy agreed. 'But don't say we must rush through it and hand it back in a day or so because I couldn't bear it. Why, I've only read a bit called *The poor little chimney sweep* and already I can tell it's just the sort of book you and I like most. We'll need at least a week and maybe more if we're to enjoy it properly.' She removed her hands from their position behind her back and began to turn the pages. 'Oh, Alice, you laughed when I said I believe in fairies, but this is a book about real people, chimney sweeps and cooks, *real* people, so since the artist has drawn water babies in the book it must mean they truly are real too!'

'I don't see how you make that out,' Alice said slowly. 'Artists paint pictures of lots of things which aren't real at all. I think this man – Mr Theaker – simply drew the things the story is about, not because they really exist. Well, little boys who scramble up chimneys don't exist now, though I expect they did when Mr Kingsley wrote the book.'

Maddy sighed. She knew her friend was practical, sensible and down to earth, whereas she herself still had a secret desire to believe the wonderful, whether it be fairies or little chimney sweeps. She glanced out of the summer house doorway and saw that the sun had edged right up over the fells. Gran would be in the kitchen by now, preparing their breakfast. She jumped to her feet, still clutching the book. 'I must go; will you trust me to look after the book until this evening? I'll take great care of it, you know I will.'

But Alice was shaking her head despite Maddy's attempt to combine an air of total trustworthiness with passionate pleading. 'I really don't think we should; it's Uncle John's book and although he didn't tell me not to lend it to anyone else I think we both know that it won't even have crossed his mind,' she said rather hesitantly. 'Of course I know you'll take great care of it, but . . .'

Maddy, poised in the doorway with the book still clutched to her chest, sighed and returned to lay the book reverently on the rustic bench. 'You're right, of course,' she said, giving the treasure a last pat before turning away. 'Oh dear, and I shan't be able to concentrate on my work for thinking about it! Can we meet later, even if it's only for five minutes?'

Alice nodded eagerly. 'Tell you what, I'll go to the market with you and then we can come back and read it after we've sold everything,' she said. She opened up the cavity beneath the bench, picked up the book and put it inside. 'There you are. Safely hidden.'

'Oh, Alice, you are so good and kind,' Maddy said gratefully. 'But don't I wish I could borrow the book to show Miss Parrott. She'd love it!'

Alice pointed out that Miss Spender, too, would like the book. 'And there must be other copies, because people don't write a whole book just for one person to read,' she added. 'You might ask Miss Parrott if she's heard of a book called *The Water Babies* and if she says she has you could ask her to bring a copy to school.'

'I'll do that,' Maddy said decidedly. 'But now I must go! See you later.' And with one last wistful glance at the hiding place of the wonderful book, she set off at a fast trot, knowing that she would have to bolt her breakfast and rush through her morning tasks or be on the receiving end of Gran's black walking cane.

'Sorry, Gran. I stopped to pick some watercress, so I'm afraid I'm a bit late.' Maddy mopped beads of sweat from her forehead. 'It's the Saturday market today, so after brekker I'll gather some plums from the tree. They always sell well.'

Gran snorted, then adjusted the tiny pince-nez on her small fat nose and gave her granddaughter a tight little smile. 'Oh well, you're not a bad child. It's a good idea to take a basket of plums down to the market, because most folk around here know we grow good 'uns.' She chuckled. 'We can't really fail to, if you think about it. Crowdale misses the worst of the winds so our fruit trees flourish. In fact if your grandfather were still alive . . . but it's no use wishing. Only my strength's gone, and you've got no weight behind you . . .' She reached over and heaved a big black saucepan off the range and began to ladle porridge into two pottery dishes. 'I baked yesterday so for our tea we'll have scrambled eggs on toast. Goose eggs, what's more.'

'Lovely,' Maddy said absently, pulling a porridge bowl towards her. 'Is there any honey left?' The Hebditch women had two small but very productive hives at the top of the orchard, but at Maddy's question Gran shook her head. 'No, not for you to use, with your soft southern ways. We'll need something to sell when winter comes, and jars of honey bring in a nice little profit. You eat your porridge as it is, and tell me what you've been up to.'

Maddy was so surprised that she stopped with her spoon poised halfway between the dish and her mouth. Gran almost never asked questions but now she was staring at her granddaughter as though she was really interested in Maddy's reply. Hastily, Maddy began to spoon porridge, though she did not make the mistake of speaking with her mouth full; Gran was a stickler for table manners and had made sure that Maddy conformed.

Gran settled herself opposite Maddy at the table and raised her bushy grey eyebrows. 'Well, girl?' she barked. 'You get about more than I do, so tell me what you've been doing so early on a fine summer morning.'

Maddy smiled but shook her head. 'If I tell you while I'm eating then the next thing I know I'll be dodging your stick and that won't do much to improve my health or my temper,' she said, quoting one of her grandmother's many sayings. 'Just let me finish my breakfast and then you can ask me any question you like.' She did not add that she would choose how to answer – fact or fiction – and poor Gran would be none the wiser.

Only a few years ago, Gran had gone into the village two or three times a week. She had kept the rent money which Farmer Sutherland paid them for the pastures they no longer used in a post office savings bank and drew a small sum weekly so that she and her granddaughter could buy things like sugar, butter and flour, goods they needed but could neither grow nor make. Now it was Maddy who visited the village, bought and sold, and kept Gran happy with talk of her occasional trips. It struck her that she really should find some means of getting the old lady down to Crowdale village once in a while to meet folk her own age. After all, perhaps loneliness was the reason that Gran sometimes got so cross. Maybe her bouts of criticism and temper were no more than the result of being cooped up, day and night, on an old farm which had once been a thriving business and was a thriving business no longer.

'Fancy a cut of my bread to round off your breakfast?' Gran's voice broke into Maddy's thoughts. 'There's a bit of butter left from the piece Mr Sutherland gave me.' The old lady smiled grimly. 'I might even spare a smear of damson jam, though the majority must go to the market when the days are short.' She drummed her fingers impatiently on the table top. '*Will* you open your budget, you wretched child. Or do I have to do it for you with the aid of my walking stick?'

Across the table Maddy stared, incredulous. Her gran had almost made a joke! But then, seeing the glitter in the older woman's eyes, she broke into hurried speech. 'All right, all right. I met my friend Alice and we agreed that she would come with me to the market.' She giggled. 'I don't know what her uncle and aunt would say if they knew their niece was selling fruit in the village, but the other stallholders have their kids running errands and nobody seems to notice that Alice is a cut above the rest of us. I think she enjoys it because it means she gets to know the kids from the village school. And she likes watercress sandwiches so I picked a bunch for her . . .'

'You make sure she pays for it,' Gran snapped. 'Those Thwaites can afford it.'

Maddy felt truly indignant. In her head she said 'You mean old besom', a term she had read in books, but of course there was no need to say it out loud because the old woman knew she was mean; was actually proud of it. She would merely snap, 'I'm careful, like all canny Yorkshire women, so don't you give me none of your cheek.' And of course in a way she was right: the Thwaites were not just comfortably off, they were rich. They had four maidservants, a long and gleaming black car driven by a chauffeur, and no end of other workers including a bailiff who ran the tenanted farms and saw to it that Mr and Mrs Thwaite were never cheated.

'Why have you never brought this girl Alice to meet me?' Gran demanded crossly. 'Oh, I know you think the sun shines out of her, but I might not consider her a suitable friend for my granddaughter. Huh! You may goggle, but you've no more idea whether the girl is a real lady than Snoops has!'

This comment made Maddy laugh out loud, though she kept a wary eye on her grandmother's stick. 'Oh, Gran, you're being quite ridiculous and I'm sure you know it,' she said. 'Just look at me! Old plimsolls, a rummage sale dress, my hair like a bird's nest because I haven't had a chance to brush it this morning . . .'

Gran got to her feet, knocking over her stick as she did so. 'Less of your sauce, madam,' she said crossly. 'Pick up my stick at once and I'll show you! Smart clothes and clean shoes aren't the only signs of a lady or a gentleman, as you should know. You think I forget, but that woman with the big nose – what was her name, Miss Crow, Miss Jackdaw – well, whatever her name is, she said you're the brightest child in the school and that makes you a lady in my eyes.'

Maddy laughed. 'Too bright to fetch your stick so that you can whack it across my legs,' she said ruefully. 'Though I've given you no cause to . . .' She stopped speaking suddenly and pointed at her grandmother's legs. 'What's the matter with your left foot? You're limping! Oh, don't say you've had a fall while I was out.'

Gran had limped over to the sink without bending to pick up her fallen stick, and now she sighed. 'No, I didn't fall, but I slipped when I put the porridge pan on the stove, and you can just stop peering at it. I admit it's bruised, but . . . What are you doing?'

'Oh, Gran, I'm pushing a chair across so you can sit down. I'll wash up and clean out the porridge saucepan ready for tomorrow. Why on earth didn't you tell me that you'd wrenched your ankle? No, likeliest it's a sprain, because I can see it's all purple, just like a plum.'

Gran sank into the chair with a little moan of relief. 'It's nothing much, anyhow,' she declared, 'and don't you pretend that you wouldn't have gone out if you'd known I'd slip, because how could you possibly tell? I don't mean you to miss market day, you know. I put a bag of eggs in the big shopping basket; if you sell them and the plums that should keep our heads above water until next week. So as soon as you've washed up and cleared away you can take the reed basket and pick the fruit.'

Maddy looked with concern at her grandmother's face, noticing for the first time how pale she was, save for two bright spots of colour in either cheek. 'Look, Gran, I have a feeling that ankle would be best raised up. You'll probably make it worse if you keep walking on it. I'll help you through to the parlour so you can lie on the sofa, then I'll go straight down to the orchard, pick some plums, and come back as soon as I've sold our stuff in the market. What am I to buy with the money? What do we need most?'

As she spoke she was trying to help her grandmother to her feet, but as soon as Gran tried to put weight on her left foot an anguished groan was torn from her lips, and the look which accompanied the groan made Maddy glad she had not yet picked up the old woman's stick. But to her surprise Gran heaved in a breath and then, for the second time that morning, smiled at Maddy. 'I'm a cross-grained old woman and I'm beginning to think I don't deserve such a kind little granddaughter,' she said. 'You can give me my stick now. With that on one side and you on t'other, I'll get to the parlour somehow, 'cos you're right, my leg should be kept up.'

Between Maddy and the stick Gran was soon established on the sofa with a large enamel mug of tea on a small stool by her side. She was still pale, and Maddy realised that she was reluctant to leave her. In normal circumstances Gran would have told her to fetch her knitting or some other homely task which would not tax her strength, but today she simply asked in a small voice if Maddy could bring down a blanket and pillow from her bed before she left the house.

As she ran up the stairs to fetch the required items Maddy wondered whether she ought to call the doctor. Normally Gran scoffed when Maddy mentioned any sort of outside help, reminding her granddaughter that they had no money to spare for such things, but today, her mood softened by her injury, Maddy thought that she might agree to a visit from Dr Carlton. He was a small, sharp little man whom Maddy had known for years, but when she went back down to the parlour and suggested they might ask him to pop in the idea seemed to give Gran back some of her strength. She had been settling the blanket around her legs but at Maddy's words she looked up, giving a snort of disgust.

'What's a sprained ankle?' she asked derisively. 'He'll maybe charge me five shillings just to look at it and tell me what I already know, that I mustn't try to walk until the swelling goes down. If it doesn't clear up in a day or so ... but it will, such things always do. And in the meantime, I've got a good little granddaughter who'll take care of me and see I don't starve.'

Maddy sighed. She would have liked to ignore Gran's wishes and ask the doctor to call anyway, but she knew this might make for ill feeling, whereas at the moment Gran actually seemed to appreciate that Maddy did her best. She decided to leave things as they were for the time being, but when she would have closed the parlour door her grandmother stopped her.

'Don't shut the door; the kitchen's where folk expect to find me and I need to keep an eye on you,' she said. 'Tell you what, I'll make you a bargain. If you'll promise not to leave me I'll promise to use my stick to help me to walk, not to slap legs. Is that fair?'

'Gran, I wouldn't leave you. Where would I go?' Maddy asked, totally astonished. 'When there's only two of you, you depend on each other. And if I don't get those plums soon I'll be late for the market. We're running very low on tea; shall I buy two ounces of that with the money?'

Gran agreed, and suggested that Maddy might see if the change would run to a bag of sugar since they had used the last of their stock. 'And anything else you fancy with what's left over. You're a good girl, Maddy Hebditch,' she added in a frail voice, quite unlike her own. 'You won't be long?'

Maddy promised to be as quick as she could, and very soon she was at the market place and slipping into her usual position. Alice was helping her to display the eggs and plums to their best advantage when Mrs Grundy came over from the next stall. 'Eh up, flower,' she said jovially, peering into Maddy's basket. 'They look champion. How's your gran?'

Maddy hesitated. She knew Gran liked to give the impression that she was still as capable and businesslike as she had always been, but she knew most of the people at the market must have guessed the truth. She was beginning to say that everything was fine when Alice cut in. 'Her gran's had a fall; slipped whilst cooking. She's awfully old, you know –

I've never met her, but from what Maddy tells me I should think she must be at least a hundred.'

There was general laughter but Mrs Grundy shook her head at Alice. 'Aha, you young 'uns are all alike; you think anyone who b'ain't young must be old as hills,' she said sagely. She wagged a finger at Maddy. 'A fall's nasty even if you b'ain't a hundred. You should get Dr Carlton to call.'

'It wasn't a fall, it was a slip, and Gran's going to rest all day on the sofa,' Maddy said quickly. 'She doesn't want a doctor, and she doesn't want people to think . . .'

Perhaps fortunately, before she could explain more fully, a customer claimed Mrs Grundy's attention, and when presently Maddy had sold the last of her plums she suggested that she and Alice should do their shopping and then go home. 'I can't read *The Water Babies* today – I have to get back to Gran. But why don't you come with me? You could stay for lunch, though it will only be bread and scrape, I'm afraid.'

Mrs Grundy, overhearing, picked up a small square wrapped up in greaseproof paper and thrust it into Maddy's hands.

'Piece of me best cheese for the old lady,' she said, patting Maddy's cheek. 'There's a heap of things you can make with cheese what's soft enough for an old lady to chaw on. Give her my regards and tell her I'd be happy to bake her a couple of loaves while she's laid up. I'll bring them to market next Saturday.' She reached across and dug Alice in the ribs. 'We stick together, you know, help each other out.' She sighed reminiscently. 'Though you may find it difficult to believe, m'dear, Mrs Hebditch were a fine figure of a woman once, running her side of farm like clockwork.' She sighed deeply. 'Ah, well, age changes all of us.' Another customer approached and she smiled apologetically before greeting the other woman warmly. 'Good morning. You'll be wanting me best cheese if I know you! And some of me unsalted butter . . .'

Chapter Two

When the two girls reached Larkspur Farm Maddy half expected to find Gran on her feet grumbling away and ready to criticise everything she had bought. Consequently she entered the kitchen with a degree of caution and was disproportionately astonished to find the room empty, the door still propped open and Gran on the sofa in the parlour snoring loudly.

Maddy tiptoed across the room as quietly as she could, followed closely by Snoops, whose nose was pressed almost on the back of her legs. He was a large and shaggy dog, bright-eyed and bushy-tailed, but despite his size and friendly nature he was a timid animal and Maddy guessed that finding Gran no longer in command of the kitchen was worrying him more than a little, so she patted his head and rubbed his pricked ears and told him in a low whisper not to bark. 'For that would wake Gran, and sleeping will be doing her good,' she told him, approaching the sofa. The mug of tea, she saw, had been drained even though she had not been able to sweeten it. Gran liked her tea strong and sweet, and the fact that she had made do with what Maddy had provided was a good indication that she had not got off the sofa. Maddy found herself wishing that she had popped into the surgery after all and asked the doctor to visit. Still, if the pain was still persisting in a day or two the idea of consulting the doctor might be more acceptable.

For a moment Maddy stayed by the sofa looking doubtfully down at the sleeping woman. However, she couldn't stand here like a stock; she had left Alice outside the back door, knowing that Gran would want to be up and properly dressed before she saw anyone save her granddaughter. She decided she would let Alice in and then shut the parlour door very, very gently before starting the preparations for a light lunch, which was all she and Gran ever had.

But unfortunately Snoops saw fit to bark the moment Alice came into the kitchen, and Maddy, in the very act of closing the parlour door, hastily opened it again. Her grandmother was looking wildly round her as though she could not recognise the room in which she lay, so Maddy crossed the floor, perched on the end of the sofa and addressed the old woman gently.

'Hello, Gran. It's only me, Maddy, and my friend Alice is in the kitchen. We're making ourselves a bite to eat. Mrs Grundy gave us some lovely cheese, and Alice is cutting a couple of slices off the loaf; she'll cut three, if you're hungry. Then there are the pickled onions you and I made last year and a few apples from the orchard.' She smiled encouragingly at her grandmother. 'It's a feast! Do say you'll eat your share, Gran.'

'What?' Gran said vaguely. 'Help me up!'

Maddy shook a chiding head. 'You mustn't get up. You sprained your ankle, don't you remember? You told me not to call the doctor, and the market folk agree the best cure for a sprained ankle is to keep it up. So just you stay there.'

Gran heaved an enormous sigh, and fixed Maddy with a basilisk glare. 'I want to pee,' she said loudly, and Maddy trembled for fear Alice would get the giggles and Gran might think herself mocked. 'Fetch me the perishing chamber pot, girl!' Poor Maddy's mind whirled. She could not imagine that Gran would find it easy to perch on the large chamber pot which adorned the old woman's bedroom, and eyed her grandmother's bulk doubtfully. Gran looked puzzled. 'I want to pee,' she repeated insistently. 'What's the matter with you, girl? Catchin' flies, are you? Don't you know a body has to pee after drinking a full mug of tea? And who's this Alice?'

Maddy, thoroughly confused, began to explain that Alice was her friend, that they had been at the market together, but she got no further. 'Oh, *that* Alice. She's the new nursery maid, isn't she?' Gran moved on the sofa, trying to rid herself of the blanket which Maddy had tucked around her, and gave an impatient sigh. 'Get this bloody thing off me,' she commanded. 'And call the nursery maid; if the pair of you give me a hand I dare say I could reach the privy in the yard easier than I could balance me bum on that old jeremiah.'

'Right,' Maddy said. What on earth made Gran think Alice was a nursery maid? But she ran across the parlour and beckoned to her friend, who was sitting in one of the old kitchen chairs with Talon, the cat, on her lap. 'Can you come?' she asked urgently. 'Gran wants to have a widdle and I can't lift her by myself. We need to help her out to the privy in the garden. Are you game to take her left side whilst I cope with the right?'

Alice looked scared. She removed the cat from her lap with obvious reluctance and stood up, shaking the creases out of her beautiful smock. 'All right, I'll have a go,' she said.

Back in the parlour the old lady had already heaved herself up and was disentangling her legs from the blanket whilst muttering curses too low, Maddy hoped, for Alice to catch. She smiled tentatively at Gran as she darted forward to take the old woman's weight, gesturing for Alice to do the same.

Alice essayed a bright smile, though Maddy saw that it was a bit wobbly. 'Good morning, Mrs Hebditch, or should I say afternoon?' Alice said in a small voice which she clearly strove to make pleasant. 'I've come to give Maddy a hand, so you must lean on me and I'll do my best to help you.'

Gran, now upright and balancing on one foot,

sniffed. 'If you're the nursery maid then it ought to be you holding me up,' she said disagreeably. 'Come along, come along, let's be having you!'

Alice giggled and Maddy realised she had probably never been spoken to in such a manner before. But she did not comment and presently the three of them crossed the parlour and were actually in the yard when, as Maddy put it to herself, their journey became unnecessary. Gran had held on as long as she possibly could, and when at last she lost the battle a positive river splashed around her bare and dirty feet.

Instincts cannot be helped, perhaps. Both girls leapt back and Gran teetered, shrieked and fell. The girls began to try to heave her to her feet, and Maddy realised that despite her efforts Alice could not prevent a stifled giggle or two from emerging. Maddy herself, on the other hand, was not amused, or at least not to the extent of laughing, particularly when she realised that they did not have the strength to get Gran back into the house. But she had not allowed for the steely determination which would not let Gran give way. 'Roll me over on to my knees and bring a kitchen chair out here,' she demanded. She gave her granddaughter a baleful glare. 'And take this silly, giggling girl away with you. You and me and the chair will manage just fine.'

Gran's criticism had brought a blush to Alice's cheeks, but though her offer of help was received with a sniff, she persisted. When at last Gran was seated in the old basket chair, it was clear to Maddy that she was beginning to feel more like her old self. She sent Maddy into the parlour to fetch the blanket, and beneath its capacious folds she shed her wet things and allowed Maddy to help her into her winceyette nightdress. Then she looked very hard at Alice. 'Who *are* you?' she demanded, and this time there was no aggression in her tone but merely curiosity. 'You aren't the nursery maid, because I remember she was . . . oh, well, it doesn't matter.'

'Nor it does; matter, I mean,' Maddy said briskly. 'Alice is the friend I've told you about, and she won't be here much longer because I'm going to ask her if she'll go into the village and pop into the surgery to see if Dr Carlton can spare us a few minutes.' She saw her grandmother's mouth open, saw the frown begin to descend, and went on quickly, 'It's no use, Gran, it'll be money well spent because you must know I have to go to school on Monday. And – and you did have a funny turn when Alice and I came in. I need advice, and the doctor's the one to give it, so don't you start arguing and throwing your weight about. Just lie back in that chair until I can give you a hand through to the parlour, and once Dr Carlton has told us what the right treatment should be we'll soon have you trotting round again.'

Gran made a mumbling grumbling noise beneath her breath but did not attempt to forbid Alice to go for the doctor. Maddy accompanied her friend across the farmyard, but before they reached the stony little track which led to the village she heard her grandmother's voice raised in a shout behind them. 'Maddy? Maddy? Don't forget what you promised! You promised you'd not leave me, so don't you go gadding off. Fetch the bellows and brighten the fire, 'cos I could do with another drink. And you'd best do as I bid you and fetch down the jeremiah from my room. A body can perch a chamber pot on a chair and use it without having to creak at the knees. Maddy? Where are you? Answer me, you little . . .'

Maddy looked remorsefully at her friend. 'Oh, Alice, do you mind? I'm sorry I didn't ask you properly first, but you saw what she's like. I don't want to do the wrong thing and make her worse.'

'Of course I don't mind,' Alice said at once. 'But how she does shout and boss you around, Maddy! And what does she mean about not leaving her? Surely she must realise you have to go to school, or come and play with me.'

Maddy pulled a face. 'My grandmother is only interested in herself,' she said ruefully. 'But a sprained ankle doesn't last for ever, and she's very strong, you know. Only for some reason she got it into her head that I might use her ankle as an excuse to run away.'

'But you wouldn't, would you?' Alice asked anxiously. 'You're my best friend, Maddy, and I don't know what I'd do without you. Tell you what, whilst you're cooped up with your gran you can have the book to keep you company.'

'Oh, Alice, you are kind, and you know I'll take great care of it,' Maddy said joyfully. 'I might read some of it to Gran, because the only reading matter we have here is old copies of magazines like *Farmer & Stock-Breeder* or *Farmer's Weekly*. I suppose . . .' Maddy was interrupted by a thin and querulous voice floating across to them.

'Maddy Hebditch, come back here this instant! I'm that parched and you've not even pulled the kettle over the flame.'

'All right, Gran, I'm coming,' Maddy said, hearing the panic in her grandmother's voice. She gave Alice a gentle push. 'You'd better go. Thank you – and you will come back soon and bring the book? You said you would.'

'As soon as I can,' Alice called over her shoulder. 'If I can get away I'll see you tomorrow morning.'

Even lucky Alice could only do as she was allowed, Maddy reflected as she crossed the farmyard. 'Coming, Gran,' she called out as she entered the kitchen. 'You can have a nice cup of tea just as soon as I've blown up the fire and boiled the kettle.' She peered through the bars of the range and saw that the fire still glowed redly. 'Do you fancy a sandwich?'

She half expected an indignant refusal, for Gran frequently boasted that she never ate much at midday, but the old woman replied that she was a trifle peckish. 'You said you'd got some of Mrs Grundy's cheese; I wouldn't mind a piece of that with a slice of new-baked bread,' she said. 'Only I don't want to be caught mumbling over bread and cheese if that girl – Alice whatshername – really does ask young Carlton to call.'

Maddy smiled to herself. Her grandmother had a set of false teeth in a cup of water by her bed, and unless she was expecting someone to call, there they would stay. 'My gums is as hard as iron; I can crack a walnut with 'em,' she was apt to boast. 'I only need those teeth for the look of the thing.' But now she turned to her granddaughter. 'Fetch me teeth, quick,' she commanded. 'I'm not having a doctor think I'm a poor old mumbling woman who can't afford gnashers. Hurry up, Maddy.'

'I'll get them as soon as I've made the tea,' Maddy said patiently. 'It's a long way to the village and Alice isn't a quick walker, so Dr Carlton can't possibly get here in much under an hour. You'll have finished your bread and cheese by then.'

Gran grinned gummily. 'And I'll breathe pickled onion straight into his face if he tries to charge me just for telling me I've sprained my ankle,' she said.

The summer holidays arrived but Gran still lay on the sofa in the parlour, though she had made several attempts to get back on her feet. Dr Carlton had made arrangements for Maddy to draw some money on her grandmother's behalf out of her pension book, so the girl was able to pay the doctor and, with the help of the farm produce, to keep their heads above water.

But she had no leisure time in which to pursue her search for water babies. She had tried reading from the book to Gran, who had declared it to be twaddle, fit only for mewling brats and not to be taken seriously at all.

'I didn't ask you to take it seriously,' Maddy had said, hurt. 'But although it's a book for children, there's a lot of good sense in what Mr Kingsley has written.' She smiled at her grandmother. 'You are very like Mrs Bedonebyasyoudid, you know.'

The two of them had been sitting at the kitchen table preparing onions for pickling and Gran had reared up in her seat, a dangerous glint in her eyes. 'Is that a dig at me?' she asked. 'If so, you can take it back. The bit you read me about that old woman was not polite at all; in fact it was very rude. She's ugly as sin and mean into the bargain, so if you're saying I'm like that you'd best watch out.'

Maddy had put down the onion she was peeling and stared across the table at her grandmother. 'I didn't mean to say that you were ugly, but you're pretty mean to me,' she pointed out. 'I'm thirteen now and yet you want to keep me in the house all the time, like a prisoner. When you could get about I used to sell our eggs and things at the market and play with Alice at the weekends and sometimes we went off for the whole day. But now, because you're tied by the heels as the doctor calls it, you think I should be tied by the heels as well. Do you think that's fair, Gran? I don't like to tell on you to the doctor, but if you don't begin to let me leave you for a few hours sometimes I shall simply have to ask him what I should do. I'm starting at the new school in a couple of weeks and I'm sure they won't let me get away with saying I'm looking after my gran. They'll tell me that if your ankle still won't bear your weight then you should be in some sort of hospital or nursing home. They'll start asking questions, and all sorts of things might happen. There's always the workhouse, or whatever they call it now.'

Gran gasped, then threw the onion she was peeling as hard as she could. It struck Maddy in the middle of the forehead, causing her to feel quite strange for a moment.

'What did you do that for?' she asked, aggrieved. 'I only pointed out that if you wouldn't let me attend school, then there was always the . . .'

Another missile bounced off her head. 'Public Assistance Institution,' Gran said furiously. 'And the day I go into one of them places is the day I'll die. You promised you'd not leave me, you promised . . .'

To Maddy's horror she saw two fat tears trickle down her grandmother's cheeks. Never before had Gran wept in her presence. She leaned across the table

44

and seized the old woman's trembling hands. 'Dear Gran, I didn't mean to distress you,' she said gently. 'But, you know, you are being very unreasonable. If you truly can't manage without having me within call all day, the ideal thing would be to employ one of the village women to come up at nine o'clock each morning and stay until four or five in the afternoon. But I'm not sure there's enough money in your post office account to pay for such a person, so I suppose we must look at the alternatives. And don't you go chucking onions at me again or I really might feel tempted to leave you,' she added with a teasing smile.

Gran heaved an enormous sigh. 'My ankle's not nearly as swollen as it were,' she muttered. 'Don't you go mentioning the perishing workhouse to Dr Carlton because I've already told him my granddaughter wouldn't hear of it. When school starts you can attend your classes, but until then . . .'

But Maddy was shaking her head. This was her best opportunity so far to talk sense into Gran and she did not mean to let it pass. 'No, Gran, that won't do,' she said firmly. 'I've already lost most of the summer holidays, thanks to your ankle. Alice and I had planned all sorts of things which we've had to miss because you've been poorly. Now I want to cram the remaining time full to bursting. I'll see to you before I go off each day, but go off I must. Is that fair?'

She half expected a firm denial and was pleasantly

surprised when her grandmother grinned and tapped the side of her nose. 'You aren't a bad child, even if a trifle hard; you take after your old gran,' she announced. 'Very well; you may start your freedom from tomorrow. Only you'd best do your chores as early as possible so you can leave me up and dressed with me lunch ready waiting.'

Maddy was so delighted that she could have danced and sung but she knew better than to do so; Gran could always change her mind. Instead, she said jubilantly: 'Oh, Gran, you are good! And don't worry, because I'm sure we'll manage things between us; we always have, after all. Only you must tell me in good time what you fancy for your meals because we can't afford to waste food.'

'If that was a dig at me leaving most of the egg custard you made . . .'

Maddy laughed, but sobered quickly. 'Honest to God it wasn't,' she said earnestly, remembering how Gran disliked to be laughed at or, for that matter, put in the wrong. 'And it wasn't wasted: I ate it.'

'And I've no doubt it did you good,' Gran said huffily. 'I was sick of slops. Now if you'd offered me a nice lamb chop . . .'

Maddy hid a grin. Gran might boast that her gums were hard as nails but Maddy knew that, even had they been able to afford lamb chops, Gran would have been unable to eat them. Every now and again someone from the village would bring them a rabbit

– poached, of course – and sometimes the butcher gave Maddy a bag of scraps, 'to boil up to make a stew for the old lady' as he put it. Such gestures were much appreciated by Maddy, but Gran valued her independence and when she was the recipient of such kindness she behaved so like a queen acknowledging a subject that Maddy felt quite embarrassed. However, she knew it was useless to tell Gran that she should perhaps reciprocate with a bag of apples or a couple of goose eggs, because that would merely cause Gran to give an affronted sniff. 'I thanked him sincerely,' she would say, staring incredulously at her granddaughter. 'And I know very well you'll go round in a day or two with a few eggs or a bag of apples. So let's hear no more about it.'

And now, the longed-for day was here at last; Gran and Maddy were in the kitchen, and Maddy was preparing to set off for a blissful day out. She had done everything she could to make sure that Gran could spend most of the day in her chair. They had already eaten their breakfast of porridge and toast, and Maddy had made a rice pudding – Gran was very fond of rice pudding – and filled the kettle and stood it on the hob so that Gran could make herself a cup of tea to go with it. She was all ready to go, her own lunch of two cheese sandwiches in a piece of greaseproof paper safely stowed away in the pocket of her shabby cotton frock, when Gran called her back. Maddy sighed. 'Yes, Gran?' she said with all the patience she could muster. 'What's wrong now?'

Gran was sitting in her favourite chair with her knitting in her lap. She was a good knitter, and whenever there was a jumble sale in the village Maddy was instructed to buy any old woollies which were not eaten up by moths. In the long winter evenings she and Gran would unpick the garments and wash the wool, and Gran knitted it up again into the warm, if somewhat loopy, jumpers which the two of them wore around the house.

'What is it, Gran?' Maddy repeated. 'Don't forget what you promised!'

Gran scowled. 'Don't give me sauce,' she said reprovingly. 'Aren't you going to take that there blamed fairy story back to the Hall? I thought you said you were.'

Maddy gasped. 'You're a gradely lass, Gran; what with making sure you had everything you wanted I clean forgot about the book, but you're quite right, I ought to take it back today. It's still in my bedroom, because I took it to bed last night meaning to have a good read, only I was so tired I dropped off before I had so much as opened it.'

Gran sniffed. 'If you think it's hard work to get ready to go off and leave me . . .' she began, but Maddy was already halfway up the back stairs. She reached her bedroom, grabbed the book and charged downstairs again. How careless she had been! She really must be a bit more organised, though how she could be when Gran deliberately made things difficult was more than she could see at present.

Back in the kitchen she waved the book at Gran. 'Here it is. Now don't forget, Dr Carlton will be popping in some time just to check that you're all right,' she said gaily. She pointed to the clock which hung on the wall near the window. 'I'll be back in time to make our tea, say at five o'clock or thereabouts. You'll be all right till then?'

'I'm not a child; of course I'll be all right,' Gran said sharply. 'Once I'd made up my mind I could manage, you were welcome to take yourself off. Always provided,' she added hurriedly, 'that you bring yourself back well before it gets dark. Evenings are drawing in now, so you'll want to return in plenty of time. I don't know why it takes me so long to get into me clothes and out of them again, but I suppose it's the arthur-itis or the sky-attica what turns my limbs agin me.'

Maddy, already at the door, nodded sympathetically. 'It's what the old fellers in the village call the screws, or the rheumatics,' she said. 'I think it happens to everyone when they begin to get old . . .'

She wished the words unsaid as soon as they were uttered, for Gran did not intend to share her afflictions with any of the villagers. 'Huh! They don't know what pain is . . .' she was beginning but Maddy, recognising yet another ploy to keep her locked in discussion in the kitchen, slipped into the yard and closed the door firmly behind her.

She stood still for a moment, considering the day that stretched before her. It was too early to go to the Hall – Alice did not usually break her fast in holiday times until nine at the earliest – but Maddy was determined not to waste a moment. The air was cool, full of the promise of a fine day to come, and when she reached the stony track she decided that she would go to the beck. Her birthday had occurred only a few days before and she knew that a great girl of thirteen was too old to believe in either water babies or water fairies – naiads, were they called? – but nevertheless, whenever she looked into the sparkling waters of the beck, she was not gazing into the depths in the hope of seeing a speckled trout, but a tiny little boy no more than four inches high who would prove that her belief in magic had been justified at last.

Maddy reached the beck and glanced all around her. To her left a willow drooped its summer-dark leaves over a deep pool; deep enough to drown a non-swimmer, rumour had it. The local children vowed it was bottomless. To her right the water cascaded over rocks, so that the beck seemed to chuckle to itself, but under the willow, because of the depth Maddy supposed, the stream was still, reflecting the green of the branches and the blue of the sky. She lay down carefully, cupped her eyes with her hands and tried to look through the water and not be distracted by the reflections, but it was no use. Unless one had the courage to put one's whole head under the water – and she was not quite that brave – it was impossible to see past the inverted willow tree. Maddy dabbled a hand in the cool water then sighed, pulled the book out of her pocket and opened it. She would enjoy a quiet read whilst keeping an eye on the beck for any sign of underwater life.

Maddy read on and on, pausing every few pages to gasp over the beauty of Mr Theaker's illustrations. In fact, she was so deeply involved in little Tom's world that when something heavy landed in the middle of her back and a harsh voice yelled in her ear, her heart almost jumped out of her chest and for a moment she truly thought that a bull must have broken out of the nearest meadow, leapt over the hedge and landed with stunning force on her unprotected spine.

Chapter Three

Naturally, she screamed like a train whistle as the breath whooshed back into her lungs, whereupon her attacker rolled off her, proving to be a boy some three years older than herself and both taller and heavier. Maddy, who knew all the boys at the village school, did not recognise this one and thought it might be unwise to say any of the things which sprang to her mind, such as 'How dare you!' or 'What the devil are you up to?' or even 'Gerroff!' Instead she sat up, clutching her chest from which every bit of air had been driven, and asked, 'Who are you, and why did you jump on me?' She was trying to stop her voice from wobbling, for her ribs still ached from the onslaught. 'Oh! Are you one of Alice's cousins?'

'No,' the boy said. 'I didn't know she *had* cousins.' By now the pair of them were sitting facing one another on the bank of the beck, Maddy gently rubbing her back and sore ribs, and the boy pushing ginger hair out of his eyes and grinning like – oh, like a tiger, Maddy thought crossly. 'It was an accident. I saw you lying there and I thought you were Alice. I was going to shout out "boo" when I caught my foot in a root and fell on top of you.' He eyed her angrily. 'I'd arranged to meet her here, only not for half an hour yet. Satisfied?'

Since he did not seem to have attacked her on purpose Maddy took her courage in both hands and repeated her original question. 'All right, but who *are* you?' she asked bluntly. 'I know everyone round here.'

The boy looked her up and down and then gave a dismissive wave of the hand. 'Mind your own bloody business, you nasty little thing,' he said rudely. 'Who are you to question me? Do you own the beck or something? You're just a village brat Alice was kind to when she had no other friends.'

Maddy felt the blood rush to her cheeks at the insult, but continued to stare at him challengingly, taking in his appearance. He had rough ginger hair, white eyelashes and a great many freckles. He was taller than she and heavily built, with greenish hazel eyes, uneven teeth and clothing similar to her own: a faded checked shirt, incredibly old trousers and black, ragged plimsolls through which his big toes peeped coyly.

Having examined him closely, Maddy raised her eyes to his face once more. 'Alice said her cousins might be coming to stay, and I thought you were one of them, but now I can see you aren't,' she said accusingly. 'The maid who looks after Alice would have torn up that shirt and trousers for dusters as

53

soon as she set eyes on 'em. So who *are* you?' For a moment the pair held each other's gaze and Maddy was pleased when he disengaged first. 'Go on, why won't you tell me? I can easily ask Alice, you know. So what's the big secret, Ginger?'

She had spoken in a deliberately provocative manner, and decided it had been the right approach when the boy gave a reluctant grin. 'I'm Tom Browning, and I'm wearing old clothes because I keep my good things for best,' he said, and then, seeing the puzzled frown on Maddy's face, explained further. 'You know that big black car at the Hall, the one parked in what used to be the stables? Well, my dad's the chauffeur, which means . . .'

'I know very well what a chauffeur is,' Maddy said repressively. 'So don't you go trying to tell your grandmother how to suck eggs.'

The boy stifled a laugh, but by the time he spoke again he had managed to school his features into an expression of gravity. 'You don't look much like a grandmother, not even one who sucks eggs,' he said blandly. 'What an odd creature you are! I don't know where Alice gets her friends from, but for sheer strangeness you take the biscuit. You're wearing old clothes, and you're as ugly as sin, so how dare you question me!'

Maddy bounced to her feet. 'Well, Tom Browning, you are quite the rudest and nastiest boy I've ever met, and the stupidest too. Why don't you bugger off

54

back to wherever you came from. I don't want you here.'

To her pleasure, Tom Browning looked as though a tiny day-old chick had bitten him on the nose. He had got to his feet when Maddy did, though more slowly, and now he burst into angry speech. 'Why, you impudent little beast! I'll box your ears. You wait till I tell Mr Thwaite you think you own the place. Just you come back here . . .'

But he was too late. If there was one thing at which Maddy excelled, it was running, and probably she ran all the faster with the devil – otherwise known as Tom Browning – on her heels. She might have actually reached the summerhouse, where she suspected Alice might be, had she not happened to glance back and seen, to her absolute horror, Tom standing with the copy of *The Water Babies* held triumphantly above his head. For a moment Maddy hesitated. If she went back he would probably not only box her ears but throw her into the beck, but if she did not go back . . . oh, what hideous revenge might he wreak on the beautiful volume which Mr Thwaite had allowed her to borrow for weeks and weeks, while she had been tied to the house!

Maddy knew, really, that she had no choice. The book was not hers, but she was responsible for its well-being. And after all, if he really was the son of Mr Thwaite's chauffeur, whom she had met once or twice up at the Hall, he could not be all bad. And she had been very rude and quite nasty: she had called him Ginger which, though true, was generally regarded as an insult . . . oh, dear, she only had herself to blame if he really did box her ears.

She turned and ran downhill even faster than she had run up, shouting as she did so, 'Tom, I'm sorry I was rude. The book isn't mine, I borrowed it . . . *please* put it down, *please* don't . . .' As she reached the bank she leapt at him and clutched the book, heard his shout of alarm as her weight overbalanced him, and before she knew what was happening found herself struggling to remain upright in a couple of feet of water, Tom having staggered backwards into the beck when she cannoned into him.

For a moment all was confusion. Maddy's one desire was to save the book from a wetting and it seemed as though Tom Browning shared that ambition, for instead of fighting her off he was thrusting her ahead of him back up the bank. Once on dry land again he pushed the book into her hands. 'You silly little twerp. I wouldn't have damaged the book; I was only kidding you,' he said. He stretched out a tentative hand to point at her soaked skirt. 'You *are* in a mess! What'll your mam and dad say when they see you?'

Maddy looked at her clothing. From the waist down she was wet, muddy and scratched, but she drew comfort from the fact that the dress was an old one, and anyway by the time she returned to the farm it would have dried out. She said as much, adding:

'And I don't have a mum or dad, I live with my gran.'
She looked consideringly at her companion. 'What
about you? Will your mother make a big fuss? Because
you're every bit as wet and muddy as I am.'

The boy shook his head. 'Don't have a mam,' he
said briefly. 'But my dad's a real stickler. Only I reckon
I'll be dry before I have to go back home.'

'Same as me,' Maddy said, nodding. 'But I've just
thought; the chauffeur at the Hall is quite young. He
doesn't look more than about twenty. He *can't* be your
father.'

The boy laughed. 'Lucas gave in his notice a few
weeks ago, and when the job was advertised my
father applied and got it,' he explained with more
than a trace of pride. 'The wages aren't bad and the
flat comes with the job, and I've still got a year to
go at a school a couple of miles along the dale, so
Dad jumped at the chance.' He raised his brows at
Maddy. 'So you see, you're landed with me, like
it or not.' He pointed at the book which now lay
innocently, and undamaged, on the grass between
them. 'So what's all this about, eh? If it ain't yours,
whose is it? Don't say a little kid like you stole the
bloody thing?'

'No I did *not* steal it and swearing's wicked;
Miss Parrott says it's unnecessary . . . why are you
laughing? I don't remember making a joke,' Maddy
snorted. 'Go on, what did I say that was so funny?'

The boy spluttered. 'No one's called Parrott; you

made it up,' he said. 'Or is it your name? Are you Polly Parrott?'

'No I am not. I'm Madeleine Hebditch and I live at Larkspur Farm with my gran. The book belongs to Mr Thwaite. He lent it to Alice and me and I go – went – to the village school and my teacher there was Miss Parrott. Satisfied?'

'Well, if you're sure . . .' the boy said doubtfully. He held out a hand towards the book, stopping when it was a few inches away. 'Can I look or isn't one allowed to touch?'

'Not if your hands are wet,' Maddy said quickly. 'It's a – a first edition and very valuable, or so Mr Thwaite says, but if you dry your hands on your shirt I suppose you could take a peek.'

The boy rubbed his hands vigorously on his much patched shirt and gingerly pulled the book towards him, opening it at random. 'Fairy stories, I suppose; kids' stuff.' He flicked over a page to reveal one of the illustrations, and let out his breath in a low whistle. 'I say, this chap can certainly draw! Oh, and it's not fairy stories; I know what it is, though I've never seen an illustrated copy before.' He closed his eyes and screwed up his mouth for a moment, then his eyes shot open. 'It's *The Water Babies*, by Charles Kingsley,' he said triumphantly. He turned to Maddy. 'Did you know Mr Kingsley wrote it when he was staying with friends here in the Yorkshire Dales? He was a vicar and a professor, a very learned man. My father told me that one day, when he's not too busy, he will take me to Cumming Cove, which is where . . .' The boy began to leaf through the pages, then gave an exclamation and returned to the beginning. 'Of course! How stupid I am to forget! Tom climbs down to sea level in the early part of the book, so if there's a picture it must be somewhere in the first couple of dozen pages . . . ah, here it is!' He tapped the illustration with a finger. 'You can just imagine how poor Tom must have felt after clambering down that, can't you?'

He was swivelling the book to face Maddy but she stopped him with a gesture. 'Don't bother; Alice and I know every picture by heart, pretty well. But I'm glad you don't think it's just a fairy story, because I think there really are strange creatures in the sea, and I mean to find them.'

'Oh you do, do you?' the boy said rather mockingly. 'Well, I bet you five bob you don't find a water baby. Not that you could, of course; water babies can't possibly exist. Tell you what, though, it might be quite a laugh to follow Mr Kingsley's wanderings and see if we can identify Vendale. What do you say to having a try? The summer hols have another couple of weeks to go and it would give us something to do.'

Maddy stared at him, two thoughts jostling in her mind. One was that it would be both fun and interesting to use the stories in the book as a sort of guide, for the Reverend Mr Kingsley – he was a clergyman, if this strange boy was to be believed –

had said right at the start of the book that Vendale was a made-up name, invented deliberately so that inquisitive little girls might not flock to it and ruin the peace and beauty of the tiny dale and its becks and rivers, where he had found not only water babies but also many other strange underwater creatures.

The second thought, coming out of the blue, so to speak, was rather more disturbing. Maddy had assumed that Alice had not visited Larkspur again after that first time because she was nervous of Gran and did not want to be involved in looking after her. Now, however, she faced the unpleasant thought that Alice had not come because she had found herself another friend, this Tom Browning, son of the new chauffeur. It was disappointing to realise that Alice, her idol, might have feet of clay, but perhaps she should not be blamed for her defection. After all, just because Maddy herself had lost several weeks of the summer holiday was no reason why Alice, also, should miss out. It was not as if Alice had other friends in the village, and if this boy was serious when he suggested trying to find Vendale then she could scarcely blame Alice for jumping joyfully at the thought of such a companion whilst Maddy herself was more or less housebound.

But Tom was staring at her, his brows still raised. Maddy pulled herself together. 'It's a champion idea, especially since my gran's agreed that I can have the rest of the hols to myself,' she said slowly. 'But what will Miss Spender say? She doesn't always have the same timetable as a regular school so Alice may . . .' and here Maddy crossed her fingers behind her back, 'already be back in the schoolroom.'

She was afraid that Tom would give himself away – give Alice away, really – by admitting that he had spent the last few weeks taking her, Maddy's, place as Alice's best friend, but he did no such thing. Instead he shrugged. 'I think Alice gets her own way more often than not, and if she wants to explore the dales with us then that's exactly what she'll do. Have you ever met Miss Spender?' And then, as Maddy shook her head, he gave a rueful grin. 'Well, she's wax in Alice's hands. But Alice will be here in person quite soon, so there's no point in discussing our plans until then.'

Maddy was beginning to agree when another thought struck her. 'Alice doesn't know I'm not still dancing attendance on my gran,' she said slowly. 'So she's expecting to see you, not me. Do you always meet by the beck?'

Tom had been leafing through the book, exclaiming softly as he reached each illustration, but now he shook his head. 'Always? You sound as if I've spent all my life here, whereas in fact I've only been here for five weeks, and Alice and her aunt and uncle were away for the first week of the hols because Mr Thwaite had promised her a seaside holiday if she passed the exam Miss Spender entered her for, which she did. Satisfied?'

'Oh, *yes*, and I'm sorry if you think me nosy,' Maddy said. 'Only Alice and I spend a lot of time together – we're best friends – so I couldn't help wondering . . .'

She left the sentence unfinished, because Tom had been staring towards the Hall and now he gestured to Maddy to follow his example. 'Here she comes. Aha, and she's wheeling my bicycle!'

When Alice had awoken that morning her first thought had been of the chauffeur's son. Though she had not yet had a chance to admit it to Maddy, for the first time in her life an interest in boys had suddenly made itself felt. He was not a handsome boy and she had never liked ginger hair, and at first he had just been someone to spend time with because Maddy was not available. As they grew to know one another, however, she found there were advantages in having a boy to do her bidding. He had a bicycle, and when he discovered that she did not have transport he had insisted upon giving her what he called 'a seater' so that they reached the village in minutes.

There were other benefits too. When Alice brought a picnic so that they might go further afield, he took it for granted that it should be he who carried not only the sandwiches and fruit but also the stone bottles of ginger beer. Most appealing of all, though, was the fact that he thought her pretty and clever, for he did not know that her reading was a recent accomplishment, and she did not mean to tell him. He might have wondered a little when her uncle and aunt took her to the seaside as a reward for passing the examination, but it was easy enough to brush this aside, saying vaguely that she didn't want to think about school work during the holidays.

The sun was coming through a crack in the curtains and it looked like being a nice day, so Alice slid out of bed and padded over to the wardrobe. She had enjoyed herself very much at the seaside, though she had missed Maddy more than she imagined she would. Every time she had begun to explore a rock pool she had thought of her friend, but it had never occurred to her to suggest to her uncle and aunt that they might invite a child from the village school to accompany them.

Her uncle could swim but refused to do so because he said Yorkshire water was too cold for a man of his years. 'One of these days, when you're older, we'll go to the south of France, where it's warm,' he had told her. 'You'll meet the sort of young men your father would want you to meet and no doubt one of them will teach you.'

'But I want to learn to swim now,' Alice had said obstinately. 'I often play by the beck near the bottomless pool, the one where the blacksmith's daughter drowned. Suppose I were to slip and fall into the water?'

Her uncle had taken her seriously, and an hour after they had returned to Windhover Hall he had called his niece into his study. 'My new chauffeur has a son a little older than you,' he had said. 'I want you to promise me, my dear, that you won't go near the beck unless you are in his company. I know you've befriended young Madeleine, but should the worst happen she would be of little assistance, I imagine.'

Alice had agreed, and now, having selected her plainest cotton smock and a pair of well-worn sandals, she hurried down to the breakfast parlour, anxious to get the meal over so that she could go down to the beck to meet Tom. The swimming lessons had never materialised but he was teaching her to ride his bicycle, though she had not proved an apt pupil, being so anxious not to fall that she clung to her teacher, only letting go when he insisted that she would never learn whilst hanging on to him. Naturally they never bicycled down by the beck, but they usually met there since Tom was a keen fisherman and normally spent the hour or so before she joined him casting a fly over the waters of the bottomless pool, where they both knew the grandfather of all trouts lurked.

'You're in a hurry this morning, my dear. I hope you and your friend are not up to mischief.'

Miss Spender's mild voice cut across Alice's thoughts. Alice smiled at her governess. Miss Spender was tall and slim with light brown hair which she wore in a bun from which strands were perpetually escaping. She had a thin, aristocratic face, a high-ridged nose and gold-rimmed spectacles perched over light brown eyes, and she wore long, limp dresses in a variety of dark shades and dark court shoes on her narrow feet. Alice had once asked her why all her dresses were so similar, to which she had replied: 'I suppose it's because I feel it marks me out as a governess, my dear.'

But now Alice did not answer her companion but merely asked politely if her teacher would care for another piece of toast or a hot cup of coffee to replace the one she had poured herself earlier and not yet touched.

'No thank you, dear. I mean to go up to the schoolroom and write a letter to my sister. Are you going into the village this morning? If so, I've some other letters I would like you to post.'

It was on the tip of Alice's tongue to say she was not, but then her conscience stabbed her. She had been forgetful of both Miss Spender and Maddy, had not even sent them a postcard from the seaside, and she could easily persuade Tom to give her a seater into the village. She smiled. 'Yes, of course I'll take your letters for posting. Tom is teaching me to ride his bicycle and Uncle John has said that when I can do so safely he will buy me a machine of my own, so riding into the village will be good practice. Can you ride a bicycle, Miss Spender?'

The governess looked alarmed. 'Well, I can ride a lady's cycle,' she said cautiously. 'But young Tom has a man's model, I presume?'

Alice looked as perplexed as she felt. 'Man's model?' she repeated. 'What's the difference, Miss

Spender? It's a nice bicycle, green with gold writing. I think it's called a Raleigh . . .'

'And you've been learning to ride on it?' Miss Spender squeaked. 'What on earth was Mr Thwaite thinking of to let you do something so unladylike?' She lowered her voice to a hissing whisper. 'You must have been showing your – your petticoat . . . oh, Alice my dear, possibly even your knickers! You see, the crossbar, as they call it, means you have to elevate one leg and swing it over the saddle.'

Alice gave a squawk of amusement, hastily muffled. 'I'm so sorry for laughing, Miss Spender,' she said. 'I have seen bicycles with crossbars, but Tom's bike doesn't have one. I must ask him why not when I see him next.'

Miss Spender gave a sigh of relief. 'I thought Mr Thwaite wouldn't countenance such behaviour,' she said. 'So you're going into the village, are you? Have you any of your allowance left?'

Alice plunged a hand into her pinafore pocket and withdrew a beautiful little drawstring purse embroidered with violets. It was Miss Spender's most recent Christmas gift and Alice loved it. She held out her palm and tipped the purse so that the money clinked into her hand. 'I've two and tenpence,' she said after a quick count. 'I shan't need more. Unless . . . do any of your letters need stamps, Miss Spender?'

'No, they're all ready to post,' the governess assured her.

As Alice crossed the courtyard half an hour later she saw Mr Browning energetically polishing the already gleaming car. He looked up and smiled at her as she approached.

'Morning, young lady! Are you looking for Tom?' he asked cheerfully. 'He's gone down to the beck to meet you.' He looked at the batch of letters Alice was clutching. 'Going into the village? If so, you'll want the bike, and he's left it in its stall.'

'Good morning, Mr Browning. I'm not sure about the bike, but did Tom take his fishing rod?'

The chauffeur shook his head. 'Not as I noticed, but if I were under the car which I was earlier I dare say a brigade of guards could have marched past without me seeing them.' He chuckled. 'Does it matter?'

'Not really,' Alice admitted. She hesitated, looking enquiringly at the chauffeur. 'I do want to go into the village to post these letters for Miss Spender. Do you think Tom would mind if I took his bicycle down to the beck to meet him?'

The chauffeur had been bending to examine what might have been a scratch on the passenger door, but now he straightened and pushed a hand up through his hair. Alice reflected that this was the first time she had seen Tom's father without his peaked chauffeur's cap and she now saw that his hair was similar to Tom's in colour, though a very much darker shade. 'I said you can take the bike, but don't you go trying to ride it. I know Tom's teaching you, but he says you've a way to go yet, and the bicycle's rather special to us both. It was Tom's mum's many years ago, and we'd hate it to be damaged.'

'I'll be ever so careful, honestly I will, and I wouldn't dream of riding it,' Alice said. 'Thanks very much, Mr Browning . . . oh, is there anything you want from the village?'

Mr Browning shook his head and tapped the car's long and gleaming bonnet. 'No thanks, duck. I'll be busy here for a while yet, but later on I'll likely go down myself and pick up a few things.'

'Righty-ho,' said Alice, wheeling the bicycle out of the stable and heading across the yard. 'I'll tell Tom you said it would be all right about the bicycle.'

'Well well well, look who's here! Alice, my love, you're as welcome as the flowers in May.' Tom grinned. 'Have you two met? If not, may I perform the introductions? Miss Thwaite, this is Miss Hebditch. Miss Hebditch, meet Miss Thwaite. Oh, and I'm Tom Browning, son of the best chauffeur in the dales!'

'Don't be so stupid,' Maddy said stiffly. 'You know perfectly well that Alice and I are best friends, only we've not met for a while because I've been looking after my gran.'

'Sorry, my mistake. You two were glaring at each other like a couple of dogs disputing over a bone so I leapt to the conclusion . . .'

'Well don't,' Maddy said crossly. She turned

awkwardly to Alice, not quite sure what to say. 'We ought to put the book back before we do anything else,' she managed. 'I've told Tom all about it. But I didn't tell him where we kept it when we weren't using it.' Her eyes fell to the letters in Alice's hand. 'Are you going to the village? Shall I come with you, or would you rather go with this – this person?'

'Hey, what have I done to deserve being given the cold shoulder?' Tom asked plaintively. 'Why can't we all go into the village? I wouldn't say I was flush for cash, but I've got about one and seven left over from last week's pocket money, so I'm quite happy to buy sweets for the three of us.'

Alice was looking at Maddy. 'You're angry with me, though I can't think why,' she said crossly. 'I *am* on my way to the village, but if you're going to get nasty then you can jolly well stay here and I'll go with Tom.'

Tom seized the bicycle by its handlebars and began to laugh. 'I don't know what all this is about but I think it's time I put a stop to it,' he said. 'Shake hands and make friends, you two, or I shall get on to my bicycle, ride into the village and leave the pair of you to walk. Otherwise we could ride and tie. Maddy, hurry up and take the book back to wherever you keep it, because you were the one who had it out last.' He turned to Alice. 'Look, get on the carrier, and whilst Maddy puts the book away I'll give you a ride down to the village and then come back for Maddy. Is that all right?' Maddy began to say that she could walk, but he brushed this aside. 'You could walk, but you're not going to because I have offered you a ride on my prancing steed and it would be very rude to turn me down flat,' he said, and this time his tone was serious.

Maddy felt her cheeks redden. 'Sorry; of course it would be lovely to have a lift down. I'm sorry if I was rude, Tom. But what did you mean by "ride and tie"?'

'Oh, it only means take it in turns,' Tom explained. 'Hop on the carrier, Alice, and we'll coast down the hill in no time. Then I'll leave you to have a good wander whilst I come back for your little friend.'

Tom was a tall young fellow, but Maddy objected to the term 'little friend' and said so, but the other two were already heading off along the stony track towards the village, and paid no heed.

Chapter Four

Miss Verity Parrott was in her classroom, trying to concentrate on her preparation for the new intake of children in September. She had checked the supplies and had a neatly written list of names of those who would start their school careers on the ninth of the month, and until ten minutes ago had been quite pleased with the way things were going. In other years the school had simply been divided into juniors and seniors but this year, with numbers increasing, she had asked for, and been granted, a pupil teacher to help her with the little ones, children aged between four and six. The Education Department had appointed someone to the post, but most unfortunately the girl had changed her mind. She had explained that she had an older sister who lived in York and that she could get a higher wage if she went there.

The headmaster of the village school, Mr Grice, had just called Miss Parrott into his office to break the news, and when she had said, comfortingly, that she supposed the pair of them could manage he had shaken his head. 'I'm not saying there is going to be a war, or that it will affect us here in Yorkshire,' he had explained, 'but I do think that such a thing is not unlikely. Germany is behaving as they behaved just before the outbreak of the last war and then, as no doubt you know, conscription speedily followed.' He had looked over the top of his steel-rimmed spectacles at the other teacher. 'I expect that to you, Miss Parrott, I seem infinitely old, but in fact I am not yet forty. If I am to join one of his majesty's forces I would prefer to volunteer, possibly for the Royal Air Force. I've a younger brother, a career aircraftman, who advises me that it's a good life. So you see, we don't want a situation in which you alone are trying to teach fifty children, and since no one will grant us another fully qualified member of staff a pupil teacher is a necessity. I spoke to the Director of Education yesterday and he suggests that we could look amongst our own pupils and see if any of them would be interested in the post.' He had looked keenly at Miss Parrott. 'Do you have anyone who might be suitable in your class? Ideally, they need to be at least thirteen years old, for obvious reasons.'

Miss Parrott had smiled. 'If you'd asked me last year I'd have had the perfect candidate, but it's too late, I'm afraid – she's won her scholarship to St Philippa's and will be starting there next month.'

Mr Grice had sighed sympathetically. 'Ah, little Madeleine Hebditch. You're right – she would have been ideal. Still, give it some thought, would you, and we'll talk again in the morning.'

Mr Grice watched the door close behind his teacher and sat for a moment lost in thought. When he had first met her he had considered her a plain, if not actually ugly, woman but now he was changing his mind. To be sure, her light brown hair was untidy and her grey dress commonplace. And to begin with he had thought her nose overshadowed the rest of her face and had never looked beyond it, but he now realised that she had a pair of large, clear hazel eyes and a mouth which, in repose, held much sweetness. Sighing, Mr Grice stood up; what did looks matter after all? She was the best teacher he had ever worked with and he frequently sang her praises to his sister, who had once held the very position which Miss Parrott now occupied. Jenny Grice had told him, on more than one occasion, that he was a lucky chap to have Miss Parrott as a colleague.

It occurred to him for the first time that he never used Miss Parrott's first name. Why had he not suggested long since that she should call him Derek? He came to the conclusion that he had not done so because he was a little in awe of her. It was that damned nose, he thought ruefully. It was the sort of nose one associated with Admirals of the Fleet or Roman emperors, not school teachers, and her Christian name didn't help either. Verity! But he knew he was being ridiculous, really, and decided that in future, when they were alone, they must use first names.

Satisfied, Mr Grice turned his attention to his own lists once more.

Back in her own classroom, Miss Verity Parrott was also lost in thought. She was remembering the day, almost exactly a year ago, when she had gone up to Larkspur Farm to confront Mrs Hebditch with the vexed question of Maddy's future. She had still been wondering how best to persuade the old lady to allow her granddaughter to try for a scholarship to St Philippa's when she reached the top of the track, pushed aside the mossy five-barred gate and, taking a deep breath, entered the neglected farmyard.

She had been halfway across it when she heard a sound like the hissing of a snake behind her, and glancing over her shoulder had seen a large flock of geese waddling towards her, led by an enormous gander whose mean little eyes were fixed, she was sure, on the backs of her knees. Verity had stopped and swung round, stamping her foot and shouting in as threatening a manner as she could, but the geese had continued to advance.

Always face up to a flock of geese, she had remembered someone telling her once. *Never let them think you are afraid or they'll take advantage. Geese are cowards and will run away as soon as they realise you aren't scared.*

But I am scared, Verity had admitted to herself. Two of the geese had somehow managed to get behind her so that she felt she was standing in a sea of birds, all of them eager to show her that whoever was afraid it was not they. The teacher had cast a wild glance around her; if only she had a stick or an umbrella, something to threaten them with! But all she had was her waterproof over one arm; she flapped it and the gander grabbed the hem whilst one of his many wives – or might some of them be his sons? – continued to advance, hissing like a sea of snakes and stabbing at the waterproof with vengeful orange beaks.

Verity had stumbled towards the back door just as a large black dog emerged, blinking and yawning, from the depths of a big kennel in front of her. He gave her a look which was almost comical. 'You can't be afraid of a few geese,' he seemed to be saying, and then, as the onslaught of the birds pushed her within a few feet of the back door, the dog had charged. There was a great deal of hissing and squawking, but the teacher had not waited to see who would win. She had thrown open the back door without even knocking and lurched into the kitchen, slamming the door behind her. The noises outside had continued for perhaps half a minute and then she had heard the dog giving an imperative little bark. Well, he had saved her bacon all right, so she must pluck up her courage and let him in even if he was not normally allowed to invade the kitchen. She had opened the door a crack, then wider, and the dog had slid in, giving her a friendly grin as she closed the door behind him. His expression was so knowing that she felt it only polite to thank him for his intervention, and even as the words 'Thank you *so* much; I don't know what I would have done if you hadn't come to my rescue' passed her lips the dog was licking her hand.

Suddenly finding herself in the house without an invitation and chatting to the dog as though it was the master here, Verity had looked round wildly. She had heard from the villagers that Mrs Hebditch was very old and not able to get about as she used to, but she had obviously managed to escape from the kitchen. Verity was just wondering where to begin the search for her hostess when a voice spoke from behind her back. 'If you'll put yourself to the trouble of turning round and telling me what you're doing in my kitchen, young woman, then I might just invite you to state your business.'

Verity had turned very slowly, not knowing quite what to expect, and seen a little old woman leaning upon a black walking cane. Her hair was sparse, her skin was wrinkled, and judging from the clothing which hung on her she had once been very much bigger, but age had shrunk her until she was now about the same size, the teacher reflected, as her granddaughter. She wore little gold-rimmed glasses on her small fat nose, and at that precise moment her mouth was set in a rather unpleasant grin. It was pretty plain that the old woman was awaiting an apology.

'Mrs Hebditch, I presume?' Verity had said.

The old woman had begun to laugh. 'Dr Livingstone, I presume?' she mimicked. 'And you might be . . .'

Talk about being at a disadvantage, Verity had said grimly to herself. She had held out her hand. 'How do you do, Mrs Hebditch? I'm Madeleine's teacher, Miss Parrott; I dare say she's mentioned me. She's a bright girl, quite a star, and I don't mind telling you that I believe with some encouragement . . .'

The old lady was staring at her with an expression she could not identify, but then Miss Parrott had remembered that she had entered the kitchen without an invitation, and though Yorkshire people are both friendly and generous she realised that her first action should have been to apologise and to explain her precipitate entry into a stranger's house.

'I'm so sorry . . . I'm afraid I was being pursued by your geese. I did not realise that the birds were so aggressive and when the big one actually grabbed my rain cape I simply threw the door open and came into your kitchen.' Once more, she had held out her hand. 'I know it was wrong, but I do trust you'll forgive me.'

She had waited for the old woman to take the offered hand, but Mrs Hebditch had suddenly clapped a hand over her mouth and spoken in a muffled tone from behind the barrier of her fingers.

'Go away. Come back when I'm more . . . oh, the devil fly away with you. I can't talk to you now.'

'Why ever not?' Verity had said, sounding as flabbergasted as she felt. She had glanced towards the door which led to the inner hallway and, presumably, to the rest of the house. 'Do you have company? Only I didn't want to discuss things in front of Madeleine in case you did not want her told. But if you'd rather, I can come back in an hour.'

The old woman had given an enormous sigh and dropped the hand which had been shielding her mouth, giving the teacher the benefit of a rueful though tight-lipped smile. 'It's me teefs; they're upstairs in a blue mug beside my bed,' she had told her astonished guest. 'No one ever visits on market days, so I never even noticed until you explained who you were.' She had ducked her head and looked up at Verity through sparse eyelashes. 'I don't find stairs too easy no more – I suppose you couldn't fetch them down for me?'

She and Verity had been facing one another whilst the dog sat between them, staring at whichever was speaking as though he could understand every word. So that was the reason for the shielding hand! Verity had leaned over to pat the furry head so that her face might not show the amusement she felt. 'Of course I can, if you tell me which is your room. Oh dear, this is scarcely how I planned our discussion! First there were your horrid geese and now ... well, which is your room? And perhaps you could pull the kettle over the flame whilst I'm gone, because I'm sure we could both talk more easily with a cup of tea to lubricate our throats.'

The old woman had cackled. 'Very true. Go up the back stairs and you'll come to a square landing. All the doors are open and mine is the second on the left. Whilst you're gone I'll mash the tea and then you can tell me why you've come a-calling. As for not telling Maddy whatever it is you're after, some hope of her not finding out! It's clear you've not been long in these parts; why, you can't take a pee without folk five miles off knowing about it. They call it bush telegraph, but I reckon it's just gossip. Ever played that game they call "Chinese whispers"?'

Verity, with her foot on the lowest step of the stairs, had laughed. 'Yes, I've played it. I think all villages are the same.'

When they had settled themselves at the kitchen table Gran had fixed her uninvited guest with a piercing stare. 'Very well, young woman – now you can tell me why you've come.'

As Verity had feared, she was not impressed by the reply. She could see no point in her granddaughter's going to St Philippa's, scholarship or no scholarship. 'As soon as she's old enough she's going to work, probably in a shop or a café in the town,' she had said decidedly. 'They're not going to ask her for qualifications for that!'

Verity had stuck to her guns. 'Look, no one expects you to make up your mind in a moment, and it is only right that your granddaughter be given a chance to choose her own path. Suppose we meet again next weekend, only with Madeleine as well, and try to sort out how we should proceed? I see no harm in her trying for the scholarship; in fact I think she should take the opportunity. You see, it comes with all sorts of other benefits – bus fares, school uniform, equipment such as tennis rackets and lacrosse sticks, school dinners and even, in some cases, school outings. If she gets it she would, in term time, be off your hands financially speaking. Would that not go some way to defraying the costs of bringing her up?'

The old woman had looked doubtful, but clearly the advantages to be gained if Maddy was offered a scholarship had impressed her. But it was immediately obvious to Verity that Mrs Hebditch was not going to give in easily. 'And how'll I manage while she's gadding off a-pleasuring?' she had demanded truculently. 'I dare say she'll have to be up at the crack of dawn to get to St Philippa's. No one to shop for me, no one to feed the hens and the geese, collect the eggs, weed the vegetable garden . . .'

Her voice had tailed away into a complaining mumble and Verity had bent her head and stroked the dog to hide her amusement. Mrs Hebditch was putting up a fight but she was already halfway to agreeing to the principle at least that Maddy should have a chance. So Verity had waited until the mumble faded into silence before speaking again. 'Naturally, all these things would have to be taken into consideration,' she said smoothly. 'I dare say there are women in the village who would be willing, for a small sum, to come up to Larkspur each day . . .'

'A small sum?' Mrs Hebditch had said, her voice expressing as much horror as though Verity had suggested that she should part with her life savings without delay.

Hastily Verity had broken into speech, though she did not make the obvious retort that it had been Mrs Hebditch herself who had said she needed help. 'I'm so sorry, I didn't mean to offend you. However, such things can be discussed next week, and Madeleine cannot sit the scholarship examination until next summer anyway. She will need to be able to tackle subjects which are not part of the village school curriculum, but if she could spare an hour or so for private coaching a couple of days a week I feel sure she will take the examination in her stride.' She had got to her feet and held out a hand which, after some hesitation, the old woman took. 'Goodbye, Mrs Hebditch; until next week. And now if you would be good enough to lend me your dog, perhaps he will keep the geese off whilst I make my escape.'

Chapter Five

Miss Verity Parrott would have liked to accompany her star pupil on a shopping trip to kit her out for her new school, but when the time came she had handed the vouchers to Maddy.

'I think you should go with someone of your own age,' she had said regretfully. 'It will be much more fun for you that way. What about that girl from Windhover Hall? She'd go with you, I'm sure.'

Maddy had considered. Before Tom had come into their lives she would have taken it for granted that Alice would enjoy the expedition, but now she was not so sure. Nevertheless, she went up to Windhover Hall to ask her friend if she would go with her, and was delighted when Alice replied at once that she would love to. But when she suggested that they should ask Mr Browning to take them into town, Maddy vetoed the idea at once. 'It's not that I don't want to be beholden, because Mr Browning's ever so nice, but I know I'd feel I had to hurry,' she said. 'I thought we'd go on Saturday, if that's all right with you.'

Alice agreed readily, and when Saturday came the

two girls walked down into the village to catch the bus to town. Maddy had promised Miss Parrott that she would be sure to pop into the schoolhouse and tell her former teacher what had been arranged, but before they could put this plan into execution they met Tom coming out of the post office. He was carrying a brown paper bag of humbugs, which he offered to the girls. 'I could have got them at the school tuck shop for half the price,' he said rather regretfully. 'What are you up to? Shopping?'

Maddy told him that they were going to see her teacher, and Tom grinned. 'What, the famous Miss Parrott?' he asked hopefully. 'Isn't she the one they call "Beaky"? Can I come with you? I'm told her nose is a sight to see!'

Maddy was about to tell him not to be so rude, for after a whole year spent in what the teacher called her scholarship class her admiration for Miss Parrott knew no bounds, and she often told Gran that without the teacher's help she might not have got a scholarship at all, let alone have come first out of all the entrants. But Alice spoke before Maddy could even begin to cut him down to size.

'Of course you can't, Tom; Maddy and Miss Parrott will be having a business discussion,' she said firmly, ignoring Tom's crack of laughter. 'You've always told me how important such meetings are, so don't you go poking your nose in.'

'Beak,' Tom said, grinning.

Maddy was so cross that she aimed a punch at his shoulder. He dodged, apologising quickly, but he was still laughing. 'Sorry, sorry, sorry,' he spluttered. 'Off you go then; you can tell me all about it when you come back out.'

'Right,' Maddy said briskly and turned towards the schoolhouse. 'Coming, Alice?'

Alice shook her head. 'No, as I said, this meeting is going to be a business one, and it's not my business. In fact it's just between you and Miss Parrott, so I'll wait for you here. Tom can keep me amused until you get back.'

'Oh, but . . .' Maddy was beginning, but then she saw the teacher standing in the open kitchen doorway of the schoolhouse, smiling at her, so she abandoned the attempt to persuade. Alice to join her and ran quickly up the path.

'Come in, Madeleine,' Miss Parrott called. 'I was looking through the window and saw you there. Was that your friend Alice you were with? Is she going with you?'

'Yes, that's right; it's all worked out,' Maddy said. 'We're catching the eleven o'clock bus into town.' She hesitated before continuing, but was encouraged by her teacher's smile. 'I thought – I thought if it was all right by you, Miss Parrott, I'd come back to the schoolhouse and show you what I'd bought before going back to Larkspur. Always assuming they've got my size,' she added.

'That would be lovely,' Miss Parrott said warmly. 'Now remember, your blazer won't have your house emblem on it; that will have to be bought separately and stitched neatly in place.' She looked shyly at her pupil. 'I know you don't like sewing so I thought, as a little present from me to my star pupil, I would stitch it on for you. But be off with you now, or you'll miss the bus.'

Maddy looked up at the clock on the wall and gave a squeak. 'Thank you *ever* so much, Miss Parrott. I'll come round as soon as we get back.' She grinned at the teacher. 'I might even give you a mannequin display.'

'I'll look forward to it,' Miss Parrott assured her. 'Now off with you before you miss that bus!'

Goodbyes were hastily said and Maddy hurried to join Alice in the short queue which had already formed. She was surprised to find Tom still hovering and said, '*You* aren't coming into town, Tom Browning. This is a girls only expedition.' She looked at Alice for confirmation, and after the slightest of hesitations Alice nodded vigorously.

'Maddy's right,' she said rather regretfully. 'You'd be bored to tears, Tom. Besides, Maddy doesn't want your opinion on what suits her.'

'And what's more, Miss Parrott's given us some money to have lunch at Betty's,' Maddy put in triumphantly. 'They do a set meal for five bob a head and she gave me ten shillings, not fifteen.'

Someone in the queue ahead of them sniggered

and Tom sniffed. 'You don't have to make excuses; the last thing I want to do is hang around the frocks' department,' he said huffily. 'I might see you when you get home, though, Alice, and you can tell me all about your day.'

'What do you think?'

Maddy, Alice and Miss Parrott were in the kitchen of the schoolhouse, Maddy wearing her recently purchased school uniform, the brown lace-up shoes which felt so very heavy to someone used to going barefoot all summer, and the smart green blazer and tunic.

'Well, Madeleine, you've got your scholarship, and now you've got your uniform, and I must say you look every inch a St Philippa's girl,' Miss Parrott said, standing back and surveying her star pupil from top to toe. 'Shall we celebrate with a slice of my fruit cake and a glass of lemon barley water, or are you in a hurry to get home?'

'I'd love a drink, because it was awful hot on the bus and Alice and I had to stand all the way from the bus station,' Maddy said. 'But I don't think we ought to linger; you know how Gran was back in the spring, and though she's pulled round a lot she's still very frail and not at all her old self.' She chuckled. 'It's an awful thing to say, but whenever Gran is ill she's much easier to cope with. In fact, she gets nicer and nicer. She hardly ever whacks me with her cane now and she says thank you when I perform any little task for her, instead of just taking it for granted that it's my duty to do it. So if you don't mind, Miss Parrott, I think I should get back to Larkspur as soon as I can.'

Miss Parrott nodded agreement. 'Yes, I suppose you've left the old lady for quite long enough,' she said. 'And I dare say Alice wants to get home as well.' She sighed. 'Don't the holidays fly by fast! It only seems like yesterday that I said goodbye to the top class, and here I am – or will be – welcoming the new intake. And you are starting on your new life, my dear. Make sure you get the most out of the experience! Pop in to see me when you have a moment . . .' she smiled, 'news from the front line, so to speak. Now, you'd best be on your way.'

The two girls set off together, but when they reached the fork in the track Alice stopped and turned to her friend. 'Why don't you come home with me and show Uncle John and Auntie Ruby your uniform?' she said. 'I know they'd like to see it, and I'm sure your gran won't mind waiting a bit longer – you didn't promise to be home by any particular time, did you?'

'Well, no, but I don't think . . .' Maddy was beginning, but Alice tugged at her hand.

'Oh, do please come,' she begged. 'I know my uncle and aunt would be interested, and besides, there might be some news . . . only I'm not going to tell you what, in case it doesn't happen.'

Naturally, Maddy could not resist such an intriguing

statement, and presently the two girls burst into the drawing room at Windhover Hall to find Alice's aunt and uncle eagerly awaiting her return, a large white envelope on the table between them.

'The letter's come at last, Alice, but your uncle refused to let me open it,' Auntie Ruby said, her tone actually excited. 'He said it was for you to decide whether you wanted to see it first.'

Maddy saw a flush creep up Alice's neck and her eyes grow bright. Just for a second the other girl hesitated, and then she tore open the envelope and pulled out the sheet of paper it contained. Her uncle John leaned forward, his face eager, but Alice clutched the page to her breast and turned a glowing face towards Maddy before holding out the sheet and indicating that she should take it. 'Read what it says, Maddy,' she said, her voice high with excitement. 'Just read what it says . . . aloud, I mean.'

Maddy obeyed. '"Dear Mr and Mrs Thwaite, it gives me much pleasure to inform you that your niece has been awarded a place at St Philippa's School for Girls . . ."'

Alice cast both arms round Maddy's neck and hugged her hard. 'We'll be in the same school at last!' she said joyfully. 'I didn't tell you, because although I passed the entrance exam I didn't come high enough to get an automatic place and had to go on the waiting list.' She turned to beam at her uncle and aunt. 'Are you pleased? Do say you are! I know you were worried when Miss Spender said she wanted to seek a post with younger children, but oh, I didn't want to board again. I'm so happy here, and the thought of being sent off to live away from Windhover Hall really frightened me. I know I'm not clever but I shall do my best to keep up.' She turned to her aunt. 'I know you didn't think I'd make it, Auntie Ruby, but I've proved you wrong, haven't I?'

'You certainly have, and your uncle and I are proud of you,' Auntie Ruby said. She turned to Maddy. 'And now you'd best go back to Larkspur so that Mrs Hebditch can admire your new clothes.' She smiled at Alice. 'Tomorrow we shall go into town again because we have to buy *your* uniform, and if you look as nice and smart as Madeleine your uncle and I will be very pleased.'

Maddy tiptoed across the farmyard, hoping to get into the kitchen without having Snoops jumping all over the beautiful new clothes she was still wearing. However, when she reached the kennel she saw at once that Snoops was not at home, and guessed that he had slipped indoors when Gran had come out to the privy. Since she had not turned him out again Maddy assumed that she had fallen asleep, so she opened the back door quietly, slid into the kitchen and shut the door noiselessly behind her.

Gran sat in her favourite chair with her knitting on her lap, a glass of elderberry wine and an egg sandwich untouched on the table behind her and Snoops curled up at her feet. Maddy tiptoed across the kitchen; she would riddle the stove, pull the kettle over the flame and mash the tea before waking Gran to admire her uniform. She carried out these tasks swiftly, put a cup of tea down on the little stool close by Gran's chair and took her hand, wagging it gently back and forth.

'Gran?' she said softly. 'It's only me, Maddy. I've made you a nice cup of tea, but before I get our supper I'm going to change out of my school kit. It would be too bad if I dropped something on it before school has even started. Gran?'

For a moment she actually wondered if Gran had been and gone and died on her, but then she noticed that the wrinkled hand was warm and saw the old lady's eyelids begin to flicker apart. 'Gran?' she repeated. 'It's me, Maddy. I've made you a nice cup of tea and I thought you might like to see my new school uniform.'

Gran moved her mouth in a series of little mumbling motions. 'Is it morning?' she asked in a thick, sleep-drugged voice. 'I don't want to get up yet, Nurse. Why are you so early this morning? I've not had me breakfast yet; you aren't supposed to come until I've had me breakfast . . .'

'You had your breakfast ages ago, Gran,' Maddy said. 'And do I look like a nurse?' Maddy was used to Gran being a little strange when she first awoke, and decided a little firmness was called for. 'Wake up, Gran,' she said loudly. 'I want to show you my school uniform but I don't want to get it mucky, so as soon as you've seen it I mean to go up to my room and change. Now don't you go falling off to sleep again or I shall be cross. Well, I'm cross anyway because I left you a nice little lunch and a glass of elderberry wine to go with it and you've not touched either.'

Gran struggled to sit up a little straighter in her chair. 'Didn't want it,' she growled. 'I don't have to eat all the slops you keep giving me. Besides, I ate my porridge at breakfast, drank me tea and had two rounds of toast and marmalade. What's wrong with that?'

Maddy felt a big smile spread across her face; she had not admitted, even to herself, how her grandmother's fits of strangeness worried her. But now Gran seemed to be her old self once more and Maddy decided she would hope for the best and not mention the occasional lapses to anyone. 'Gran, do you know what these clothes mean?' she asked.

She half expected Gran to look at her blankly but the old woman's face wore its usual knowing look. 'It means you'll be starting at that damn fancy school,' Gran said resentfully. 'Just an excuse to go gadding off at the crack of dawn every morning, leaving me to manage the best I can, thinking only of your own enjoyment . . .'

Maddy felt her cheeks grow warm; there was

enough truth in her grandmother's assertion to make her blush, but on the other hand no one but Gran would call starting at a new school an enjoyable experience. However, she knew there was no point in saying so, merely putting her arm round the old woman and helping her to her feet. She was sitting her down in one of the straight-backed chairs at the kitchen table when the back door opened, after the briefest of rattles, and Dr Carlton came into the room. 'Afternoon, Mrs Hebditch, afternoon Maddy,' he said cheerfully. 'I see you're about to have your tea, but I wanted a word with you and since I was passing I thought I'd pop in.' As Maddy straightened he pretended to have just noticed the new uniform and stepped back, feigning astonishment. 'So the rumours *were* true!' he exclaimed. 'I heard on the grapevine that clever little Madeleine Hebditch had got a scholarship and now I can see it was a fact. But don't let me interrupt your tea . . .' he glanced at the clock, '. . . or is it supper?'

Maddy giggled. She liked Dr Carlton and appreciated the fact that he visited her grandmother almost every day. 'It *was* Gran's lunch, actually, and I bet you've known about the scholarship for ages,' she told him. 'And now you're here, do try to persuade Gran to eat the food that I leave for her, because once school starts I shan't be here to give her a meal around noon. It's so depressing when I get back to Larkspur and find she's not touched her grub. Is it Gran or me you wanted to talk to? Only I'm just going upstairs to change into old clothes before I begin preparations for supper.'

The doctor grinned at her. 'Both,' he said promptly. 'But Gran and I will have a chat while you change so I'll still be here when you come down. You needn't rush, because you're my last visit before I shut up shop. Is there anything I can do? Put the kettle on? I could do with a nice cuppa.'

Maddy grinned back. 'I've already made the tea,' she said, heading for the stairs. 'Help yourself – I shan't be a tick.'

Coming downstairs again five minutes later in her oldest clothes, Maddy saw, with some surprise, that Gran was sipping her tea and that the doctor had settled himself comfortably in the second basket chair. 'I've just been discussing the future with your grandmother, young Maddy,' he said. 'We've agreed that you'll have to have some help once school starts.'

Gran had been hunched over her mug but at this remark she sat upright and stared at the doctor, eyes blazing. 'Some friend you are,' she said bitterly. 'Me and the girl manage all right without any help from anybody and I don't see why things should change just because she's going to attend some fancy school. I don't mean to get poorly again, but if I do she'll just have to stay off and you'll have to send a note explaining she's ill.'

The doctor shook his head sadly. 'So you expect

me to lie for you? It won't work, Eleanor Hebditch. It's summertime now and you've coped pretty well, all things considered, but winter's coming on and our winters in the dales can be pretty severe. Oh, I know you and Maddy have managed in the past, but the older you get the more prone you will become to infection. And it's not just your health . . .' He glanced around him, seeming to take in, through its open door, the almost empty pantry, the dwindling pile of wood stacked up by the stove and, it must be confessed, the eager interest with which Snoops, who had got to his feet when the doctor entered the kitchen, was eyeing the remains of the loaf. His gaze returned to Maddy. 'This place needs at least one adult, as well as you and your gran,' he said gently. 'There's an Irish couple searching for work in the surrounding villages, a Mr and Mrs O'Halloran. They lost their job as caretaker companions when their employer decided to leave his country house and move to London. I've sounded them out and they would be prepared to give you a hand with housework, cooking and so on in return for their keep, and a small wage which you could afford from your savings.'

At his words, Maddy was conscious of an almost overwhelming feeling of relief. Though she had tried not to worry about the future it was idle to pretend that the addition of a grown man and woman to their small household would not be a welcome one. She opened her mouth to ask what sort of wage the couple would want but Gran spoke before she could do so. 'Whatever they want, they ain't getting it,' she said wrathfully. She glared at Dr Carlton. 'And you've found out about my savings account, eh? Well, you're not touching that, whatever you may think, because it's for my old age.'

The doctor gave a rude crack of laughter. 'Eleanor Hebditch, you'll never see seventy again. Don't you consider that old? No, it's no good protesting. Your granddaughter is at the threshold of her life and I won't see her sold into slavery, so since you're too mean to part with your savings Mrs Foulks at the post office has given me your pension book and I've brought it with me. You can sign it in my presence and on Monday Maddy can take it to the post office and collect your money.'

Gran had sunk back in her chair but now she reared up once again, eyes flashing. 'She shan't take another penny of my pension,' she said furiously, letting her glance dart from the doctor to her granddaughter. 'You say I'm old . . . well, maybe I am, but I'm not on the way out yet. When I can't cook myself a meal or pull a few veg from the kitchen garden then maybe I'll use a few shillings, but until then, no, no, no! Just you let me be, doctor; Maddy and myself manage very well, I'm telling you.'

The doctor sighed. 'What will you do when you've used the last of that wood?' he enquired, pointing to the small pile of logs by the stove. 'How will you dress yourself in the morning and undress yourself in the evening when Maddy isn't here? You say you can make yourself a meal but it's Mrs Grundy who baked that loaf I see sitting on the table, and it's young Maddy who searched out the eggs, boiled them, shelled them and mashed them so you could enjoy them at lunchtime.' His patience suddenly seemed to run out. '*Will* you listen to reason, woman? I'm telling you, I can't leave you here in your present state of health with only a schoolgirl to help you. I'm fond of you, you foolish old woman, so I'm telling you plainly that you've a choice: accept paid help or go into an institution! Which would you prefer?'

Chapter Six

It was no contest, of course. Gran, however, startled and dismayed both her listeners by pretending to burst into tears. 'I'd sooner die than go in the workhouse, and you know it,' she said through stifled sobs. 'You're a wicked old man, Dr Carlton, because you've heard me say many a time that I wouldn't so demean myself. And has Maddy complained that she can't manage? I'll warrant she's done no such thing.'

She dragged a handkerchief out of her sleeve and dabbed at her cheeks and the doctor and Maddy, who had both noticed the absence of actual tears, exchanged guilty smiles; there had been sobs in plenty, however, and Maddy knew her grandmother was genuinely upset, so she did not even suggest that the mopping-up action was somewhat unnecessary. Instead she said briskly: 'Blow your nose, Gran, but the truth is, if you fall or need help when I'm in school . . .'

Gran shot up in her chair, eyes flashing. 'Two months ago I had one fall and we managed fine, with no mention of shutting me up with all those old fogeys,' she said bitterly. 'Why should it be any different now?'

The doctor shook his head chidingly at her. 'It's different because Maddy's going to be away from the house for much longer each day, and when she is here she'll be busy with her homework. The O'Hallorans seem a steady, reliable pair and God knows you've enough empty rooms in this barn of a house to spare one or two. They've a reference from their previous employer which speaks in glowing terms of their efficiency and reliability, but of course I wouldn't expect you to agree to employ folk you've never even met. I can bring them up tomorrow, if that would suit.'

There was a long silence; then Gran blew her nose resoundingly and spoke. 'I suppose there's no harm in my letting them have the use of a couple of rooms if it'll get you off my back,' she said, glaring at the doctor. 'This feller, this Mr O'Halloran, is he a man of the soil? If Maddy insists on going to this posh school I could do with someone to give an eye to the kitchen garden. And if the woman flicks a duster round the place I suppose I wouldn't object.' She cocked an eye at the doctor. 'I dare say he'd agree to sell the garden produce and maybe do odd jobs around the village if he's a handy sort of feller. Yes, it might work out.'

Maddy had watched her grandmother's face and seen the little flicker of satisfaction in the old woman's eyes. It was clear to her, and probably to the doctor as well, that Gran was beginning to see the advantages which the O'Hallorans could bring.

There was a moment's tense silence, and then Gran said decidedly: 'Well, Dr Carlton, you'd best bring them up tomorrow – both of them mind – and we'll see what we can arrange.'

The trio arrived promptly at ten o'clock. Maddy had penned the geese so that their guests were not worried by them, and she and her grandmother, both neatly dressed and sitting facing the back door, had scarcely had time to feel nervous before the doctor rattled a brief tattoo and flung the door wide. He ushered into the room a large woman in a print dress, with a mass of dark hair tied back from her face by a piece of blue ribbon, and a small wiry man whose age, Maddy thought, was impossible to guess, although the woman looked to be in her late thirties or early forties. Both had dark eyes and sallow skin, and the glances they shot round the kitchen were appreciative.

Maddy automatically assumed that it would be the larger partner who gave the orders, but she revised this opinion as they took their places round the kitchen table and the doctor performed the introductions. It was Mr O'Halloran who was the first to hold out his hand and shake Gran's reluctant paw. 'The top of the mornin' to you,' he said jovially. 'Dis is my good lady, Eileen O'Halloran, and you'll be Mrs Hebdyke . . .' He swung round to face Maddy and she saw he had a charming smile. As they shook hands he said: 'So you're the clever young lady what won a scholarship

99

to the posh school; lucky for Eileen and meself it is, 'cos we'd not be needed otherwise, I swear.'

Gran smiled graciously. 'Very true,' she observed. 'And the name's Heb*ditch*. Now, let's get down to brass tacks. My granddaughter will show you round the house and you can decide which rooms would suit you. Then we'll discuss what I'll need help over and what I can perfectly well manage myself.'

'Sorry, my mistake.' Mr O'Halloran smiled apologetically. 'I've a poor memory for names, so I have.'

The meeting was going well, though Maddy was surprised at the O'Hallorans' choice of rooms. They decided they would be happiest in the attic, despite the fact that this meant they would have two quite steep staircases to mount daily, but the reason for this became clear when they returned to the kitchen. 'Me husband's got a terrible snore and we wouldn't want to disturb you,' Mrs O'Halloran explained. 'I doubt whether you will hear a sound from the attics 'cos isn't this a grand big house now?'

Gran had pulled a doubtful face. 'If we do hear a sound you'll be out on your ear, so you will,' she said, imitating Mrs O'Halloran's soft Irish accent in a very rude way, Maddy thought. But when she took Mrs O'Halloran out into the garden and tried to apologise for Gran's behaviour Mrs O'Halloran laughed and told her that she thought nothing of it.

'Sure and our last employer had his old mother

livin' with him and she was a naggy old woman; if we could put up with her and still get a grand reference, Mrs Hebditch won't be hurtin' our feelings,' she said reassuringly. She turned a beaming smile on Maddy. 'Dis place is the answer to a prayer and I can see we'll all get on like pigs in muck.' She glanced around at the kitchen garden of which Maddy was understandably proud, for no matter how tired she was she had kept at least half of it weed-free and productive. The vegetables she grew here were a large part of their diet.

She turned an appreciative glance on the older woman. 'Does that mean it's you who does the gardening?'

The Irish woman raised her brows. ''Tis the pair of us, but my husband can turn his hand to anything, so he'll be after looking for any little job what'll earn him a shilling or two.'

Maddy laughed. 'He'll likely get employment up at the Hall, then,' she observed. 'Mr Thwaite is always after someone to do bits of work and he's a fair man and pays what the job's worth.' She had been leading her companion back through the farmyard, and now she gestured round her at the waist-high weeds and general neglect. 'And if he doesn't find paid work away from Larkspur he can always have a go at the weeds in here!' They were approaching the back door when it suddenly occurred to her to ask Mrs O'Halloran when she and her husband would be joining them. 'No doubt there's a heap of stuff you'll be bringing over, either in a hired van or a horse and cart,' she added. 'Would you like me to give you a hand?'

Mrs O'Halloran stopped short, sniffing the air, her nostrils flaring with pleasure. 'What's dat I can smell?' she said. ''Tis a perfume as sweet and strong as any I've ever smelled! Ah and isn't it the scent from dis wonderful dark red rose? Oh, I could stand and smell it all day, so I could.'

'Yes, it is lovely,' Maddy agreed. 'Long ago, when I was small, Gran used to make potpourri and these were the rose petals she liked the best. But I was asking you when you would be bringing your luggage up to Larkspur. How would next weekend suit you, or do you have to consult your husband?'

Mrs O'Halloran shook her head. 'Declan and myself will be of one mind,' she said. 'We'll bring our stuff at the weekend.' She pushed the back door open as she spoke and walked in on a cosy domestic scene: Gran dispensing tea and biscuits to Mr O'Halloran and the doctor, whilst chatting on the very subject Maddy had just brought up.

'. . . so you'll be bringing your stuff next weekend?' Gran was asking, and Maddy was relieved to hear that she had apparently accepted the Irish couple. 'We've got a deal of blankets and there are a couple of bedsteads in the attic.' She chuckled. 'Is that why you chose the rooms up there? Because you didn't fancy trying to carry bedsteads and mattresses down the attic stairs?'

Everyone laughed, and Dr Carlton got to his feet and addressed the O'Hallorans. 'I must go; will you come with me, or stay here for a while and walk down later? I'm sure Maddy will show you the quickest path. Will you need help with your luggage, by the way? How much will you be bringing?'

'Not a great deal; we're not overburdened with stuff,' Mr O'Halloran admitted. 'We travel light, me and the missus; two suitcases, that'll be it. 'Twas all found whilst we worked for Lord Bromfield, but we've everything we shall need.'

'Lord Bromfield! Well, you'll find it very different working for Lady Hebditch,' Gran said with a dry chuckle. She waved a hand at her visitors. 'Off with you; and mind you're on time on Saturday 'cos your first task will be to help me do a bake.'

Gran hardly waited until the O'Hallorans were out of the door before turning to Maddy. 'What do you think?' she asked rather querulously. 'She was bold enough, giving her opinion on this and that, but he scarce opened his mouth. They say when a fellow's been in prison and comes out he's unnatural quiet; I hope we've not agreed to take a jailbird into our home! And why so little luggage? Fishy, I call it.'

Maddy heaved a sigh. 'If you didn't like them why didn't you say so?' she asked bluntly. 'It would have been easy enough to make up an excuse. Only I see nothing wrong in a man being quiet, especially when he has a wife who never uses one word when ten will do. And that's all tosh about ex-prisoners being quiet; it's what they call a generalisation, and that means . . .'

'I know what it means,' Gran said quickly. 'Don't you go lecturing me, young woman, else I shan't teach that baggage to make your favourite gingerbread. And now I suppose you're going off to the Hall to tell young Alice that we've been and gone and let strangers into our house.'

Maddy grinned guiltily. Gran was a wily old bird; she had indeed had every intention of going up to the Hall and explaining, not only about the O'Hallorans but also what a difference their presence would make to her. She would have time to do all sorts of things with Alice now, but with Gran's beady eye upon her she shook her head sadly. 'All right, all right; so I was going to nip up to the Hall. But there's no point because I've just remembered the Thwaites attend church on Sundays, so I suppose the sensible thing to do would be to get the attic ready for its new occupants. And why did you tell Mrs O'Halloran that awful whopper? You never do a bake at the weekend; you know you don't.'

Gran flung up her hands. 'That's right, pick on your old grandmother and make out that I'm a liar,' she said resignedly. 'I just want to see if she's got a light hand with pastry and knows her favourite recipes off by heart. How are we off for ingredients?'

'Haven't got 'em,' Maddy said bluntly. 'And until you let me collect your pension – and you know I can, now that you and Dr Carlton have signed your book – there won't be any. So you'd best make up your mind really fast, otherwise the O'Hallorans won't just think you're a liar; they'll know you are.'

Gran made an angry noise like a cat growling. 'All right, all right; you've had your laugh,' she said bitterly. 'You may take yourself off with *my* pension book tomorrow morning, and buy whatever we need for a bake.'

A week later the O'Hallorans moved into Larkspur Farm, and for the next few days Maddy was fully occupied with settling them in and explaining what Gran could not do, how much she could do, and how much she thought she could do. However, she did manage one hasty trip over to the Hall, only to find neither Tom nor Alice present, though Mr Browning assured her that they had only walked into the village and would be back soon enough. Maddy and Mr Browning were in the immaculate stable yard, Mr Browning in the overalls which he wore when he was not about to drive his employers somewhere. Looking a little self-conscious, he cleared his throat and cocked an eyebrow at Maddy. 'My son tells me that you and your gran are employing a couple of migrant workers to give a hand. Tom says you're lodging them free in return for work, which I must say the old place could do with. Last time I passed, I saw the yard alone was waist-high in weeds. I enjoy gardening, and it wouldn't take myself and your new chap more than a couple of hours to clear it. It'd make life a lot easier for your hens and geese when they forage for the corn you throw out of an evening.'

'Oh, thank you. What a kind offer. But I'm afraid we couldn't afford ...' Maddy began, only to be interrupted.

'Did I say anything about payment? Mr Thwaite pays me a pretty good wage, but to tell you the truth I don't have enough to occupy me and I'd be glad of a chance to meet your new worker.'

Maddy had begun to say that it was early days yet but she was sure Mr O'Halloran was equal to the task of clearing the farmyard when something occurred to her. Mr Browning was lonely! Doubtless he had been too busy to meet many locals since he and Tom had moved to Windhover. So she smiled at him, and said that the O'Hallorans would doubtless welcome Mr Browning's help once they had settled in. The chauffeur nodded; clearly this was a man who could take a hint. 'I'll give it a couple of weeks and then come calling,' he said. 'There's a nice little pub in the village called the Craven Heifer; we might toddle down there and have a drink together.'

'I'm sure Mr O'Halloran would like that,' Maddy said politely, preparing to take her leave. 'Tell Tom and Alice I called, would you?'

The baking day to which Gran had referred did not occur until the O'Hallorans had been at the farm for a few days, and was only a moderate success. Mrs O'Halloran looked doubtfully at the ingredients which Maddy had set out on the big kitchen table and then spoke apologetically. 'Sure and I never made a loaf like that in me life. I t'ought, when you axed me if I knew how to bake bread, that you meant sody bread.' She flicked the pot of yeast with a disdainful finger. 'We don't use yeast to make sody bread; don't need it. And 'tis better for the digestion, so it is.'

Eager to please, Maddy would have let their new worker make her soda bread, but Gran was made of sterner stuff. 'We don't want no slapdash ways here,' she said firmly. 'A good loaf of bread is easy to make once you know how. Oh, I know it's an all day job because the loaves have to be proved, but at the end of it you'll have bread for a week and still as sweet and fresh on a Sunday as it were the previous Monday.' She assumed the attitude of someone tottering on the brink of the grave. 'I thought you were going to do the bake for me, with just the odd bit of advice, but it looks as though I'll have to roll my sleeves up and give you a demonstration.'

'Oh, there's no need,' Mrs O'Halloran said quickly. 'A fast learner, I am. Tell me what to do and I'll do it . . .' she smiled at Maddy, 'and sure won't you be having yourself the best loaves of bread in the whole of Yorkshire.'

107

But this Gran would not allow. 'It won't be Yorkshire bread if it's made by a perishin' Irish flibbertigibbet,' she muttered, heaving herself out of her chair and going over to the kitchen table. 'Stand clear,' she said irritably. 'And watch what I do and do the same yourself. Maddy, divide the ingredients into two piles. Fetch me a jug of water from the pump in the yard – I want it fresh, not standing. And when we've baked the loaves we'll see who makes the best bread.'

Mrs O'Halloran sighed deeply and then turned and winked at Maddy. ''Tis idle to pretend I've ever baked bread in me life, but I still say sody bread's the nicest,' she whispered. 'The old lady's a tartar, but 'tis clear she'll teach me, whether I like it or no. Ah well, 'tis always hard when a body starts a new job, but as I say, 'tis a quick learner I am and I reckon I'll soon get into the way of it.'

'I'm sure you will,' Maddy said, with a confidence she was far from feeling. She had tried to make bread under Gran's tuition before; her loaf had been soggy in the middle and since then Gran had barred her from the kitchen on baking days, so now she watched closely while the Irish woman kneaded and punched and manhandled the dough before dividing it between the tins and placing them in the hearth so that they might prove in the warmth from the stove.

That done, Mrs O'Halloran stepped back, shooting a triumphant glance at Gran; too soon, as it turned out. 'Now we'll make a family fruitcake and an egg custard for our dinners,' Gran said briskly as her helper turned away from the stove. 'Off with you, Maddy; I dare say there's a hundred things you ought to be doing, and you can safely leave Mrs O'Halloran and myself to finish off the bake.'

Maddy was glad to go, for her time of freedom was growing short. At first she had been quite happy to concentrate all her spare time on the O'Hallorans, but she very soon realised that she and Gran, thanks to Dr Carlton, had fallen on their feet. Although Gran ruffled up like an indignant turkeycock when Mrs O'Halloran offered to dress her, there was little else which the old lady did not expect her helper to do. The kitchen garden, however, remained Maddy's pride and joy, but when she headed there now, meaning to pick some runner beans, she found Mr O'Halloran at work with a will, double-digging the uncultivated half. As Maddy approached him he leaned on his spade, wiping the sweat from his forehead with a large red and white spotted handkerchief. 'Mornin', miss, and ain't it a grand one?'

Maddy agreed. 'I've come to get some beans,' she told him. 'I didn't expect to find you here, Mr O'Halloran.'

The man cocked an eyebrow. 'Ah, by the time you've been in your new school a week I'll have the whole place nicely dug over for when the frosts come. There's nothing like a good frost to break down heavy soil. And me next job were to ask if I can have some of that manure heap in the corner of the pasture. It's the best grub for improvin' the soil. Sad it is that we can't plant the whole area with spuds, but they should have been in by Easter, or April at the latest, so's the haulms would have swelled in the soil by the time we'd want to harvest them.' He grinned at her and she thought, suddenly, that it was a pixie grin, full of mischief. In fact, Maddy realised, he reminded her of an illustration in Miss Parrott's big fairy book of a little man sitting on a spotted toadstool, in a magic wood. She must have smiled involuntarily as the thought entered her head, for Mr O'Halloran raised his brows. 'You agree that to put down the land to spuds would enrich the soil? Value your opinion I would, for you've kept this garden as well or better'n any man could; we both love the land so we'll get along fine, so we will. When does school start?'

'In a few days,' Maddy said briefly. 'I'll pick some beans and take them to your wife in the kitchen, and then I think I'll nip over to Windhover Hall to see my friend Alice. She's starting at the school at the same time as me.'

However, a shock awaited her at the Hall. Alice had been engaged in arranging her brand new books in a smart leather satchel, but when Maddy was ushered into her sitting room by a smiling maidservant she jumped up from the window seat. 'Let's walk into the village; I need a pencil sharpener,' she said, then giggled. 'With all the things my aunt and uncle said I would need – a beautiful fountain pen, a geometry set, and all kinds of pencils – no one thought of a tiddly little thing like a pencil sharpener.' She tucked her hand into Maddy's arm. 'Do *you* want a pencil sharpener? They don't cost much, and Tom says they're important, so we'd best get one each.'

'I've got one already, thank you very much,' Maddy said loftily. She indicated the numerous objects which Alice had spread out on a small table. 'Gosh, if you try to take that lot to school the weight will break your shoulder!'

Alice's soft brows shot up towards her hairline. She was wearing one of her smart summer frocks, pale green cotton with matching sandals, and looking even prettier, Maddy thought, than she usually did. 'Break my shoulder? What makes you think I'll be carrying it myself? It'll be Browning's job to carry it until we reach my classroom . . . I expect he'll carry yours as well, if you ask him.'

Maddy frowned. 'What on earth makes you think *Mr* Browning will be anywhere near the school? You'd better explain.'

As she spoke both girls had been crossing the hall and now Alice stopped by the coat-stand and took down her jacket, taking it for granted that Maddy would help her into it. 'Well, of course Uncle John's chauffeur will drive us to and from school,' she said impatiently. 'How did you think we would get there?'

Maddy felt annoyance well up within her. Alice behaved as if she, Maddy, were just another servant, standing by to help her into her coat and possibly even to hold the door for her, and now she was actually daring to sound put out. 'Are you listening?' Alice demanded. 'Browning will be taking us to school. Uncle John says we must leave early because it's a good drive from here, but Browning doesn't mind. Tom says his father often grumbles that he doesn't have enough to do, so ferrying us to and from school will fill in his time.'

'Ferrying *you* to and from school, you mean,' Maddy corrected her hotly. 'I'd rather go on the bus.'

'Oh!' Alice said blankly. 'If you insist . . . but surely you'll let Browning take you into the village? And back again after school, of course? Oh, do think again, dear Maddy. Think of the winter when the snow's a foot deep and the backs of your legs get covered in chilblains!'

Maddy knew Alice had a point; it would be madness to refuse the offered ride into town when the weather was truly awful. But other girls and boys didn't have a Mr Browning, and they managed to get to school in all but the very worst weather. Come to that, there was no guarantee that the car would get through when the weather was really bad. In fact they probably stood as good a chance, or better, on the bus than in the Daimler, so despite Alice's pleading eyes Maddy refused to capitulate.

112

'I don't want to be different,' she said obstinately. 'I shouldn't have thought you'd want to be either. And honestly, Alice, we don't know a soul – apart from each other – who's starting at St Philippa's when we do. Wouldn't it be easier to go in on the bus with lots of other girls?'

'Well, maybe,' Alice said after a considerable pause. 'But Tom thinks we should go with his father and Tom's usually right.' She had been looking thoughtful but now she turned a hopeful face towards her friend. 'Tell you what, we'll get Brow— I mean Mr Browning to take us to the village really early, then when the bus arrives we'll be first aboard and can be sure to sit together. Will you agree to that?'

Maddy was tempted, but she knew Alice's wheedling ways. All it needed was a day of rain or high winds and Alice would insist that they go all the way to school with Mr Browning, and it would be difficult to change her mind. She temporised. 'Tell you what, Alice, we'll let Mr Browning take us to the bus stop for the first week, and the second week we'll go all the way by car and then decide. Will that satisfy you?'

After some thought Alice said, rather grudgingly, that she supposed Maddy must have her way as usual, a remark which was to say the least somewhat unfair, for Alice took it for granted that she should have her way over most things. However, it turned out that both Gran and the O'Hallorans thought

Maddy was mad to turn down the offer of a ride in the Daimler, so for the time being Maddy held her peace. She was pretty sure that if Alice enjoyed the bus ride and made a few friends on their journeyings she would probably agree to travel by bus for the rest of the term.

On the first day of school Maddy got up while it was still dark. She dressed with special care, plaited her long, light brown hair into two shining braids, and reminded herself that she needed a couple of oatcakes and a chunk of cheese for her elevenses. But early though she was, when she went down to the kitchen she found that Mrs O'Halloran had already cooked the porridge and made a pot of tea, and when Maddy greeted her she indicated a small package, done up in greaseproof paper, on the end of the table nearest the door. 'I t'ought you'd be wantin' a mouthful come break-time,' she said rather awkwardly in response to Maddy's delighted thanks. 'And I know your gran wouldn't have you goin' off wit' only a jam sandwich betwixt you an' starvation, so get outside of that porridge quick, 'cos you don't want to be late on your first day.'

Two minutes later, porridge eaten and tea drunk, Maddy was putting on her brand new blazer. She had thanked Mrs O'Halloran profusely for getting up so early, but assured her that it had not been necessary. 'I'm used to early rising, and in fact I like it,' she said.

'It's awfully nice to have company, but don't feel you have to do this every morning.'

The older woman smiled. 'You aren't the only one what enjoys early risin', me darlin',' she said. 'This way, by the time the sun comes up I'll be at work in the house or the garden. Off wit' you now.'

Maddy opened the back door and sniffed the wonderful country smell, a mixture of the sheep on the hillside and the rich September grass, with the added little chill of the mist in which the sheep stood, their fleeces steaming as the day warmed. She set off at a smart pace towards the lane where she was to meet the car, but when she reached it she was rather surprised not to hear the purr of the Daimler's engine. She frowned. Surely she had not got the arrangements wrong? She and Alice had agreed that Mr Browning would pick her up first and then return to the Hall to collect Alice on the way down to the village, which would give Alice a good twenty minutes' extra time in bed. But there was no car gliding along the lane, so Maddy was forced to conclude that something had gone wrong and she must make her own way to the bus stop.

When she got there she saw a couple of girls already waiting, but there was no sign of either Alice or the Daimler. Something really must have gone wrong, Maddy concluded, and was more certain than ever when the bus chugged to a halt and the conductor shouted at them to get aboard since he knew they would not want to be late on the first day of term.

Maddy hesitated. She knew cars sometimes broke down but she did not think that the Daimler, after all the loving care lavished on it by Mr Browning, could possibly have done so. Mentally, Maddy shrugged. The bus driver was consulting a large gunmetal watch which hung by its chain just below the steering wheel. Tentatively she put a foot on the platform, then climbed into the bus. She knew how much Alice liked getting her own way, but surely even she would not let her friend down in such a manner?

However, conjecture was useless. She would find out what had happened when she reached school.

Because his term did not start for another two days, Tom thought he would go to see the girls on to the bus on their first day at the new school. He waited in the passenger seat of the Daimler whilst his father fussed around, checking that all was as it should be, before settling himself behind the wheel. 'You've taken Miss Thwaite's place,' Mr Browning said, only half laughing. 'Madam likes to sit in front, you know.'

Tom felt his face grow hot; he knew his father thought Alice somewhat above herself and would have liked to see Tom take her down a peg or two. However, now was not the time to start an argument so he just grinned and said apologetically: 'It's all right, Dad. I'll stay here if you like, but Alice and I are friends, even if she does act a bit "Lady of the Manor" from time to time; I bet you she'll be quite happy for me to come into the village and see her aboard the bus.'

His father shrugged, and started the engine. 'Well, I dare say you're right.' He turned the car towards Larkspur. 'And anyway, little Miss Thwaite will be so excited at the thought of her new school that she probably wouldn't notice if you drove and *I* sat in the passenger seat!'

They were still chuckling over the thought when the car suddenly veered, and before either of them could react the front of the Daimler buried itself in the bank and the engine spluttered and died. 'What the devil . . .' Tom began, thoroughly startled. He had never known his father have even the slightest of accidents. But Mr Browning was already out of the car, running round to examine the damage, so Tom opened his door and went to join him.

'Whatever made her suddenly leap into the bank like that?' he said plaintively, staring at the long bonnet, now buried in mossy earth and wild flowers.

Mr Browning gave his son a withering look. 'Look there – the perishing tyre's burst,' he said bitterly, pointing to the offending wheel. 'I checked every nut and bolt, every spark plug even, and yesterday she was fine. She must have caught something sharp that simply ripped the tyre virtually in two. Still, if we can get her back on the road then I can change the wheel and still be in time. We shan't be able to call for little Madeleine, but I dare say if you run you can

117

get to Larkspur in time to explain what's happened. Fortunately the walk into the village is all downhill, so even if she waited a while for me to pick her up she'll still have time to catch the bus.' He grinned at his son. 'All I can say is thank the Lord this didn't happen with Mr and Mrs Thwaite aboard. Mr Thwaite would have laughed it off, but his wife wouldn't have liked it at all. Still, neither of them need know. Now you take the left-hand side, Tom, and I'll take the right, and we'll both heave on three. One, two . . .'

Twenty minutes later, father and son stood back and exchanged rueful glances. 'We'll have to get a tractor and chains; it's going to take more than the two of us to get her free,' Mr Browning said, glancing at his watch. 'It's far too late to go to Larkspur now, and anyway the bus will have left. Mr Thwaite will have to arrange for a car for Alice, so we'd best go and tell him so's he can ring the garage. Then we'll go down and fetch old Fred from Mallard Farm to the rescue; he'll soon have her out.'

Maddy took one last glance around her and then selected an empty seat near the front and slid into it. She pushed her neat little satchel down by her feet, and even as she did so the bus began to move. Maddy sighed; for whatever reason, Alice had let her down. Maddy could not help remembering the face that Alice had pulled at the mere thought of catching the bus; no doubt she had always intended to get her own way with no thought for the position it would put her friend in. Well, two could play at that game. When the Daimler arrived at the school gates, Alice would find no Maddy awaiting her; no indeed! Maddy would go straight into school, looking neither to left nor right, and leave Alice to discover for herself which classroom she was expected in, and where she was meant to go first. And unless she had a very good reason for not sticking to their plan, she could jolly well make her own friends. She need no longer think that Maddy wanted to be one of them.

Even as the thought crossed Maddy's mind, the bus jerked to a stop and another passenger jumped on to the platform. She was a small girl with curly, ash blonde hair, laughing blue eyes and a little satchel that was the twin to Maddy's own. She was also wearing an identical green blazer with silver braid. Maddy wondered whence she had come, for she was breathing heavily and had clearly had to run to catch up with the vehicle, though why she had not been at the bus stop Maddy could not conjecture. Perhaps she was a new girl, like herself, or perhaps she was one of those people who are never on time for anything.

The girl slid into the empty seat beside Maddy, turned, and gave her a beaming smile. 'Hello,' she said cheerfully. 'Your uniform looks new, like mine. Does that mean this is your first day at St Philippa's?'

'Yes, it is,' Maddy said. She wished she had even half the confidence this girl displayed. 'I won a scholarship.'

'Did you? I did too! How odd that we should sit together – we're probably the only two scholarship girls on the entire bus,' the blonde one said. 'My name's Marigold Stein; what's yours?'

'Madeleine Hebditch,' Maddy replied at once. She glanced curiously at her companion and decided that she liked this girl. Since it was the first day for them both, they would possibly be in the same class, which would be nice. Maddy could not help smiling a little. If Alice expected her, Maddy, to be lonely without her, she would be disappointed. But her new friend was speaking.

'Madeleine. That's a really lovely name. My name is quite pretty too, don't you think?' And then, not waiting for a reply: 'But I meant to ask you whether you were saving this seat for someone?'

'I was, but she didn't turn up,' Maddy acknowledged. 'Maybe her father's car broke down. But don't worry about it – I know Alice and she'll somehow manage to get to school in time, car or no car. To tell you the truth, she wanted to be driven all the way, so maybe that's what's happened. She's used to getting what she wants; she's had a governess till now and Miss Spender wasn't very strict with her.' Suddenly Maddy felt ashamed of discussing her friend with this unknown girl. 'She's all right, is Alice,' she added rather feebly. 'You'll like her, honest to God you will. She's very pretty and has lovely clothes and – and though she wouldn't claim to be clever she worked very hard to pass the entrance exam and she's always shared the nice things she has with me, so I shouldn't be critical. We both live a good way from the village so we spend quite a lot of time together.'

Marigold smiled. 'Are you warning me off?' she asked cheerfully. 'Can't you have two best friends? Think of all those Angela Brazil stories of the Triumvirate. In fact lots of her stories have three main characters, come to think.'

The two of them chatted as the bus rumbled on, sometimes stopping to pick up a girl in green or a lad in the purple and cream uniform of the neighbouring boys' school. 'Do you read much?' Maddy asked. 'We had a wonderful teacher at the village school, Miss Parrott, who used to lend us books so I've read all sorts, and then over the summer Alice's uncle John – she lives with him and her aunt Ruby – lent us *The Water Babies* by Charles Kingsley. Have you read that?'

'I did try once,' Marigold said rather dubiously. 'But it was full of moralising, so I gave up. Then I found another edition which was better, only for younger children, I think; at least, one of the teachers asked me why I had an edition meant for the under tens, so I explained about the moralising one and she said she'd try to find me what she called "something more suitable", only she never did. Why?'

Maddy hesitated, then turned a searching look on her companion. Scanning her from top to toe and dropping her voice, she asked in thrilling accents: 'Do

121

you believe in magic? It's important that you tell me the truth.'

'What sort of magic?' Marigold said promptly. 'Elves on toadstools? Or little people with wings who can grant wishes? Or old women in pointy hats, who live in gingerbread houses? There are all sorts of magic, you know.'

'Not fairies, or at any rate only very special ones. I was thinking more of water babies,' Maddy said. 'In the very first chapter of the book Mr Kingsley talks about Vendale, which is where he says he found them. He doesn't give the place its real name because he says if he does curious young ladies would turn it upside down looking for naiads, so Alice and I, and our friend Tom, decided to try to find out where he meant. We know he visited Cumming Cove, which was where the little chimney sweep climbed down the cliff when he was being chased by the people from the big house who believed he was a thief.' She thought she saw a sceptical look in her new friend's eyes and hastened to explain. 'But of course I know we shan't find water babies. What we want to find is Vendale itself, so that we can look in the pools and waterfalls there and possibly see a flash of whatever it was Mr Kingsley saw which led him to write his story.' She hesitated, and when she spoke again her voice was uncertain. 'If . . . if you'd like to join in our search I'd love to have you.'

'I think that's a grand scheme,' Marigold said, her

blue eyes sparkling. 'Tell me more about your friend Tom. I can't think of a single boy I know who would even pretend to search for a secret dale, let alone water babies.'

But at this point the bus drew up betwixt the two schools, and Maddy noticed, with an inward grin, that whilst the boys slung their satchels over their shoulders and galloped off without a backward glance, amongst the girls there was much fluffing up of hair and straightening of ties and stocking seams. Appearances were clearly important at St Philippa's.

As soon as she and Marigold entered the schoolyard, Maddy forgot her vengeful intentions and began to cast around for sight of Alice. When she saw her friend, who was clearly waiting for her, the last traces of her recent animosity disappeared, for the anxiety on Alice's heart-shaped face made her ashamed of her lack of faith. And after all, if Alice had not let her down she would not have met and made friends with Marigold. Grabbing the other girl by the hand, she towed her across the playground until they reached Alice's side.

'What went wrong?' she asked. 'When Mr Browning didn't come I decided I'd best start walking, and when I reached the village and the bus arrived I couldn't wait any longer.'

'One of the Daimler's tyres burst, so Uncle John had to telephone for a car from the garage. When I got here one of the older girls saw me hovering and asked me which class I was in, and when I said I didn't know she laughed and said that in that case waiting for my friend was the sensible thing to do.' She raised her brows at Maddy. 'How *do* we find out what class we're in?'

'I think we get into lines and the teachers call the roll, or at least that's what they did on the first day at the village school,' Maddy explained in a rapid undertone. 'But I should introduce you two to each other before we do anything else. Marigold, this is my friend Alice Thwaite; Alice, this is Marigold Stein. She's new too, so we might all be in the same class.' The two girls eyed each other warily and Maddy was dismayed to see that Alice's eyes flicked rather disdainfully over her new friend. However, she told herself that it was probably shyness. 'Ah, here comes a teacher; she'll explain what we're supposed to do.'

The teacher, arriving at Marigold's side, smiled down at them, then looked round the schoolyard. 'New girls, over here, please,' she called. 'You are bound for class 3A. Your form teacher will be Miss Bendon. Get into line, please, and I'll take you straight to your classroom. Follow me, everyone.'

School finished at four o'clock, by which time Maddy was worn out. She had been allocated a desk, a peg in the cloakroom and a little key to a locker where she could keep personal possessions. She had met a bewildering number of teachers, had received a bundle of dinner vouchers and enjoyed a meal of mince and mashed potatoes.

The girls were allowed to sit anywhere they liked for the meal, and Alice and Marigold had settled on either side of her. The girl sitting opposite had grinned cheerfully at them as the plates of rice pudding, each with a dollop of red jam on top, were passed along the tables. 'We call this "Death in the Alps",' the girl had said. 'We've got nicknames for most of the school dinners, but you'll find out for yourselves soon enough.'

Maddy had giggled, but did not reveal to anyone how nice it was to have a meal in whose preparation she had not been involved. Indeed, she had been pleasantly surprised at break-time that morning to be given not just a small bottle of milk with a straw but two biscuits, one shortbread and the other a ginger nut. She had waited with some apprehension for a teacher or a prefect to demand payment for such luxuries, but it had soon become obvious that no money was to change hands, so she had been able to enjoy her milk and biscuits without a qualm.

Most of the day had been spent in learning their way around the school, meeting the teachers and receiving text books, yet Maddy felt as weary as though she had run a marathon, and when she crossed the playground with Alice and Marigold at the end of the day she admitted that she was worn out.

'I'd like to be able to say come back with me in the

Daimler,' Alice said ruefully. 'But I can't, because the beastly car won't be back on the road, Mr Browning says, for the best part of a week. I thought Uncle John might borrow the car from the garage for the whole week, but they can't spare it so I shall be coming by bus like the rest of you.'

'Good,' Maddy said. 'And did you hear Miss Bendon say we'd best get ready for a bit of a rush? Someone told her the boys simply push their way through the waiting girls and bag all the best seats, so we shouldn't expect any gentlemanly behaviour from them because we won't get it.'

The bus arrived and Miss Bendon's informant was proved right. Girls who had stood patiently waiting were brushed aside in the mad rush, and found themselves climbing aboard a bus on which the vast majority of seats were already taken. Some of the older boys, leering horribly, suggested that a girl might like to make use of a boy's lap, but such remarks were ignored. Maddy sighed aloud at the thought of having to stand all the way to the village, but was heartened by a short and stocky boy with a cream cap on the back of his head and a broad grin on his freckly face. 'You'll be all right, kid,' he told her patronisingly. 'Me and my pal get off at the next stop, so if you look sharp you can nab our seats.'

Maddy nodded; what with the noise of the engine as it began to grind up a hill and the shouts and the yells of the passengers, even hearing oneself think was a problem, but she got the gist of what the boy was saying and passed the message on to Marigold who, like herself, had failed to get a seat and was strap-hanging. Alice, to no one's surprise, had secured a window seat.

When the bus was about to stop, Freckle-face poked Maddy in the back. 'Get ready or you'll be given the bum's rush,' he warned her. 'I gave your pal the nod, so if you move fast you can sit for the rest of the journey.'

'Thanks,' Maddy mumbled. It had just occurred to her that not finding a vacant seat had been a mixed blessing. Alice's attitude to Marigold had got frostier and frostier as the day went on. At first Marigold had not seemed to notice the drop in temperature and had prattled on, eager to discuss how she would like Maddy and Alice to come down to her house in the next village so that they might do their homework together. But gradually she had realised that Alice was trying to freeze her off, and being only human, Maddy supposed, had begun to resent it. If I *had* got a seat and Marigold had sat beside me, I think Alice might have got really unpleasant, Maddy told herself. Oh lor, I'm like a bone between two dogs . . . no, more like a mouse between two cats! Whatever am I to do? How silly that Alice is jealous, but I think that's what it is. Oh dear, I can see trouble looming and no way of averting it, or not without being downright rude at any rate.

She realised she had been right when Freckle-face and his companion began to rise in their seats and Alice, who must have been watching them in the reflective window glass, got to her feet too. She caught Maddy's eye and raised her voice in something perilously akin to a yell. 'Madeleine! Keep that seat for me.' Being Alice, she ignored the grumbles as she pushed her way past standing passengers, arriving at Marigold's side just as the other girl slumped into the aisle seat next to Maddy's window one. Alice stamped her foot. 'I *told* you to save that seat for *me*, Madeleine Hebditch,' she said, her voice loud enough to be heard even above the general hubbub. 'I *did* tell you that I wanted a bit of help with my homework.'

Marigold looked indignantly up at Alice, who was now strap-hanging, just as Marigold and Maddy had previously been doing themselves. 'If you want help with your homework, ask someone else. Maddy and I have got our own to do.'

Alice sniffed. 'Mind your own business,' she said rudely. 'If I want advice from you I'll ask for it.'

Maddy hunched lower in her seat, ignoring them both. Alice and Marigold were like a couple of boxers, slinging punches at each other and not caring who got hurt in the process. If I sit here quietly and say nothing to either of them perhaps they'll shut up, she thought. In fact, if I read one of my text books I needn't say a word; I'll just let them get on with it and see how they like that, but oh what a pity it is! Here am I, with two really nice girls, both wanting to be my best friend, and all they do is snipe at one another. But oh, what a lot I shall have to tell Gran . . . and Mrs O'Halloran, of course. I do like her. She's kind and sensible and she works every bit as hard as I do, probably harder.

So, taking her own advice, Maddy delved into her satchel, brought out a copy of *A Midsummer Night's Dream* and began to read. She was soon absorbed, answering only 'Mm-hmm' whenever one of the others spoke directly to her, and when two seats became vacant in front of them and Alice took one of them she refused to move. 'I'm fine where I am, thanks,' she said. 'If you're bored, find yourself a book.' And with that she buried her nose in the text once more.

Because it was a school bus, nobody took any notice of the three girls, though the sixth former seated next to Alice had caught Maddy's eye and winked. At last the bus entered the village where Marigold lived. Maddy waited for her new friend to stand up, and when she did not move said, 'Marigold, this is your stop! You'd better get up, or you'll miss it!'

'Can't,' Marigold said briefly. 'I promised our landlady I'd pick up a couple of loaves and some butter which the lady at your post office is keeping for me.' She twinkled at Maddy. 'So don't think you can get rid of me quite so easily, Miss Hebditch.'

Maddy laughed, trying to ignore the fact that Alice was pulling a grim face, and peered out of the window as the bus approached Crowdale. 'I say, look who's come to meet us!'

Alice ignored the remark, but her gaze followed the other girl's pointing finger. 'Oh, it's Tom,' she said, surprised. 'And, he's brought his bicycle. I suppose he's come to give me a seater back to the Hall.'

When the bus drew up Alice was the first to disembark. She went straight up to Tom, and though Tom raised a hand in acknowledgement when Maddy and Marigold descended on to the lane he and Alice set off at once in the direction of the Hall.

Maddy was disappointed; she and Tom now got along very well and the more she knew of him the more she liked him, but of course Alice had met him first. Still, their ways lay together, and it would have been nice to have company up the two-mile climb.

But Marigold was talking. '. . . never told me he was so nice-looking,' she was saying. 'You said he had ginger hair, but it's not ginger, it's a dark auburn, almost chestnut – wish mine was like that! And he isn't as freckly as some boys who have the merest trace of red in their hair. Look at that feller who gave up his seat to us; you'd be hard put to it to stick a pin in an unfreckled bit of his face.' She tugged impatiently at Maddy's arm. 'Get a move on, Maddy! You can introduce us.'

'If you don't mind I don't think I will,' Maddy said apologetically. 'I'm not saying Alice wouldn't like it, but . . .'

'Don't care whether she'd like it or not,' Marigold said impatiently. 'She doesn't own him. Oh, *do* come on, Maddy, or we'll lose them.'

Maddy, however, stood her ground. 'You told me that you had to pop in to the post office to fetch something for your landlady,' she said accusingly. 'Or was that just an excuse to stay on the bus for an extra stop? Remember, Marigold, I've met you for the first time today and for all I know you might be the biggest liar in the Yorkshire Dales. I'm not saying you are,' she added hastily, 'I'm just saying you could be.'

Marigold pouted, but to Maddy's relief she was also smiling. 'You're quite right, of course, but I'm astonished that you've clearly never noticed how handsome your friend Tom is. Are you coming with me to the post office? Mrs Timothy – she's the lady we lodge with – said the post office woman would have the shopping all ready for me. She's ever so nice, and if you come back home with me – to give me a hand with the shopping, you know – then I'm sure she'll offer us a bun or one of the little cakes she makes, as well as a glass of her home-made ginger beer.'

Maddy was tempted, but she knew Gran would be waiting for a blow-by-blow account of her first day. If she hurried home now she might still have enough time to come back to the village later, because Gran was not the only one eager for news; Miss Parrott had said, rather wistfully, that she would be delighted if Maddy could find time to pop in and tell her how she had got on. Of course the most sensible thing would be to go to the schoolhouse first, but Maddy feared Gran would be upset if she knew her granddaughter had visited the teacher before returning home.

Marigold was staring at her. 'Will you or won't you?' she said. 'You say Alice is your pal, and I'm sure she is, but she didn't wait for you, did she? Not her! She went off with that gorgeous feller . . . oh, sorry, you think we're too young to notice a chap's looks. That ginger-headed moron – is that more like it?'

Maddy giggled. She really couldn't help it and she supposed it was silly to resent her new friend's noticing that she had been blind to Tom's looks. But though she comforted herself with the reflection that it was natural not to pay particular attention to the appearance of someone who was just a friend, she did feel an explanation was called for. 'Tom's father is Mr Thwaite's chauffeur; they live in a flat over what used to be the stables, so it's only natural for Tom and Alice to walk home together.' She gave the other girl a shove. 'Go and collect your shopping,' she said. 'I'm going to nip into the schoolhouse – the village school finishes at a quarter past three, so Miss Parrott will have been home for a while. Another time you must come with me and I'll introduce you, but not on the first day.'

Marigold smiled. 'All right, another time will do,' she said airily. 'And another time, Miss Dog-in-the-Manger, I mean to get an introduction to that delicious pal of yours.' She had stood her satchel down while they talked but now she picked it up and slung it over one shoulder. 'See you tomorrow! Tell your snooty pal that you're going to save me a seat. Bye!'

Maddy's heart sank into her boots. How on earth could she save a seat for Marigold – the implication was the seat beside herself – when Alice would take it for granted that they would sit next to one another? There was always the back seat, of course, but on any bus that was usually bagged by boys, and they would think her an odd sort of girl if she tried to sit there. But that problem would only arise next day; no point in worrying about it now, though she supposed she could see what Miss Parrott advised. The teacher was a sensible woman and might easily come up with a compromise.

Cheered by the thought, Maddy set off across the playground, through the little wicket gate, into the schoolhouse garden and up to the back door. She did not even have to knock, since her teacher had once more seen her coming and ushered her straight into the kitchen, her face reflecting the pleasure that she felt at her ex-pupil's visit. She had laid lemonade and biscuits out on the kitchen table and now she indicated that Maddy should help herself. 'Tell me everything,' she said eagerly. 'From the moment you got off the bus this morning until you got back on it again this afternoon.'

Chapter Seven

Gran and Mrs O'Halloran had laid the table for tea. Gran had not wanted to do anything special because she still felt in her heart that it would have been better for herself had she refused to let her granddaughter take the scholarship, let alone have a celebratory tea, but Mrs O'Halloran had insisted.

''Tis a grand thing, so it is, to get your schoolin' free,' she said reproachfully. 'I remember my mother tellin' me that if I did well in the schoolin' I'd either make a good marriage or get a good job, but I never got a chance. Schoolin' costs.'

The Irish woman surveyed the table with pride. After some urging, Gran had made a batch of Maddy's favourite cheese scones, and Mrs O'Halloran had baked two fine loaves of bread and made an apple pie from the Bramleys which still remained on the tree. Because the weather was still warm and sunny there was home-made lemonade as well as tea. When the door opened both women looked up expectantly, but it was only Mr O'Halloran. He grinned cheerfully at them. 'I were down in the village when the school bus arrived. The girl went straight to the schoolhouse, so if she's givin' her old teacher the story you don't want to put the kettle on yet.'

Mrs O'Halloran nodded. ''Tis natural, so it is, that she should want to tell the woman what sort of a day she's had,' she said. 'You and me, Mrs Hebditch, we don't know nothin' compared with the teacher. There's questions Maddy'll want to ask which we couldn't possibly answer. But that don't mean she ain't longin' to tell her gran every detail of her first day, so I reckon she'll be here in ten minutes or so. I'll wet the pot now.'

Gran grunted. 'Bloody posh school,' she muttered. 'I'm a fool to myself, always was. She'll make posh friends, get on in the world, forget her poor old gran. It'll be the workhouse for me as soon as she sees I'm nothing but a weight on her back.'

When the door opened for the second time, Gran thought bitterly that it was probably someone else again, but it proved to be the girl herself. Gran was pleased, but did not intend to let it show. She glared at Maddy, chumbling with her lips, an action she had taken to performing lately when annoyed. 'You're late!' she snapped. 'Don't think that just because I can't get down to the village no more, I don't know what time of day it is. The school bus is reg'lar as clockwork, which means you could have been home half an hour ago.' She stamped with her walking cane, causing Maddy to flinch. 'Where were you? Don't tell me the bus broke down, because I shan't believe you.'

'Oh, Gran, I'm sorry if I frightened you . . .' Maddy began, but was immediately cut down to size.

'Frightened? Me?' Gran snorted. 'If you imagine I was worried, you're wrong. You can come in any time you choose, I suppose, now you're at perishin' senior school. Ho yes, you don't have to think of your old gran, watching the clock, jumping every time she hears a sound outside . . . well? Now you're here, you can tell me what's been going on.'

Mrs O'Halloran cleared her throat. She had been standing at the head of the table, ready to pour the tea, but the tirade seemed to have taken the wind out of her sails. She opened and closed her mouth a couple of times, and when she finally spoke her tone was almost apologetic. Maddy realised it must be the first time that Gran had shown the least pleasant side of her nature to the younger woman and Mrs O'Halloran did not know how to deal with it.

Maddy smiled to herself. It was better that the O'Hallorans should know what they were up against, so she did not immediately smooth Gran's ruffled feathers. Instead, she added fuel to the fire. 'What on earth are you going on about, Gran?' she asked. 'Did you think I would run all the way up the hill from the village just to get home five minutes sooner, with scarcely a breath left in my body? Because if so, you've got another think coming.' She smiled sweetly at the old woman, then turned to Mrs O'Halloran. 'But before I say another word I think we ought to give Gran her tea. I'll have ginger beer, please; I'm that dry I could drain the beck.' She turned to her grandmother. 'Tea, Gran? Or would you rather have a glass of ginger beer?'

'Tea,' Gran snapped. 'And you can stop trying to butter me up. Where did you go after school?'

Still with the praiseworthy intention of forewarning the O'Hallorans, Maddy sat down at the table and reached for the glass of ginger beer which Mrs O'Halloran was proffering. To annoy Gran more than anything else she took a long draught, wiped froth from her upper lip and heaved a sigh. 'Gosh, that was good,' she said, and then, seeing Gran was almost hopping with impatience, spoke rather more hurriedly than she would have liked. 'I popped in to the schoolhouse. Miss Parrott has been so good, and of course she was very anxious to know how I got on. She understands what's involved much better than you do.'

She had been watching Mrs O'Halloran's face as she spoke, and now saw the woman's eyes open in surprise; clearly, Mrs O'Halloran thought the remark provocative, as indeed it was meant to be. But Mr O'Halloran was handing round the cheese scones, so his wife hastily poured the tea, telling Gran that she was lucky, so she was, to have such a clever granddaughter.

'Huh! I don't know about that,' Gran muttered. 'Before this scholarship hullabaloo started we got along very nicely, me and the girl. And don't forget I can still have the last word.' She turned a face, already beginning to suffuse with temper, towards her granddaughter. 'You know that, don't you? I come first. If I feel poorly or need you here . . . why are you shaking your head? Answer me that, you uppity girl.'

'I'm shaking my head because it's you who's got the wrong end of the stick,' Maddy said calmly. 'Why are the O'Hallorans living here with us? It's so that you have someone at your beck and call all day. It's so that the kitchen garden has someone to weed and sow and harvest it; it's in order to get the shopping from the village, draw your pension . . .'

But at this outrageous suggestion Gran had had enough. With her colour dangerously heightened, she said sharply: 'No one touches my pension but myself, understand? Nor my savings book, nor anything of that nature.' She pointed an accusing forefinger at her granddaughter. 'When money's needed you will tell me and I shall take out whatever is necessary. Dr Carlton will bring his car right up to the back door, I shall get into it like a queen and he will drive me down to the post office to withdraw whatever's necessary. Is that clear?'

'As crystal,' Maddy said rather thickly through a mouthful of cheese scone. 'Now I have a bit of a problem which I'd be interested in your solving, if you can. Mr Browning couldn't pick me up this morning, and when I got on the bus another new girl came and sat beside me . . .'

But though the three adults listened with interest, at the end of the recital, when Maddy said rather plaintively: 'Well, what would you do if your old friend and your new one wouldn't even try to get along?' she received blank stares from all three.

Finally, it was Mrs O'Halloran who spoke, and she cast an anxious glance at Gran before she did so. 'You could take turns to sit wit' Alice and Marigold,' she suggested diffidently. 'Or you could sit on the back seat, where you can get five or six people if you squeeze up a little. 'Tis a knotty problem, but didn't you say the girl from Windhover Hall offered you a car ride in both directions? Won't that solve it?'

'Ye-es,' Maddy said slowly. 'But I don't want to be dependent on either Mr Browning or Alice. She's grand, is Alice, and so's Mr Browning, but if the car's needed for some other purpose and Alice has to catch the bus . . . oh, I don't know! Why can't we all three be friends?'

'It'll work out,' Gran said shortly, and Maddy saw that the old woman did not like losing the O'Hallorans' attention. 'And now you can stop gabbling, young woman, and pass me a slice of that fruit cake.'

Despite Marigold's interest in Tom, Maddy did not introduce them until the schools were about to break up for the Christmas holidays. Tom was working towards his School Certificate, and though he did have some time to himself on Sundays he seemed disinclined to do anything but study, and the atmosphere between Alice and Marigold continued frosty.

A week before the end of term, Maddy and Marigold who had been working pretty hard themselves, decided that they ought to go down to the town centre after school one afternoon and see what they could find in the way of presents. They had been advised by one of the senior prefects to visit the Christmas market in the square by the war memorial, and were standing at the bus stop discussing which day they should go when Alice joined them. For once she did not take exception to Marigold's presence, but said at once that she would accompany them on the next market day. 'Because don't forget, we all have to buy dip presents for the form bran tub,' she explained. 'Haven't you heard? We each buy a gift costing around a shilling, wrap it nicely and pop it into the tub, and then on the last day of term everyone gets a dip. So we might as well go together and get any bargains going. Tom's already broken up, so he'll probably come with us too.'

Marigold's eyes lit up. 'Goodee!' she exclaimed. 'So I'm to meet the mysterious Mr Browning at long last.' She grinned at Maddy. 'You've done your best to keep us apart, but you couldn't hide him for ever!'

Maddy giggled. 'I've never tried to keep you and Tom apart,' she protested. 'It's his being a weekly boarder that has prevented him spending time with me and Alice. Anyway, you'll meet him now, and much good may it do you.'

At this point the bus arrived and in the usual scrimmage Maddy and Marigold got separated whilst Alice, who had eased Maddy's problem by seldom travelling by bus, ran across the road, slung her satchel on to the back seat of the Daimler and climbed hurriedly in after it. Once settled she waved violently to the bus in general, not being able to pick Maddy out from the dozens of similarly uniformed girls, and settled back.

On the bus the conductor tinged the bell and the vehicle moved ponderously forward. Marigold, perched on the seat behind the one upon which Maddy sat, leaned forward and jabbed her friend between the shoulder blades.

'That was a nasty moment,' she observed. 'I thought your posh friend was going to get on the bus for once and I wanted to ask you whether you thought she might unfreeze a bit if I bought her something really pretty for Christmas? I keep trying to make her like me and sometimes I think it's working, but usually it doesn't.'

Maddy smiled. 'I don't know, but she might. There's a lot of niceness hidden beneath that touchy exterior; maybe she'll loosen up a bit on Thursday. Let's wait and see, shall we?'

It was a wonderful afternoon and all four of them, Maddy thought, were thoroughly enjoying it.

The shops were lit up, their windows gay with decorations and tempting goodies, and everyone was in a holiday mood. As the prefect had predicted, the market traders were already lowering their prices, and the four of them bought penny cones from Mr Delamere's Ice Cream Parlour and licked with enthusiasm whilst walking between the stalls.

Rather to Maddy's surprise, as she was pondering over the purchase of a small bone-handled penknife for Tom, she saw Mr O'Halloran chaffing a fruiterer and then holding out his hand for what looked like a couple of notes, which he hastily thrust into his pocket. Though he could scarcely be blamed for selling off unwanted produce, at this time of year they needed everything they could grow. She was about to hail him when he turned away from the stall, taking the arm of a tall woman whom Maddy immediately recognised as Mrs O'Halloran. She would not normally have hesitated to hail either party, for over the weeks since they had moved in she had grown easy in their company and got on well with them both, but it did occur to her that on this occasion it might be tactless to greet them. Surely, though, they would not have left Gran alone in the house, particularly when Maddy had announced her intention of being late home herself? No, Dr Carlton must have popped in and promised to stay until they – or she – returned.

Fleetingly, she wondered why Gran had permitted

them to come into town at all, but then she smiled to herself. Gran dearly loved Christmas, and any small gifts which came her way were greeted with enormous enthusiasm. She was particularly fond of chocolates; indeed, Maddy had already visited Skipton in order to stock up on a Claire's Variety Box. No matter how short money was, ever since she had been old enough to earn a little extra she had saved up and bought Gran the small selection box, and had enjoyed her grandmother's delight in the gift almost as much as the old woman had enjoyed the chocolates.

For the rest of the afternoon the four of them split up, examining and buying with care, for Alice was the only one with an apparently unlimited supply of money. Maddy still sold watercress and eggs and such so she had money for presents, but it was money hard earned and she did not intend to spend two pennies if one would do. At one stall her hand and someone else's closed over the same object simultaneously, and Maddy, laughing, looked up to find that her rival for the prize – a small leather purse priced at the exact sum for a bran tub gift – was Alice. She expected her friend to remove her hand at once – she had enough money to buy up half the stall – but the other girl shook her head and hung on. 'I don't want it for the bran tub, I want it for *me*! I have to take dinner money to school every Monday so it would be very useful.'

'But we aren't shopping for ourselves, and that

purse was to be my dip gift,' Maddy exclaimed. 'They have lots and lots of purses, but all the others are more expensive than this one.'

Alice must have read Maddy's feelings in her reproachful glance, for she suddenly thrust the purse into Maddy's hand. 'I meant it for you anyway; I was going to tell you to pick the pink and white parcel out of the bran tub, and now you've spoiled my surprise,' she said reproachfully. 'Never mind, you have it anyway; I'll think of something different for the tub.'

Maddy turned back, her faith in her friend restored. 'I'm sorry to spoil your surprise,' she said remorsefully, and it was only afterwards that she remembered Alice knew that she, Maddy, never brought money to school since her school dinners were free. And Alice had distinctly said that she wanted the purse for herself.

Oh, but she only said that to make sure the purse was a surprise, Maddy told herself, but the lingering suspicion that Alice had intended to keep the purse niggled away at the back of her mind until Tom appeared with four toffee apples. When they were all gathered together, he handed these round and said he thought they ought to be getting back to the steps of the town hall where they had arranged to meet Mr Browning, who was giving everyone a lift home.

Mr Browning's first question was to ask if they had managed to finish their Christmas shopping. 'I'll be coming in again on Christmas Eve to pick up the turkey, a nice big ham and a sack of sprouts,' he said, 'so if any of you ladies want a lift, all you have to do is come up to the Hall right early. Around eight thirty would be best.'

Maddy and Marigold exchanged glances; they had both thoroughly enjoyed the shopping trip and had already arranged to meet on Christmas Eve to catch the bus into town and look around at their leisure. Maddy wanted to see the cathedral, and though Marigold pulled a face and said 'dull stuff', she agreed that if they were there for any length of time it would be interesting to visit such a landmark.

'And next summer, when the long evenings arrive, we must come into town at nine o'clock and see the wakeman doing his stuff,' Maddy told her now. 'He's dressed in very beautiful old-fashioned clothes and he carries a long horn thing, which he blows four times, once in each direction, I suppose, north, south, east and west. Then he does a lovely bow towards the house on the corner – I think it was where the mayor once lived – and he says "The watch is set, Mr Mayor." He's been doing it for over a thousand years.'

Marigold's mouth dropped open. 'Are you trying to make me believe a man is a thousand years old?' she said incredulously. 'Pull the other one, Madeleine Hebditch.'

Maddy laughed. 'No, of course not! It's the ceremony that has been going on for a thousand years, with different wakemen of course. But you really should see it, because it's very impressive and no other town in the whole of England has anything like it.'

Tom, seated on the passenger seat alongside his father, twisted round to grin at the three girls. 'But what about Christmas Eve? If you're all going with Dad I might join you, though I won't be able to run to any more toffee apples; it's only Alice who's in what you might call affluent circumstances. You have pocket money, don't you, Alice? I mean pocket money that you don't have to earn. Does your father send it from India or does your uncle John simply shell out?'

'Don't know; never asked,' Alice said through a mouthful of toffee apple. 'But if you're all going into town, I'm coming too; I'm not having you three ganging up against me.'

Tom looked a little taken aback, but at that moment the car drew up in front of Marigold's lodgings and Mr Browning nudged his son. 'Get out of the car and open the door for the lady,' he said, giving him a wink. 'It's the done thing.'

Tom groaned, but got out of the car and held the door for Marigold to alight, saying as he did so: 'I see no lady, only a little blonde kid who should be quite capable of opening a door for herself.' The truth was he had been knocked sideways by the girl's golden good looks, but now he grinned at Marigold's indignation, then staggered as she swung her satchel, catching him a good blow in the midriff.

'Thank you, vassal,' she said loftily and then, seeing

reprisal in Tom's face, set off at a fast trot towards her landlady's front door.

She had almost reached it and Tom was getting back into the car when Maddy called after her: 'Hang on, Marigold! Are you coming into town on Christmas Eve?'

Marigold turned back. 'Of course, because if *she's* going, I'm not having the three of you ganging up on me behind my back!' she said, imitating the very tone that Alice had used.

Tom laughed. 'I take it then that all four of us will be going,' he called. 'See you on Christmas Eve.'

After what had happened last time Mr Browning did not wish to drive right up to Maddy's door, so she got out of the car when Alice did, hefting her heavy satchel and shaking a reproving head at Tom when he offered to walk her home. 'No, you go indoors with your dad; I've got a good torch, and besides, I know the way between Larkspur and the Hall like the back of my hand.' She giggled. 'I'd probably end up walking *you* home if you insisted upon coming with me.'

'Well, if you're sure . . .' Tom began.

'I'm sure,' Maddy said firmly. She had no intention of allowing Tom to walk four miles, for having accompanied her to Larkspur he would then have to retrace his steps. And it was true that she knew every inch of the path she trod so regularly. Indeed, the little scuttlings and squeaks which accompanied her steps were as familiar to her as the voices of her classmates. As she set off she hummed a little tune beneath her breath, telling herself that if Gran objected to her going out on Christmas Eve she would simply make certain that the O'Hallorans would be in and then slip away anyway.

She was a good walker, taking the steepest part of the lane in her stride, but her satchel was heavy and slowed her down quite a lot. She had bought her bran tub gift as well as some small things for particular friends, including a soft and silky length of pink hair ribbon which she intended to bestow upon Alice. She had hidden the ribbon away at the very bottom of the satchel, not wanting Alice to see it. She was just wondering what Alice had bought for her when she suddenly felt a tingle in her spine, almost a warning; something was different, something in the lane ahead of her – no, to the right – had altered the composition of the shadows. For one moment Maddy was gripped by panic. The urge to run, to look neither right nor left but simply to reach home and safety, almost overcame her, but then common sense came to her aid. She looked searchingly to her right and saw not so much an intruder as a thickening of the shadows on the bank, which could have been caused by a sheep or a cow or some other largish farm animal. And yet . . . and yet . . .

Maddy stood her heavy satchel down, stretched and yawned, trying to give the impression that she had stopped to ease her aching arm for a moment, then picked the satchel up and stood there, swinging it hopefully before she spoke. After all, if it was only a stray animal . . . but she was sure it was not; she would not have felt the warning tingle if it had been merely a straying creature standing so still in the shelter of the hedge. Maddy summoned all her courage and spoke, her voice loud and firm.

'I can see you, so you might as well come out.' She was conscious of a gust of cold air and thought for a moment that she saw movement on the far side of the hedge. When she looked harder, however, she could see no one. 'What the devil are you doing here anyway? These pastures are private property. And let me tell you that if you think you're hidden . . .'

There was a moment of silence and then someone slid down the bank and stepped into the lane and Mr O'Halloran smiled ingratiatingly, producing a small torch and shining it into his own face. ''Tis meself, missy. I heared you a-comin' and got out of your path 'cos I didn't want to frighten you. But mebbe 'twas the wrong t'ing to do.'

'Mr O'Halloran!' Maddy said crossly. 'What on earth do you think you're playing at? I don't frighten easily, but seeing someone pressed into the hedge and keeping quiet is enough to scare anyone. How silly you are! Why didn't you just call out when you heard me coming up the lane? And now you can jolly well carry my satchel, because it's heavy.'

Mr O'Halloran took the satchel and in the tricky moonlight Maddy thought his smile was almost malicious. 'I telled you, missy; I didn't want to frighten you,' he repeated. 'Knowin' what a one you are for ghoulies and ghosties, I t'ought I'd not put ideas in your pretty l'il head. And now let's get into the warm, for I'll be knockin' icicles off me nose if us stays out here much longer.'

Maddy began to say that her one-time preoccupation with water babies could scarcely come under the heading of 'ghoulies and ghosties', then decided against it. The more she thought about it the more certain she became that the figure on the other side of the hedge had not been either a ghost or her imagination, but a flesh and blood man or woman, who had melted soundlessly into the black and silver of the moonlight and disappeared before he or she could be challenged. 'But what were you doing in the lane, Mr O'Halloran?' she asked rather sharply. 'I thought you were looking after Gran.'

There was a perceptible pause before Mr O'Halloran answered. 'I was returnin' from Haywain's poultry farm, after arrangin' to buy a goose for our Christmas dinner,' he said. 'I'm to pick it up on Christmas Eve.'

They reached the gate and Mr O'Halloran swung it open, setting off across the yard at a smart pace, but Maddy tugged at his sleeve. 'And who were you with? There was someone else on the other side of the hedge.'

She had hoped to surprise Mr O'Halloran, but when he answered his voice was calm. 'Ghosties you're seein', miss, if you t'ink there was anybody in the lane barrin' us two,' he said. 'And now no more nonsense. We don't want to frighten Mrs Hebdyke with talk of ghosts.'

'Ditch,' Maddy said automatically and smiled to herself. She knew how it irritated Gran when Mr O'Halloran got her name wrong. 'You're right about the weather. I can't wait to get into the warm. Let's hope there's a good fire in the grate.'

Chapter Eight

Maddy and Tom were working on an old sledge which Tom had discovered in the hayloft at Windhover and decided to bestow upon Madeleine to help with her shopping. It had scarcely stopped snowing for more than a couple of hours at a time since it had started on Christmas Eve, and carrying supplies up from the village was becoming a problem.

'So what do you think?' Maddy said with assumed casualness as Tom, who had been securing one of the steel runners which had come loose, stood back and wiped his brow.

'Phew,' he said. 'I know it's cold but I'm sweating cobs, as they say up here.' He eyed his work appraisingly. 'That's more like it. In fact, you're going to end up with a nice light little sledge, far better than the Thwaites' humping great thing. It'll take both Dad and me to tow that one home once it's fully laden.'

'Oh, dear. I suppose I ought to say you'd better keep this one, only I've already told the O'Hallorans that they can use it for their shopping trips,' Maddy said, dismayed. 'But you've worked so hard, Tom, that if anyone deserves to benefit from the result of your labours, it's you.'

Tom shook his head. 'No, I was only teasing. You know what the Thwaites are like; they'll get us to fill the big sledge to the limit. So you're safe to consider this one your own. I doubt if the Thwaites even know it exists.'

'Well, thank you,' Maddy said gratefully. 'But you haven't told me what you think about the O'Hallorans being in town that day.' It was something that had been worrying her on and off ever since the expedition to the Christmas market.

Tom grinned. 'I wasn't exactly listening, but I rather gathered you'd asked yourself the question and haven't had a satisfactory answer.' He leaned over and tweaked a loose lock of hair which had fallen forward on to her forehead. 'What was it you said?'

'Tom, you are the most exasperating boy I've ever met,' Maddy said. 'I told you – I saw Mr and Mrs O'Halloran in the market when they ought to have been at home with Gran. I should have asked them what they were doing, but I didn't want to upset the applecart.' She looked appealingly at Tom. 'You see, life's been so much easier for me – and so much pleasanter – since the O'Hallorans moved in. Gran treats them just the way she used to treat me – she shouts at them and waves her stick and threatens to cut their wages if they don't do as she bids them – but I don't think they really bother much; they're very independent, you know. So I'm really glad they've come to live with us, and I didn't want to cause trouble by asking how they'd managed to leave Gran alone without her kicking up the most enormous hullabaloo.'

Tom sat down on a straw bale and eyed Maddy quizzically. 'So you never even asked?' he said incredulously. 'Madeleine Hebditch! And I've always thought you as brave as a lion! Are you telling me that your gran never complained that she'd been abandoned? From what you've told me, that isn't much like her.'

'It isn't much like her at all; that's what's got me a bit worried,' Maddy admitted. 'And there's another thing: I met Mr O'Halloran in the lane that night, and I thought I saw someone with him, but when I asked him who it was he said I was imagining things. But I wasn't, Tom, I'm sure I wasn't, only before I could say so he'd opened the kitchen door and there was Mrs O'Halloran, and Gran asleep in her chair. She woke up when we went in, and she didn't complain about being left, or say her tea had gone cold, which it had; she just said she'd had a lovely sleep and since I'd decided to abandon my posh friends and come home at last would I kindly put the kettle on and fetch her a few biscuits because she was fair clemmed. So, I went to the pantry to get the biscuits and Mrs O'Halloran followed me, saying she'd made a couple of jam tarts especially for Gran and me. I did ask her, casual like, where she had been all day, and she looked me straight in the eye, bold as brass, and said: "Why, Maddy, in this very kitchen, giving an eye to your gran and baking a dozen mince pies and them jam tarts I mentioned."'

'Hmm,' Tom said thoughtfully. 'So what did she say when you told her you'd seen her at the market?'

After a pause, during which Maddy felt the hot blood invade her cheeks, she gave a shamefaced shake of her head. 'I didn't say anything, Tom. Only now I know she tells lies and that makes me feel uncomfortable. Oh, I knew she did tell the odd fib to Gran, just to keep her quiet, but I didn't think she would lie to me about something like that. And then there's another strange thing . . .'

'Fire ahead then,' Tom said when Maddy hesitated. He cocked an eyebrow. 'Why are you asking me, though? I'd have thought you'd want to know what Alice or Marigold thinks.'

Maddy shook her head. 'I'm not sure; maybe it's because you're older, and I know you won't laugh at me, or scoff, because I really am worried. You see, I *like* the O'Hallorans, and I trust them, or I did. But now Mr O'Halloran has suggested to Gran that she might buy a heifer calf from Mr Sutherland so that we could have milk without needing to walk all the way to and from the farm, and when I said we didn't have enough money he winked and said that Gran's post office book would scarce notice the price of such

155

a calf. I didn't think Gran had ever let anyone else handle her savings book, but when I questioned her she admitted quite cheerfully that the O'Hallorans had both withdrawn money for her from time to time. She said she always checked what had been taken out, so I needn't worry that my inheritance was shrinking.'

Tom grinned. 'She's a cunning old woman; she knows a remark like that would make it seem self-seeking to enquire further,' he observed. 'Well, all I can say is, watch them, though I don't suppose you need that sort of advice.' He chuckled. 'Whether they know it or not you'll be on your guard from now on, and *do* you know how much your gran's got in her savings book?'

Maddy pulled a face. 'I haven't the faintest idea,' she said cheerfully. 'Save that it's enough to pay the O'Hallorans a small wage for some time.' She jumped to her feet. 'And now we ought to try out this wonderful sledge of yours. Shall we have a sneaky go before we tell Alice that you've mended the runner? She's always fair so she'll take turns all right, but she may only want to try it out down a small slope, and I'm keen to see how it goes high up in the fells. What do you say?'

'Why not?' Tom said. He was bright-eyed and flushed. 'Tell you what, you're only a slip of a thing, so you sit on the sledge and I'll pull you to the top of the long meadow; then I'll get aboard behind you and we'll see how far we can go before the snow gets too soft and we grind to a halt. Then we'll be more or less on the same level as the Hall and you can nip over and tell Alice that we're all set for a morning's sledging. She'll be looking at her blessed magazines in the library, I expect, and she'll need five minutes or so to kit herself out with a thick coat, scarf and woolly hat, so while she's selecting her warm things you can ask Mr Thwaite whether they've any skates hidden away somewhere. The pond down by the village is frozen and as soon as it's safe to do so half the village will be skating on it.'

'I might have some skates,' Maddy said thoughtfully. 'Gran used to talk about wonderful skating parties by the light of the moon, and I believe she was very athletic when she was young. We hardly ever go up to the attics now the O'Hallorans sleep there, but I'll make time to do so and see if I can find a pair of skates which would fit me.' Tom had been pulling her along on the sledge as they spoke, and now she looked round. 'Is this the top of the long meadow? It's difficult to tell with the snow hiding all the landmarks.'

Tom nodded. 'It'll do,' he said briefly. 'Are you ready?'

Maddy noted how tiny the Hall looked from here and wondered what sort of landing they would have if they set off from such an exalted position. She was beginning to voice the thought when she felt Tom's weight land on the sledge behind her and before she could do more than squeak they were off, travelling faster and faster, the wind whipping her hair out into a long tail behind her, to Tom's annoyance.

'Your perishing hair's in my mouth,' he shouted. 'Start braking now, or we'll end up in the Thwaites' library, which would be a surprise for Alice and no mistake!'

Fortunately, Maddy was able to enter the library in a more conventional manner, being ushered in by the maid who had admitted her to the house, and found Alice sitting in front of the fire with a pile of women's magazines on a small table by her side, flicking through the fashion pages. She looked up as the door opened and smiled at her friend. 'Oh, lovely. I've just been wishing I had someone to help me choose a warm winter frock or maybe a coat and skirt to wear when I'm invited out,' she said. She tapped an illustration with an elegant finger. 'See this? It's made of cherry-coloured jersey cloth, trimmed with white angora, and I'd wear it with cherry-coloured court shoes ... or they also do it in lime green. It's available in most departmental stores, so next time we go into town I shall visit Blenkinsops and try on anything which takes my fancy. You'll come with me, won't you? I feel a bit mean, because you can't afford party frocks and so on, but you don't really care, do you? You're not interested in clothes at all ...'

'Oh, Alice, do shut up. Tom's mended the little

sledge and it's champion,' Maddy said. 'We've had one run on it just to make sure it worked all right and now Tom says you can join us. It's quite safe and the most tremendous fun; I'm sure not even the Daimler can go as fast as that sledge.'

Alice shuddered. 'Who wants to go fast?' she asked pettishly. 'I *hate* being cold, and . . . oh, Maddy, look at yourself ! You're streaked with mud and wet through. Is it still snowing?'

Maddy went over to the long windows to look out, then sighed and shook her head despairingly. 'Honestly, Alice, you're as capable as I am of looking out of the window. It stopped snowing half an hour ago, only then Tom was still fixing the runner. Do get your coat and boots, and Tom says bring a scarf as well as your bobble hat, because when you're travelling at high speed on a sledge you'll want to pull your scarf up over your nose and mouth, or the air feels like knives.'

Alice, who had half risen to her feet, sank back into her armchair once more. 'Oh, does it?' she said disagreeably. 'Then I'm staying in here. I never did see the point of slogging up a hill, dragging a heavy sledge, just in order to slide all the way down again. If the sun was out I dare say it might be quite fun, but from what I can see it's cloudy and cold and probably just waiting for me to go outside so it can start snowing again.'

Maddy giggled. 'You make it sound as though the

snow falls deliberately to spite you,' she said. 'Oh, do get up, Alice, and get . . .' she smirked, 'your skates on!'

Alice pulled a discontented face. 'I don't want . . .' she began, just as the library door opened and the Thwaites came into the room to announce that they meant to go into town and suspected that Alice might like to join them. 'We're going to buy our niece skates,' Mr Thwaite told Maddy. 'If this freeze persists, every little pond will be utilised for skating, and Alice won't want to be left out of that sort of fun, but she's had no experience and won't want to make a fool of herself on the ice. I used to be good at skating, so I'm going to teach her.'

'But I don't want to learn to skate,' Alice wailed. 'Auntie, do I have to? I'm sure my father would agree that I needn't do something I hate.'

Mr Thwaite began to protest, to say that Alice would enjoy it once she'd made up her mind to do so, but Mrs Thwaite intervened. 'Alice is just like me, my dear John,' she explained. 'We are a couple of delicate hothouse blooms who do *not* excel at winter sports. But why don't we organise a really exciting party before this big freeze ends?' Just for a moment her eyes met her husband's, and she chuckled. 'You've told me often enough how, in the old days, your father would build a bonfire and provide, oh, I don't know, sausages, jacket potatoes, that sort of thing. He gave prizes, didn't he, for figure skating and dancing the polka on the ice?' She contrived to make her face look wistful, an expression which Maddy had never seen on it before. 'If I remember rightly, it had to be when the moon was at the full, though I do believe the light from the bonfire lit up most of the festivities.' She clasped her hands in a very theatrical gesture, making Maddy stifle a gurgle of merriment. 'Couldn't we do that again, John? I'm sure you could teach Alice just enough to enable her to take part in the fun.'

Mr Thwaite looked doubtfully at his niece. 'If she really doesn't want to . . .' he began, but was swiftly interrupted.

'It's a grand idea,' Alice said, beaming at her aunt and uncle with real affection. 'I don't want to be a spoilsport, so I'll do my very best to learn to skate. Gosh, a party! Who shall we invite? Oh, I'm already *so* excited, and I bet Maddy is too.'

Maddy glanced at Mrs Thwaite and this time she saw the wink and knew it was not her imagination. Mrs Thwaite was as keen as her husband to persuade Alice to join in. Mr Thwaite said jovially: 'Whom shall we invite? Why, we'll throw it open to the whole neighbourhood. We'll have sausages and potatoes, mulled wine for the adults and something hot for the youngsters; Cook can consult her recipe books. Well, well, well. It'll be our first party since Alice has come to live with us, and we must make sure it's a good one.'

When Mr and Mrs Thwaite had disappeared,

161

telling their niece to be ready to accompany them into town in ten minutes, Alice turned impulsively to her friend. 'I'm going to ask Auntie Ruby if she can buy me a new coat for the party,' she said. 'What do you think of bright red, or bright blue for that matter? Something striking, anyway. And if she buys me a new scarf and cap you may have my old ones. The angora is beautifully soft.' She stroked the collar of her navy coat.

'Thanks, Alice,' Maddy said with real gratitude. 'Well, I shall leave you now, because poor Tom is waiting at the top of the long meadow. See you!'

When told of the conversation in the library, Tom gave it as his opinion that things had worked out for the best. 'And you never know, when Alice looks out of the window and sees us having fun she might easily change her mind and join us,' he said. 'And don't forget you're going to see if you can find some skating boots; I'm sure Mr Thwaite would be happy to teach you as well as Alice, but personally I think you'd be better off with me. You'd be stiff and shy with Mr Thwaite, and embarrassed if you fell; even more embarrassed if you dragged him over as well! So you and I will take ourselves off to the bottomless pool and I'll teach you enough to save you from breaking a leg.'

But it was soon obvious that Alice had no intention of sledging. And though Maddy and Tom made a point of inviting her to join them on several occasions, she resolutely refused to do so, saying loftily: 'My uncle is teaching me all I need to know.' Maddy thought, a trifle guiltily, that had Alice realised how much friendlier she and Tom had become her friend might have thought twice about refusing their invitations, for Alice considered Tom to be very much her property.

Being so wrapped up in her own affairs, Alice had still not noticed the strong friendship which was blossoming between her best friend and the chauffeur's son by the time she came down to the bottomless pool on the night of the party. All the youngsters from the village were there, showing off their skills, and though it would not be truthful to say that Alice was an expert, she put on her skating boots and allowed Tom to encircle her waist with his arm, and the two of them went merrily off on to the ice, though Tom's efforts to teach her to make a figure eight were unavailing. 'But there's always next year,' he said comfortingly, though he winked at Maddy as he spoke and she had to turn her head away to hide her smile.

Alice went along with Maddy to the bonfire and buried her potato in the glowing embers, and even toasted a sausage impaled on a sharply pointed stick. Looking around her and trying to shield her face from the heat of the fire, she nudged Maddy in the ribs. 'Haven't my aunt and uncle done us proud?' she murmured. 'It's not only that they've provided masses of grub, but they're giving really good prizes for the skating competitions. Who do you think will win the polka?' She giggled. 'Did you see who has entered? Your pal, Miss Parrott, and Mr Grice! Can you imagine your old teacher polkaing across the ice with the headmaster? He must be twice her age!'

Maddy pulled her sausage away from the flames and regarded it critically, and then looked to where Mr Grice and Miss Parrott were swooping gently across the ice, so at home on their skates that they were talking and laughing as they circled. Maddy raised her brows. 'He doesn't look old – and he doesn't skate old either,' she said rather confusedly. 'And Miss Parrott looks almost pretty. Did you see her in the figure skating? Your aunt Ruby says she beats the rest into a cocked hat.' She sighed wistfully. 'Wish I could skate like that!'

Tom, coming up behind them, seized Alice by the nape of her neck, making her squeak and giggle. 'When you've finished admiring those two, how about putting our names down for the polka?' he said. 'Think how pleased your uncle and aunt will be, even if we don't win. But you are quite a competent skater, so it might be worth having a go.'

Maddy swallowed her disappointment; she had been practising on the sly whenever she had the opportunity and had thought that she and Tom might put up a good performance. But of course, she reminded herself, Alice had known him longer than she had, so she sat on the bank and watched.

Later in the evening, when all the prizes had been awarded, the sausages eaten, and people were beginning to drift off homeward, Miss Parrott, breathless from the exertion of another spirited polka, came over to say goodbye to her one-time pupil. 'I don't know when I've enjoyed anything more!' the teacher said, smiling. 'Haven't we been lucky? The cold has continued and the frost is still as hard as iron. I wonder if Mr Grimshaw was wrong when he said there was a thaw coming?' She peered at the small bag Maddy was clutching. 'What's in there? I heard Mr Thwaite calling your name; is that your winnings?'

Maddy nodded vigorously. 'That's right; speed skating for beginners. I came first and got a bag of humbugs, which just happen to be Gran's favourite sweets, so I'm taking them home for her . . . well, apart from the one in my mouth.'

Miss Parrott chuckled. 'Good for you. Oh, Maddy, isn't it a fabulous night? What with the glow from the bonfire and the moonshine, it's almost as light as day. I don't think I shall ever forget this evening if I live to be a hundred. Mr and Mrs Thwaite have done more than throw a delightful party; they've given us memories which will last our lives long.' As she spoke, she tapped the white angora scarf and bobble hat Maddy was wearing. 'And you so smart!' she added. 'You look very pretty, as well as snug as a bug in a rug. But how are you getting home? The party invitations said the fun ended at midnight, and it must be well past that already.'

Maddy smiled. 'Tom says he'll walk me home; it's a lot quicker going by the fields than it would be going in the car. I don't want to put him out, but his dad's going to pick him up from the top of the lane and I must admit I'll be happier to have company, even on such a magical night as this.'

'And I shall be happier knowing you're not alone,' Miss Parrott said, smiling. 'You young things are so impetuous; you simply don't take into account that accidents do happen. If you fell and broke a leg, how would you expect to get home? Oh, I know what you'll say: you know every inch of the lanes and meadows between here and Larkspur, and that may be true in daylight, but moonlight, I assure you, my dear, is a very different kettle of fish.'

As she finished speaking they were joined by Tom. 'Miss Parrott, Mr Grice said to remind you that he's giving you a lift into the village,' he said. 'Most of the villagers will be walking home by the beck but he says you've had a very tiring evening, what with the polka competition and everything, so he's waiting for you in the stable yard.'

Miss Parrott laughed. 'Hoity-toity young man; I was just having a word with my star pupil, making sure that she wasn't walking home alone, but she tells me that you've offered to accompany her and she has accepted, so I needn't worry that she'll go wrenching her ankle or tumbling into a ditch.' She turned to Maddy. 'I've a little bit of news for you, my dear; I shan't be living at the schoolhouse in Crowdale after the end of next term.'

Maddy began to express dismay at the thought of not having the teacher nearby, but the older woman shook her head, laughing. 'Don't look so dismayed, my dear – I haven't had the sack. In fact my reason for the move is the best possible one. Mr Grice has been offered the headship of a large boarding school near Ripon and he's asked me to be his wife.'

'Oh Miss Parrott, I'm so happy for you,' Maddy said at once. 'I thought – well, I did wonder, when I saw you skating together – but will you stop teaching? It would be an awful waste if you did, because you're the best. I'd never have got into St Philippa's if it hadn't been for you. But when are you getting married? Will you be having bridesmaids?'

'Stop, stop,' Miss Parrott said, laughing. 'Give me time to answer your questions, at least! First, yes, I intend to continue teaching; Mr Grice's school have offered me a place. What would I do by myself in the house all day? And we shall have a register office wedding, since we're neither of us in what you might call the first bloom of youth, and that means no bridesmaids, nor long white dresses. The wedding ceremony itself will take place at Easter, when I'll have worked out my notice at the village school, and

I hope you will be one of our first visitors in our new home. But now I really must bid you good night, my dear. Mr Grice is a patient man but I can't keep him waiting any longer. Sweet dreams.'

As the teacher left them, Tom slid an arm round Maddy's waist. 'That's one very nice woman. I'm sorry I was so rude about her nose; you hardly notice it at all when you're talking to her, do you? I wish my dad could meet someone he cared about, because when I'm at university – if I get there, that is – he'll really miss me. We'd better get a move on, though. Do you think the O'Hallorans will wait up for you? I saw Mr O'Halloran hovering around the bonfire a couple of times so I picked out some spuds for him – I thought he might like them with a knob of butter in for his supper – but when I went to look for him he had disappeared.'

'It seems disappearing is his long suit,' Maddy said ruefully. 'He certainly isn't lazy – he works extremely hard in the kitchen garden, for instance – but he's a past master at the art of melting into the landscape. And you're right – I saw him several times too, but then he did his disappearing trick, though I do believe he "disappeared" some sausages at the same time. Still, I'm sure Alice's uncle and aunt won't grudge the O'Hallorans and my gran a few sausages.' She felt as though she was floating on a sea of dreams, and when she said so and Tom tightened his hold around her waist she knew a moment of pure happiness. She looked up into the dark bowl of the sky above her. 'Have you ever seen the sky so dark or the stars so big?' she asked softly. 'I never have, and I'm the one who shuts the poultry up each evening so that the fox doesn't get them, so I see the stars every night of my life . . . when there's no cloud about, of course.'

She snuggled closer to Tom's side and then, unable to prevent it, gave an enormous yawn, causing Tom to chuckle deep in his throat. 'You poor little kid, you're exhausted,' he said. 'You'll sleep like the dead tonight; I can guarantee it. But you mustn't fall asleep yet, because I don't fancy having to carry you the rest of the way to Larkspur Farm. I'd be bound to step on a loose stone and drop you and then we'd both be in trouble. But keep hold of me, because we're coming to the bit of the lane which is like a tunnel . . . hey up!'

'Hey up to you,' Maddy said, still sounding sleepy. 'Don't say you've seen a ghost, Tom Browning?'

'No, not a ghost, but I felt something hit my head and it means old Mr Grimshaw got it right as usual. The thaw has started, my little water baby, and soon the beck will be running again and the fish in the bottomless pool will come up to the surface to snap for the flies. Ever tickled a trout, young 'un?'

'No-o-o, but I've tried,' Maddy admitted. 'Is it something that can be learned? If so, how about teaching me when the summer holidays come?'

'I'll see,' Tom said cautiously. 'Do you remember how we used to talk about finding Vendale one of these days?' Tom gave her a little shake. '*Do* you remember, little sleepy-head? Gosh, weren't we a credulous trio? And come to think, it was you who started the whole thing off with your conviction that because Mr Kingsley was a clergyman every word he wrote must have been true.'

Maddy shook off the sleepiness which was causing her to drag on Tom's arm, and conjured up indignation. 'I did *not* believe in water babies. Or if I did believe in poor little Tom, that wasn't believing, that was wishing.' She looked round and was genuinely startled to realise that they were crossing the farmyard and heading for the kitchen door. She said so, which made Tom laugh. 'There's nothing like being half asleep for making a journey shorter,' he said. 'Yes, I can see the headlights of the Daimler coming round the bend at the top of the lane. Night night, Maddy; I expect we'll bump into each other again before term starts and I promise I won't tease you about water babies.'

'Thanks ever so much for bringing me home, Tom. I've never been nervous of the dark but it was really nice to have your company.' Impulsively she took his hand and squeezed it. 'Goodnight – and thanks again.'

Tom sketched a bow and she could see his teeth flash into a broad smile in the moonlight. 'It was a pleasure, madam,' he said formally.

Maddy had the strangest of feelings that she had

left something unsaid, but he had swung away from her and was heading for the road. She watched the car's tail lights until they disappeared, then went into the house. She half expected to find Gran and the O'Hallorans still settled at the kitchen table, but the room was deserted. Gran must have toddled off to bed at her usual time and, presumably, the O'Hallorans had followed suit.

Maddy laid the table for breakfast, banked down the fire and headed for bed, but tired though she was she did not fall asleep at once. Ever since she had confided in Tom about seeing a stranger in the lane he had urged her to question the Irish couple, and the problem of how to do so still nagged at her at night. 'It's not that you're suggesting they abused your trust,' he had told her earnestly. 'It's just, first, that you have every right to know how they came to leave your gran alone – if they did – and, second, that a stranger so near your property might be up to no good. Unless they are prepared to answer a couple of innocent questions, one must conclude that they have a reason for their silence on the subject. You are a young girl and Gran is an old woman. You can do without mysteries which may have perfectly respectable solutions, but on the other hand may put you at risk.'

It was good advice, but Maddy had not taken it. For a start, she knew that Gran would be furious if she cast any doubt on the O'Hallorans' characters. Gran, despite her occasional outbursts, got on well with the O'Hallorans and championed them at every turn. At first she had been suspicious, had tested every word the O'Hallorans spoke to see if it was true, but latterly she had grown more and more fond of the Irish couple. Maddy had been at first amused and then a little put out to discover that the O'Hallorans were trusted before herself, as in the case of the savings book.

But when she taxed Gran with it, her words had been brushed aside. 'Eileen and Declan are my very good friends,' she told her granddaughter. 'You must know I pay them only a tiny wage and yet there's nothing they wouldn't do for me. So you think they went off to the Christmas market and left me alone, do you? Well, you're wrong. They wanted to buy me something special for a Christmas treat, so Eileen stayed with me while I had my nap and Declan went to the market and bought me that lovely box of chocolates and a pot of goose grease, enough to spread on all my joints and help ease the aching. So don't you go bad-mouthing them to me or anyone else.'

She had shut her mouth like a trap at almost the same minute that Maddy's own mouth had closed sharply. For a moment the two had glared at each other, then Maddy had relaxed and actually dared to laugh. 'All right, all right, you silly old Gran,' she had said affectionately. 'The O'Hallorans are a couple of saints and I'm a sinner for asking questions. But Gran, it's for your own sake . . .'

'Ho, yes, and I'll thank you to keep your nose out of my business, you nasty little snooper,' Gran had said wrathfully. 'Let me tell you, they've made *your* life a lot easier. How do you think you'd have got on at that posh school if they'd not been here, hey? How would you have coped with trying to get to and from town so's you could give me my meals?' Her eyes had sparkled with all their old malevolence. 'The O'Hallorans never complain and they do whatever I happen to ask. If *he* can't do it, *she* will. And as for you, you conceited little madam, you ought to be down on your bended knees thanking them. The money I pay them is peanuts yet they never grumble, so just you be grateful and don't let me hear you criticising my friends ever again . . . hear me?'

'I'd have to be deaf not to hear you,' Maddy had said drily. 'But about your savings book . . .'

But that had been enough to set Gran off once more, and in the middle of a tirade about serpent's teeth and ungrateful granddaughters Maddy had slipped quietly out of the room. Curiosity was all very well, but a fully fledged ticking-off could wait until she had a bit more time.

Chapter Nine

It was a glorious summer, and when the Thwaites returned from the promised trip to the south of France Maddy, Tom and Marigold had listened with envy to Alice's description of the days of sun and sea which she had enjoyed.

'I wish we could go away, like you did,' Maddy sighed as the four of them slogged across the Hall gardens and headed for the beck. 'It would be such fun to learn to swim! Isn't it just like fate to give us super sunny weather and make the beck shrink so no one can possibly swim in it? Oh well, at least we can paddle.'

'True,' Marigold said. She and her mother had been to stay with relatives, and had only returned the previous day. 'But we might go off on an expedition.' She turned to Maddy. 'Didn't you once say you wanted to look for Vendale? That might be quite fun.' She spoke to Tom, pointedly turning her back on Alice. 'You'd come with us, wouldn't you, Tom? We could take a picnic . . . we could even camp out!'

'No we could not,' Alice said coldly. 'And it's our cook who makes up the picnics and my aunt who provides the nice things to eat. Your mother . . .'

'My mother gives us chocolate bars and shop cakes,' Marigold said quickly. 'She does what she can; she's a working woman, don't forget. And what does Maddy contribute, hey? Nothing! But you don't pick on her.'

'I'm not picking on anyone,' Alice said untruthfully. 'But if I'm honest, Marigold Stein, I'd rather you stayed at home. The three of us got on pretty well before you came along . . .'

'Stop sniping this minute,' Tom said suddenly. 'Haven't you heard that there's almost certainly going to be a war? Isn't it bad enough to be on the brink of what could prove to be every bit as bad as the last lot without you two not only competing in school but competing at home as well?' He scowled at Alice. 'There's your aunt Ruby bottling half the orchard and putting the other half down on straw in the apple loft, and the only thing you do to help is deride everyone else's efforts. Why, Maddy is the only one of you with a grain of sense.' He glared wrathfully at Alice and Marigold. 'Will you two shake hands and make up? Because if you won't, I'm off.'

Alice and Marigold stared at Tom as though they could not believe what he was saying. Alice was the first one to break the uneasy silence. 'I'm sorry you think I'm argumentative,' she said stiffly. 'It's Marigold; everything I say she contradicts, and as for Maddy not being argumentative, that's just because she wants to be your little favourite. But if it will make you happy, Tom, I won't open my mouth for the rest of the day.' She turned to give Marigold the benefit of an icy smile. 'Will you say the same, Marigold? Though I doubt if it's possible for you to shut up for five minutes, let alone five hours.'

At this point Tom gave a shout of laughter and Maddy joined in. Laughter is infectious and soon all four were rolling around on the bank of the beck, unable to sober up. When eventually they did stop laughing, Tom spoke before either of the combatants could do so. 'That's better!' he said approvingly. 'Are you going to shake hands and be friends? I know you thought I was just kidding, but I meant it; either we have a permanent truce or I'm going to help Dad clean the car or something.'

Maddy watched with considerable amusement as Alice and Marigold, both looking extremely sulky, conferred, moving a little way off in order that whatever they had to say to each other would not be overheard. But she knew both girls wanted to please Tom and was not unduly surprised to see them shake hands. Alice was the first to speak.

'Sorry, Tom. You're quite right, of course; it's downright daft to fight amongst ourselves. How about going up to the house, persuading Cook to make us a few sandwiches and then deciding what to do.'

By the time they reached the kitchen several ideas had been put forward, but it was Cook, making sandwiches with incredible speed and packing them into a handy bag, who made the suggestion that proved to be the most popular. 'Rare hot both in and out today,' she said placidly as she worked. 'Where are you goin'? What you want is somewhere cool. Ever been to the limestone caverns? Can't say I've ever been myself, but folk say the fells is riddled with caves and that, and the deeper in you go the colder it gets.' She chuckled richly. 'Just the ticket for a day like today. They say there's an underground lake with white fishes in it what have got no eyes 'cos it's always dark down there. Now, if you could find that there lake you could cool your little tootsies in it before comin' home with one of them eyeless fish to prove where you've been.'

They left the kitchen and set off towards the little stone bridge in whose welcome shade they sheltered as they began to make plans to visit the caves the following day. 'We'll have to meet at the crack of dawn – well, no later than eight o'clock – because it's a fair walk to the limestone cliffs,' Tom said. 'And we'll want to get there before the heat of noon. We'll ask Cook to make up a picnic basket this evening and then we shan't have to wait around in the morning. What else will we need? Oh, I'll bring my big torch along as well. See you all here at eight o'clock, then – Alice, don't forget the picnic basket – and in the meantime we can get all our chores done.'

'Alice doesn't have any . . .' Marigold began, her

tone distinctly spiteful, but Maddy saw Tom raise an eyebrow, and Marigold deflated. 'Sorry, sorry . . .' she said, and Maddy thought she meant it. 'I forgot. I will be good even if I can't stay silent for five hours!'

Within an hour of setting out, the heat was beginning to get to all four of them. So high in the fells there were no trees to cast any shade, and very soon Alice began to say that they might as well start on the picnic Cook had packed. 'Because if I don't have a drink soon I shall expire,' she said pathetically. She turned to the others. 'Anyone with me?'

But to her dismay two heads were shaken in a strong negative, though Marigold looked a little wistful. However, Tom, who was carrying the basket of food, announced that anyone who wanted to raid the picnic before they reached the caves would have him to tackle. 'There's a beck with lovely clean water bubbling past and you want to sully your lips with ginger beer?' he asked incredulously. 'I thought better of you, Alice. It'll only make you thirstier, you know. Now be a good sensible girl and dip a mug into the beck; there's nothing as sweet as cold fresh water bubbling up from its source in the high fells.'

Alice hesitated, but Maddy dipped her mug in the water and drank thirstily and soon everyone else followed suit. They perched on rocks in the stream and enjoyed the respite for a moment, but Tom did not intend to let them linger for long.

'Come on, troops!' he said cheerfully. 'Cook said if we followed the beck we'd be able to see the caverns quite clearly above us and I think I can see the cliffs, so best foot forward and the last one there's a sissy.'

Maddy shielded her eyes with one hand and peered ahead and up. 'I can see them – the cliffs, I mean – and they look really close, almost as though I could reach out a hand and touch them,' she said. 'The sun is burning my head and I'm sure my shoulders are on fire; the sooner we can get into the shelter of the caverns the better. I do hope we're not following the wrong beck!'

'Would I, the leader of this expedition, get my route wrong?' Tom said indignantly. 'Of course we're on the right track; another twenty minutes of hard walking and we'll be there, and when we arrive we'll celebrate by getting into the caves where it's cool, and starting our picnic.'

But when they reached the cliff face, at first they could not see a single cavern or cave. The four explorers stopped short and three reproachful pairs of eyes turned to their gallant leader.

'We *are* in the wrong place,' and 'We *did* follow the wrong beck,' Alice and Marigold said in chorus. 'Oh, Tom, whatever do we do now?'

Maddy wiped sweat from her eyes on the piece of rag she used as a handkerchief and peered at the cliff. Suddenly, as though it had only just come into focus, she saw a crack. It was narrow and camouflaged by a growth of various weeds and wild flowers, but it was there all right; an entrance, of sorts, to at least one cave. She pointed it out to Tom, who promptly saw another crack, and though it was a tight squeeze even Tom, the tallest and broadest of them, managed to get himself through the small aperture. They found within a large and airy cavern, divided in two by a bubbling beck, and realised that though it could be described as a cave there was a space at the top through which they could see a sliver of sky framed by tossing, wind-blown grasses. It was very cool. Maddy could feel the sweat drying on her; she even shivered a little. Looking round her, she saw that there were several passages, or at least openings, which led deeper into the cliff. Tom approached the nearest and was brought up short by a shriek from Alice.

'Tom, you're the only one with a torch; come back at once! You know Cook said there was an underground lake; one of us might run straight into it and be drowned dead before we could scream.'

Maddy gave a muffled giggle. 'Don't worry – I brought my torch too. But I don't believe in that underground lake,' she said. 'I was at the village school, remember, and though there was always quite a lot of talk about Grumbling Gill – you have to get all roped up to enter that and be lowered through quite a small hole – I never heard anyone say anything about an underground lake. I expect that was just one of Cook's tales.'

Tom stood up. 'I'm going to see where the biggest passage goes,' he said. 'Ages ago I was talking to old Fred in the village, and he told me about a cave as big as a cathedral which was completely open. If we could find that we could eat our picnic there.'

Everyone agreed that this was a good plan and presently they entered the largest of the fissures. Tom went first, shining the torch ahead of him and commenting as he did so that the path was smoother now, though there were still a few pieces of fallen rock, best avoided. They had not gone very far, however, when Marigold, who was clutching Tom's arm, suddenly pulled him to a halt, giving a small shriek as she did so.

Tom sighed. 'What's up, Marigold? There's nothing frightening ahead, so will you please stop grabbing my arm and behave sensibly?'

But Maddy, having heard the note of panic in her friend's voice, told him to hang on a minute. 'Not everyone likes being underground, with hundreds of tons of rocks above them . . .' she began, but apparently this was too much for Marigold.

'I don't like it; I'm going back, Tom, and I don't care if you think I'm a coward and a sissy,' she wailed. 'I thought we were going to explore caves, not narrow little passages which might lead anywhere. I'll wait for you in the first cave but I won't, I *won't* stay in this horrible little passage.'

Tom shone his torch into Marigold's face and what

he saw there clearly changed his mind. His tone had not been entirely sympathetic, but now, Maddy realised, he could see for himself that Marigold was not just being difficult. She was pale with terror, her eyes like dark pools and her mouth trembling.

'I'm sorry if I'm spoiling your fun, but I just can't go on,' she said wildly.

Maddy, who had no fear either of the dark ahead or of what might possibly appear round the next bend, grabbed at Marigold's flailing hands and held them in what she hoped was a consoling grip. 'It's all right. Lots of people don't like confined spaces,' she said. 'I'm not too keen on lifts either, come to think. I'll come back with you, Marigold.'

'Oh, thank you, Maddy. You are a friend . . .' Marigold began, but Tom interrupted.

'I'll go back with you and make sure you're safe, Marigold, whilst the other two wait for me here. If you want to go a little further you can, you two, but if you do find another cavern don't go wandering off into it until I get back.'

It was not easy turning round, for the passage had narrowed as they came further in, but they managed it. A hand at her waist, Tom shepherded Marigold in the direction of daylight. Alice tugged at Maddy's arm. 'I bet she just pretended she didn't like enclosed spaces so that she could get Tom to herself,' she whispered. 'It would be typical of Marigold, scheming little cat.'

'Don't be so nasty,' Maddy said automatically,

though she thought it was quite possible that the other girl was right.

Alice started wandering aimlessly up and down. 'What on earth are they doing?' she asked fretfully when five minutes or so had passed. 'I hope they're not tucking into the picnic. I hadn't thought of it before, but now I realise I'm quite hungry.' She gave a sharp exclamation. 'Ouch! There's a pebble or something in my shoe . . . no, not a pebble, something sharp! Oh, if I'm crippled for life it'll be Marigold's fault, making Tom take her back to the outside world and leaving us in the dark with only your little torch.' She took it from Maddy as she spoke, then flopped down on the nearest rock and took off her shoe to examine the sole of her foot. 'Look at that . . . blood! Well, that will put a stop to any talk of exploring further.'

Maddy sighed, but when commanded to do so lifted Alice's foot cautiously and looked at the sole. There was a little blood, to be sure, but it really was only a small amount. However, she knew Alice always made a huge fuss over the tiniest hurt, so she said bracingly: 'Oh, poor Alice! But you'll be all right. I'll go and see what's holding Tom up.'

'Wait for me – oh, it hurts to put my foot on the ground,' Alice whimpered. 'You go ahead then, Maddy, and make sure they aren't eating up all the sandwiches and things. I'll come as fast as I can.'

'Right,' Maddy said brusquely. When she reached the original cave there was no sign of Marigold or

Tom, and she was almost at the entrance before she saw them. When she did she stopped short, for Tom and Marigold were in one another's arms outside, and they were kissing.

Maddy turned so quickly that she collided with Alice, who had come up behind her, and trod on her injured foot. Alice fell to the floor with a shriek like a train whistle.

'My foot, my foot,' she wailed. 'Oh, I think my back's broken! How shall I get home? Oh, my poor foot.'

Tom, looking worried, came panting back into the cave. 'What happened?' he asked anxiously. 'Did someone attack you, Alice? Or did you slip on the wet rock? Do stop yelling, though. You'll burst my eardrums and then I shan't be able to hear a thing.'

Maddy gave an artificial laugh; her one thought was that Alice must never know what she, Maddy, had seen. She must behave normally, or as normally as was possible in the circumstances, for Alice was still lying on the ground having refused, when asked, to get to her feet and let Tom examine the damage. Maddy gathered her wits and spoke sternly. 'Alice Thwaite, just you pull yourself together and behave! I'm very sorry I trod on your foot – your injured foot, I should say – but it was only a stone getting into your shoe, after all. As for your back, if you'd really broken it I don't believe you would be able to shout. So shut up and get up before we decide to go home and leave you here.'

She kept her gaze averted from Tom, reminding herself, fiercely, that he had planned this to be an expedition they would all enjoy. There was, after all, no law which said a boy could not kiss a girl. It was only that Alice would be furious, and Maddy had no desire for the 'truce' Tom had insisted on to come to a premature end. She must forget what she had seen and make sure that Tom and Marigold never knew they had been spotted. Above all, Alice must never discover that Tom felt anything but friendship for Marigold Stein.

As they prepared to eat their picnic and fill their mugs with cold water from the beck, she told herself that you cannot lose what you never had, in this case Tom Browning. He had never shown the least sign that he was aware of her feelings. Well, how could he be? She had not been aware of them herself until she had felt that sharp stab of almost unbearable jealousy as her astounded gaze took in the sight of her friends' embrace.

The conflicting emotions that had occupied Maddy's thoughts as she walked home that night must still have shown on her face as she entered the kitchen, for Gran said inquisitively: 'What's got you all in a lather you silly girl? Been kissed by the boyfriend, eh? Ah, well, boys will be boys, and though that Tom is a nice young feller they're all out for what they can get, even him, so just you remember that and don't go comin' back here wailin' you're in the family way.'

Mrs O'Halloran, sitting in a fireside chair and placidly knitting, raised her brows, but her husband, who was whittling at a piece of wood with his penknife, said chidingly: 'That's no way to talk, Mrs Hebditch. Maddy's a respectable young lady, and don't you forget it.'

Maddy glared at Gran. 'Just you apologise, Gran,' she said wrathfully. 'You've got a nasty, dirty mind. Why, I'm not even fifteen yet and I don't have a boyfriend.'

Gran sniffed, but Maddy saw a spot of colour appear in her cheeks. 'All right, all right, a girl can fall for a feller's charms at any age,' she said gruffly. 'But you're not a bad girl, Maddy, so maybe I shouldn't have said what I did.' She got creakingly to her feet and then cursed as her knitting rolled off her lap. 'Did you reach the caves? I'd forgotten all about them.'

'Yes, but Marigold got frightened so we didn't do much exploring,' Maddy said. 'And Alice hurt her foot and made an awful fuss – you know how she is – so it wasn't what you'd call a total success.'

Gran opened her mouth to make a scathing comment and then changed her mind. 'Ah, well; I dare say you enjoyed the company,' she commented. 'And now you can help me up to bed because I've had a busy day as well.'

'I can't think what you have done to tire yourself out since you hardly ever move from that chair,' Maddy said indignantly. 'And you're right about one thing: Tom *is* a nice boy and he doesn't want to take advantage of anyone. I'm going to bed.'

And with that she crossed the kitchen, seized Gran's arm and led her to the hallway. For the best part of a year now Gran had needed someone to help her up the stairs, but it seemed to Maddy that she walked more easily tonight. She said as much, and Gran looked round as though suspecting that walls had ears before replying. 'Eileen's been making me walk ten times round the kitchen table whenever she says,' she confided. 'It's that damned Dr Carlton's fault. He told her that unless I kept my joints mobile I'd be bedfast by Christmas, so now she chivvies me round the table and won't give me my elevenses until me poor legs is near to falling off! But I reckon Eileen has my best interests at heart, which is more than I can say for you, you selfish little madam!'

Maddy, whose spurts of temper with her grandmother never lasted long, giggled; it was typical of Gran to turn an ordinary remark into a cause for complaint! But on the whole she was pleased, because she was sure that Eileen's previous habit of leaving the old woman in the same position for hours at a time had been increasing Gran's reluctance to leave her chair, and indeed reducing her ability to do so. A couple of visits to the privy in the yard and one ascent of the stairs had been the sum total of her movement over the course of a full day. But now, it seemed, Eileen realised it was in her best interests to keep Gran mobile. After all, even though the wage Gran paid the O'Hallorans was small, Maddy was seeing more and more how much the couple valued the advantages that went with it. Oh, yes, Mrs O'Halloran had obviously realised that what they must regard as a cushy option would come to an abrupt end with Gran's demise.

Maddy awoke late the day after the expedition to the caves. Realising it was mid-morning by the position of the sun, she lurched out of bed, swished back the curtains and began to dress; washing would have to wait. If she went down at once she could have her elevenses instead of breakfast and then cope with her chores.

It was the work of a moment to splash her face with water, drag a brush through her tangled hair and make for the stairs. She was about to descend when she remembered that Gran rose late on a Sunday, and popped her head round the old woman's door. But no Gran met her eyes, only a rumpled bed and a tin mug which had shed its water on to the old black-stained floorboards. Maddy shrugged. She knew Gran well enough to realise that if she had not got someone else to help her dress she would have woken Maddy herself without compunction. So she hurried downstairs and exploded into the kitchen, apologies for her tardiness already on her lips.

They were all there, as she expected, Mr O'Halloran drumming his fingers on the table, Mrs O'Halloran with her long, grey-streaked hair released from its bedtime plait but not yet twisted into the bun she usually favoured, and Gran, looking oddly alert, positively trim compared with Mrs O'Halloran, who appeared to have dressed by guess since her blouse was buttoned up wrongly and was rucked up at one side.

Maddy got no further than the first couple of words. Mr O'Halloran got up from his chair and indicated that she should sit down. 'You missed the announcement, alanna,' he said, and his voice was almost gentle. 'That there Chamberlain has just told us the bad news. He give them Huns an ultimatum: agree to get out of Poland by eleven o'clock or we'll drive you out. He ain't had no reply, so it seems we're at war with the perishin' Huns all over agin.'

Chapter Ten

December 1939

Maddy was walking up the track which led from the village to Larkspur when she met three young boys coming in the opposite direction. Their arms were full of holly, their faces bright with anticipation, and though this was the first time she had met them they greeted her as though she were an old friend.

'I reckon you're Mrs Hebditch's granddaughter, what she said was comin' to see how we goes on,' the tallest of the trio said cheerfully. He wore a ragged cap on the back of his head, an even more ragged jacket, too small for him, and a pair of boots, very much too large. 'I'm Herbert, Herb to me pals; the little 'un with the snub snitch is Sid and t'other, him with the muffler round his scrawny little neck, is Monty. Old Ma Hebditch told us you were comin' 'cos your factory has give you a coupla days off for the first time since you started workin' there.' He flourished his bunch of holly. 'We're takin' this for Miss Evans at the school. We likes her, don't we, fellers? We've already got a load to decorate Larkspur; the old 'un keeps on about makin' this Christmas a real grand 'un, because of rationin' you know. She says by next Christmas everything'll be on ration, not just sugar and butter and that.' He smacked his lips. 'The farmer's give us the promise of a chicken and Mr O'Halloran is goin' to take a boat to Ireland to bring back supplies, mebbe even a cake.' His eyes glistened at the prospect. 'We ain't ever had a Christmas cake, but the old 'un says we'll have our share this time, especially since two of the 'vacuees has gone home – more fools they are, says us, eh, lads?' He chuckled hoarsely. 'Me mam's all right, but me dad's a docker and come Christmas he an' the booze get together and no one ain't safe. So we'll be stoppin' at Larkspur till they kicks us out, ain't that right, lads?'

The two smaller boys agreed enthusiastically and were beginning to edge past Maddy when Herb stopped them with a gesture. 'I say, I've just thought; *are* you the old 'un's girl, what's called Madder-something?'

'Maddy. Yes I am,' Maddy said. 'And I shall be at home for Christmas because my leave is for a whole week. And a friend will be coming to join me . . .'

'A feller?'

That was Sid, the one with the snub nose, but Maddy, though she laughed, had to confess that her friend was just another girl. 'No, her name's Marigold, and we lodge together in the town.'

'Oh! Well, I suppose it don't make much difference,' Sid said. 'Only we's goin' to join the army as soon as we's old enough, so whenever we go into town we look out for the soldiers … ain't they just smart? Dontcher wish you had a uniform, miss?'

Maddy thought of the stained and disreputable overalls the girls who worked in the munitions factories wore, and agreed with Sid that a uniform would be nice. 'We're goin' to join the army too, when we're old enough,' Maddy told them. 'Well, the Auxiliary Territorial Service, anyway.'

Herb nodded wisely. 'ATS,' he said. 'Good on you, miss. And now we'd best gerron, else we'll miss us dinners.' He chuckled. 'Your old gran is a real tartar, but I like her better'n that Irish woman, even though she's the one what gets our meals. See you later, miss.'

The boys continued down the lane and Maddy carried on towards Larkspur. So much had happened, she reflected, since she had moved away from the farm. In fact, looking back, she realised that everything had changed, not just for her but for everyone. Within three days of war being declared, Alice had been bundled off to India aboard a troop ship taking five or six hundred British soldiers to help to secure India's borders, for that mighty subcontinent was very much a part of the Empire. On the fifth of September she had come rushing across to Larkspur, pedalling inexpertly on Tom's ancient bicycle. She had been tear-streaked and furious, but nothing she could say had saved her from banishment.

'I told Daddy that the voyage itself was likely to be

more dangerous than being hit by a bomb,' she had said tearfully. 'Daddy is afraid of what people will say if he leaves me in England, because everyone's sure the Germans will invade. Oh, Maddy, I'm so dreadfully unhappy! India was all right when my mother was alive – though actually I always saw more of the servants than I did of my parents – but I'm happy *here*! Uncle John says he and Auntie Ruby are moving down to London because he's been given an important job in the War Office. But I could stay here; oh, not at the Hall, that's already been requisitioned by the army, but at Larkspur? Oh, I'm so unhappy!'

'What did Tom say? He's the one with ideas, and I'm sure he doesn't want to see you packed off to India,' Maddy had said. 'I'm sure he'll agree that you'll be more at risk on an ocean voyage in wartime. Where are you supposed to be sailing from, anyway?'

Alice had dabbed at her eyes with a small handkerchief which was already drenched with her tears, saying bitterly: 'I don't know and I don't care. And as for Tom, a fat lot of good he's been: he's already left. Apparently he joined the army even before war was declared and got the letter he's been waiting for yesterday, telling him to report to Catterick a.s.a.p.' She had gulped and rubbed fiercely at her reddened eyes. 'Why didn't he think of *me*? I thought he was keen on me, but if so he's got a strange way of showing it, running off without a word. He could at least have tried to say goodbye!' She had mopped again at her tears, then sniffed defiantly. 'He's cooked his goose, I can tell you; not that I ever intended to marry a chauffeur's son, but now I wouldn't even give him the time of day.' Despite herself, Maddy had laughed, earning a glare from Alice hot enough to fry an egg. 'All right, all right, I suppose he had no choice, but he must have known I'd be angry and upset. But, dear Maddy, will you ask Uncle John to let me stay with you, for as long as the war lasts?' She had looked appealingly at her friend. 'Everyone's saying it'll all be over by Christmas.'

But pleading had been useless, of course, and Alice had had no option but to leave on the troop ship, accompanied by a great many soldiers, several of whom had not hidden their admiration for the pretty, weeping girl, which Maddy thought Alice would find comforting.

Now, as she walked up towards the house that had been her home for as long as she could remember, Maddy continued to ruminate on the changes war had brought. The absence of Tom had been painful at first, for she had begun to think that she might become an important part of his life, but the fact that he had left without saying goodbye seemed to indicate that this was unlikely. Worse, Marigold had told her that on his way to the station Tom had stopped off at her lodgings and given her the address of his training camp, promising to write to her as soon as he got there.

But I could have written to him as well as Marigold, Maddy told herself now. After all, I've been his friend for longer than she has. But then she remembered the expedition to the caves, and the kiss. If you kissed someone did you instantly become boy and girlfriend? She had heard girls talking in the village, but could not make up her mind about the significance of the embrace she had witnessed. And presently, as the lane grew steeper and rougher, she tried to distract herself by thinking about the invasion which the Germans had promised and every member of the United Kingdom must be prepared to repulse.

But the war was three months old now and though there had been various false alarms – rumours of nuns floating out of the sky on parachutes, only identified by their lack of petticoats and the addition of jackboots – the threatened invasion had failed to materialise. Some things were rationed, to be sure, and their number would greatly increase on the eighth of January, when the new restrictions came into being, but other than that things jogged along very much as they had always done.

At the beginning of the war Marigold and her mother had discussed the possibility of returning to their relatives in the south, but this Marigold had been reluctant to do. She and Maddy had applied for factory work, and decided to find lodgings in town.

I wonder what the O'Hallorans are going to do now, Maddy asked herself as she reached the old gate which led into the farmyard. For the hundredth time she went over the advantages of the O'Halloran occupation. Gran liked them, and they were both patient and pleasant to the old woman. Mrs O'Halloran, though she admitted that she had never preserved fruit before, had allowed Gran to instruct her in the art of bottling fruit and veg when she discovered piles of empty Kilner jars under the pantry shelves. They did Gran's laundry as well as their own, and when Mr O'Halloran shot a rabbit or caught a couple of trout there was no question but that Gran should have her share. They shopped for her in the village, sometimes going as far as the town for something she needed, and they saw that she took her medication and was visited by the doctor, taking his advice and seeing that Gran did too.

In the beginning Maddy had sometimes wondered why Mrs O'Halloran did not write lists of what Gran wanted, seeming to prefer to simply memorise her requirements. But it had soon struck her: neither of the O'Hallorans could read or write! This had surprised her, but she had been far too tactful to let it show. She was sure they thought they had hidden their inability pretty well, because whenever he went down to the village Mr O'Halloran bought a newspaper. He would sit in the old basket chair of an evening, apparently reading the headlines and then fetching a funny little pair of wire-rimmed spectacles to cope with print which he said was too tiny for him to read with the naked eye. But it was a small deceit, reminding Maddy how anxious Alice had been to hide her own inability to read. After all, she had accepted Alice's secret, so why should she not accept the O'Hallorans?

She leaned on the gate, contemplating the farm and wondering idly what was different. Apart from the fact that it looked even more disreputable than it had when she left – the gate she was leaning on, for instance, had finally shed its rusting hinges and was tied to the post with string – she could see no particular changes. Her eye ran swiftly from the roof tiles to the cobbles; nothing new there. Perhaps it was something to do with the evacuees, though she could not think what it could be.

She was halfway across the yard before it occurred to her that the geese had not rushed out, honking, to drive her off. Maddy paused; that was odd! Then she realised that without its hinges the gate had given no revealing squeak to warn the birds that a stranger had entered the yard. Maddy tutted beneath her breath. She would have to tell Mr O'Halloran that it must be repaired, because geese, as everyone knew, were even better than a guard dog for keeping strangers at bay. She headed for the back door, and something made her beat a tattoo on the door panel before she flung it open. She told herself that it was only good manners to warn the occupants of Larkspur that she had arrived, but she resented the necessity. Nevertheless, she pinned a bright smile in place as she entered the deliciously warm kitchen with its well-remembered scent of cooking, but had she been looking for an ecstatic welcome she would have been disappointed. Fortunately, she had had no such expectation.

Gran had never been demonstrative, and the fact that her granddaughter had been living away from her for the past three months did not merit any special greeting. To be sure, she looked up, but if anything like a smile crossed her countenance it was speedily gone. 'Oh, so you've decided to come a-callin', have you?' she said disagreeably. 'About time too – it's a good thing that at least Mr and Mrs O'Halloran have spared no pains to see I'm not affected by this war. And it may interest you to know that though you've not seen fit to come home and see how I was getting on, one of your friends hasn't been so neglectful. We've had a visit from young Tom Browning, and very smart he looked in his uniform. The evacuees mobbed him as if he were a fillum star. He stood there, on the very spot where you are standing now . . .'

'But I thought he was miles away from here! Oh, don't tell me I've missed him. Is he home for Christmas? But where will he stay? The Hall's full of soldiers and somebody in the village said the evacuees have taken every available bed, so the local children have been forced to sleep on sofas, or to share beds with brothers or sisters . . . oh, Gran, don't say I've missed seeing Tom!'

Maddy's obvious disappointment had one thing

in its favour: it brought a smile to Gran's face. 'Yes, you've missed him,' she said, with evident satisfaction. 'He was on . . . oh, what the devil was it called? It was something to do with dogs . . . yes, I remember, barkation leave.'

'*Em*barkation leave,' Maddy said, unable even to raise a smile over her grandmother's inadvertent humour. 'Oh, damn, damn, damn . . . if only I'd known I'd have wangled some time off, by hook or by crook!' She noticed Mrs O'Halloran for the first time and turned an imploring face towards her. 'Sorry, Mrs O'Halloran, I didn't see you over there. Did Tom stay here?'

Mrs O'Halloran gave Maddy a rather wintry smile. 'We're full up with them dratted evacuees,' she said. 'He didn't give us no warning any more'n you did, miss! I think he stayed in the old flat above the stables at the Hall. I disremember when exactly he were here, but he's been gone a long while, two or three weeks at least. And if embarkation leave means what I think, it'll be many a long day before we see him again – always provided he survives the voyage to wherever he's bound, of course.' She looked across the room at Maddy and there was something strangely secretive in her expression. 'We couldn't put your pal Tom up, and the same goes for you,' she said. 'You'll have to look for somebody else to take you in – you and your friend.'

Maddy stared at her. 'Can't take us in?' she asked

incredulously. 'You must be joking, Mrs O'Halloran! Apart from anything else, I met three of your evacuees coming up the lane – they were taking holly down to decorate the schoolhouse – and they told me that the other two had gone back home for the holiday. So there's at least one attic room – which will be unoccupied for the next week or so. Besides, this is my home, mine and Gran's, and it's not as if I didn't give you notice; I sent a telegram to say when we would be arriving.'

Mrs O'Halloran opened her mouth as though to reply, then shut it again as Gran cut across her. 'Have you lost your sense of humour, girl?' she asked, her tone aggressive. 'Of course Eileen's joking you – coddin' you as they say in Ireland. It might have been awkward if you'd not sent that telegram, but you give us enough notice to stock up on a few extras. You'll be in your old room next to mine with your friend, toppin' and tailin' it. Where is she?'

'She'll be here later,' Maddy said. 'She's called in to see her mother – she'd be staying there for Christmas, only the house is so full of evacuees there isn't a spare bed in the place, their landlady says.' She glanced towards Mrs O'Halloran. '*Were* you only joking when you said there was no room? It didn't sound like it, and you looked deadly serious.'

'What, me refuse to let you stay here in your own home, miss?' Mrs O'Halloran said. 'As if I'd dare! It's just – just that them evacuees takes up all of me time. What with keepin' them out of the pantry and guardin' the apple loft from the little demons, I scarce have time to sit down, so you don't want to take no notice of what I say.'

Maddy turned to Gran. 'Did Tom ask for my address? I don't suppose he left a message?'

Gran rooted in her overall pocket and produced a sheet of paper torn from a notebook. She handed it to Maddy. 'He writes as he's going abroad but will drop you a line as soon as he arrives at his destination.'

Maddy took the note and after a quick glance at it she thrust it into her pocket. 'Thanks, Gran. Thank heaven we've not lost touch.' She had thrown down her haversack as she entered the kitchen, but now she picked it up and went over to the stairs. 'I'll just take my things up and then come down and have a look round; shan't be a tick.'

But in fact she was more than a tick, because the moment she got to her room she threw herself down on the bed and began to beat the pillow with her fist. He had thought of her, had wanted to say goodbye before going off to wherever the army was sending him. And she had missed him! If only she had known . . . but of course he had had no address for her, just as she now had no address for him. Why didn't I write to him at Catterick, she thought despairingly. Oh, dear God, if only, if only! But she had not thought that he might be sent abroad, and now her heart sank into her shoes. What a fool she had been!

Maddy had been lying face down on her bed, but now she sat up. She glanced at her reflection in the mirror on top of the chest of drawers and saw that she was pale and red-eyed, her cheeks still tear-wet. Despite herself, she gave a snuffly little giggle. What a sight she looked! If Tom could see her now he probably wouldn't even recognise this pathetic creature, and would look around for the cheerful smiling girl he had so cruelly abandoned.

This thought made the sobs rise up again in Maddy's throat, and she dismissed it quickly. You are a stupid, miserable, whining girl and Tom would be ashamed of you, she told herself. Pull yourself together, Madeleine, and give your face a wash. Forget your grievances and go downstairs; Marigold will be arriving soon and by then all traces of tears must have disappeared.

But, oh, I do wonder what Tom is doing now! I don't believe he's a good sailor, so he's probably leaning over the rail being horribly sick. Oh, poor Tom! But at least he didn't join the Navy, so once he reaches his destination he'll have other things to worry about, which will take his mind off his stomach's behaviour. In her mind's eye she saw mosquitoes the size of seagulls, snakes the length of the farmyard and many other horrors from which Tom might have to suffer. Seasickness would suddenly seem like the least of his worries though she was pretty sure, even if one did not die of it, it could reduce one to a wreck in a couple of weeks.

Wrecks! Suppose his troubles were already over? Suppose his ship had been spotted by an enemy submarine – the Germans called them U-boats – and had been torpedoed with the loss of all aboard? The thought was almost enough to start her crying again; she could feel tears welling up. Then she chided herself. Mr O'Halloran had been right; she really must learn to control her imagination. Tom might indeed have to become an expert in jungle warfare and learn all about snakes and mosquitoes, but it was too soon to worry about that. She set off for the kitchen, a determined smile on her face, but despite all her efforts to be sensible, Tom's face, with misery and pain in his eyes, swam before her vision for the rest of the day.

March 1940

Aboard the troop ship *Beaumaris Pride*, Tom was writing letters – or rather he was trying to, for as he remembered telling Alice, Madeleine and Marigold, he had never been a good sailor. At first he had only felt slightly uneasy, but when the ship got into rougher waters – they had to take the long route round, having been informed that the Med was alive with U-boats and enemy shipping – all hopes of a calm voyage ended. Not that he intended to tell any of his correspondents how he really felt, which was queasy most of the time. Writing, of course, was no help; the minute he bent his head over the page nausea attacked him in waves. But he knew that their first landfall was imminent, so he planned to send his letters off as soon as they docked. The powers that be had not told the troops where they were bound, but word had gradually spread that they would be docking at Cape Town to refuel and, with luck, would not only be able to post mail home but also have some time ashore.

So Tom was writing to his father, who was now serving somewhere, Tom thought, in Egypt; to Alice who would be settled in India by this time, and to Maddy and Marigold who were working in a factory until they were old enough to apply to join up.

At first he had intended to write identical letters to all three girls, but had changed his mind on learning that Madeleine and Marigold shared the same accommodation and would undoubtedly read one another's correspondence. Alice, however, was now with her father somewhere in Bombay, so he could copy his Alice letter to Marigold without fear of being found out.

Tom sighed, and regarded his pen with loathing. It was a relic from school, old and spluttery, and Tom made up his mind that when they went ashore he would buy himself a decent fountain pen, even if it cost a bob or two.

He was only on the second line of the letter to Alice, however, when someone smote him on the shoulder. 'Hello, hello, hello, who's a good little soldier boy then? I thought you'd written to your dad and the girl who lives in the farmhouse with the funny name . . . don't say you're playing Miss Letshavealark false!'

'And I thought I was lucky to find someone I knew aboard the ship,' Tom said ruefully, glancing up at the face now bending over his correspondence. 'Gerroff, Ricky Thompson! Don't you know it's rude to read other people's letters?'

'Not when the letter writer is you, old sport,' Ricky said. He was a tall, dark-haired young man, handsome, Tom supposed, in a swashbuckling Douglas Fairbanks sort of way. He bent over Tom's shoulder again.

'Who's Alice? You'll be in trouble when these women discover you're two-timing them.'

'And I was so delighted, when I first saw you hanging your hammock next to mine, to find I wasn't as alone as I thought, that there was another past pupil of the good old school aboard,' Tom said, blotting his letter with care. 'Odd that we never really saw much of each other there, despite both being in the OTC.'

'Ah, but I was a whole year ahead of you, and a good deal cleverer, naturally,' Ricky said, puffing out his chest. 'I was one of the upper class and you were just a dirty little fag . . .'

'Say it louder; someone might actually believe you,' Tom said sarcastically. 'I'd like to see the day dawn when any boy at St Oswald's had, or was, a fag. We left that sort of thing to Eton and 'Arrow, of which you, dear Richard, know nothing. And now go away and let me finish my letters. According to one of the deckhands, we'll be ashore in a couple of hours and I want to get these ready for posting, so's the folk back home don't worry.'

'You may post them, but that doesn't mean to say your fan club will ever receive them,' Ricky said darkly. 'There's an awful lot of hostile sea between us and them.'

'Yes, I know, but if none of us wrote letters because of that there'd be no such thing as a post office,' Tom said. 'Anyway, we got here, didn't we? And now go before I lose my rag and give you a bloody nose.'

Ricky gave a derisive laugh but went away, and Tom got down to the serious business of writing to what his friend had referred to as his 'fan club'.

He pulled the letter to Alice back towards him and began to describe the voyage, his fellow travellers and those members of the crew with whom he was best acquainted. Rather to his surprise it turned into a three page epistle, writing on one side only of the flimsy paper with which the men were provided. At the end he signed off with a flourish, and turned to the next sheet and wrote *My dear Marigold*. Copying was easy, and as his disgusting pen spluttered out the words he conjured up an image of Marigold's golden prettiness as he had taken her out of the caverns. He could not recall what she had been wearing, yet every line of her face and the tumble of golden curls was clear as though he had her picture before him. He sighed reminiscently. Ever since the visit to the Christmas market he had wanted to get Marigold alone, but there had been no opportunity until the day of the caves and then what a sweet and cuddly armful she had proved to be! She had not pretended for one moment that his kisses were unwelcome but had cuddled closer, murmuring into his ear how much she liked him and how hopefully she had looked forward to that very moment.

Such thoughts, however, reminded him of a conversation he had had with his father the previous summer. Tom had said he had been thinking of saving up so that some day, far in the future, he might be able to buy a car and take Alice, Maddy and Marigold for a spin; he could drive, after all, and had passed his test, so the girls would be in no danger.

Mr Browning had raised his eyebrows. 'I always thought you liked Alice best: a good choice. The little blonde – Marigold, isn't it? – is already measuring up every young male she looks at and will probably be a right little handful by the time you've saved up for a car.' He looked thoughtful. 'Maddy's still young for her age, but Alice, unless I'm much mistaken, will turn into a delightful young lady once she has to stand on her own two feet.'

Tom had been surprised. 'Stand on her own two feet? Doesn't she do that already? I've always thought she was quite independent . . . after all, she's an only child with no parents in this country, and a father pretty well indifferent to her by all accounts.' He considered, then nodded slowly. 'Though, come to think, she does tend to get someone else to perform any task which she doesn't fancy. I suppose you could say she was both spoilt and selfish and you wouldn't be far wrong. But I do like Alice, and it's a long time since she's put on her lady of the manor act with me.'

'Or with me,' Mr Browning had agreed. 'Oh, she tried once or twice, but I soon put a stop to that. I told her that whilst I didn't object to calling her Miss Alice I would thank her to remember that I too had a handle to my name and would prefer to be addressed as Mr Browning.' He chuckled. 'She went as red as a turkey cock, but she never called me "Browning" again. So you see what I mean? Oh, I know she's a very rich young lady, but after that she always considered my feelings and never tried to ride roughshod over me.' He grinned at his son. 'Look, you're young yet, and no doubt you'll meet many other girls over the next few years, but you could do worse, when you're a bit older, than to take up with Alice Thwaite. As long as you never marry for money. Remember, there's very little warmth in a handful of coins, and money can disappear leaving you with nothing.'

Listening to his father's words, Tom had remembered life before the Thwaites. Jim Browning had not always been a chauffeur. Once he had been the owner of a thriving business, a small but successful grocery and off-licence, in a small but equally thriving town. They had had a nice flat over the shop and in addition had owned a smallholding which, Tom knew, his father had meant to expand. But then the Depression had begun to bite. Suddenly, the rent on the shop had doubled. Tom had been seven or eight at the time and had not really understood why they had to sell the smallholding, though his father had tried to explain that the money from the sale would be all they had to keep them afloat until he got a job. Later, they had moved out of the flat into what his father had called a bedsit, and it was in that cheap and unattractive room that his mother had died. Tom could remember his father's tear-stained face and the way he had begged their landlord to let them remain in the bedsit. The landlord had been sympathetic but had pointed out that he could not waive the rent for more than a couple of weeks and young Tom – not so little now – had reproached his father, telling him that though mummies might cry, daddies never did so.

It had made Jim Browning smile, and when his son had won a scholarship to an excellent independent school in the Yorkshire Dales he had truly rejoiced, but there had still followed a series of jobs, a series of bedsits, a series of towns, until the happy day when he had applied for, and been offered, the comparatively well-paid job of chauffeur and general handyman to Mr John Thwaite of Windhover Hall. Tom, too, had loved the place from the first moment, and when he had discovered that there was a girl not very much younger than himself living at the Hall, who appeared to look up to him and take his advice, his happiness had been complete.

His father had been right, to a certain extent; he had liked Alice very much, and had been reluctant to include Maddy in their comfortable little twosome. Maddy had disliked him intensely at first – with some reason, he admitted to himself, remembering how rude he had been to her at their first meeting – but had come round when he had agreed to search for Vendale, even if he could not pretend to search for water babies. And just as he had grown accustomed to their threesome, Marigold had come along. She was quite as sophisticated as Alice and far prettier than either her or Maddy, and she had fitted in with all their plans. But the truth was, Tom had never considered a more permanent relationship with any of his 'fan club' and had said as much to his father.

Thinking over that summer conversation, however, Tom found that he was really glad his father could not read his thoughts at the moment, because he could no longer doubt his own feelings. Marigold – and her willingness to be kissed and cuddled – was all he wanted. Maddy was . . . well, Maddy was just Maddy, and Alice was wrapped up in herself, and only herself, and anyway she was in India. In fact for all he knew both Marigold and Alice might have fellows of their own, might not be interested in him any longer.

He signed off the letter to Marigold, which he had been absently copying from Alice's sheet, and pulled another piece of paper towards him; this last would be to Maddy. Although he did not think of her in the way he thought of Marigold, or even Alice, he was fond of her, and admired her too. She had looked after that miserable old grandmother, worked hard on that tumbledown old farm, growing a good half to three quarters of their food, and still won the top scholarship to a prestigious school. He knew she distrusted the O'Hallorans, though without them her life would have been hard indeed, and now she had taken on war work in the nearby town, which would make her life even harder.

He seemed to have been writing letters for hours, and he briefly considered just scrawling a few lines, explaining that he was too busy to write at more length, but would make up for it when he had more time. Then he hesitated. To palm Maddy off with a short note seemed pretty despicable. Tom groaned, and, dipping his pen into the inkpot once more, began to write.

The rumour was correct; the good ship *Beaumaris Pride* did indeed stop in South Africa to refuel and revictual, though their time there was short. All too soon the troops were herded aboard a replacement ship and saw the *Beaumaris Pride* steam out of the harbour, presumably on its way back to Britain for another complement of troops.

The new ship was a French vessel and the men were aboard her for long enough for Tom to begin to conquer his seasickness, although the length of the journey was beginning to get everyone down. It seemed never-ending, and when they finally landed and were marched across to a small but extremely dirty little station and piled into dusty railway carriages there were mutterings on every side.

'We joined the army to see the world, so I suppose we shouldn't complain, but who could have imagined a more slow and long-winded journey?' Tom grumbled, as the small train chugged towards the receiving camp. 'Did you want to travel, Ricky? If so, someone's taken you literally!'

Ricky shrugged. 'I was studying languages, so of course as soon as I'd made some money I intended to go round the world,' he said airily. 'Other men from our school did it, so why shouldn't we?'

They were sitting on slatted wooden seats and staring out of the dirt-grimed windows as the countryside laboured past, and Tom tried to interest himself in glimpses of what life was like in this very foreign land. Like most young men he, too, had wanted to travel but had always been put off by the thought of the sea voyages necessary to get anywhere interesting, and of course by the cost. Chauffeurs' sons, even the sons of men as resourceful and intelligent as his father, did not have the sort of money to even consider foreign travel, but it now

212

looked as though his dream might come true, and at the army's expense.

At last the train stopped and porters, grinning widely, ushered them out of the carriages and into lines.

'Not far now,' a sergeant told them comfortably. 'It's a hell of a journey but we're almost there. Got all your gear? Right; then off we go.'

By the time they reached their destination they were too travel-weary to pay much attention, but when they had recovered from the journey they speedily realised that the camp was a soldier's dream.

'At last we've got something to write home about,' Tom told Ricky as the two of them were given the number of the two-man tent in which they would spend their nights. They were already wearing tropical kit: shorts, shirt, socks and puttees, as well as stout boots.

Ricky had grumbled over the boots but been told sharply, by a man already experienced in desert warfare, that sand and Germans were not the only enemies. 'Of course if you ain't afraid of snakes and would quite welcome being bit by one, then just you trot around barefoot,' he had added sarcastically. 'The army ain't mad, you know. Even the silly hats they make us wear have a purpose – to keep you from getting sunstroke. The sun's rays get reflected back at double strength once you're out in the dunes.'

The camp was an enormous one, and a haven to

soldiers who had just suffered a long sea voyage and a dusty train journey from the coast to end up here, in Ismailia, where their 'hardening off' training would take place. They had expected tough conditions but here there were trees to cast shade, ice-cold lemonade to drink whenever they were thirsty and small, cool buildings full of comfortable chairs, where they congregated for classes in engine maintenance, Morse code and signalling. Very soon they had discovered that there were even dhobi men to do their laundry, carrying it off when they handed it over, and bringing it back stiffly starched six hours later.

They had also soon discovered that it was an agreeably short journey to the centre of Cairo, and as soon as they had finished their lectures they were free to visit the city. Here they could buy almost anything: razor blades, sunglasses, postcards, pens and bric-a-brac. Tom had treated himself to the promised pen, whilst Ricky, who had had his wristwatch stolen within seconds of arriving in the city, had bought himself a new one which he always left behind on subsequent visits, having learnt how neatly his original timepiece had been cut from his wrist as he lolled in a tram with one arm dangling through the glassless window.

'I never thought life in the army could be like this,' Ricky said dreamily one evening as he snuggled down beneath his blanket, for despite the heat of the day nights were cold, sometimes unpleasantly so. He reared up on one elbow and stared at Tom through the thickening gloom. 'Have you seen some of their women? Oh, I know the only thing you really see is a couple of eyes and an outline, but what eyes! Deep pools a fellow could drown in, and somehow only seeing a suggestion of the figure beneath the robes is enough to set a fellow dreaming.'

Tom snorted. 'I don't need to imagine what the women here look like; I've got a beautiful blonde waiting for me back home,' he informed his friend smugly. 'You can have your sloe-eyed beauties. But if you want to be kept on the straight and narrow, imagine that there's a toothless gob grinning behind the veil, or a nose like the prow of a ship, or cheeks pitted with smallpox scars . . .'

Ricky aimed a punch, Tom dodged and the pair wrestled amiably for a moment before lying down again. 'It's our turn to start training tomorrow, so we'd best get what sleep we can,' Tom said. 'I wonder how they'll wake us? If they sound the reveille, they'll wake the whole camp, and I don't imagine they'll want to do that.'

Ricky turned over on his creaking camp bed. 'No sense in meeting trouble halfway; we'll find out soon enough,' he commented. 'And now for the Lord's sake stop nattering and let's get some sleep. If there's one thing the army has taught me, it is that tomorrow comes soon enough.'

For some time after Ricky's snores filled the air,

Tom lay curled up in his blanket, thinking rather wistfully of home. He had wanted to join the war effort and the desire of his heart had been to fight that war abroad, but his imagination had only carried him to France; the war in North Africa – the desert war – was something he had never envisaged or dreamed of. He examined his innermost thoughts and decided that though he naturally felt fear, even more strongly did he feel excitement. The mere presence of so many fighting men convinced him that the North African war had already started, and he found he wanted to be a part of it. It would test his newly discovered fighting spirit; he just hoped he could carry it off.

But he knew Ricky was right and that they should sleep when they could, for the training of soldiers to fight in the desert was a hard one. Old hands – men who had been over here for several months – advised one to start cutting down on drinks, because the day would come soon enough when even a trickle of water would be a rare pleasure; if one let oneself wallow in tall glasses of cool beer or lemonade whilst in camp one would be ill-prepared to eke out half a pint of water, if that much was allowed, during a day in the desert.

Tom sighed and slid into sleep, and it was no wonder, perhaps, that he also slid into dreams; endless sands, burning blue sky, the sun as hot and bright as a copper warming pan. And suddenly there was Maddy, walking delicately and barefoot across the

216

burning sand. She was giving him her sweet, three-cornered smile, telling him that she was looking after Marigold for him and, sounding almost apologetic: 'We're going to join the forces, you know, me and Marigold; we've been making parts for Spitfires, but it's very boring work. We want to be a part of it – the real war, I mean – not just on the fringe. Oh, Tom, I do miss you. It's not the same here without you.' And suddenly she was no longer walking across the red hot sand in little bare feet, but treading lightly on the turf at the side of the beck, stopping to dip her cupped hands in the water and offering him a drink . . .

And then he was woken by a hand shaking his shoulder and a voice in his ear reminding him that it was a five thirty start, and if he wanted his mug of tea he'd best get himself dressed before the rest of the unit drank the lot.

Later, it occurred to Tom to wonder why he had dreamed of Maddy, plain little Maddy, when it was glamorous and gorgeous Marigold who possessed his thoughts. But it didn't really matter; he had dreamed of home, and at that moment in his life home had seemed a very good place to be.

Chapter Eleven

February 1942

It was a bitterly cold day, and as Maddy and Marigold passed through the gates of the enormous Durham training camp snow started to fall, stinging their faces and causing them to slow and blink. Marigold heaved a sigh and turned to her companion. 'We should have known better than to join up in one of the worst winters in living memory,' she shouted crossly above the howl of the wind. 'It's all your fault, Madeleine Hebditch; if we could have waited until the spring at least it wouldn't have been so cold.' She grabbed Maddy's arm and pulled her to a stop. 'Where do we go from here? All it said on the rail pass was that it was a one-way ticket to this place; it didn't even tell us that we'd be picked up by a lorry at the railway station and brought the rest of the way in the oldest, noisiest vehicle the army could discover.'

'Oh well, you must have heard as often as I have that the army never tells one anything except what one needs to know, and as for what we do next, isn't it obvious? We follow the crowd,' Maddy said.

'Suppose it's like the Pied Piper and the people

at the head of the line walk straight over a cliff?' Marigold suggested. 'Oh, how I wish I had a thicker pair of shoes. My feet are getting wet, which isn't going to do much for my chilblains.'

The two girls were at the end of a long line which was gradually making its way into the largest of the brick buildings they could dimly see through the now whirling flakes. 'Do stop grumbling, Marigold,' Maddy said impatiently. 'We're committed now. I remember someone telling me that a young lad who had volunteered for the army decided he didn't like it, and when no one was looking he turned round and went home.' She chuckled. 'He was brought back the next day by two redcaps – they're the military police – and was made pretty miserable by his fellow entrants, so if you've any idea of changing your mind you can just forget it. And anyway, it was you who forced the issue and said you didn't mean to spend the rest of the war making parts for Spitfires . . .'

As she spoke they reached the shelter of the largest building, and now a sergeant emerged through the big double doors and began to shout out orders in a broad Liverpudlian accent. 'Gerrin line, you useless perishin' gairls,' he shouted. 'We's a-goin' to make somethin' like soldiers of you whether you like it or not, so stop whinin' and complainin'. Straighten up an' foller me.'

It wasn't particularly warm in the enormous building, but at least it was dry, and they were happy to be simply out of the snow, which was now whirling so thickly that when Maddy glanced back the parade ground they had crossed was just a hell of white. Marigold stood on tiptoe to look ahead, then nudged Maddy. 'Where are we heading?' she hissed. 'You used to be the same height as me but ever since we started working at the factory you've shot up like Jack's beanstalk. You must be able to see what's happening ahead, you great beanpole.'

Maddy giggled. 'Uniforms,' she said briefly. 'The girls are being given large paper bags, and they're writing something on them – their names, presumably – and then they're being taken off to the far end of the hall. Oh-oh, you aren't going to like this, Miss Perfect. They're taking all their clothes off, except for vest and knickers, and putting the new stuff on, and there isn't even a curtain they can hide behind.'

Marigold gave an outraged gasp. 'It's disgusting, but I suppose we'll have to go along with it,' she said resignedly. 'And I know all the services are the same. That girl who was invalided out of the Wrens when she threw up every time she got into a boat said she had to strip to the buff to have her FFI, whatever that is, and she said you had it every six months.'

Maddy nodded abstractedly, remembering the many arguments which Marigold had put forth against all three of the services open to them. She had refused completely to even consider the Land Army, and Maddy knew very well why this was. Marigold was physically lazy and had baulked at the mere suggestion of tackling a field full of sprouts when the rain was pouring down and the only other workers were either females or elderly men. She had said she wouldn't mind driving a tractor but would refuse to do so in adverse weather conditions, and at the mere thought of milking a cow she had shuddered with revulsion.

'But you can't tell what the ATS will ask you to do,' Maddy had protested when Marigold had finally declared her choice, for she thought her own experience on the land would be valuable to the war effort.

Marigold had giggled and raised her eyebrows. 'Yes, I know, but at least whoever was supervising me wouldn't be an old farm worker with no teeth and black fingernails,' she had insisted. 'And I've heard land girls grumbling in the pub on a Saturday night. Why, for all their hard work and the promises the government have made, they don't get any extra food. No, you won't persuade me, especially when I think of the uniform: great baggy breeches, enormous clodhopping shoes and overalls which go over your shoulders and button at the back so you can't pop behind a hedge if you get caught short and want a pee. Well, you could, but by the time you'd got yourself out of the overalls everyone would know damned well where you were going and why.'

Maddy had sighed deeply, and nodded agreement

when Marigold had put forward her most cogent argument. 'My birthday's practically a whole year before yours; we'll tell whoever's in the recruiting office that we were at school together,' she had reminded her friend, 'so if we hand over our birth certificates at the same time, with mine on top, and tell the sergeant or corporal or they aren't going to so much as glance at yours, particularly now you've grown so tall; in fact they'll probably think you're older than me. So if you're truly determined to become an army lass it'll have to be in the ATS with me. And anyway, though I know you were secretly hoping to be a land girl at Larkspur, it wouldn't happen, you know. Everyone tells you that all the services like to put square pegs in round holes, and I'm sure the Land Army is no exception.'

'All right,' Maddy had said reluctantly, and had accompanied her friend to the recruiting office, reflecting gloomily that she might have guessed how the disagreement would end. Marigold was famous for always getting her own way. Within a week, both Marigold and Maddy had received a letter telling them that they had been accepted by the ATS and were to report to Durham Barracks, where they would receive their official training. It was here, too, that they might choose a trade, though whether they would get their choice they doubted.

Now, as they approached the long counter, Maddy looked at the girls ahead of her. They were a very mixed bunch. A number had clearly decided to wear their best clothing, which included high-heeled pumps and saucy little hats dipped over their eyes. Others wore skirts and jumpers and elderly mackintoshes, and yet others were in school uniform, though they had done their best to disguise the fact. Marigold and Maddy wore what they had worn to the factory, since they had been told that their clothing would be taken away and only given back at the end of hostilities.

'So wear something you can afford to be without,' the recruiting sergeant had advised them. 'What you'll get give is practical warm clothing, just like everyone else, so no point in tarting yourself up.'

As they neared the counter behind which a number of elderly men were sorting out clothing, Marigold nudged Maddy. 'Some of these girls look really rough,' she whispered. 'You'd better not talk posh, Maddy; you know what happened at the factory.'

Maddy shuddered. All the girls in the factory had spoken with broad Yorkshire accents, and until she and Marigold had been advised by the supervisor to imitate their co-workers they had been more or less ostracised; an unpleasant experience which neither had suffered from before. 'But I'm sure that won't apply in the ATS; if you look at the girls picking up their uniforms they're a pretty mixed lot,' she said. 'And they aren't by any means all Yorkshire. I've heard Cockney, Liverpudlian, Norfolk and Welsh at least, so I don't think they'll gang up against us.'

She was about to expand on this theme when Marigold gave a squeak of dismay. 'Oh, Maddy, I never even thought we might get separated so early, but the sergeant on the end of the counter is sending some girls to the left and some to the right. Oh well, when he isn't looking we'll match up again.'

Presently, they reached the head of the queue and a short, fat sergeant, wearing steel-rimmed glasses and a sour expression, passed one glaring glance over Marigold, sorted out a pile of clothing and pushed it across to her. 'If something don't fit, come back,' he ordered. Then he glanced up at Maddy – five foot nine in her stockinged feet – and gasped. 'Big 'un here, Greg,' he shouted over his shoulder. 'Have we gorra skirt what'll fit a geeraffe?'

There was mocking laughter from the men sorting uniforms in the background, but one of them, a tall, fair-haired man with a humorous face, grinned at Maddy and handed her a skirt which would be, she judged, just about the right length. 'There you are, beautiful,' he said. He dropped his voice to a whisper. 'The sarge is just jealous; he'd give a month's pay to have a few more inches.'

Maddy smiled at him. 'Why are they dividing us up?' she asked. 'I want to be with my pal.'

The man called Greg looked slightly embarrassed. 'You'll join up again once you leave the building,' he assured her. 'First you have a few inspections . . .' He cast an appraising glance over Marigold's glowing golden locks and then at Maddy's straight and silky hair. 'Don't worry, it's a bit like being a horse before a sale. They check your hair for nits, your teeth for fillings, your skin for scabies . . . well, I dare say you know the sort of thing.'

'Yes, I suppose I do,' Maddy said doubtfully. 'We had a physical of sorts when we volunteered, and they told us we'd be having something called an FFI every six months or so. What does that stand for?'

Greg hesitated, but there was still a twinkle in his eye, though his cheeks had reddened. 'Er . . . Free From Infection,' he said finally. 'We get a rum lot wanting to join. But you and your pal will be just fine. And now grab your irons and move along or you'll be getting me into trouble.'

Marigold started to ask what her irons were but Maddy elbowed her in the ribs. 'Don't you *read* Tom's letters?' she hissed as with a final wink Greg turned back to his piles of clothing. 'He told me that if you lose your irons in the desert you'll be eating like monkeys, from your hand, because you won't get replacements; it made me laugh.'

'He might have put it in your letter but it wasn't in mine,' Marigold said grumpily as they waited for their medical inspections, which they were able to face much more calmly than they would have done had Greg not warned them what lay ahead. Dismissed, they were sent straight to their hut with their bedding rolls, issue pyjamas and toiletries.

Apparently the army did not provide soap or toothpaste, and when they visited the ablutions hut they realised that it was pretty stingy with hot water as well. They washed themselves in cold, brushed their hair, collected their irons and the tin mug with which every new entrant had been presented, and with a deep sigh from Marigold, and an almost deeper one from Maddy, they set off to the cookhouse. This was a large wooden building, well provided with metal chairs and tables, and needless to say there was already a queue of soldiers heading for the long counter behind which stood the catering staff, armed with large ladles and other kitchen equipment. Watching what the men and women in front of her did, Marigold helped herself to a tin plate and held it out rather in the manner of Oliver Twist. The first man sloshed what was probably stew on to it, the second contributed mashed potato, the third added cabbage and the fourth slopped a gooey mess on another tin plate.

'That's your puddin', queen,' he informed her, seeing her puzzled face. 'It's plum duff. Want some custard?'

Marigold took one look at the bright yellow goo and shook her head. 'No thanks. I'm sure the duff will be delicious without it,' she said mendaciously. 'Come along, Maddy. We've got to get outside this lot before we can make our beds, and someone told me there's a really good NAAFI on this site where they sometimes hold dances. Feel like treading the light fantastic?'

Maddy felt more like diving straight into bed, but this was the first time her friend had shown any enthusiasm for anything so she said, rather reluctantly, that she would be happy to find out what sort of dance they were holding. Presently, food eaten and beds made up, they asked directions to the NAAFI and slogged through the snow to the building indicated.

As Maddy had known she would, Marigold made a great hit with all the men present and clearly enjoyed both dancing and flirting with them, but Maddy could not help wondering what Tom was doing. Marigold was making no secret of her liking for Tom and did not show Maddy his letters to her, although his epistles to herself, Maddy reflected dismally, were pretty harmless. He must know I like him, she had told herself after one rather stilted letter, and I shouldn't mind who *he* likes so long as he comes home safely. Now, glancing out of the windows of the NAAFI building, she wished fervently that she could send him, sweltering in the desert, a sack full of snow and ice. Her imagination, never far behind the rest of her, conjured up a magic carpet – no, two magic carpets, one of which would carry snow to Tom and the other to ferry back the burning hot sand to spread all around their horribly cold quarters. But it was no use wishing, and no use either to blame Marigold, who was flirting delightfully with a handsome aircraftman. Apparently there was an airfield not two miles away. When they had worked in the factory, Maddy had been shocked at first by the way her friend behaved. She had taxed her with it but Marigold had merely widened her eyes and assured her that it was all a bit of fun. Then she had stunned Maddy by announcing that she would probably marry Tom when the war was over.

'Not if he finds out about the way you've been behaving in his absence,' Maddy had said waspishly, after a brief pause. 'No one would ever guess you had a boyfriend fighting Rommel in the desert.'

She had looked accusingly at Marigold as she spoke, but Marigold had merely giggled. 'I'm not engaged to Tom, you know; he'd be the first to tell me to enjoy myself while I had the chance. But of course I know that you're in love with him yourself – or would be, if you knew what love was.'

The idea of being in love with Tom had come as a complete surprise. There had, of course, been that stab of what could only have been jealousy in the caves, and the wild disappointment she had felt on learning she had missed his visit to Larkspur, but still, the thought of being in his arms on the dance floor was all wrong. Somehow she had managed to get this across to Marigold and was rather surprised when her friend had nodded sagely, lowering her voice and saying she understood. 'I'm a bit like that over our supervisor. I know he's not in the forces because of having his foot blown off during the evacuation of Dunkirk, but sometimes I think he's the best and kindest man I've ever known . . .'

'And the only one you know with a wife and three children,' Maddy had snapped. 'Don't you go messing with married men or you'll find yourself in real trouble. Stick to Tom; and anyway, Tom is much, much handsomer than Mr Crowdy.'

But that had been a long time ago; right now the gramophone record had been taken off its turntable and the dance was over, so Maddy and Marigold joined the rush of girls heading for bed. From what they had been told, the time they spent here would probably be the toughest they would ever spend anywhere, so they should always sleep when they could.

When they got to the door a sergeant was blocking their way. 'Tomorrow morning you must be up at reveille,' he told them. 'You've got a deal of training to do so you'd best not be late. Reveille's at seven in the winter and breakfast is served from seven thirty. It'll be followed by a medical which will include a fair number of injections.' He grinned at them. 'They say first come first served, but that ain't what we say in the army. It's first come gets the sharpest needle, and believe me there's a deal of difference between being stabbed early and having the MO struggling to get the needle in if you're amongst the last. Now off to your huts.'

It was still snowing and after the relative warmth of the NAAFI Maddy's chilblains flamed with dismay as the cold bit into them, but it was no use standing out here gazing around. Dimly, in the distance, she could see the row of wooden huts, and grabbing Marigold's arm she made straight for them.

'I bags the bottom bunk,' Marigold said as soon as they had shut the door behind them. She shivered. 'My God, it's as cold in here as it is outside. Isn't there a stove of some description?'

A stockily built girl with dark hair cropped short and a cheery grin pulled a face and shook her head. 'No, nothing so civilised,' she said in a strong Welsh accent. 'My orders were to bring a rubber hot water bottle but there's no means of heating the water to put inside it so I suppose this is what the men call "hardening off". I've put my pyjamas on over most of my underclothes just so's I shan't freeze; advise you to do the same, I would. We'll indent for one of them tortoise stoves as soon as we're up tomorrow.'

Most of the girls were either already in bed or preparing to be so, but the one nearest to them shook a sorrowful head. 'This is a training camp especially for the ATS. Dozens and dozens of girls have slept in these huts, wrapped in their blankets, only to find their washing water frozen solid in the morning. Do you think none of them tried to persuade the authorities to give them a stove of some description? Of course they did, but the army's mean as hell to their soldiers and twice as mean to us, because they've been trained to believe we're the weaker sex. Now go to sleep and remember we're only here for a month; after that things must surely get better.'

Maddy dived beneath her blanket and was about to prepare for sleep when she was reminded of the old rule: last in puts the light out. Reluctantly she wriggled out again and dropped on to the icy linoleum. A quick sprint up to the door, a snatch at the switch which doused the one small electric bulb and a hasty, toe-curling scamper and she was back in bed. 'Goodnight all,' she shouted. 'See you in the morning; and let's hope it's a better one!'

There was a chorus of goodnights and one voice rose above the others, that of the corporal who slept, curtained off from the rest of the girls, at the very end of the hut. 'Thanks for remembering to turn off the light. Goodnight, everyone,' she said drowsily. 'We'll get to know one another in the morning. Sweet dreams.'

Gran heaved the extra blanket Eileen O'Halloran had given her up over her shoulders, then opened one eye to peer at her alarm clock. The light coming through the window was what she would have called 'snowlight', for it had been a shocking winter and though it was mid-February there had been no sign of a thaw, the snow simply continuing to fall and build into mighty drifts through which Declan O'Halloran made his way weekly to fetch their rations from Mrs Foulks at the shop. They had chosen to register with her even before the bad weather started, and now they were glad they had done so. It saved them the long trek into town, and if anything was available off ration, Gran was sure that the postmistress made certain that they got their share. But now, as she lay in her cosy nest, Gran considered what her next move should be. The previous autumn Eileen had encouraged her to get up and cook their breakfast porridge, make a large pot of tea and do any other small tasks of which she was capable.

"'Tis good for you. 'Tis what the good Dr Carlton calls "keeping mobile",' the Irish woman had said instructively. 'Them blessed 'vacuees will give a hand if forced to do so, but 'tis easier all round if we keep the cooking in our own hands. Kids can't cook, and what wi' rationing and shortages us can't afford to let the kids experiment, not when it means ruining good grub.'

Gran had heartily agreed with this sentiment, for she was a good and inventive cook herself, but she was not so sure about getting breakfast. She hated early rising and thought wistfully that, had Maddy still been at home to prepare it, she herself could have remained in her warm bed until hunger drove her down the stairs and into the kitchen. Declan always lit the stove as soon as he was up, and Eileen would have been on hand to help her dress.

But Maddy, impudent granddaughter that she was, had taken herself off, first into that aeroplane factory and now into the ATS. Gran tutted and punched her pillow. Self, self, self, that was the young of today; if Maddy wanted to help with the war effort why couldn't she have come back home and worked at Larkspur? True, they did have a couple of land girls, but they lived in one of the farm cottages which had once belonged to the Hall. Gran scarcely ever saw them, and when she did, though they were polite enough, they took little interest in an old lady whose sole contribution to the war effort seemed to be ordering the evacuees to collect eggs, take food to the pigs in the sties or, when the weather was clement, attack the weeds which grew up between the rows of vegetables in the kitchen garden.

Gran sighed deeply, and was still considering whether she might put a toe out of bed and shout for Eileen when her bedroom door shot open – without so much as a knock, she thought sourly – and Herbert's comical face appeared in the aperture. 'Are you goin' to gerrup, Miz Hebditch?' he enquired. 'Only the porridge is ready and Miz O'Halloran wants us to take the sledge into the village for to get our rations. School's still closed, so Sid, Monty and meself said we'd go, and we want a note and your pension book, 'cos you've not drawn it, your pension I mean, since the snow got bad.'

Gran sighed and sat up. She had begun to say that

the postmistress would sign for the pension when she remembered that her teeth were still reposing in the glass by her bed and drew the sheet up across her mouth. 'All right, all right, I hear you,' she said rather thickly. 'And now just you bugger off and send Eileen up here, 'cos I can't dress in the kitchen if you kids are still in there.'

'Why not? I suppose you think the sight of your glorious body would strike us blind,' Herbert said, giggling. 'Want any help to get down them stairs?'

Gran drew herself up haughtily and the sheet fell down, revealing her toothless gums. Herbert, a thoughtful boy, bent down and lifted the sheet into its position just above her button nose. 'You forgot your yashmak,' he said kindly. 'Oh, and I forgot to tell you there's a letter for you from Maddy. I 'spect it's to give you her new address. That Marigold has joined up as well, and her mam told Miz Foulks that she was in a training camp somewhere in the north.' He chuckled hoarsely. 'Bet it's even colder up there than it is down here! Now, are you going to get up, or should I tell Miz O'Halloran you'll be down later?'

Gran wriggled her toes and thought about it, but her hot water bottle was as near cold as made no difference, and though Eileen was always careful to accede to any requests she might make, her disapproval could take the form of a refusal to give Gran a second helping of porridge, or a decision to withhold from the old woman the scrambled goose eggs which the O'Hallorans might be about to enjoy. She was still considering the miseries of dressing in her ice-cold bedroom instead of in the warm kitchen when Herbert decided to take a hand. He seized the blankets in one grimy hand and ignored Gran's horrified squawk. 'Are you going to get up or not?' he enquired baldly. 'Me and the lads mean to get to the village and back by elevenses time so you'd best make up your mind pronto.'

Gran narrowed her eyes at him; she longed to say something cutting, something that would teach him not to try his luck too far, but she was hampered by her lack of teeth. Only Maddy and that teacher of hers – what was her name? Miss Budgie, was it? – had ever seen her with her gnashers not in place and she did not intend the impudent Herbert to join their number. So she retained her grip on the sheet and ordered him to leave the room at once. 'Bugger off, you cheeky varmint,' she said thickly. 'Tell Mrs O'Halloran I shall start to dress immediate, but could do with a hand.'

Herbert giggled. 'And a full set of choppers,' he said cheekily. 'I 'spect Mrs O'Halloran will be up as soon as I tell her you're gettin' dressed.'

'Shut the door behind you when you go,' Gran ordered haughtily, but what with the sheet across her mouth and the absence of teeth it didn't sound nearly as impressive as it was meant to, and neither did Herbert obey her command. Gran sighed and swung her feet in their fluffy pink bedsocks on to the floor.

The cold bit like a knife and she seized her dressing gown and bundled herself into it, then went to pour water from the jug into the ewer, only to find it solid ice. Oh, bugger, she thought irritably. She trundled out of the room and stood at the head of the stairs. 'Eileen, I need you,' she called peremptorily. 'Come at once, *hif* you please.'

There was an appreciable pause before Eileen answered her, and Gran thought the other woman's tone was one of suppressed impatience. 'It's all right, Mrs Hebditch, you can come down now,' she called. 'The lads have took your pension book and me list of grub what we need and gone, so you can dress down here in the warm, same as you do when they're off to school.'

Gran gave a grunt of satisfaction, picked up her clothes and descended the stairs with all her usual caution; she had hurried once, long ago, and could still remember the pain of her wrenched knee. She did not intend to let that happen again. She reached the kitchen and glanced approvingly at the fire roaring in the stove and the big pan of porridge bubbling gently on the hob.

Eileen greeted her politely but added cheerfully: 'Bad weather for bombers; bad weather for fighters come to that an' all, Mrs Hebditch. In fact, you might call it bad weather for war.'

Gran grunted. She knew they had been lucky because they lived deep in the country, which was why they had been blessed – or cursed – with evacuees. No government in their senses would send children to safety without first checking out the area, and though over two years had elapsed since Mr Chamberlain's announcement, life at Larkspur had gone on much as usual. To be sure they had suffered from rationing and shortages – Gran had made that horrible object, a Woolton pie, on more than one occasion – but they had not suffered from the constant bombing raids which had become a way of life to Londoners. Along with a great many other country folk, they had a secret pig, unknown to the Ministry, which provided them with bacon and salt pork for most of the year, and though they had to hand over a proportion of the food they grew Declan always made sure that the majority of such food was hidden away when the inspectors called.

Eileen, standing at the range, raised her brows at Gran. 'Are you goin' to have porridge first, or get dressed? The kids won't be back for an hour or two, so you can choose.'

Gran considered. Eileen was not much of a cook, her pastry was hard and her loaves were uninspired, but anyone, Gran told herself, could make porridge. She crossed the room slowly and sat down in her favourite chair. 'Breakfast,' she said briefly. 'I need my grub to keep me going.'

For one awful moment Eileen was tempted to rap on the table with her serving spoon and say 'Whatever happened to "please"?' But then she remembered that this was Gran's house and she herself was, after all, simply a paid – underpaid – employee.

'Porridge it is,' she said therefore, biting back the unwise words. 'And we might run to a boiled egg afterwards, provided the kids don't come back early and demand their share. Can you eat a boiled egg?' She saw how the old woman's eyes gleamed at the prospect and grinned to herself. The way to Gran's heart was certainly through her stomach, but the older woman did not give her the satisfaction of showing enthusiasm.

'Hens must be laying well for you to offer me a breakfast egg,' she said, and there was suspicion in her tone. 'Still an' all if you're offering, it'd make a change from burnt toast.'

For the first fortnight at the Durham camp, Maddy and Marigold told each other that the factory had been a piece of cake compared to this. They worked, and worked hard, from the moment reveille sounded until they fell into their beds at night. That first NAAFI dance looked like being their last, for neither of them had the energy to do anything but sleep once the day's activities were over.

At the end of the second week, however, whilst they ate the never-ending stew provided by the cookhouse, they discussed what they had learned and how useful or otherwise their training had been so far with a couple of other girls from their intake. Every day started with drill, regardless of weather conditions, and would do so for their entire time in the ATS, even though the drill was becoming so familiar that they could have performed it in their sleep. Then there was learning the Morse code, and naturally they could see the point of that, though they wished the sergeant in charge wouldn't talk to them as though they were idiots.

'By the time you leave here you will read the Morse code as easily as you read a letter from your mum and dad,' he had told them. 'It's the same with aircraft recognition; you'll know not just our planes but the German ones too, because there's talk of some of you going to the ack-ack batteries.' He had laughed. 'Personally I doubt that – girls on perishin' guns indeed! But if it did happen you'd simply have to know friend from foe, 'cos we're in enough trouble without some stupid girl shouting "On target" when a Spitfire strays across the beam.'

'I hated drill at first, but now I don't mind it so much,' Maddy confessed. 'If only we didn't have to drill in all weathers . . . and we'd be a lot healthier if they could let us have brekker first . . .'

The girl sitting next to Marigold, Jane Shepherd, laughed bitterly. 'If only the high-ups were forced to drill in a snowstorm, you mean,' she said. 'Some things you can see a reason for, but others . . . well, you begin to wonder if most of the officers and NCOs have a grudge against women, the way they treat us. And I'd like to know why we have so many injections . . . my arm nearly fell off last time. I was at the end of the line and the needle was as blunt as anything . . .'

'My feller joined the army in '39, and he moaned about what he called "bull", but that was just because he didn't like having to polish his buttons and keep his uniform tidy,' a tall girl with roughly cropped black hair – she had cut it herself with blunt nail scissors – said ruefully. 'Sometimes I think you're right and the officers and NCOs do have a grudge against women – all women – because they seem to *enjoy* treating us like dirt, even when we're doing something right.'

'But everyone says the first month – the training month – is always the worst,' the small girl who had the bed next to Maddy's put in rather shyly. 'My sister Mavis joined up the day after war was declared and she's had a pretty rough ride, or did have, rather. But she had a lucky break, at least I suppose you could call it that; she does, at any rate. She had to drive a major to an important meeting because his regular driver was taken ill with a funny tummy, and halfway to the meeting the car broke down. The major started effing and blinding, saying there would be hell to pay if he didn't reach the camp in time to attend the meeting, and was all for thumbing a lift, but it was a minor road and deserted, so Mave hopped out of the car, lifted the bonnet, cleaned the spark plugs, hopped back into the car again, pulled the starter and the engine fired. The major was so impressed that he made her his permanent driver, and now not even the other officers dare to get on the wrong side of her. So you see, you can be lucky.'

'But we shouldn't have to rely on luck,' the dark-haired girl said thoughtfully. 'Have you heard the one about the executive who needed a secretary, so he went to the personnel officer and asked for a recommendation? The personnel officer sent him three girls, one who had a shorthand speed of one hundred and forty words per minute, one who spoke four languages so fluently that she sounded like a native and one who had a degree in English language and was, in fact, a professor. The executive interviewed all three and then sent for the personnel officer. "Well, which one would suit you best?" the personnel officer asked the executive, "the young lady with four languages, the one with excellent typing skills or the one with the degree in English language?" And the executive said: "I'll have the blonde in the pink jumper."'

Everyone laughed, though with some reluctance. 'Yes, we get the point,' Maddy said. She indicated the girl whose sister drove the officer with a jerk of her thumb. 'I don't deny that Pasfield's sister got the job because she was an efficient motor mechanic as well as a good driver, but it might easily have gone the other way. The major might have blamed her for the car's bad performance – it happens all too often, as we know – and then where would she be? Back in the motor pool and you can bet your bottom dollar that she would have been picked on by every man in the unit.'

The girl called Pasfield sighed. 'You're right,' she said resignedly. 'Mave's major treated her well, but the other drivers – the men, not the Ats – made nasty remarks which were totally unfounded. It was jealousy, I suppose, but I think we all agree that the men should have to prove themselves too, and not simply assume superiority.'

'Oh, well, we're halfway through our training now and beginning to get the picture,' the dark-haired girl commented, pushing back her chair and scooping up her irons, ready to dip them in a bucket of extremely dirty water and dry them on the rag of a dishcloth. 'Tomorrow is another day, as my dear old gran used to say, so comfort yourself, girls, with the fact that it can only get better.'

It had been warm, almost muggy, in the cookhouse, but the moment Maddy and Marigold followed their companions out through the open doorway they walked into a snowstorm. Maddy clutched Marigold's arm and bawled directly in her ear, tilting her friend's cap in order to do so. 'Want to go to the NAAFI and write letters?'

Marigold shook her head and they dived into their hut and slammed the door behind them.

'Tomorrow there's kit inspection immediately after drill, then a hair inspection and then a hearing test,'

Maddy said. 'The corporal said that at this stage in our training we'd usually have to go into the gas hut, but not in the snow – too dangerous – so that's one thing we can discount. But I ought to write to Alice, because she really does try to keep in touch.' She sighed. 'There's Alice and Tom complaining about the heat and you and I complaining about the cold! So what's it to be? Letters or bed?'

'Bed, I think,' Marigold said, after a moment's hesitation. 'If I'm to get up at reveille I need all the sleep I can get. I keep waiting for someone to ask me what trade I mean to apply for, because I fancy being a driver, the same as Pasfield's sister. If I could just find a major important enough to have his own chauffeur, I'd find some way of wangling myself into his good graces. Oh, I know it's wicked of me to want to jump the queue so to speak, but I'm sick of being ground down and mocked by every man in uniform just because I'm female and a lot prettier than they are.'

Maddy heaved a sigh. She had always enjoyed letter writing, but the thought of fighting her way across the parade ground to the NAAFI, penning a letter to Alice and then fighting her way back to her hut had very little appeal at the moment. And bed wasn't all that attractive either, she told herself, eyeing the three straw 'biscuits' which made up the mattress of her bunk bed with loathing. Life would have been so much pleasanter if at the end of a hard day you could have relaxed on a decent bed, but that wasn't the army way. Presumably the men, too, had to make and remake their beds morning and night.

She began to remove her clothing, spreading skirt and battledress out on the end of her bed in the hope – usually vain – that they would add to the warmth for which her frozen feet longed. She put on her issue pyjamas, added the thickest pullover she possessed and made up the bed, something she could now do with incredible speed. Then she wriggled underneath the blanket, beating Marigold to it by the skin of her teeth.

She fell asleep almost at once, only to be awoken in the early hours by some sound or movement which she could not at once interpret. She lay listening for a bit and then realised that the relentless drips as the snow filled every gutter on the hut had stopped. It was not the thaw for which they had longed, she realised, sitting up and peering out through the thickly frosted window above her bed, but the storm did appear to have blown itself out. Maddy gave a loud yawn and the voice in a bunk nearby said: 'It's stopped snowing! Wouldn't you bloody well know it! Just when I was hoping to get out of being gassed, the bloody snow stops.'

Maddy giggled. 'That's life!' she said. 'And all this time we've been praying for the snow to stop. Isn't that what they always tell you? Be careful what you wish for; you might get it.' And with these words she slid down beneath the blanket again, adjusted the woolly cap she always wore at nights now, and fell instantly asleep.

Next morning the girls drilled for the customary thirty to forty minutes, finding it difficult to obey the sergeant's commands since they could scarcely hear his voice above the howl of the wind. Then they formed two lines and returned to their hut for kit and hair inspection.

'I'd like to see the nit which dared to try and establish a colony in *my* squeaky clean locks,' Marigold said as the corporal moved along the line, cursorily examining the girls' heads. 'Mind you, having seen Morton scratching like a maniac I suppose anyone can be targeted by the little beasts.'

'Oh, Morton's all right,' Maddy said hastily. Morton was a large and aggressive girl, who would be a bad enemy. 'Come on, let's get into the queue for this wretched hearing test, though anyone who's a trifle deaf is to be envied when the sarge starts shrieking commands into the wind.'

Cleared of deafness, the two girls went straight to the cookhouse. 'I'm bloody starving,' Marigold moaned as they entered the warm and fuggy atmosphere. 'If the porridge is burnt I swear I'll empty my plateful over the chief cook's miserable bald head.'

Maddy laughed. Marigold was always threatening to pay the cookhouse back for its many mistakes, but though she often voiced her disapproval she was still popular with the staff, who often saved her odds and ends of food, warning her that if she got fat she would only have herself to blame.

'I will; I'll empty it over his head, so help me God,' she repeated dramatically. 'What's next on the agenda? After brekker, I mean.'

Someone ahead of them in the queue turned round and grinned. It was the tall dark girl, Plethin. 'You could have toast,' she remarked. 'Oh, I know there's no marmalade or Marmite, but there's margarine and marrow jam, if that's your fancy. Oh, and did you know? They've decided to test us in the gas hut today after all, provided it doesn't start snowing again.' She grinned at them. 'What a wonderful treat,' she said sarcastically. 'If I die, girls, I shall leave my body to medical science, and I trust you will see that Sergeant Wetherspoon gets his come-uppance.'

Later that morning Maddy and Marigold joined the queue of girls, respirators in hand, who were awaiting their turn in the gas hut. This was an empty hut, similar to their own and with entrance and exit doors, but of stronger construction, with a corridor marked out down the middle. Sergeant Wetherspoon waited at the entrance and an ATS corporal barred the way to the far door. The sergeant collected them in groups of ten and gave them their instructions. 'First go off, you wear your respirators and proceed in an orderly fashion halfway down the length of the hut until you reach the corporal – she'll be wearing her respirator the whole time – whereupon you will remove your respirators and proceed *h'again* in a orderly fashion towards the exit. Do not run or gallop or do anything but march, holding your breath so as not to take on board no noxious fumes. Do not breathe in or out until you emerge from the hut. Remember, I shall be observing your progress . . .'

'Do not stop. Do not collect two hundred pounds, but go straight to jail,' Maddy murmured wickedly. 'Trust the army to turn gas drill into a board game!'

'Do you think they really fill the hut with poisonous gas?' Marigold said nervously as they neared the front of the queue. 'Surely it would escape whenever the door was opened?'

'I expect it's just a trick,' Plethin said knowingly. 'Be comforted by the fact that if they kill us they'll have to face a court martial . . . oh, crumbs, what if your respirator has a leak? I mean, we've not tried them out, have we? I wish I'd thought of testing mine earlier.'

But it was too late now; the sergeant was checking each girl, ensuring they were all wearing their respirators, and when he was satisfied he stepped back, giving them a peculiarly saturnine grin as he did so. 'Forward march!' he bellowed. 'And take them respirators off as soon as you get level with the corp. And remember, no runnin' allowed, else you'll have to go through again.'

The first part of the test was easy because they

were wearing the respirators – gas masks to civilians – which they had been carrying around unused ever since they were first issued. But getting the mask on was a lot easier than getting it off; Marigold, eyes watering, managed to tug quite a lot of her hair out by the roots in the process, which caused her to gasp and thus inhale some of the noxious fumes against which they had been warned. Maddy saw what had happened and grabbed her friend's arm, forgetting that, in order to communicate, they had been told to use sign language only. Needless to say, they held up the line and confused the other girls, so that when they emerged through the exit, taking huge breaths of the clean, cold air, they were ordered, brusquely, in the sergeant's stentorian tones, to return to the dreaded hut and this time to do it properly.

After the second ordeal the girls were permitted to go to the cookhouse and get their midday meal – sandwiches, a very small piece of cake and a very large mug of strong, unsweetened cookhouse tea – and in the afternoon Sergeant Wetherspoon decided it was time they all learned to march. Maddy, having wrongly assumed that drill was marching and marching was drill, soon discovered her mistake. A platoon of soldiers who were being marched from one place to another would not deviate from their forward motion unless whoever was in charge of them ordered them to turn right or left, or to halt.

Once they had got the idea, and in some cases had

learned to tell their left foot from their right, marching was not too bad, and in the following weeks the girls took turns to act as corporal and give the orders as they marched through the streets of Durham, causing a good deal of amusement as they shepherded their obedient troops up and down narrow alleys and across main roads. The only disadvantage was the fact that the ATS shoes were heavier than those most of them usually wore, so that blisters burst and chilblains burned and itched, sending the girls to sit shivering on their beds in their huts whilst trying to repair the damage.

'I wonder if Tom has to march in the desert?' Maddy asked Marigold, one dark afternoon when they had been practising aircraft recognition with the rest of their set. 'I could ask him next time I write, but I don't suppose I shall. It's a silly question really. We are only doing so much marching because we're in a training camp.' She smiled reminiscently. 'Can you remember how green we were, Marigold? I know we've grumbled and moaned, particularly over all the medical stuff and the gas hut, but it has had a purpose. When we came in we were starry-eyed kids, imagining ourselves in romantic uniforms, doing romantic things. Why, I even thought I might get to the front line, having been taught how to use a Bren gun. I imagined soldiers queuing up to take us to the flicks. I even imagined marrying one of them, or being dropped in France as a spy to discover what Hitler's latest plans were. Gosh, I was green!'

'Yes, you were,' Marigold said rather too quickly. 'And if you go even further back you believed in Tom the chimney sweep and the water babies . . .'

'Hey, unfair!' Maddy said indignantly. 'I did *not* believe in either Tom or the water babies. I did believe in Vendale, and thought we might find where the Reverend Mr Kingsley pretended he'd seen water babies, but I'm not sure, now, that I even believe in Vendale any more. You are mean, Marigold, to rake up all that old business . . . but at least the ATS has brought us both down to earth with a bump. It's disappointing to have to admit that the army seems to have decided that we're an inferior sex, which considering that they make us work twice as hard as the men seems very unfair. But I intend to go through with the examinations when we've completed our four weeks' basic training, and if I pass I shall put in for an ack-ack or searchlight battery. I know that passing examinations and doing work that men don't want us to do won't prove anything, but it will make me feel better.'

'Oh, but you can't – take those examinations, I mean,' Marigold said, her voice rising. 'I don't intend to spend my army career stuck out on some miserable gun site in the middle of nowhere. For one thing, they say you have to be really good at maths to work with the guns, and for another, I've always wanted to learn to drive, and they won't teach you if you're on an ack-ack site.'

'Oh, Marigold, don't be such an ape,' Maddy protested. 'The War Office wanted girls to go on the gun sites months ago but the men didn't like it, said women wouldn't be able to cope. I'd like to pass the exams and become a girl gunner just to prove that they were wrong. If you take the exams too – and I'm sure you're as physically strong as I am – we could go on being together, and wouldn't it be a feather in our caps to wear the white lanyard and work alongside men on the ack-ack sites!'

Marigold hesitated, and Maddy thought, with an inward grin, that she could see various options struggling within her friend's curly blonde head. Finally the other girl nodded reluctant agreement. 'All right, I'll have a go,' she said. 'I don't suppose for one moment that I'll pass, but as you say, if we do, there will be a lot of crestfallen faces on our male colleagues. It's awful how keen they are to make fools of us and how they constantly shoot themselves in the foot when we're seen to do well. One or two of the officers are quite nice, and the one with the little blond moustache told me that women consistently come out streets ahead of men in written tests. Of course he told me in confidence, but I know you won't repeat it, and anyway, once the results are known, they'll simply have to accept the findings.'

'True; but can you imagine the chagrin?' Maddy said with a small smirk. 'Well, they'll find a way to get even, you may be sure, only once we've proved ourselves it will be a lot more difficult to keep putting us down.'

They had been having this discussion in the classroom, finally empty save for themselves, and now Maddy got up from the desk upon which she had been perched. 'I'm as bad as the fellows, boasting about how we mean to come out on top,' she said cheerfully. 'But the proof of the pudding is in the eating, as my old gran used to say. Onward and upward, Private Stein!'

'Right,' Marigold said. 'I'll take the exams, because if you're going to dig your heels in . . . only if I do pass I needn't agree to be what you so charmingly describe as a "girl gunner" on an ack-ack site, I suppose.'

'We'll see,' Maddy said cautiously. She had a feeling that the army would not take to the idea that a girl might choose her own posting, but no need to tell Marigold an unpalatable truth. Instead, she turned the subject. 'I wonder where Alice is now?' she said casually. 'Fancy her actually becoming a nurse and *liking* it! All those horrid wounds and diseases, and being moved from one field hospital to another, to say nothing of the uniform. She always used to say that if she joined anything it would be the Wrens, because they wore black silk stockings!'

'Oh well, that's the rich Miss Thwaite for you,' Marigold said tolerantly. 'I'd love to go abroad, though, and the only way to do that is through nursing. Have you heard from her lately? It's ages since I've had a letter from Tom – he apologised for not writing more regularly but I gather his surroundings are primitive, to say the least. And anyway, all I need to know is that he's still alive . . .' she giggled, 'and still longing for me . . .'

'Oh, shut up,' Maddy said quickly. 'Let's go and put our names down for this examination you are so sure you'll fail. And whilst we're in the Mess we'll take a look at the notice board and see if anyone's written to us lately. It's quite possible that Alice might have penned a few lines, describing her latest feller!'

Chapter Twelve

Alice was dressing an enormous ulcer on a soldier's leg. She was cleaning it thoroughly, knowing it was painful for the man but also knowing that hygiene was essential, for Egypt swarmed with unpleasant diseases, many of which she had treated over the past couple of years.

When she had first arrived in India and was staying at her father's house she had been unhappy and, to put it mildly, unhelpful. Her father had wanted her to work with him in his office, but after three boring weeks, during which time she had done almost nothing, she had rebelled. Without telling her father, in case he tried to prevent her, she had gone along to the local hospital and volunteered as a trainee. She had been welcomed enthusiastically, put in a class in which Anglo-Indians predominated, and had begun to work harder than she had ever worked in her life before.

Letters from home – mostly from Maddy, Marigold and Tom – were rare and at first, hearing of their trials and tribulations, she had been almost ashamed to write back. But once she had passed both practical and written examinations and was actively training other women to do the work she had only just conquered herself, she found that she was proud of her particular war effort, even though for the most part she worked in civilised surroundings, whereas poor Maddy and Marigold, once they had joined up, seemed to have landed themselves in a hell of cold, misery and hard work.

And then there was Tom. She had always liked him, admired him even, but now she realised that he had meant more to her than just a companion. He was better than a brother, someone on whose championship she could totally rely. And very soon she began to long for his letters and plan how they would greet one another when the war was over. With the resilience of youth, she never even considered that one of them might be killed.

'Nurse! Nurse Thwaite! When you've finished with that dressing I'd like a word. Come to my office.'

'Yes, Matron,' Alice said automatically. Once she would have drawn herself up and demanded that a "please" should be inserted, turning the command into a request, but now she knew better. Mrs Fortescue-Smy had once been the matron of a large London hospital and had brought her air of authority with her when she married her lieutenant colonel. That had been in the thirties, of course, but she had volunteered her services when war was declared. And the War Office soon realised they were lucky to have her.

255

'Gawd, she scares me more'n the bleedin' Jerries,' the soldier upon whom Alice was working said through gritted teeth. He peered down at his shin and the blackened hole caused by the ulcer. 'It don't look no different from the way it looked yesterday and I don't mind tellin' you, nurse, it's bleedin' agony.'

'I know, and I'm sorry for hurting you, but cleaning up the infection is essential before your leg can begin to heal,' Alice said soothingly, beginning to bandage the dressing she had just applied to the man's shrinking leg. She smiled as her patient relaxed, knowing from experience that once the dressing was in place the worst would be over . . . until the next day, of course.

She straightened up and began to collect her paraphernalia. 'I wonder what Matron wants?' she asked idly, not really expecting an answer. 'I'm sure I've done nothing wrong. I wonder if it's another posting? I've been moved around an awful lot since I joined the Queen Alexandra's, so if they need nurses somewhere else . . . but I dare say Matron will tell me the score presently.' Her face brightened. 'Or it might be leave; I've not had leave for absolutely ages, not since I came to Egypt, in fact, so it'd be grand to wear mufti for a change.' She smiled at the young soldier and patted his shoulder. 'I'll let you know when I know myself, provided it's not classified,' she said, beginning to wheel her small dressings trolley off the ward.

Outside Matron's office she discovered her friend Susan about to knock on the door and they went into

256

the room together, to find Matron seated at a small desk with a pile of papers in front of her. She looked busy, but as soon as they entered she pushed down the little steel spectacles she wore and indicated that they should sit down. 'Now, I've been catching up with my paperwork and find that neither of you has had leave for . . . well, for some considerable time. If you would like to take advantage of the fact that we're within reasonable reach of Cairo, it should be possible for you to spend some time in more civilised surroundings. How do you feel? It's a fair journey from here, but not impossible, and there is a rest camp only a couple of miles from the city.' She smiled very kindly at the girls. 'Hot showers, a swimming pool, good food, a chance to relax . . . Nurse Thwaite, are you listening to me?'

Alice jumped, brought her attention back to the matron's small room, and began to concentrate on the older woman's description of the journey they would have to endure. It sounded long but perfectly possible, and the thought of a hot shower and a decent meal, a proper bed, time to relax and maybe a bathe, to one who loved swimming was like the gold at the end of the rainbow. But Matron had stopped speaking and was looking at them enquiringly. Alice swallowed hard twice, then spoke for them both. 'Yes please, Matron,' she said in a small voice. 'How long would we have, though? You aren't thinking of a forty-eight . . . ?'

Matron smiled. 'I think we can do without you for a week, maybe even a little longer,' she said cheerfully. 'I suggest you set off as soon as you can arrange for someone to take over your wards. You can reach the camp in a day or two . . . a nice change to be travelling, young ladies, from the hours you've been putting in here. Now off you go and start making your plans, because you won't want to waste a moment of your leave.'

Alice and Susan left Matron's office feeling, quite literally, as though they were walking on air. Leave! Alice had not fully realised how very tired she was until this moment, when the weight of responsibility was lifted, if only temporarily, from her shoulders. All the nurses had been working incredibly hard – twelve-hour shifts were the norm – for all hospitals were subjected to influxes of wounded men as they got nearer the Front. But Alice had heard from a number of the newer patients that the constant to-ing and fro-ing of the troops was, at present, in the Allies' favour, so the stream of wounded had become a trickle. This was clearly why they were being allowed leave – Matron was seizing the opportunity to give the nurses time to themselves for a change.

She said as much to Susan, who enlightened her further. 'You're right, of course. Matron is sending everyone, by turns, to the rest camp; Dr Hassan told me so earlier. She really values her nurses – not like some – and knows that we will work all the harder when we come back from our break. Won't it be lovely to get out of uniform, and into a swimming pool ... oh, I can't wait! Let's start packing at once. I'm off shift; Nurse Greaves will be standing in for me, I expect.'

Alice didn't answer. She was busy dreaming of some additions to her wardrobe – a floaty dance frock, a daring swimsuit, perhaps a brief white tennis dress – when it occurred to her that Susan was also blissfully contemplating some future fun. She poked her friend in the ribs. 'Look, I know you're already planning to play masses of golf, or tennis, or maybe even netball, but I'm not as sporting mad as you.' She pulled a rueful face. 'My only worry is that I might spend the entire time sleeping! But I dare say a couple of nights' proper rest will set me up to enjoy the rest of my leave.'

Susan smiled at her. She was a plump and pretty brunette with an infectious giggle, and now she laughed delightedly at the other girl's words. 'Hole in one,' she squeaked. 'I'm off to start packing!'

Alice was halfway back to the nurses' quarters when she remembered her promise to let the young soldier with the ulcer know why Matron had summoned her, and turned back to the ward. It wouldn't take a minute and fair was fair; he was a nice lad and would appreciate her bothering to say goodbye. She began to hurry.

Tom was dreaming. The dream had started with that first – and last – exploration of the limestone caves the day before war was declared, and since, in the way of dreamers, he knew how it would end, he was looking forward to what he always thought of as 'the Kiss'. What he did not anticipate, however, was finding himself clasping to his manly bosom the wrong woman! He looked down on Alice's well-remembered, heart-shaped face, at the wide blue eyes gazing so trustfully up at him, and felt a heel; it was scarcely Alice's fault that she wasn't Marigold – or was it? Had she deliberately invaded his dream?

In his sleep, Tom moaned softly. Where was Marigold, where her gleaming gold curls and bright blue eyes? But even as the thought made him turn towards the cave entrance he saw, coming towards him, the right girl, an inviting smile on her lips. Tom moaned again and tried to run towards the cave mouth, but it was as though he ran through treacle, or perhaps sand . . . yes, it was sand, and oh, curses, curses, curses, he was waking, the dream was fading, and he was back in the hateful desert, his blanket heavy with dew, for nights in the desert were icy cold, and slipping off his shoulders.

Tom lay still for a moment, trying to recapture the dream, but it had gone. Ruefully, he snuggled down, but before he could try to conjure sleep there was a tremendous explosion and he was wriggling as far as he could into his bolthole before he was more than half awake. Another enormous explosion rent the air. Someone screamed; no, it wasn't human, it was one of those hellish dive-bombers – Stukas, weren't they? – which had probably seen the Jeep, though how the pilot had known friend from foe in this tricky dawn light was a puzzle, Tom thought. He lay very still, in one of the gritty tunnels which he and Ricky had dug the previous evening, till the sound of the aircraft had faded into silence, then crawled out of his retreat and looked around for his pal, reflecting that they had not expected to be attacked at this particular spot. After all, they had dug the vehicle in as well as they could and their boltholes should have been impossible to pick out from the air. He supposed that the Stuka was simply shedding a last bomb rather than aiming at anything in particular and it was just bad luck that they had been in the way.

The war in the desert had been a series of advances and retreats and this time they had seen the German army doing more retreating than advancing. So we Brits have been getting cheekier and cheekier, Tom reflected with a grin, remembering a recent incident when, short of supplies, including water, he and Ricky had taken one of the staff cars, whose engine it had been their job to get back into fighting trim, and blasted off into what was described as the wide blue yonder. They had searched for and found a German supply depot, guarded by a couple of soldiers, and driven straight in. Both guards had straightened up and heil-Hitlered, and after a second's pause Tom and Ricky had returned the enemy salute. Then they had jumped down and begun to help themselves, taking tins of corned beef, canned fruit, tea and a large quantity of something which turned out to be dried milk, as well as several cartons of cigarettes and some loose shag. They had just filled their water containers when Ricky had suddenly gasped, pointing to the vehicle which had driven in ahead of them. The Jerry soldier in the passenger seat had jumped down and checked the contents of his restocked vehicle against a list which hung on a wooden post by the exit. Tom had waited until the other vehicle had driven off into the dusty distance and then walked over to the list. With true Teutonic efficiency, the list had instructed *Detail items taken, then sign* – or at least that's how Tom's schoolboy German had interpreted it. Fortunately, they had not had to speak but merely to fill in figures – the cigarettes and tobacco, a dozen tins of corned beef, the same number of canned fruit, several bags of tea and four large boxes of dried milk.

Tom's heart had beaten rather faster than usual, but he had thought the risk worthwhile, for their supplies had almost gone. However, when he told Ricky that they were lucky the guards had not been the keenest, his friend had pointed out that their chances of being recognised and challenged had been pretty slight. 'That's one thing about desert warfare, with everyone casting uniform aside in favour of khaki shorts and army boots: you wouldn't know Marlene Dietrich from Gracie Fields, though I dare say if you replaced our Gracie with Tommy Handley, that might raise a few eyebrows!'

But that had been several days ago and now there was anxiety in Tom's voice as he called his friend's name and heard no answering shout. 'Ricky? Where are you?' he yelled, and was horrified to hear a mumble and then a groan coming from the bolthole next to his own. He dived and grabbed his friend's arm, saying, 'Ricky! Are you all right?' and was appalled to hear a sharply indrawn breath and to realise that the arm he had grabbed was slippery with blood.

For a moment Tom was literally struck dumb. He and Ricky had stuck to each other like Siamese twins, and had somehow managed to regard the war, if not as fun, definitely as an adventure in which victory would always reward the bold. Neither had yet suffered so much as a scratch, though God knew they had had plenty of narrow escapes. Indeed, had it not been for the amount of blood, Tom would have taken it for granted that his friend had merely received a scratch, perhaps from shrapnel, for judging by the sound the bomb had exploded some distance from them.

But now was no time for conjecture. There had been three of them gathered round their little campfire the previous evening, the third a fat and jolly sergeant. Tom looked round, but couldn't see him anywhere, so he returned his attention to his friend. Ricky had got into his bolthole with no trouble the previous evening, but Tom knew that getting him out, badly wounded as he appeared to be, would be a different story. He began to dig as a terrier would when unearthing a rat, except that he took a good deal more care not to scatter his quarry with the sand he was disturbing. At intervals, he shouted the sergeant's name, but getting no response he concentrated all his efforts on digging Ricky out.

When at last he had his friend's body clear of the sand, he could see that whatever had hit him had been quite unpleasant. The wound ran diagonally from the top of his left shoulder across his chest and abdomen to his right hip, but Tom did not think it was deep. Taking it in at a glance, however, he realised that unless he got his friend to hospital with all possible speed Ricky could die from loss of blood, and the idea of continuing to fight the war with no Ricky to guard his back was unthinkable.

'Rick? There's an awful lot of blood and Sergeant Baldock seems to have disappeared, so we're in it alone. Old sarge can look after himself, but I'm going to wrap you as best I can in what's both our shirts, and then drive like hell to the nearest hospital, so if I seem a bit rough it's in your interest to grit your teeth and bear it. Ricky, do you understand what I'm saying?'

Tom waited, then put his hands beneath Ricky's shoulders and began to heave. He saw the wounded man's face suddenly contort and knew he must be causing him considerable pain, but he knew also that the most important thing was to stop the bleeding if he could and then get his friend to a hospital, so he began to pull him towards the staff car.

If it hadn't been for Sergeant Baldock, Tom thought afterwards, he could not imagine how he would have got Ricky into the jeep. When the sergeant had rolled into view and seen Tom heaving uselessly at the blood-boltered figure of his friend, he had wasted no words but put his large, fat forearm under Ricky's knees and commanded Tom to 'lift when I give the word'. The insurmountable task became simple when there were two of them to share it. And then the sergeant had gathered everything of value into the jeep, jumped into the passenger seat and leaned round to give Ricky a wide smile, seeing the younger man gritting his teeth to prevent a shout of pain. 'Now your pal's managed to stop the bleeding, you'll be all right and tight,' he had said cheerfully. He had turned to Tom, driving the vehicle as fast as he could whilst avoiding potholes and other obstacles. 'Isn't that so, old feller?'

Tom had agreed, and once they had left their makeshift camp behind he had turned to the sergeant, saying, 'Where were you? I did look for you when I was digging Ricky out but there was no sign of you. Your bolthole must have been too good; it looked just like the rest of the landscape.'

'And you would have driven off, leaving me with no vehicle and not even a camel to get me back to civilisation,' the sergeant had said. 'How would you have explained what had happened to me, hey?'

Tom had felt the hot blood rush to his cheeks and glanced sideways at the sergeant. 'What would you have done, sarge, if you'd been in my position? No point in searching for you when I thought you must have taken a direct hit and be scattered all over the campsite. Besides, me and Rick, we're good as brothers, almost. We went to the same school, signed on the same day, went on the motor mechanics' course together and have been watching each other's backs ever since. If you had been wounded, I promise you, we'd have done the same for you . . .'

'Thanks very much,' the sergeant had said with more than a trace of sarcasm. 'As it happens, I'm a very heavy sleeper. I heard the air attack, but to tell you the truth I thought I was dreaming. Still, you did all right, and now you must concentrate on giving your friend as smooth a journey as possible. We'll want to be out of the sun in a couple of hours, so let's hope we've reached one of the field hospitals by then. No more recriminations; let's drive.'

Tom and Sergeant Baldock had managed to get Ricky to a hospital in time for the operation he needed, and now, a week later, Ricky was sitting up in bed eating the hospital food, which he said was horrible but, even so, more palatable than the makeshift meals they had made themselves in the desert.

Today, Ricky was still festooned with tubes, but

even the anxious Tom could see that his friend was very much better. After his operation he had seemed sleepy and lethargic, uninterested in everything, and although the doctor had assured Tom that it was only the loss of blood and not an attack of something dreadful such as sleeping sickness Tom had only been partly reassured, until today. Ricky had been positively animated when describing the horrors of hospital life, and for the first time had shown an interest in what had been happening in the outside world, where the Desert Campaign was slowly winding down in the Allies' favour. Tom and Ricky began to discuss what it would be like if they pushed into Tunisia, as everyone assumed they would.

Alice stopped by the soldier with the ulcerated leg and sat down cautiously on the small camp stool which stood beside the bed. She smiled into the young man's weary face, which had lightened when he saw her. 'It's all right; I'm not in trouble, in fact quite the opposite,' she told him. 'Believe it or not, I've been given a whole week's leave, possibly even a little more. Apparently there's a rest camp only a few miles away from Cairo which has a swimming pool . . .'

'Lordy, lordy, I've heard about them rest camps,' the soldier said wistfully. 'I thought they was probably just for officers, but apparently it seems I were wrong. Other ranks get to go there and the blokes what've been say it sets you up nice for wharrever is to come.

That young doctor, Hassan I think his name is, says as soon as my poor bloody leg heals I'll be off there meself for at least four days.' He grinned cockily up at her. 'Wharrabout that, eh, nurse? You might find yourself dancin' the light fantastic wi' me, as soon as this perishin' ulcer does as it's told.'

Alice was about to reply when she saw someone stand up and stretch from his position beside one of the other patients' beds. She stared. It was just a likeness, of course; everyone knew how easy it was to believe you had spotted a friend, only to run up to him or her and realise that you were addressing a total stranger. It was the man's hair colour, she thought guiltily. She had thought Tom's hair was aggressively ginger when they had first met, but later she had realised it was really chestnut; his father's was the same.

The man leaned down and gripped the hand of the patient in the bed, then straightened and turned away. It *couldn't* be Tom, Alice told herself. That was carrying coincidence too far. If Tom had had a brother . . . but she was certain that he did not. The only other man she had met with Tom's colouring was his father and she knew for a fact that Mr Browning was somewhere in India.

Alice took a couple of tentative steps towards the man just as he raised his head, and for a dizzying moment their glances locked. And then Alice gave a small shriek and was in his arms and being lifted up and twirled round, whilst the man repeated her name over and over. 'Alice, Alice, Alice! What in God's name are you doing in Egypt? You're in India, I know you are. I got your letter telling me you'd started training as a nurse . . . oh, Alice, it's so very good to see you again!'

Alice was beginning to reply when an acid voice spoke from the bed beside which their reunion was taking place. 'Can I gather from this rather strange conversation that you two know each other?' it said. 'If so, nurse, I think it only fair to warn you that Tom is notorious for having a girl in every port. Or perhaps every oasis would be more appropriate. But let me introduce myself.' He scowled at Tom. 'When you've stopped dribbling over this delightful young lady you might tell her that I'm your old school pal, Richard Thompson.' He turned to face Alice. 'And you, you lovely lady, will be . . . ?

'Alice Thwaite,' Tom said quickly, too quickly, for he had suddenly remembered that Ricky might easily assume Alice was either Marigold or Maddy and address her accordingly. He turned to Alice. 'And don't you listen to him . . .'

'I see,' Ricky murmured, staring very hard at his friend. 'Well, go on, I can see you're dying to tell Nurse Thwaite how you saved my life. Don't mind me.'

Tom laughed and addressed Alice. 'Ricky was hit by shrapnel; nearly bled to death. He's still convalescing; will be for another week or two, and then I'll take him back to the desert and we'll chase Rommel all the way back to Germany. But until he's well enough to return I shall be kicking my heels around Cairo. My officer has said I can take official leave at the rest camp there.'

'No! My friend Susan and I leave for the camp tomorrow,' Alice cried. She fixed hopeful eyes on Tom, who could not help remembering, ruefully, the difference in their circumstances: she, the rich Miss Thwaite, and he the chauffeur's ginger-headed son. 'Any chance of spending our leave together, Tom, or are you secretly engaged to some Egyptian beauty?'

As she spoke, Tom had a fleeting vision of Marigold as he had last seen her: softly curling golden hair, big blue eyes and a figure . . . he swallowed. By God but she was beautiful! And she had something which lifted their relationship from mere friendliness to something warmer; he had heard the men talking about sex appeal, and supposed that Marigold had an extra dollop of it. But Alice was a dear – it might be nice to spend time with her. After all, spending a leave together – two old friends in a foreign land – could surely not be misconstrued as encouraging Alice to believe he was in love with her.

But Alice was still staring up into Tom's face; too much time had elapsed and he had no intention of hurting her by letting her see his uncertainty. He broke into rapid speech. 'Oh, Alice, that would be wonderful! I've heard the rest camp's grand and the pool – imagine a swimming pool so near the desert

– is large enough for all but the most dedicated swimmers. But wouldn't your friend mind if I tagged along? I don't want to put her nose out of joint.'

He squeezed her hand as he spoke and Alice, to his great embarrassment, returned the pressure. 'I'm sure Susan will soon find herself some exciting companion,' she said contentedly. 'Where did you come from, incidentally?'

'Oh, somewhere in the desert,' Tom said vaguely. 'Our camp, if you can call it that, was attacked by a Stuka, which is how Rick came by his wounds. The hospital won't let him go until the stitches are out and the wound has healed, but if all goes well I'll be setting off for the rest camp tomorrow.' He grinned at Ricky, sitting up in bed now and clearly listening. 'My leave looked like being pretty dull without old Rick here to keep me up to the mark. I thought I wouldn't know a soul and would feel very out of it, but if you'll befriend me, Alice, it would be a real kindness. And that's our story. What's yours?'

'Oh, nothing exciting happens to nurses; we're too stretched,' Alice said truthfully. 'Oh, Tom, you don't know how happy you've made me! Of course Matron is sending us off in pairs, so I would have had Susan, but if you and I are together I'm sure I'll enjoy every moment of my leave.'

Alice and Susan were packing in the cool, stone-built room with its patch of tropical garden which they had been allocated for the duration of their leave. And what a leave it had been, Alice thought dreamily, carefully folding a beautiful pale green evening dress in sheets of tissue paper before laying it in her cream-coloured suitcase. The shops in Cairo were wonderful. She and Susan, having had nothing upon which to spend their salaries for months, suddenly found themselves surrounded by a multitude of shops, some extremely British and others fascinatingly Egyptian. To their delight the prices were low, so they had been able to indulge in an orgy of spending. Both girls had fallen for tennis dresses with skirts made up of a thousand tiny pleats ... and the bathing costumes! And then there were cotton frocks made to measure, smart suits for daywear, and even shoes. On the wards one wore flat shoes or sandals, but here, with dances being held somewhere every night, they could indulge in totteringly high-heeled pumps, or sandals disguised as mere wisps of leather.

'I wonder when we'll wear these again.' Susan flourished a long pink gown as her voice cut across Alice's musings. 'Oh, Alice, hasn't it been wonderful? I shall never forget the beautiful sunsets. I've often heard folk remarking that when the sun goes down in Africa darkness follows immediately, but I suppose I thought it was an exaggeration. It isn't, is it?'

Alice remembered skies streaked with scarlet and gold, emerald green and palest blue, and smiled across at her friend. 'No, it's no exaggeration,' she said, recalling how when the sun sank the sky had almost immediately become a black velvet curtain pricked with stars, and an enormous moon, gold as a sovereign, had shone down upon the land.

Susan gave an ecstatic sigh and clasped her hands. 'And the camel rides; I thought it would be dreadfully uncomfortable, but it wasn't, was it? And the pyramids! They won't believe us back home when we say we went inside a pyramid and visited the Cairo museum to see the bodies of kings and queens in their sarcophaguses. And Paul was so knowledgeable; he made it come alive, almost as though they had died yesterday. For me, at any rate.'

She spoke dreamily and Alice, folding a skirt carefully on top of the dance dress, nodded sympathetically. 'He did know a lot,' she agreed. 'You had Paul, but of course for me it was Tom who made it all so special. You did like him, didn't you, Susan.'

She made the comment more as a statement of fact than a question, but Susan answered enthusiastically. 'Oh, yes, your Tom's really nice, but what a pity he had to go back before we finished our leave. Still, as he said, he and Ricky have got a war to fight. Only he said he now had something to look forward to, meaning seeing you again, I suppose.'

Alice tucked in a last pair of shoes and began to close her suitcase. 'Do you know, I've never been certain how I felt about Tom. When we first met we were just kids, and though there was much I admired about him I sometimes thought he liked Maddy more than he liked me, so of course I treated him rather coolly. Then there was this other girl, Marigold. She definitely liked him, but how he felt about her I couldn't be sure . . .'

'And are you sure now?' Susan said, closing her own case – or rather trying to do so – with a bang. 'Oh, hell, it won't shut.' She smiled beguilingly at Alice. 'Do you have space for a tiny bathing costume, and possibly some of those extraordinary sandals which lace right up to your knee? Because if you can't get them into your case I don't know *what* I shall do!'

Tom and Ricky re-joined their unit in time for the worst weather they had encountered since leaving England. As they moved forward into Tunisia, the rain fell steadily and constantly. Freezing cold, it soaked into blankets, clothing and, horribly, food, so that even when the NAAFI supply vehicles drove into camp they brought little comfort. Tom and Ricky told each other that unless there was a Noah's Ark round the corner the rain was simply bound to ease, and ease it did, eventually, as the long line of men and materials continued to slog onwards. And then, at last, the sun came out. Blankets steamed, mud began to dry on clothing and boots and hot food was once more delivered daily. The NAAFI, Tom remarked, had its faults but the issue of hot bully beef stew and tinned potatoes went a long way towards cheering up the column.

The night after the rain ceased, Tom and Ricky lay for the first time for ages in dry blankets, smoking cigarettes which the NAAFI had thoughtfully provided and thinking back to their leave. In the end Ricky had only had three days at the rest camp because the doctors had not released him until his wounds were completely healed, but he had arrived there in time to attach himself firmly to Tom and Alice, though he had speedily added another nurse, Lucy, to 'even up the numbers' as he put it.

Now, Tom stretched lazily. 'Are you going to write to Lucy?' he asked. 'The two of you seemed to get on awfully well.' He took a drag of his cigarette and watched his friend's face in the tiny glow.

Ricky was grinning reminiscently. 'Lucy is a very generous girl, and runs her life like clockwork,' he said. 'Yes, I've no doubt we shall exchange letters. One of the reasons we got on so well is because she's not the clinging type.' He gave a subdued chortle and lowered his voice to a conspiratorial whisper. 'She's had an exciting sort of love life. First she was engaged to a bomber pilot, only he bought it over Berlin. Then she took up with a Frenchie in de Gaulle's little lot; he left her and probably joined the Resistance. Then there was a petty officer aboard a merchant vessel going to and fro between New York and Liverpool, and after that . . .'

'My God, she's certainly experienced,' Tom said, laughing. 'What number are you, twenty-five?'

Ricky chuckled. 'I tell you what, that girl knows a thing or two, and even if I am number twenty-five, probably half the nurses' boyfriends are in the same position. Do you know how old she is?'

'About a hundred, I should guess, judging from her history with men, only she's most awfully well preserved for her years; like those mummies we saw in the pyramids at Cairo,' Tom said. 'Go on, surprise me! I suppose you'll say she's seventeen.'

'As a matter of fact she's thirty-eight; she really doesn't look it, does she?' Ricky said. 'And if that surprises you, hard luck! Little Lucy taught me more in three days than I've learned in my life so far. How about you? Did Alice come across? It was pretty obvious she thinks you're something special, though God knows why. *Did* she? Did you . . . ?'

'Don't be so bloody nosy,' Tom said. 'Alice is a decent girl, not the sort to go bestowing her favours on any Tom, Dick or Harry. To tell you the truth, I had a thing about a girl called Marigold – I'm sure I told you – but by the end of our leave Alice had sort of taken over. In fact, when I try to visualise Marigold, Alice's face keeps getting superimposed on hers . . . know what I mean?'

Ricky pursed his lips and then expelled air in a shrill whistle. 'I know what you mean, but I doubt if you know yourself,' he said. 'If you ask me you're in love with the girl. Not Marigold – Alice. Has it never crossed your mind that liking might have turned to love? Could you bear to spend the rest of your life with her?'

'I'm not sure, but I think you may be right, and I am in love with Alice,' Tom said slowly. 'But can someone love a girl when they've never . . . oh, you know, gone all the way, as you'd put it.' He leaned out of his blanket as a tiny snore escaped from his friend's open mouth, and flicked his shoulder. 'Ricky! Wake up, will you? I'm asking you a very serious question because you're older than me, and your Lucy is older than either of us. Do you honestly think that I could be in love with Alice Thwaite?'

Tom waited, but Ricky did not stir. Thinking about it, Tom realised that his question had been a foolish one anyway. Ricky had only known Lucy properly for three days, and although he was clearly going to keep in touch with her if it was humanly possible to do so, in every other way their two cases could hardly be less alike. From what Ricky had said, he must at least have slept with Lucy, but when Tom and Alice had parted he had given her a chaste kiss and promised to write. Apart from anything else, he realised now that he knew the adult Alice scarcely at all, because she had changed almost out of recognition in the three years since they had seen each other. He decided he would write to her, meet her whenever the exigencies of war allowed, and make a mature decision when they had shared more than one shy kiss.

He wriggled further down into the cocoon of his

blanket and thought about Alice. Wide blue eyes, a straight little nose, and a way of looking at him which made him feel he was really one hell of a feller. I believe I really do love her, Tom thought. But when the war's over and I can see her more often, I shall find out for sure how I feel.

He was on the very verge of sleep when an unexpected thought flashed into his head: won't Dad be pleased? Then, surprisingly, a mental picture of his father formed in his mind, and Jim Browning did not look pleased at all, but quite the opposite. Odd! Tom tried to claw back the image to examine his father's expression more closely, but it was too late. *For better for worse, for richer for poorer, in sickness and in health*, he thought confusedly.

And Tom was asleep.

Chapter Thirteen

1945

Maddy walked across the parade ground, heading for the Mess. The war was surely in its final stages, with the Allied troops now chasing the enemy, taking prisoners, and closing on Berlin, where everyone assumed the war would end. It was a difficult time for the girl gunners, Maddy mused. But with the easing of hostilities it was no longer necessary for her battery to spend every night targeting enemy aircraft. Even the unmanned doodlebugs they had been shooting down lately had disappeared, although the rockets which had replaced them seemed to be causing great devastation.

Maddy knew she was not the only one who felt flat, almost let down, as a result of the sudden change in their lives. Yet they were still all members of the forces, still programmed to obey orders, and when there were no orders being given, and the war had not officially ended . . .

But it was the same for all of them. Maddy and Marigold had gone their separate ways after Marigold had failed the examinations which would have enabled her to become a gunner, and at first it seemed as though the army did not know what to do with her. She was in the cookhouse for a couple of months, but had then rebelled and been given a desk job. She had not minded the work, she had explained to Maddy, but felt she was not doing anything particularly useful. Then, the previous year, the censors had been overwhelmed with mail and Marigold had been posted to an office in the far north of Scotland. She had said grandly, in her first letter after the move, that she was doing an extremely hush-hush job, though she could not say what until the war ended, but Maddy believed her old friend had been one of the many in the ATS to be seconded as what the girls irreverently called 'censor-snippers'. Marigold often bemoaned the fact that she was in Scotland, in a location too remote to allow her to get home to Yorkshire, where her mother still worked, or to visit Maddy, who had been constantly on the move until very recently.

At this point in her musings Maddy opened the door and went into the Mess. The first person she saw was a tall young infantryman who had been injured in the last stages of *Operation Overlord* and was now fretting to be off to re-join his unit. The MO had said he could leave when he no longer needed his crutches, but that day had not yet come, so now Maddy raised her brows. 'Have you been to the cookhouse yet, Cassidy?' she asked. The young soldier's name was actually Ben Travers, but he was nicknamed 'Hopalong Cassidy' after the cowboy film star. 'I thought I'd pick up my mail – if I've got any – and then go along to get something to eat whilst I read.' She grinned at him. 'I've heard there's a rasher of bacon to go with the dried egg; aren't we the lucky ones?'

Cassidy returned the grin. 'I wondered why you were so early,' he said. 'But I can't accept your kind invitation to brekker as I had mine half an hour ago. And as for letters, you've got several.'

'Oh, marvellous,' Maddy said happily. 'Sounds as though they've all caught up with me at once.' If working out just where Marigold had been posted was hard, Maddy's correspondents must have been driven half crazy by her constant moves. Once the girls knew the drill by heart, they could be sent to any gun site in the country, and Maddy's battery had one of the highest records of hits in the regiment, which made them popular.

She began to take her letters off the board, smiling as she did so. Lovely! One from Gran; her impeccable copperplate handwriting was unmistakable, Maddy thought, and was probably the reason why Gran's letters were always short. Then there was one from Marigold – a nice fat one. Taking it off the board, Maddy reckoned that the envelope probably contained at least three of her friend's closely written sheets. There was one from Alice – no, two – and one from Tom. Maddy's heart gave an excited little hop. Despite telling herself that Tom meant nothing to her, save as a good friend, she always read his letters slowly and luxuriously, whilst a picture of him formed in her mind.

Since becoming a gunner she had been far too busy – and too tired – to even think about forming relationships amongst the men with whom she worked. Besides, almost all of them were elderly. They had been seconded to the gun sites so that younger men might go to the front line, and they often resented the girls who were quicker, more intelligent and keener than they were themselves. A rather nice – and happily married – man in his forties, on a searchlight battery, was the only one Maddy could recall who gave the 'girl gunners' their due. 'You're young and keen,' he had once told Maddy. 'You aren't afraid of making mistakes, yet you hardly ever get the maths wrong. I do my best, but I can't mimic your speed and accuracy on the guns.' At the time Maddy had beamed at him and thanked him for the compliment.

She was turning away from the board when she saw that there was one more letter bearing her name. It was not an official brown envelope – thank God, oh, thank God! – but a blue envelope which she did not recognise, addressed in a hand that was strange to her. Was it a mistake? But then it was perfectly possible that one of the friends she had made in her wanderings might have decided to get in touch. Maddy took the last letter off the board and placed them all in her gas mask case, then set off for the cookhouse.

'Well, and ain't you the early bird!' The corporal doling out breakfasts grinned widely at Maddy as she reached the head of the queue. 'Did you hear as how there were bacon this mornin'? I've only got another five pieces, so anyone what arrives after I've doled them out has only theirselves to blame.' He stabbed a weary-looking slice of bacon and dropped it on Maddy's tin plate. 'There you are, chuck! That'll put hairs on your chest!'

Maddy heaved an artificial sigh. 'I do believe I've heard that one a mere thousand times before,' she said, helping herself to a slice of cold burnt toast. 'No thanks, Cooky, no jam.'

As she left the queue, several people called out to her to share their table, but Maddy shook her head. 'I've got a pile of letters to read,' she explained. 'And one of 'em's from my feller, so excuse me if I grab a table to myself.'

It was the one excuse which would be acceptable, she knew, and presently she began to eat whilst reading the letter from Marigold. Dear Corporal Stein, Maddy thought affectionately, I miss you most dreadfully, but it won't be long now before we meet again. Everyone says the war's all but over, and once we're in civvy street we'll be able to resume normal relations, and that means friendships.

The letter began with the usual grumble; it was

colder in Scotland than it had any right to be, considering that spring was well advanced. Then Marigold demanded why Maddy hadn't written more often and said that she had had to rely on Alice, who was not even in the country, to find out what was going on back in dear old Blighty. Which, when you considered that Alice was nursing in field hospitals all over the Continent and had very little time for herself, was fair criticism of Maddy, who wrote very rarely.

Reading Marigold's reproaches, Maddy thought of long nights on remote sites, when the planes had raced overhead and she and her fellow gunners, soaked to the skin and icy cold, had worked out the maths, adjusted the angles, shouted 'On target!' and watched as the planes they caught in the searchlight's beam crashed to the ground. If that wasn't hard work . . . but it was no use getting into a state. It was typical of Marigold to assume no one else held an important place in the war effort.

Maddy sighed and continued to read, for now her friend had got into her stride and was talking about a fascinating man, a Spitfire pilot, who had asked her out . . .

. . . *of course I told him I was already practically engaged to Tom, who has gone before his commissioning board and no doubt will, in future, be Lieutenant Thomas Browning, but he refused to be put off, which is fortunate, considering what apparently happened at that rest place outside Cairo* . . . the letter went on.

Maddy's heart gave an enormous leap. What had happened at a rest place outside Cairo? She had received only one letter from Tom since his return to what she supposed was called the Italian Campaign, and she was sure it hadn't mentioned Cairo; oh, what had she missed? She was gripping Marigold's letter so hard that her knuckles were white. Oh, God, don't say Tom found himself a woman whilst I was stuck on a gun site in the middle of nowhere, she prayed. She thought back frantically. Had there been the slightest hint . . . ? But conjecture was useless; she must finish reading the letter and hope that light would presently dawn.

Marigold's missive, however, simply rambled on, and Maddy realised, not for the first time, that her friend not only suffered from verbal diarrhoea but did not always read the letters her friends penned so carefully. But surely, she thought, whilst Tom had what army friends rudely called 'the hots' for Marigold he was unlikely to go finding himself another woman. And when he came home and Marigold let him down by producing a Spitfire pilot or some high-ranking officer as her latest conquest, she, Maddy, would be on hand to prove to him that *her* friendship was real and, what was more, everlasting. Like those horrid flowers which have petals like paper and no scent, Maddy thought now, grimacing . . . and turned to Marigold's missive once more.

But whatever had happened in Cairo was not

mentioned again until it was broadly hinted at on the last page. *I knew Alice was a sly one right from the start*, Marigold had written rather unkindly. *It looks as though she will be the first of us to get married – bags I be her bridesmaid – though I don't know whether Tom's actually popped the question yet. Did you think I was head over heels in love with him, like you? Because if so . . .*

Damn her eyes, Maddy thought furiously. How dare she insinuate I was ever in love with Tom Browning, or anyone else for that matter! Oh, how typical of Marigold to assume that everyone else feels just as she does. I could wring her neck! She screwed the letter up into a ball and guessed she was probably red in the face from sheer indignation, for half the occupants of the cookhouse were staring at her and the other half regarding her screwed-up letter with more than usual interest. She told herself not to be an idiot and carefully unravelled the crumpled pages, quickly scanning the rest of the unread sheet. Nothing of interest here, except that Marigold asked if Maddy knew that Tom's nickname was Gravy (because of gravy browning, of course), and said she just hoped that his wife wouldn't mind being called Mint Sauce because she was such a lamb!

Maddy shoved the letter into her pocket, got up, and walked over to the large tub which stood by the cookhouse door. She waggled her irons vaguely in the rather greasy water, which had once been hot but was now cooling rapidly, and left the cookhouse.

When she reached her hut she remembered that today was kit inspection and groaned, but a glance at her watch showed her that another twenty minutes would elapse before drill, which they suffered every morning even now, when they no longer had to rush to the bulletin board to see where their ack-ack team would be operating tonight.

But kit inspection, like the poor, is always with us, she reminded herself as she began to make her bed and lay out her uniform in the prescribed fashion. She had just arranged her stockings so that the hole in the toe of the left one was hidden when she remembered, with a guilty start, that she had not even begun to read the rest of her mail. Curse Marigold, she thought, for worrying me. Was it possible, though, that Alice would really marry Tom, as Marigold insinuated? It seemed unlikely, but unlikelier things had happened in war. Hastily, Maddy delved into her gas mask case and withdrew the contents. She sat down on her bed, being careful not to upset her kit, and forced herself to begin reading the letters whose envelopes she had not so much as opened.

Gran's came first.

Dear Madeleine,

Mr Sutherland killed our pig for us, so next time you come home there may be bacon. Ivy Sutherland is marrying Willy Jones next time he comes on leave. Not before time, judging by the bulge. Mr and Mrs

O'Halloran have planted King Edwards because they
are my favourites. I cooked a spotted dick last Sunday.
Mrs O made custard. You are a good girl. I'm sorry
for what I did.

At this point, Maddy remembered Gran's black walking cane and had to stifle a little giggle. It was just like Gran to bury an apology in the midst of quite ordinary bits of news, though why she was harking back, literally years, to the time when she had had to dodge Gran's cane Maddy could not imagine. She was still smiling when she realised the letter ended rather abruptly. *You've not had leave for a long while*, her grandmother had written. *Write soon, your loving grandmother.*

Maddy stared at the letter for several moments, then shrugged and dropped it back into her gas mask case. Though Gran was a crotchety old thing she seemed to have understood that because Maddy had almost always been on gun sites in the south of the country she had been unable to return home for any of her leaves. I'll write to her this evening, Maddy told herself, beginning to open Alice's envelopes. She extracted the letters, which were numbered, and arranged the sheets so that she could read them in the order they had been written.

Dear Maddy,
    Lovely to hear from you. My friend Susan and I had
four days off recently, which was great. Can't tell you

where, or when, or why – if I did the censor would snip
it out – but we met an old friend (no names, no pack
drill) which made my leave perfect. I can't remember
whether I told you that we'd met up a couple of times
before, and each time it was better. Oh dear, there's so
much I'm longing to tell you, but of course it's not
allowed. Oh, hell, I've got to go; continue in my next.

Frowning, Maddy re-read the short letter. A shared
leave? But with whom? They – she and Alice – had a
good many friends in common, but . . . Maddy turned
to the next letter, aware of a sinking sensation in her
stomach and trying to ignore it. She began to read.

Dear Maddy,
Sorry for the scrappy letter, but I suppose we're
all in the same boat, getting caught up in events and
having to put our own lives on hold. I can't remember
exactly what I said in my last but suffice to say that
when this wretched war is over it looks as though I shall
be changing my name from Thwaite to Browning! I'd
ask you to be a bridesmaid only I hope we may tie
the knot before we get back to Blighty; we've wasted
enough time as it is, so why waste more? Take care of
yourself, Maddy, and one day you'll be as happy as I
am now. From your loving friend, Alice.

Maddy was struck dumb, and for a moment could
only stare at the page in her hand, whilst the words

disappeared in a blur of tears. She remembered vaguely that Alice had mentioned in one of her letters – a couple of years ago, surely – that she had met Tom by chance in an Egyptian hospital and spent some of her leave with him. Could that have been at the 'rest place outside Cairo' Marigold had alluded to? And I wasn't even upset or jealous, Maddy thought now. I always thought Tom had a 'thing' for Marigold. Oh, I can't believe it, I simply *won't* believe it; Tom and Alice, Alice and Tom! How could they do this to me? Well, at least they haven't actually tied the knot, so I suppose I can still hope. But then she realised that it would be downright wicked to hope that her two best friends might not marry. It was tantamount to saying that she would be pleased if a bomb fell on Alice, whereas what was much likelier was that Tom would be killed – she shuddered all over at the thought – and if that happened she would blame herself as long as she lived.

Still blinded by tears, she pushed both letters back into her gas mask case and pulled out the remaining two envelopes. She opened Tom's, aware that she was hoping for a denial, yet knowing this was impossible . . . it would be too much of a coincidence to get a letter from Alice proclaiming her joy in the marriage to come at the same time as another from Tom saying that the wedding was off. And indeed, Tom's letter did not mention marriage, or weddings, or anything very much. He talked wistfully of the time when peace would be a fact, when he would be discharged from the army and could begin to build a new life, which he meant to spend out of doors if possible, for he had discovered in himself a keen interest in the land.

I've talked it over with other chaps in my unit, and having spent five years of war mainly out of doors, most of us would like to work on the land. Did you know Alice's uncle John had died? He was a grand chap and I'm truly sorry, but it may mean that Windhover Hall will come on the market and if it does several chaps, including me, might try to form a syndicate to run the place as a business venture. I understand something similar, if a good deal smaller, is going on at Larkspur, but you'll know all about that.

Maddy gave a rather watery smile. She thought you could scarcely call the O'Hallorans and Gran a syndicate, but she knew what Tom meant, or supposed she did. She skimmed through the rest of his letter, but it was all about farming, which once would have interested her deeply but now seemed to have no bearing on the future to which she had once looked forward.

From outside she heard the clatter of shoes on concrete and realised that the girls were assembling for drill. Hastily she pushed the letters, including the mystery one, back into her gas mask case and hurried towards the door, which swung open to admit most of the members of her battery. 'Hi, Hebditch. Drill first, then kit inspection,' Maddy's friend Evie shouted boisterously. 'Cassidy told me you'd had some letters . . .' she must have suddenly realised that Maddy was looking less than happy and stopped in her tracks. 'What's up? Not bad news!'

'No, not bad news . . . in fact very good news,' Maddy said with determined gaiety. 'I've just heard that my two best friends are getting married. It was a bit of a shock, because the feller used to be head over heels in love with another of my friends, but it's good news, honestly it is, Evie.'

'Oh; well that's nice,' Evie said uneasily. 'But you can't sit in here whilst we drill; sarge is bound to notice you're missing.' She raised her voice to a shout. 'Come along, girls, sarge is waiting!'

It was not until very much later that day, when Maddy was getting ready for bed, that she remembered the 'mystery letter', still unopened, and pulled it out from under her gas mask case. She frowned at the envelope for a moment, not recognising the handwriting yet feeling that she should know it, before tearing it open and extracting the two sheets it contained. She flicked over to the second page and saw that it was signed *from your good friend Herb*.

Maddy stared for a moment, then smiled. Of course! Gran's evacuees. Herb had been the oldest, the most responsible of the trio and also, she thought, the one who had made it plain how much he loved Larkspur.

But that did not explain why he was writing to her; he had certainly never done so before.

'Maddy, got a letter from your sweet'eart?' a voice suddenly interrupted. 'Or 'ave you won the sweepstake? It'd be just like you to draw the winnin' number and not tell a soul. G'on, what does luvverboy say?'

'M.y.o.b.,' Maddy said automatically. But the other girl, Daphne Swift, was large and aggressive and though Maddy now held the rank of corporal she had no intention of making an enemy of her, so she went on, 'But I've not won the sweepstake – didn't know there was one – and this letter, alas, is from a young man who can't be more than ten or eleven. One of the evacuees, in fact, who's been billeted with my gran.'

'Oh,' Swift said, losing interest. 'Come along, girls, get into your pits, though it's been a while since Moaning Minnie made us scamper for the shelters. Lights out in ten minutes. Last one in's a sissy!'

Everyone began to strip and get into their issue pyjamas, and Maddy remembered, with a touch of nostalgia, how she and her fellow Ats on the batteries had looked upon Moaning Minnie not as a sign to make for the shelters, but to head for the gun sites and begin the always hard, and often muddy, work of training the guns on the enemy and making sure, before a shot was fired, of the identity of the planes overhead!

As soon as she was in her pyjamas, Maddy began to read the letter from Herbert, first detailing the girl nearest the door to turn the light off once everyone was in bed.

Dear Maddy,
   Maybe its a cheek for me to write to you but I thort I should. Your grans been in a rare taking and theres folk here on Larkspur as mebbe shouldnt be. Its been a long while since you was here last, and me and the fellers doesnt think that you know whats goin on. I asked Gran when Mrs O were out of the way and she bit me head off – Gran not Mrs O. Me and the fellers talked it over and you mite say I drew the short straw, so I'm writin to ask you to come home. I know your on the ack-ack, wes real proud of you, Gran an all, but I'm no hand at letter writin so if you can come home that would be best. I know me spellin aint perfect, but I done me best. Please come, from your good friend Herb.

Maddy was still frowning over the letter when the light went off and the last girl climbed beneath her blanket. She guessed that Herbert would only have written to her if he was truly worried, and knew that she should make every effort to get home. But at present she and her fellow gunners were on a site just outside Southampton, which meant she was a long, long way from Larkspur. Despite the fact that everyone thought the war would soon be over, leave was not easy to obtain, but she rather thought that her commanding officer, if she read the letter, would grant her corporal at least a week to go home and find out what was wrong. She would jolly well ask for leave the very next day, and considered she was unlikely to be refused. She had worked continuously for the past two years and the letter, it seemed, was urgent. Sure that she had made the right decision, Maddy turned on her side and slept.

Next day, as soon as drill was over, Maddy made for the orderly's office, having asked for an interview as soon as she got up. She took the letter with her, determined to stress Gran's age and numerous disabilities, but no explanations were necessary. The officer had looked up Maddy's service history, discovered that she had had no leave for two years, and granted her absence for ten days without a blink. 'Because of troop movements travel by rail is pretty complicated,' she said. 'That's why I would advise you to go as soon as your leave starts, which is officially at midnight tonight, though you'll not be needed after six o'clock.' She stood up and held out a hand. 'Good luck, Corporal. I hope you will find the situation at home less worrying than you fear. Your grandmother has survived so far, and we all know the end of the war is approaching.' She smiled very kindly into Maddy's anxious face. 'Off with you now, and I'll see you in ten days' time; get a rail pass from the front office.'

Gran woke when the sun found its way through a crack in the curtains, though that was not what had woken her; it was worry which had done that. When

Herbert had told her frankly that he thought she ought to get in touch with Maddy, she had been absolutely furious and had shouted at him so loudly that Eileen O'Halloran had come in from the dairy to ask what was the matter. Herbert had turned and given Mrs O'Halloran a long, cold look. 'All sorts of things is the matter,' he had said brusquely, when the woman had repeated her question. 'I'm tellin' Mrs Hebditch here as how she ought to gerrin touch with Maddy. But she's that obstinate . . .'

Mrs O'Halloran had given Herbert a look laden with spite. 'There's no need for Mrs Hebditch to do anything of the sort,' she had said, bristling. 'Now as we've got our relatives to help, we can manage very nicely without no interference from anyone. And I might tell you, Master Nosy, that if anyone's needed here, it ain't yerself. You're here on what they call "sufferance", and me and Dec could send you back to London tomorrer. I'd do it too, rockets or no rockets, only I dare say we're stuck wi' you until the war ends official like.' She had turned to go back to the dairy and Gran had seen Herbert stick his tongue out and waggle his ears in a very rude way, but she had said nothing.

Had Herbert been right? But he was only an evacuee, little more than a child. When the time was ripe she would get in touch with Maddy, but the time was not yet anywhere near ripe.

Gran lay for a while watching the strengthening

sunshine as it poured through the crack in the curtains, and wondering when she should get up. Eileen always helped her to dress now, but today Gran had decided to be independent. After all, if Herbert had been right . . . but it was pointless thinking like that. Maddy hadn't bothered to come back to Larkspur for two years, and though Gran hadn't said so in any of her letters she thought her granddaughter had chosen not to return.

Could have come if she'd really wanted to, Gran told herself now. And when she does come, if she dares to try and tell me off, say I shouldn't have done what I did, then I'll tell her to keep her breath to cool her porridge. It's none of her business anyway. What does she expect to happen if she walks out on me, leaves me to the mercy of the O'Hallorans? What did she expect, eh?

Gran sniffed and began to tug her long winceyette nightdress over her head. She looked at the basin and ewer and decided, in a spirit of defiance, not to wash today. Then she began to struggle into her clothing. It was quite a struggle, too, and when at last she was fully dressed she had to wipe away tears, telling herself she was shedding them because she was getting slow and old and didn't like it. But she knew in her heart that the tears had come because she was thinking guiltily that maybe Herbert was right. Maybe she should have told Maddy – not asked her permission, but told her – that things had to change, and if Maddy had reproached her, so what? My shoulders are broad, Gran told herself. I can take any amount of criticism because I know I've done right. And then she had to sit down on her bedside chair and mop her eyes again, because Gran didn't intend that anyone, anyone at all, should see her crying.

Maddy turned into the familiar lane and felt a clutch of pleasure at the well-remembered and much-loved views of their own particular dale. Almost immediately, she felt a stab of pain because this country was where she had been happiest and, because of her best friends' projected marriage, could be happiest no longer. She had not bothered to pack very much, guessing that she would be expected to do her share of any work which Gran and Mrs O'Halloran deemed necessary, but even so her kitbag was heavy. After a quarter of a mile or so she swapped the weight from one shoulder to the other and told herself brusquely to concentrate on what she meant to say to Gran.

Herb's letter, though it had had the desired effect of bringing her back to Larkspur, had given her little clue as to what, if anything, had gone wrong. Who were the strangers at Larkspur? Maddy scowled as she tried to guess what had caused the boy to write to her, for it was obvious from his letter that writing did not come easily to him. Then she smiled to herself; Miss Evans was clearly no Miss Parrott – Mrs Grice – for she had been a stickler for spelling and punctuation, neither of which appeared to have troubled Herbert unduly when he wrote.

Presently Maddy came to the five-bar gate through which Mr Sutherland's sheepdog herded his charges when they were changing pastures. Maddy stopped and leaned on the top bar; she was realising more than ever before how she loved this place and realised too, in virtually the same thought, that she was longing to come back here so she could put right all the things which had led Gran to rent out Larkspur land.

But you couldn't blame Gran, because she was an old woman, and knew very little about farming. When her husband had been alive, Gran had had the full responsibility of the house. She had cooked and cleaned and made do and mended, and though her grandfather had been dead for many years when Maddy had first come to Larkspur, there had been signs that the farm had once been well run and extremely productive. Alas, the war had not helped; the O'Hallorans had done their best but they had been forced to concentrate most of their efforts on the vegetable garden and the pigs and poultry. Ploughing, reaping, sowing and even haymaking had been beyond them. Mr Sutherland had been glad to take on the rest of the Larkspur land in addition to the few acres he had rented nearest his own farm, for once the war had started the Ministry of Agriculture and Fisheries dictated who should grow what and where. Fields which had lain untended for many years became productive under the stern eye of the Min of Ag, as it was known, and Maddy had accepted that this should be so. Once the war had got into its stride Britain could not rely on foreign imports but must feed itself, and indeed had done so very successfully.

But very soon things will return to normal, Maddy told herself, and that meant she and Gran would have to talk over how they would tackle Larkspur. She imagined that Mr Sutherland might want to buy the land he now rented and found, to her own surprise, that she did not want this to happen. Once, she would have taken it for granted that she would marry someone who wanted to farm; now she was not so sure. She knew Tom and his father had once owned land and had intended to do so again, but obviously Tom's marrying rich Alice changed everything. She and Gran could of course get themselves a bailiff and work with him on the reclaiming of the Hebditches' acres, but that was for the future, and Maddy realised she was still reluctant to look into a future which did not contain Tom.

At this point in her musings she reached the gate which led into the Larkspur yard. She swung it wide, passed through it and latched it behind her, noticing that it had still not been mended, despite her repeated requests.

She was beginning to cross the farmyard when she realised something was different and hesitated, trying to think what it was. The geese! She stared about her, astonished. She and Gran had always kept geese, partly for their eggs and also, it must be confessed, because they were such good watchdogs. Snoops might stay in his kennel – though he was not in it now – but the geese would attack anyone, friend or foe. Maddy still had marks on the backs of her shins where she had not been quite quick enough to keep the gaggle at bay. She whistled and stamped loudly on the cobbles, hoping that either the dog or the geese would appear, but when she remained the only occupant of the farmyard she shrugged and headed for the back door. She would start by demanding to be told what had happened to their fine flock of waterfowl.

She pushed open the back door and poked her head round it. 'Coo-ee!' she called. 'Anyone at home?' The words died on her lips and she stood there for a moment, shocked to see a total stranger standing at the sink. It was a girl of about Maddy's own age, or perhaps a little younger. Her dark hair was tied back from her face with a bright head-square, and she seemed to be cleaning vegetables.

She swung round when she heard Maddy's voice and spoke reprovingly. 'Why didn't you knock? It's not manners, ye know, to walk into someone's house wit'out bein' invited.'

Maddy was so astonished that for a moment she was quite literally speechless, and in that moment the girl had crossed the kitchen and shouted up the stairs: 'Auntie, will you come? There's some young gal here . . . oh, I'd best go up. She's probably dressin' the old 'un and can't hear me.' She turned to wag an admonitory finger at Maddy. 'Don't you go touchin' nothin'; just stay where you are. Auntie will be down in a minute.'

Once more Maddy's mouth opened and closed but no sound came out. What *was* going on? As the girl thundered upstairs she looked around the kitchen, dismayed. She and Gran – and Mrs O'Halloran for that matter – might not have been perfect housewives but they had always kept the kitchen sparkling clean. Now it was grimy, the wooden furniture in desperate need of polishing, the vegetable racks overflowing and an indefinable smell emanating from the deep stone sink and the wooden draining board. Maddy went over to the sink at which the young girl had been working. It was full of potatoes and it occurred to Maddy that there were a great many more than seemed necessary for Gran's small household.

Before she could investigate further, heavy footsteps descended the stairs and Mrs O'Halloran appeared. 'What do you want? You come in here, throwin' your weight about— Oh, it's you! Well, your gran will be surprised, since she were sayin' only yesterday that you scarce ever wrote to her no more.' The woman glanced quickly round the kitchen, then back to Maddy, a gleam of spite in her eyes. 'Has your gran been tellin' tales? I know there's some as feels it their duty to noise our doin's abroad . . .'

Maddy stared at her. 'Where's my grandmother?' she asked brusquely. 'It's almost eleven o'clock; is she ill? Kept to her bed?' She paused as the young girl came down the stairs and headed for the back door. 'Hang on a minute,' Maddy called. 'Come back here! I want to know just what you were doing . . .'

But the door, shutting with a bang, closed behind the girl whilst Maddy was still speaking. She turned back to Mrs O'Halloran, who said quickly, 'So you've decided to come back, have you, and no doubt you expect to take your place amongst us. Well, you can forget that. You're neither wanted nor needed, but I dare say it would be best if I let your gran tell you so herself.' She sat down in the creaking old basket chair and stared defiantly up at Maddy.

Once again, Maddy was left speechless. But first things first, she told herself. Without waiting for an invitation, which she was very sure would never be given, she crossed the kitchen and pulled out one of the ladder-backed chairs, seating herself firmly upon it. 'Why is my grandmother still in her room, Mrs O'Halloran? Is she ill? If so I shall go up to her immediately.'

These words acted upon the Irish woman as though she had sat on a thistle. She leapt up from the basket chair, crossed the room in a few strides and stood protectively on the bottom stair, a hand on each of the banister rails, thus making it impossible for Maddy to get past. 'There's nowt wrong wi' Mrs Hebditch; she's just been havin' a lie-in. She'll be down in a minute,' she said aggressively. 'She's a lot slower now than she was in your time, but my sister went up there half an hour ago to give her a hand, so she won't be long now. Mind you, she may not want to see you . . .'

This was too much. 'Just who do you think you are, Mrs O'Halloran?' Maddy said stiffly. 'You have no right to stop me going upstairs in my own home.'

Before Mrs O'Halloran could reply both women heard shambling footsteps crossing the upper hall and beginning to descend the stairs. Gran came down slowly, and with all the care that was necessary on the rather narrow flight. When she saw Maddy her expression changed from its initial welcoming smile to a look which Maddy found difficult to read. Was it embarrassment? Anger? Possibly a touch of fear? But Gran isn't afraid of anyone, as she's very fond of asserting, Maddy told herself.

In view of Mrs O'Halloran's strange attitude, Maddy began to say she would like to speak to her grandmother alone, but she was only halfway through the sentence when she saw another woman descending the stairs, a woman whose striking likeness to Mrs O'Halloran proclaimed her to be that lady's sister. She had greying black hair, thick bushy eyebrows and a determined chin, but she helped Gran solicitously down the last two stairs and guided her to what had always been her seat. Only then did she glance towards her sister. At a jerk of Mrs O'Halloran's head, she let herself out of the back door, closing it quite softly behind her. There was a moment's silence before Mrs O'Halloran pointed an accusing finger at Maddy.

'Ho, so you think you can just walk back in here and take over, do you? Well, you've done little enough for your grandmother these past two or three years – longer, likely – so me man and meself decided to tek a hand. We've worked like slaves, doin' all that was necessary, but we warned Mrs Hebditch that we couldn't go on. Why should we work from dawn to dusk, in someone else's gaff, and take home a pittance? So we looked into alternatives. Dec's always been a sociable sort of feller and he got pally with this 'ere chap what said if Gran could no longer work the land, which it's obvious she can't, then she might will it to us, or hand it over as a Deed of Gift.' She grinned suddenly; a triumphant grin. 'So we decided it 'ud best be a belt and braces affair. Your gran's signed a Deed of Gift, which will cover us taking over here, and she's also made up a will in our favour.' She chuckled. 'Belt and braces, see?'

Maddy stared at her grandmother. 'Oh, Gran, how could you?' she said in a low voice. 'But I do hope you've told these – these people – that you don't own Larkspur outright. You told me years ago that only a member of the family can own it. And I'm your only living relative.'

In actual fact, Maddy had no idea whether or not such an arrangement was legally binding, but Gran was wiping away a tear, and then blowing her nose noisily. 'I told them it couldn't be right to take your home,' she mumbled. 'It's been in our family since ancient times, going from generation to generation; sometimes a feller inherits, sometimes a woman. It doesn't matter so long as they're a Hebditch by blood.' She banged rather feebly on the arm of her chair, turning her head back towards Mrs O'Halloran. 'I *warned* you; I said Maddy's dad should have inherited when I die, only as it happens there was the accident and he were killed, leaving his share to his little daughter.'

'Well there you are; plain as a pikestaff,' Mrs O'Halloran said triumphantly. But Maddy could hear the twinge of doubt in her voice. 'A child of five can't inherit.' She rounded suddenly on Maddy. 'Did you think we'd go on working, and you and your gran the only ones to benefit? Neither of you have done a hand's turn for years and when you did' – she pointed at Maddy – 'it was such simple things as feedin' the poultry and fetchin' in vegetables for the market . . . something anyone could do. So now you can take yourself off.' The older woman smirked as she spoke, but Maddy was heartened to recognise her uncertainty. 'The papers your gran signed were signed by us as well, to say that as long as she kept her promise to give us the farm we would work for her on the present terms. But there was no word of you, Miss Madeleine Hebditch, not the tiniest mention, so you've no right here, and the sooner you get out the better.'

Maddy got to her feet. 'Just a minute. I've a few questions which need answers,' she said. 'Who are all these people living here? One is obviously your sister – you're like as two peas in a pod – and I suppose the other may be a niece, but what are they doing here?'

As she spoke, the back door opened and Declan came in. He greeted her politely enough but she saw his eyes dart from Gran to his wife and back again, and read the anxiety there, so she addressed him directly. 'Mr O'Halloran, it's not that I want to argue with you over who owns what, but you will understand that I can't simply let you take what belongs to my grandmother and myself. I realise the state we would be in without you, but you had no right to introduce your relatives on to Hebditch property, and still less right to tell my grandmother that she could cut me out of my inheritance.'

Declan O'Halloran's smile was ingratiating and Maddy was pretty sure that he and his wife had not agreed over the legality of their claim. 'I said you'd not like it; well, who would?' he said softly. 'But I'll come into town with you any time you want, and we'll both read the Deed of Gift, make sure it's legal like. If we really do own Larkspur then we'll continue as we are, except you and your gran must pull your weight. But if we aren't the true owners of house, grounds and acreage, we'll not be stoppin', which will put you in as much bother as if it were all ours.' His grin became downright wicked. 'So it seems to me that us'll win whichever way the truth lies. You'll never manage this place with just your old gran, not even with a couple of them evacuees what's growin' too old for school.' His grin widened. 'I gives you the truth, missie. Which will you choose?'

Maddy gulped. 'I'll come with you to see the deed when I've talked things over with – with friends who know the law . . .'

Mr O'Halloran grinned. 'Any time's fine by me, but you'll find all's in order, you'll see.'

It was clear to Maddy that the O'Hallorans believed they had the upper hand. What could she and Gran do, after all? But some time before she left Yorkshire she would have to see what could be done about Gran's unreliable behaviour. Fancy giving away her granddaughter's birthright as well as her own. Declan seemed positive that all was legal and above board, but Maddy was not so sure and meant to look into things as soon as she could do so.

When she announced that she intended to sleep on a camp bed in Gran's room, however, she was speedily disillusioned. 'There ain't no camp bed to spare; me sister and two of me nieces have come all the way from the south to help out at Larkspur,' Mrs O'Halloran interrupted. 'You'll find there's plenty of bed and breakfast places only too willin' to take you in. We have our main meal around six, and you'll not want to hang around here for all that time when you could be lookin' up old pals. You'll want to tek a look at Windhover Hall, no doubt; no end of soldiers were billeted there but a good few have moved on now. Did you know Mr Thwaite were dead?' She clicked her tongue and pulled a sad face, but Maddy thought there was little sorrow in her sloe-black eyes.

'Yes, I knew,' she said, 'and I don't need a camp bed; I'll sleep on the floor.' Then she turned to Gran. 'But now I might stroll over there, have a word with anyone I know. Didn't you say in one of your letters that Dr Carlton had arranged for you to have a bath chair? I could wheel you to Windhover Hall and back again if you fancy a change of scene?'

Gran brightened. 'Dr Carlton said . . .' she was beginning when Mrs O'Halloran cut across her words.

'Your gran ain't been out of the house for a twelvemonth; it don't do to rush things,' she said decidedly. 'You'd have to take it slow, wrap her in a shawl – it can be nippy even in springtime if you're not used to going out . . .' She pretended to consider. 'Perhaps you should leave it a while till you've had some practice with that there chair.'

Maddy sighed; she could see the sense of this but was secretly sure that Mrs O'Halloran's words were just an excuse to keep her and Gran apart. She looked steadily at the older woman before turning to her grandmother.

'If you've not been using the bath chair then I dare say it could do with a clean and perhaps some air in the tyres and oil on the joints. You stay here with Mrs O'Halloran whilst I go and strip it down.' She turned to the Irish woman. 'And since, whatever you may say, I still regard this as my home I shall invite myself to lunch and to the evening meal; I *do* hope you don't mind.' As she spoke she gave Mrs O'Halloran her most charming smile and was pleased to see the other woman bristle a little, showing clearly that she had never even considered that Maddy might have any claim on the house.

She guessed that, one way or another, she would be discouraged from taking her grandmother anywhere which was out of the O'Hallorans' hearing, and later she was proved right. When she quietly suggested to Gran that she should pop on her coat and hat, saying she would help her into the now sparkling clean bath chair when they were clear of the farmyard, Gran shook a reluctant head. 'Better not; Declan says there's a sharp little wind and my old bones like warmth,' she said. 'You go off to the Hall; did you know it's a military hospital now? I've not seen it myself, of course, but I believe it was a terrible mess, took a whole team of Tommies two or three weeks to get it suitable for wounded men, though they tell me that now you could eat your dinner off the floor. There's them as says it's even cleaner than it was in Mr Thwaite's time. What about that, eh?'

Maddy waved goodbye to Gran and set off, but

halfway towards the gate she remembered something and stopped. 'Where are the geese?' she demanded of Declan, who had just come out of the stables. 'Don't tell me you've gone and sold the whole flock! They were worth any amount of money, because their eggs were huge and always sold for a good price. What's more, you couldn't get better watchdogs if you searched for months. And come to think of it, I didn't see old Snoops when I passed his kennel.'

She had stopped in the middle of the farmyard to cross-question Declan and saw what might have been a slight blush redden his cheeks, though he spoke confidently enough. 'Them geese! Everyone who came to Larkspur got bit or attacked in some way; seems they don't like visitors. So we sold 'em at a market a couple of years back to some feller who liked the look of 'em.' He tilted a defiant chin. 'And how could them possibly be valuable? They was the same as the poultry, only bigger . . .'

Maddy stamped her foot; she knew it was foolish to cry over spilt milk, but there had always been geese at Larkspur and this man had no right to sell them without permission, which she was sure he had done. Moreover, they would not let a stranger approach the house, which had been comforting when she and Gran had been alone there. She turned on Declan, her eyes sparkling with annoyance. 'And what about Snoops? He was a first-rate sheep worker. Don't tell me you've sold him too?'

Declan sniggered; there was no other word for it. 'Sold him to Mr Sutherland; got a tidy sum for *him*,' he said laconically. 'And now you can just stop asking questions and tek yourself off.'

Maddy gave him a look of blazing dislike and turned her shoulder on him, setting off once more towards Windhover Hall. She had always rather liked Declan, certainly had thought him preferable to his wife, but when they had worked together it had always been out of doors, generally in the vegetable garden. Tom had advised her long ago not to be taken in by Declan's occasional friendliness when it suited him to imply they were in league together against what he had called 'them indoors', by which he meant Gran and Mrs O'Halloran. 'He isn't just two-faced, he'll run with the hare and hunt with the hounds, that one will,' Tom had said sagely. 'I dare say he is easier to get along with than his wife, but don't you go trusting him, young Maddy.'

At the time, Maddy had laughed at him. 'Oh, Mr O'Halloran's all right,' she had said airily. 'It's his wife that rules the roost, but me and him get round her sometimes. For instance, Mrs O once wanted us to plant lots of peas, but we took no notice and put in early potatoes instead. Mr O said it was better for the soil, and when she grumbled he just grinned at me and we planted earlies just the same.'

Tom had shrugged. 'Please yourself, but watch him,' he had repeated, suddenly smiling broadly.

'And one of the things I like most is new potatoes, hot from the pan, with a dab or two of butter, so I certainly wouldn't have argued in favour of peas!'

Remembering that long ago conversation, Maddy decided that she would write to Tom, when she had got to the bottom of what was going on here, and tell him that he had been right all along. Dec had proved with every word he had spoken that so far as taking sides was concerned he was lined up with the enemy and would probably lie, cheat and steal for the gold at the end of the rainbow: the farm which had been in her family for centuries. Sighing, Maddy paused on the bank of the beck where she had stood so often with Tom or Alice and gazed into the depths hoping to catch a glimpse of a water baby. She remembered Charles Kingsley's book with warm nostalgia and suddenly remembered that it might well still be in the summer house, in the hiding place they had made for it; would it be stealing to go into the garden and, if the book was still there, to take it? She had a longing suddenly to see once again the pictures which had so enchanted her. And seeing the book would somehow be a link with Tom, and with Alice too.

Maddy began to tread the well-remembered path then stopped, giving herself a shake. Ridiculous, to simply accept the O'Hallorans' word that Larkspur Farm was as good as theirs. Gran had admitted to signing over the property as a Deed of Gift, but judging by the expression on her face she had been trying to intimate to her granddaughter that she had signed under duress. After all, Maddy herself had more than once heard Mrs O'Halloran threatening to leave if Gran made a fuss about something. It was no light matter, when one was as old as Gran, to suddenly find oneself alone in a ramshackle farmhouse, a good two miles from any shops or public transport. She decided that instead of going to the Hall, after looking for the book she would walk into the village and arrange for a taxi to call the very next day to take her and Gran into the town. Once there, they would go to the office where the Deed of Gift was held and explain to the solicitor that for one thing the farm was not Gran's to give and for another she had signed the deed under duress.

Having made up her mind on which course to take, Maddy felt a good deal happier. She had ten days' leave and so far had only used up two of them. By the time she had to return to her battery she felt sure she would have solved the problem, and how she would enjoy the crestfallen looks on the O'Hallorans' faces when they realised she had not been duped. Of course she would have to make some sort of arrangement so that Gran would not be left alone, but for the time being it would be sufficient just to make certain that the Deed of Gift was null and void, as she was sure it must be. Maddy began to hurry, thanking Providence that it seemed likely she and Gran would escape from this horrid tangle without too much difficulty. How right Tom had been. Without her husband's wholehearted approval of her devious plans Mrs O'Halloran would never have dared to walk into a solicitor's office, far less to pay an unnamed sum for his services. Good old Tom! If she had taken his advice years ago the present situation would never have arisen, but at least she and Gran would soon be on the right road.

Maddy went down the path which led first to the summer house and then to the Hall itself. The garden was grievously neglected, with weeds waist high in places, but the summer house must have been used by the patients, for the floor had been swept and the benches too, so it was still a pleasant retreat. Maddy peeped in the window nearest her and, seeing nobody, went to the old hiding place which she and Alice had used for the book. She lifted the loose plank and was disproportionately disappointed to find that the dusty hollow was empty. For a moment she could only stare; she had managed to convince herself, as she had pushed through the multitude of weeds and wild flowers, that neglect alone would have saved the book from discovery, but it was plainly not so. The book had disappeared and with it, Maddy realised, her right, if you could call it that, to be in the summer house. When Alice had been about to be packed off to India, her uncle had told her that she might keep the book, but Maddy was pretty sure that Alice had left the volume hidden for any one of the remaining trio to take possession of, should they so wish.

She pushed the loose plank back into place and headed for the door, which she had shut behind her as she entered the summer house. As she opened it and slipped into the weedy garden, she wondered which of them was now the guardian of young Tom the chimney sweep's adventures. Had Alice changed her mind and decided to pack it in her big cabin trunk? Had Marigold been told about the book and decided to read it for herself? Or had Tom, who had teased her so frequently, actually wanted the book to remind him of home? But Maddy, retracing her steps, told herself that it didn't matter a jot; Mr Kingsley's book had gone.

She reached the beck and turned towards the village. The book is not important, she told herself severely. It was Gran who mattered now.

Chapter Fourteen

Tom was with his unit, brewing up after a long and tiring day. The war in North Africa was over and the troops had been brought back to Europe in order to 'chase the Jerries back to where they belonged' which, Tom presumed, was Berlin. There was constant activity going on overhead as planes both British and American droned towards their target which was also, Tom presumed, Berlin.

Earlier in the evening there had been a pleasant interlude between a lean French farmer and the British soldiers. The farmer, carrying a milk pail in one hand, had approached them cautiously, obviously not sure to which side they belonged. But then he must have recognised their uniform or heard them speaking English, for he had walked towards them with more confidence, smiling shyly, and as soon as he got close enough had broken into voluble French. Tom had grinned at him and begun to speak French himself; reflecting that there had been some point after all to all those language classes he had attended at St Oswald's!

Ricky, who had taken sciences and spoke almost

no French, had grinned at the farmer, demanding in a whisper as he did so that Tom should translate. 'He's telling us that the Boche have stolen everything but his cows, cattle being too heavy to carry. The herd is still productive and he thought we might like to have real milk in our tea.' The farmer had held out his bucket and the men had accepted gratefully, reciprocating by giving him some of the chocolate bars which the American soldiers – who called them candy bars – had insisted their English counterparts should accept.

But now, sitting by a fire upon which bubbled a very large pot of vegetable stew, Tom and Ricky discussed the war as they saw it. 'The maddening thing is that officers order but never explain,' Ricky said restlessly. 'But it was interesting to hear what the doughboys thought of our equipment.' He chuckled. 'Some of 'em just couldn't believe we'd already had five years of war and not been blown off the planet. Why, even their chuck wagons, as they call them, are more up to date than our gharries, and their tanks put ours to shame.'

Tom pulled a wry face. 'Did you see that German Tiger tank parked on the brow of a hill this morning?' he asked. 'For all that it had probably been abandoned there, I got the impression it was actually sneering at us, knowing we couldn't possibly hit it at that range, and not bothering to shell us because we were no threat to its army. I wonder what it's like to fight a war with equipment like that? Interesting, anyway.'

He sighed. 'Is that stew done yet, do you think? Oh Lor', we forgot the spuds. Well, we'll just have to dip the bread in the gravy as usual.'

Ricky grunted and leaned forward to jab his knife into the nearest carrot. 'I think it's cooked,' he said rather doubtfully. 'Is it Oxo gravy again? If so, you can put my bread on hold. I'd rather have it wrapped round some of that cottage cheese we won earlier in the day. All right by you?'

'If it's Oxo gravy I'll do the same,' Tom said, beginning to ladle out the stew, and reflecting as he did so how lucky he and Ricky were to be together. In his army career so far he had made many friends – and lost some, too – but he and Ricky had always managed to stick by each other. In the desert it had been important to have a pal on whom one could rely, as it had been when they had moved on through Tunisia to tackle the Italian campaign.

But now that the war in Europe was also nearing its end, the best thing about having such a friend was the conversation in the quiet hours after whatever meal the supply wagons had managed to deliver. Then one could reminisce about home and family, and discuss whom one most admired amongst the female film stars. Tom talked often of Alice and Marigold, conscious of his good luck in having two such glamorous girlfriends. At one point, whilst he was still in the desert, Marigold had sent him a small crumpled photograph of herself which he had placed in his wallet, carrying it in the top pocket of his shirt and feeling heartbroken when it had disappeared after he had forgotten to hide the wallet before going to sleep one night. 'So much for the brotherhood of man,' he had said resignedly to Ricky. 'I never thought there was anyone mean enough to steal from a feller out here in the sticks. What can they spend the money on anyhow?' Next day, however, he had had to eat his words, for the wallet had been discovered and handed back to him by the finder with the money still intact. He did not discover for several days that the photograph was missing.

He had told Ricky he meant to marry her when the war was over, and his friend had raised unbelieving eyebrows. 'I don't remember the photograph at all, but I'll take your word for it that she's a real dazzler. But what about Alice? Now she's a very pretty girl, and she won't be best pleased if you throw her over.'

Tom had felt guilty and mumbled that he and Alice had never mentioned marriage. 'My trouble is I'm a little bit in love with three girls – well, two really, because Maddy's just a friend – but the only one I had a photo of was Marigold,' he had told his friend, adding rather melodramatically that losing the photo really didn't matter, for the picture of his golden-haired Marigold would live in his heart for ever.

Ricky had given a rude chortle. 'Along with Bette Davis, Mae West and Veronica Lake,' he had said derisively. 'I can see you're in love, but you needn't tell such whoppers. In my opinion no girl could hold a candle to the incomparable Miss Davis.'

But that had been months ago and now, if he was honest, Tom would have to admit that he no longer found it easy to call Marigold's beauty to mind. In fact, again being honest, he really didn't think much about women; he had other subjects on his mind; winning the war, for instance.

'Everyone at home seems to think it's all over,' Ricky said gloomily. He held out his tin plate. 'I don't believe it is Oxo gravy, so give me my share and then we can both get some sleep.'

Next morning, when Tom rolled up his blanket, there was a light wind blowing and a drizzling rain. Breakfast as usual was anything the supply wagons had managed to find and Tom, despite eating his share of the stew the night before, had awoken hungry. With the remainder of the milk that the farmer had given them, and a couple of large cups of oatmeal, he made a sort of porridge which he sweetened with sugar captured from a German unit. 'Who's going to take the wheel first today?' he asked his companion.

Ricky shrugged. Ever since arriving in Europe they had been seconded as lorry drivers, for men were desperately needed to handle the big Bedford trucks of which the army seemed to have a never-ending supply – which was fortunate, for the big vehicles, heavily laden, soon began to develop faults and had to be replaced by other vehicles which had not yet suffered from being driven through rivers, cornfields, copses and other unlikely pathways – and on this particular day Tom and Ricky had been detailed to collect food from one of the depots. They were looking forward to a trip which would not leave them stinking of petrol, or prey to the constant fear that a passing soldier might throw a cigarette stub into their load, thus sending them all to Jericho by the nastiest route of all.

The day started cool and damp, but within half an hour of their setting out on the three-hundred-mile round trip, the sun had come out and they found themselves passing through attractive countryside. Woods, meadows and streams edged the road, cocks crowed and somewhere they could hear the tinkle of sheep bells. Tom wondered where they were. It might be anywhere; unless you knew the language, or recognised the place names, you had no idea through which country you were driving. The men simply drove, only consulting the map upon which their route was already traced when they came to a crossroads or feared they might have missed their way.

'It must be beautiful country in peacetime,' Tom said longingly as the lorry thundered through a little whitewashed village. 'When this lot is over I mean to farm. Someone said we'd be given some sort of resettlement grant to help us back into civvy street, and mine will purchase land, and stock as well if the money will run to it. What about you?'

Ricky grinned. They frequently discussed what they would do when peace came and both young men were apt to change their minds at random, depending upon where they were and what they were doing. 'I've decided at last to go to university and try to get a law degree. I know I said I wanted to join an experimental laboratory, but I've decided I don't fancy the idea after all. So I'll go for law, partly because I believe it's where most money is made and partly because experimentation – any sort – will be connected in the public mind with what German scientists have been doing.' He gave an eloquent shudder. 'You know what I mean.'

Tom nodded. 'And you're going to say I'm wasting the valuable asset of my brilliant mind,' he said gloomily. 'But if you ask me, the universities will be full of older men twitching whenever they hear a motorbike engine, and diving for cover under their desks whenever something backfires. I want to forget all that and concentrate on becoming a normal human being again. And don't say I never was, or I shall be forced to punch you on the nose. And now let's get back to camp, because if you ask me we'll be back on petrol-ferrying tomorrow and I'd like to get a good night's sleep first. Apart from the danger, the smell of the petrol when we're crossing rough country goes straight to my stomach.'

Next day, however, their orders had changed. They were to visit the main distribution depot and stock up with an enormous list of supplies which made Ricky chuckle and remind Tom how they had raided the German store in the desert.

'At least we shan't have to watch for young fools chucking cigarette ends about,' he said. 'And once we're loaded with goodies we'll be able to snitch a fag or two and have ourselves a bit of a break, which we couldn't do if we were ferrying petrol; too dangerous.'

They had a successful trip, and by the time they neared the end of the return journey it was growing dusk. Tom, who was driving, was simply ambling along, feeling at peace with the world. Gentle hills, not unlike the fells of Yorkshire, greeted him as he drove, and they splashed across a ford which might have been the very one they crossed when leaving the Hall in Mr Thwaite's Daimler. As they turned into the next village he slowed down, gazing at the houses and suddenly realising that they were not houses at all, but shells. He slowed a little more.

'It's deserted,' he said, raising his voice to be heard above the truck's engine. 'I wonder what it means when people tie ribbons to the trees? I know it has some significance . . .'

'My God, it's a minefield. That's why the place is deserted,' Ricky shouted suddenly. 'Don't you remember? White ribbons, or skull and crossbones; the whole village is a bloody minefield! Let's get out of here fast. Oh, God, stick to the road! If you go on the verge the chances are . . .'

Tom obeyed, feeling his heart leap in his chest. He thought they had stuck to the main road but now he realised that, distracted by the gentle weather and pleasant countryside, he must have gone astray without noticing. He turned to Ricky, and even as he slowed to go as smoothly as possible there was a tremendous explosion and blackness descended, wiping out the dusky evening, the peaceful countryside, and the pinprick of stars.

Maddy had to wait until she and Gran had gone to their bedroom that night to have a talk, for Mrs O'Halloran's aunts, sisters, nieces and even the occasional nephew seemed to be everywhere, and had clearly already made Larkspur their home. So it was almost midnight before Maddy, who was sharing not only Gran's room but also her big double bed, felt they could safely talk without being overheard. Finally she explained to her grandmother what she intended they should do next day. 'We'll get a taxi to pick us up at ten o'clock and take us into Ripon, right to the very door of the solicitor's office,' she said. 'Then we'll ask to speak to this Mr Tebbit, who you said witnessed your signature on the original document. You must tell him that you only signed your inheritance away because the O'Hallorans threatened you, and you were afraid . . .'

Gran snorted. 'I'm not afraid of the O'Hallorans,' she said boastfully, but Maddy noticed that she said it in a very small voice. 'I'll soon tell them off if they try to bully me.'

Maddy opened her mouth to remind Gran that she had not talked so big down in the kitchen with the O'Halloran family listening, but then closed it again. Pointless to upset the old lady, so she spoke softly. 'I know you're very independent, Gran, and of course you're not frightened of them, but that is not the point of our visiting the solicitor. I want you to rescind the Deed of Gift – that is what you want as well, isn't it, Gran?'

There was an appreciable pause before Gran replied, and when she did so it was with a certain amount of doubt creeping into her voice. 'But Maddy, if I take back the Deed of Gift they'll up and go; the whole perishin' tribe of them. I suppose I could sleep in the parlour rather than try to climb the stairs by myself – it took you all your strength to get me up here tonight, wouldn't you say? – but I'm out of practice with everything but cooking. I doubt I could tackle any of the outside chores like collecting eggs, or feeding the pigs. But of course if *you* were here to do what the O'Hallorans have been doing we might manage. Only the war makes things difficult; all the young men have gone for soldiers, and the old 'uns can pick and choose. Can you leave the army right away?'

Maddy had blown out the candle as soon as she had climbed into bed but now she reared up on her

326

elbow and stared at the lump in the blankets. 'Leave the army?' she said blankly. 'Just like that? Oh, Gran, I wish I *could* just walk out, but I'd be court-martialled. I'm sure if I explained to my commanding officer they'd arrange for me to be given compassionate leave whilst I sort things out here, but I can't possibly desert my whole battery. I'm sure you wouldn't want me to, would you?'

In the stuffy darkness Maddy could not see much, but she guessed that Gran's mouth would have turned down at the corners, and a furrow appeared between her brows. 'Fine talk,' she said jeeringly. 'So your battery comes before your dear old grandmother, does it? Ho, yes, I can see you being glad enough when your commanding officer doesn't give you passionate leave and you find some village idiot to help me cope what'll probably murder me in my bed. It's rather the devil you know than the devil you don't, and Eileen and myself got on fine until you decided to turn up.'

'Oh, but Gran . . .' Maddy began, dismayed by the turn the conversation was taking, but she stopped speaking as Gran suddenly reared up and gripped her arm.

'Did you hear that?' she hissed. 'That'll be the tatty-headed niece; she's in your old room next door and she's got ears like a donkey. Now she'll go and tell Eileen and there'll be hell to pay.'

'I don't see . . .' Maddy began, but Gran snorted and wriggled under the covers once more.

'Let well alone,' the old woman said crossly. 'You go ahead and get that taxi, because I could do with a day away from this damned place, but I won't promise to try to change things, not if it means the O'Hallorans will take themselves off. It 'ud be different if you could swear on the Bible that you'd take their place, but I reckon you can't, can you? And now I'm going to sleep, so you can just shut your gob.'

Maddy sighed, and following Gran's example was very speedily asleep.

When Maddy arrived back at Larkspur in the taxi she had hired, she had a secret fear that Gran might have chickened out and gone back to bed, for Mrs O'Halloran had made it plain at breakfast that she disapproved of their expedition. Gran had said firmly that it was not every day her granddaughter planned a day out for her old gran, but Maddy had placed no reliance on her sticking to her guns once she herself was out of the house. However, when Maddy jumped out of the taxi and ran to the back door, it shot open to reveal Mr and Mrs O'Halloran, wreathed in smiles. They had already got Gran into her coat and hat, and now they helped her tenderly across the yard and into the waiting vehicle. Maddy half expected that one of them would try to get into the taxi as well, but this was not the case.

'You enjoy your outing, my dear,' Mrs O'Halloran said, giving Gran a kiss on the cheek. She turned to

Maddy. 'There's rabbit pie and maybe even a few fried taters for supper,' she announced. 'I'll serve up around six. Can you be back by then?'

'Oh, sure to be,' Maddy said airily, wondering just what had been said whilst she was out of the way.

After putting the old bath chair in the boot and strapping it in place, Mr Gray, the taxi driver, told Maddy that it would be cheaper if she took the bus from the village to the town, but Maddy shook her head.

'I want my gran to have a proper little holiday and not to have to worry about bus times,' she said. 'We'll have our lunch at the Court House Café, and a cup of tea and a bun at Betty's before leaving. If you wouldn't mind picking us up say at five o'clock, we'll be home in time for rabbit pie and a nice big mug of tea.'

'Right,' Mr Gray said breezily. He turned his head to wink at Gran. 'I've not seen thee outdoors for heaven knows how long, Mrs Hebditch; 'appen that'll be a nice change for you.'

When they reached the town square Mr Gray unstrapped the bath chair and helped Gran into it. Then he drove off, promising to pick them up at the same place at five o'clock, and Maddy smiled at her grandmother. 'Lead me to the solicitors,' she said gaily. 'We'll soon have that Deed of Gift rescinded and then we can get on with our lives. After all, we don't have to tell the O'Hallorans what we've done, so they won't be any the wiser. And as soon as we've finished our little bit of business we can take a look at the shops.'

'Oh, is that your plan?' Gran said disagreeably. 'You're as devious as the O'Hallorans, in your own way. As I recall, the lawyer's office is in that old building over there, the one with the green painted door and a brass plate on the side. Good thing it's on the ground floor.' She chuckled unkindly. 'I'd like to see you carting this bath chair up a staircase.'

As they crossed the square and opened the green painted door, a question occurred to Maddy. 'When you signed the Deed of Gift you must have come into town to do so. Did you come by taxi? Only Mr Gray would have said, and he's the only one I know of.'

'Then you don't know everyone, or everything,' Gran said derisively. 'Mr Tebbit came to Larkspur, if it's any of your business, but I know his offices from way back. Your grandfather said he was the best solicitor in town, and so I told the O'Hallorans when they asked if I knew one.'

'Oh, the Hebditches only deal with the best,' Maddy said breezily, pushing the bath chair along a short corridor into what was probably the reception area, though it was just a small and dusty room with a desk bearing an elderly typewriter upon which an even more elderly female was typing.

Here Gran hesitated, so Maddy stated their business in a firm voice. 'We've come about a Deed of Gift which was drawn up by one of your partners

330

and needs an alteration,' she said. 'Is it possible to see Mr Tebbit?'

The woman looked doubtful. Maddy thought she must be in her late sixties, judging by her old-fashioned tweed skirt, starched purple blouse and sensible brogues. 'I'll have a word with someone, if you'll wait a moment,' she said, pulling a notebook towards her. 'Name? And your business?'

Maddy gave both her own name and Gran's, and repeated that they had come about a Deed of Gift. The woman disappeared through a door at the back of the room, which opened again to reveal a small and harassed man wearing steel-rimmed spectacles and a navy suit, shiny with age, who beckoned Maddy and Gran into his office.

Maddy had thought it would be a simple matter, but it turned out to be anything but. The little man, who said his name was Arnold, explained that Mr Tebbit had been called up late in the war and he himself had been brought out of retirement because everything was in a bit of a muddle, but he would see what he could do. Naturally, he had not had time to check the files, but he could tell them in general terms that Gran could only rescind the agreement if the recipient was also present. This rocked Maddy back on her heels, and when she asked if they might have a copy of the Deed when he found it the little man pushed the small spectacles further down his nose and looked at her over the top of them. It was not a happy look. 'I'm afraid Mr O'Halloran would still need to be present . . .'

Maddy stared at her grandmother and was just in time to see a little self-satisfied smile cross that lady's face before Gran had wiped it free from any expression. 'Gran? Did you know that Declan would need to be present?' Maddy asked, and could have shaken her grandmother when she replied tranquilly: 'Well, I didn't know, but maybe I suspected. Not that it makes any difference, because I've been thinking, and I don't mean to rescind it. I gave my word that the O'Hallorans should have Larkspur, provided they kept me in good health. Should I fall ill and there be any question that my health had been jeopardised by any member of the family, then the Deed would be null and void anyway.'

'But Gran, we discussed all this last night and I told you that Larkspur is not your property to dispose of at will; it's mine as well, my very own home, and I explained that as soon as the war was over I would be coming back to look after you myself. Don't you see? I remember you telling me once that you came from a long-lived family. I've no idea how old you are, but I've sometimes thought you aren't as old as you pretend. All sorts of things could happen; things which could leave me having to work for the O'Hallorans, if indeed they would employ me! Oh, Gran, can't you see what you've done? If only you'll let me re-draft the Deed . . .'

But her grandmother only tightened her lips. 'I won't have you drive Eileen and Declan away,' she said. 'Maybe they've been good to me for their own ends; but they were there when I needed them. And now let's go and look at the shops; you promised, you know you did!'

This time it was Maddy's turn to tighten her lips. 'All right, I did promise, and we shall visit the shops, but that doesn't mean to say that I admire the way you've behaved,' she said. 'And if you think that's the end of it, you're very much mistaken, because we must arrange a meeting in this office . . .' here Maddy tapped the desk, 'where we can all see the Deed of Gift and discuss my own claim. That's right, isn't it, Mr Arnold?'

The little man nodded nervously. 'You can make an appointment with the secretary in the outer office,' he said, 'at any time which is convenient for all parties, of course.'

As they left the office, Maddy turned to Gran. 'Don't you see? After you die my inheritance will belong to the O'Hallorans. You can make a will leaving it to me, but as long as the Deed of Gift is in place I shall have no legal claim, any more than you have. Larkspur Farm has been in the Hebditch family for over three hundred years, and you've given it away to strangers!'

Tom awoke to darkness and intolerable pain. He could hear someone groaning. Where was he?

Who was he? He turned his head a fraction and felt something touch his cheek for an instant. A pillow? Desert sand? He did not know, could only guess. If only the groaning would stop! He wanted to call out, to ask the other fellow what was the matter, but his lips seemed sealed in some mysterious way, and the blackness was frightening. Desperately, Tom fought to move his head, but it was heavy as lead and could only move an inch or so, and even the slightest movement brought the pain ripping through him, so he stopped trying. They had captured him, he was imprisoned in his own body . . . oh, God, who *was* he? It was not until he stopped attempting to move that he realised the groans were coming from him.

At that, another consideration, even more bizarre, rose through the muddled sea of turbulence which was his mind. I'm the only survivor, the only person left in the whole world of war, he thought. And I'm blind and paralysed, so what is the point of crying out except that everyone wants to be in contact with another human being? But if I'm the only person left alive, even if I could scream as loud as a train whistle no one would come. He made one more effort to force a sound from between parched dry lips. A tiny croak was the only result, but suddenly he had the impression that there was a way out of his nightmare. If he could just remember the magic, then he might at least know who and where he was. Pictures flashed before his inner eye – places he had been, people he had known – and even this little glimpse of his one-time reality cheered him immensely. There might be no life in this terrible place of darkness and fear, but there had been life once, proper life, the sort that one wanted to return to. If he could only concentrate, force the darkness back . . . but for now, at any rate, darkness reigned.

Tom woke again, or at least he thought he did. He was still in darkness and even the slightest attempt at movement sent the excruciating pain knifing through him, but if he hung on grimly to what passed as his consciousness he could begin to make sense of things, even as he slipped down once again into the dark pit. His name was Tom! He could not remember his surname, but at least he knew he was Tom. Desperately, he tried to stop himself sliding back into the darkness and fear from which, it seemed, he had managed to escape, if only for a short period. What was I when I was alive, he asked himself desperately, knowing it was an unanswerable question, yet putting it to himself all the same. What was Tom?

Just as he gave up and let go and swam back into the darkness, an answer popped into his head. I'm a chimney sweep! That's why I can only see black. I'm not blind or paralysed, I'm just stuck in a chimney, waiting to be rescued by – by someone who loves me, loves me enough to come up the chimney and guide me back down into the real world. I hope my rescuer comes soon, but at least I know where I am.

335

Once more he tried to move his head, and this time, staring upwards, he thought he saw, high above him, a pinprick of light; a light so brilliant that he had to close his eyes. Closing them, he fell into the darkness once more, but this time hope flowered within him. He was *not* alone. Someone knew he was trapped in this chimney, unable to move without triggering the pain, so help would come eventually. When he felt stronger, he would try once again to cry out so that they knew where to look when they came to bring him back into the light.

This time he registered that the worst pain was in his left leg, up his left side and into his left arm. Vaguely, he thought that this side of him must have snagged on something in the chimney, which was why he could not change his position without awakening the snarling beast of pain. Keep still, his mind told him. Don't make things worse for yourself. Wait for rescue with all the patience you possess and it will come.

And even as he forced himself to relax, willing his mind to recall pleasant interludes, he heard a voice. It was a small, steady voice and one he recognised, though he could not, for the moment, say whose voice it was. He listened eagerly, but it seemed to be in the far distance, though it was rapidly growing closer. Then he could hear it; hear it distinctly what was more, and understand its message. '. . . only me; I've come to see you and tell you that you'll soon be well. Can you hear me?'

Tom tried to nod, but even that slight movement broke the thread which joined him to the voice, which grew smaller and smaller until he could hear it no longer. But its message was clear: the owner of the voice would help him out of the chimney, would understand his fears, would be on hand to comfort him.

Slowly Tom relaxed once more, and suddenly he knew that he was not stuck in a chimney, though he still had no idea where he was. Oddly enough, it no longer seemed to matter. Help was at hand. Presently, he slept.

Maddy and Gran returned from their visit to the town in very different frames of mind. Gran chatted about the purchases she had made, the light lunch she had enjoyed, the tea and toasted crumpets at the smartest café in Ripon, and the plans she was making to persuade Mr Gray to pick her up next week and take her on another shopping spree. 'I need a light little jacket now that spring's arrived. I've got my clothing coupons and enough money to get something pretty. So you can wheel me into the village and Mr Gray can take us to town. Ripon market's bigger than the village one, so I'm sure I'll find something there.' She sighed happily. 'I fancy a nice soft pink; the colour they used to call "Baby's Blush". Older people should always wear pastel shades, don't you agree?'

'If you like,' Maddy snapped. Gran might have had a lovely day, but having failed to so much as see the Deed of Gift which dispossessed her, Maddy had felt distinctly peevish. However, as the day had worn on, she had begun to realise how it must have irked Gran to be confined to Larkspur for so long, and she decided she was being downright mean to spoil Gran's day out by quibbles. So, after their lunch at the Court House Café, she had thrown herself into Gran's plans with as much enthusiasm as she could muster, and by the time five o'clock came they were once more on the best of terms. 'Only you mustn't try to stop me examining the Deed of Gift to see if there's any way out,' Maddy had told her aged relative. 'Any day now Mr Churchill is going to declare Victory in Europe Day and when that happens the boys will all be coming home – and the girls too, of course – although no one will be able to leave the army until they get demobbed. But that's a matter of weeks now rather than months.'

At this point the taxi had drawn up alongside them, so Maddy was able to ignore Gran's grumbles whilst she helped Mr Gray to heave the bath chair into the boot and secure it with straps. Only when they were once more heading for Larkspur did the topic of the war come up again. 'Hast thou heard the news, ladies?' Mr Gray said, as they left the town behind them. 'Likely your leave will be extended, petal, to take in this VE Day what Mr Churchill's talking

338

about. Fellers is having bets on it in the Black Bull, but I reckon tha's as good as out of uniform already.'

Before Maddy could answer Gran put her oar in. 'Don't you go encouraging young Maddy here to say she'll be out of the army as soon as all that,' Gran said warningly. 'It's all very well for her to talk big about this here passionate leave, but I've yet to see a sign of it. Why, if Mr Churchill himself popped into Larkspur and said my granddaughter would be moving back to the farm in two or three weeks, I'd need his written promise before I would believe him. When they started towing the Mulberry harbours across the Channel to invade Normandy they said the war would be over in no time, yet here we are, nearly a year later, and still there's only *talk* of peace. No, I want facts, not fairy stories!'

Mr Gray, who knew when he had met his match, slowed down behind a huge army lorry. 'At any rate, it'll be gradely when all these troop movements are over,' he said pacifically. 'But has thou visited Windhover Hall since it became a hospital? The fellers there are rare bad cases; made me sick to my stomach to see 'em, poor devils.'

'What made you go to Windhover Hall?' Maddy broke in quickly. She felt she had 'supped full with horrors' and did not particularly want to hear any more, but she thought that Mr Gray's observations would be easier to bear than further grumbles from Gran.

'Me and the missus belong to a choir what goes

339

round hospitals and convalescent homes and the like,' he explained. 'We entertain the patients, as they say, and there's nowt that cheers 'em up like a nice sing-song. We give 'em all the old favourites – "Greensleeves", "Danny Boy", "The Skye Boat Song" – and it helps 'em to show emotion and say it were caused by the music.' He turned in his seat to look again at Maddy. 'There were a feller in, when we last visited, what you might know. Remember the chauffeur's son from the Hall? Browning was the name. Seems he drove over a landmine . . . but there, I dare say you already knew, seeing as how you was friendly with Miss Alice . . .'

Maddy was literally struck dumb. She could only gaze at Mr Gray whilst she went cold with shock and horror. For a moment speech was beyond her, but fortunately Gran chipped in. 'Well, fancy that! I remember young Tom coming to Larkspur at the beginning of the war to tell Maddy that he had barkation leave, but she wasn't here, so she missed him. Not that it mattered,' she added, with unconscious cruelty. 'He wasn't one of her boyfriends, or anything like that, just a pal, you know. I believe he was sweet on young Alice, or that blonde gal with bright blue eyes. Well, whichever it was, it wasn't on Maddy. She was still practically a schoolgirl, weren't you, dear?'

Maddy forced herself to give a weak smile, and then she caught Gran's eye and felt a rush of affection.

Gran understood! It wasn't in her nature to show it, but the very speed with which she had picked up on Maddy's shock proved to her granddaughter, for the first time, that there was more between them than mild family feeling.

But Gran had asked a question and it was her duty to answer it, however feebly. 'That's right,' she managed. Mr Gray had turned back and was grumbling about the army lorry, which was not giving him a chance to overtake. In a fever of impatience, Maddy waited until he had squeezed past and then broke into urgent speech. 'Mr Gray, was Tom – was he very badly wounded? I didn't even know he was in England! But as Gran said, we were good pals. Would I be allowed to visit him, do you think?'

At this point they reached the gate and Mr Gray got out of the car, opened the boot and began to unstrap the bath chair. 'You'd have to ask Matron, but I don't see why not,' he said. He looked at her curiously. 'I'm sorry to give you bad news, Miss Hebditch, and I can't tell you much; we've not been to Windhover for a while. But I'm sure a visit from you would cheer him up.' He stood the bath chair down and went to help Gran out of the car. Maddy had paid him in advance, but when he would have climbed into the driving seat again, she caught his arm.

'I'm sorry,' she said, trying to keep her voice from trembling, 'but I think you said something about a mine . . .'

'That's what I heard,' Mr Gray said uneasily. 'But you go ahead and visit; likely I've got it all wrong. As I said, we've not been to the Hall for a while. He may have been discharged to a convalescent home by now.'

'Yes, I'm sure that's possible,' Maddy said through dry lips. She did not mention the grim spectre which Mr Gray's news had raised in her mind: that Tom might have died of his wounds. Instead, she scolded herself for unnecessary worries; if Tom had died she would have surely known! So she waved goodbye to Mr Gray and then returned the bath chair to its place in the stables. Only when it was safely stowed did she turn towards the back door.

Chapter Fifteen

When they entered the kitchen they found Mrs O'Halloran putting potatoes into a large black pan on the stove. She bustled over to them, proffering cups of tea and reminding them that supper would be served in half an hour. 'Good,' Gran said succinctly. 'But my granddaughter may be a little late. She's off to visit an old friend.'

Mrs O'Halloran had been beaming, obviously very pleased with herself for some reason, but at these words an angry flush stained her cheeks. 'Did that there lawyer show you the Deed?' she demanded. 'If so, he had no right. We was told no one could see it without us being there.' She glared at Maddy. 'I knew you was trouble the moment I set eyes on you,' she said spitefully. 'You'd like to do us out of what's ours by right, but you can't. We've been good to your gran; we've worked like slaves and brung our relatives to work as well. Not a word of complaint have we heard from your gran, or anyone else for that matter, until you turned up. Did you honestly think we'd do all that for nothin'?' She laughed. 'You must have thought we were fools,' she added harshly.

But Maddy was already letting herself out of the house. 'It doesn't matter. Don't wait supper for me, I may be some time,' she said. 'You all right, Gran?'

Gran was tired and began to say so, but the slam of the door cut across her grumbles. Indeed, Maddy was running even as her feet touched the farmyard cobbles, so that she was entering the big tiled hallway at Windhover Hall scarcely twenty minutes after arriving back from Ripon. It was strange to find herself in once familiar surroundings that had changed completely. The rooms had been given names and numbers, and all the rugs and pictures had gone.

An elderly woman in a white overall was sitting behind a reception desk, and when Maddy entered she looked up and smiled. 'Good evening! You're a little early for visiting, but since I can see you are a member of the forces I expect we can stretch the rules,' she said. 'Who have you come to see?'

'Lieutenant Browning – Tom Browning,' Maddy said breathlessly. 'Is he – is he still here?'

The woman got to her feet. 'I'll take you to Matron. Yes, he's still here,' she said, crossing the floor and beckoning to Maddy to follow her. 'I understand he's a local lad; are you a relative?'

Maddy was tempted to reply that she was indeed, but her treacherous tongue refused to lie, even in a good cause. 'No, but I'm an old friend; I've known him for years,' she explained. 'I believe his father is abroad, and so far as I know Tom – Lieutenant Browning, I mean – has no other relatives.'

They had reached a door bearing a plaque announcing that this was Matron's office, and Maddy's companion knocked and entered, Maddy following close on her heels. The room had once been the breakfast parlour, but now the walls were shelved and the shelving was full of box files, and behind a large desk sat an enormous woman whose navy dress and white apron would have told Maddy that this was the matron even had she not worn a badge proclaiming the fact. She had been writing on a large sheet of paper when the pair had entered the office, but now she laid her pen down on a pad of pink blotting paper and said, 'Yes?'

The receptionist cleared her throat and began to speak, but Maddy broke in before she'd uttered more than a few words. 'I've come to visit Lieutenant Tom Browning; I'm an old friend,' she said briefly. 'I'm only here for the duration of my leave and it's essential that I see him before I go back.'

The big woman bent down and extracted a slim file from a desk drawer. She perused it for a moment in silence and then spoke. 'You're an old friend, you say – not a relative?'

'No. What happened to Tom? I heard from someone in the village that he drove over a landmine, but perhaps you can tell me a little more.'

Matron indicated that Maddy should sit down in

the chair opposite her. 'Lieutenant Browning received various injuries, some of which were severe,' she said. 'His left leg and arm were extensively damaged.' She looked very hard at Maddy. 'However, his wounds are healing nicely. What worries us is that he was concussed, and though he's been with us for several weeks he has still not gained consciousness. In fact, Miss er . . .'

'Corporal Madeleine Hebditch,' Maddy said quickly. 'Is it normal for someone to remain unconscious for so long?'

'No,' Matron said frankly. 'And that is why I think you may be able to help us, Miss Hebditch. Usually a parent or a sibling would be asked to come in and talk to Lieutenant Browning, but it seems he's not a local boy by birth and has only lived in the area for a few years.' She looked doubtfully at Maddy. 'Do you think there is a chance that you might be able to get through to him? It may take some while, however, and if you're only here for the duration of your leave . . .'

'I've got ten days,' Maddy said, completely forgetting that she'd already used up three of them. 'But I'm sure there are other people who could help as well, people who knew Tom and would be glad to come in and talk to him. One of his old girlfriends, for instance.'

Matron brightened. 'An old girlfriend! That would be ideal. But can you contact them?'

'Yes!' Maddy said excitedly, then drooped a little. 'Oh, but I was forgetting; one of them is a nurse with the Queen Alexandra's RANC and she's abroad at present, and although I know that his other friend, Marigold Stein, would come like a shot if she knew Tom needed her, she's miles away too, in Scotland . . .' She saw the expression on Matron's face, and for the first time since she had heard of Tom's injuries she gave a little smile. 'Don't look like that, Matron – he wasn't a sailor with a girl in every port. It's just that the four of us, Tom, Alice, Marigold and me, were close friends before the war, and we've kept in touch with each other.'

Matron smiled. 'And very nice too – it's good to hear that there are some things the war hasn't torn apart. Now, come with me, and I'll take you to him. Don't be alarmed by the way he looks – I'm sure your visit will do him good, even if you don't see any change.'

As they arrived on Tom's ward and stopped by Tom's bed, Matron put out an enormous hand and shook Maddy's heartily. 'Sit on the stool by his bed and speak softly to him,' she advised. 'Don't go on for too long, though, because we mustn't tire him, but try to think of nice things which happened to him before the war. We find concussed patients respond best when listening to talk about their childhood, and no doubt you will remember good times when you and he were just best pals. Come to my office before you

347

go home and I'll give you a pass so that you can visit him whenever you're able to do so.'

Standing by the bedside, Maddy looked around, seeking for something – a photograph, a card, a letter – which would link the man in the bed with the Tom she knew. But the room was completely anonymous, and indeed the waxy face on the pillow might have belonged to almost anyone, for all that was Tom, she thought, was waiting, scarcely alive, for something to happen. It occurred to her then that this was like the story of Sleeping Beauty, except that the prince, who should have woken the princess with a kiss, was waiting for his princess to kiss *him* awake. But which princess? He had been in love with Marigold, but he intended to marry Alice, and she herself . . .

But she found that in this desperate situation it simply did not matter who awoke the prince, provided that someone did. And at least I can help him by bringing back good memories, she told herself, settling on the hard wooden stool that Matron had pointed out. She took his hand and squeezed it, but his fingers remained flaccid in her own. Sighing, she settled down for a long wait, and it was only then that she began to examine the patient. His left arm was in a sling, which seemed to Maddy altogether needless since he made no effort to move it. There was a dressing on his head, the bandaging no paler than the face beneath. She let her eyes stray further and noticed for the first time that there was a hump in the blankets, presumably caused

348

by some sort of device to hold the bedding away from the worst of his injuries. Matron had said something about his left leg . . .

But she had been given a job to do and she was not doing it. Maddy squared her shoulders and began to talk, keeping her voice low and steady. 'It's all right, Tom, it's only me; I've come to see you and tell you that you'll soon be well. Can you hear me?'

There was no sign that he had heard, yet somehow Maddy sensed a change in the atmosphere, a lightening of the mood. She leaned closer to the still figure in the bed. 'Tom, are you listening? Do you remember how we used to watch for water babies? Oh, I know you never believed we'd see one, but you were so kind, Tom; you never made me feel like a silly kid, though I know I sometimes behaved like one.' She chuckled beneath her breath. 'Oh, Tom, we didn't realise how lucky we were to have the beck and the dales as our playground! If only we were up on the fells now! But once the war is over . . . Tom, I'm sure your eyelids flickered then! Dear Tom, I only want to help you, that's all I ever wanted. Please come back to us!'

Later, when Maddy went into Matron's office to collect the promised pass, she noticed a book in a brown paper cover lying on the desk. She did not know what made her reach for it, but as soon as she touched the cover her fingers tingled and when she flicked the volume open it was no surprise to discover that it was the very copy of *The Water Babies* which Alice's uncle John had given them. She must have gasped, for Matron, handing over the pass, raised her eyebrows.

'Yes, Nurse – I mean Corporal?' Matron corrected herself. 'Is there anything wrong with the pass? You can show it to your superior officer . . .' she smiled, 'and perhaps it may soften his cold heart!'

She laughed, and Maddy smiled too. 'No, it's just the book, *The Water Babies*. Tom and us girls always wanted to look for Vendale, the place where Mr Kingsley saw the water babies,' she explained. 'Where did you find the book, Matron?'

'I didn't; it was handed in by one of the convalescent patients. I think he said it was in the summer house and it's such a fine copy – a first edition, you know – that I told him to give it a brown paper cover and leave it in the room which used to be the library. But if it's yours, my dear, you can take it away with you.' A bright idea seemed to strike her. 'Next time you come perhaps you could read extracts to young Lieutenant Browning. Anything which might get through to him can only be good, and if he remembers these illustrations that would be good too.' A bell rang somewhere and Matron, who had taken the book from Maddy and flicked through it as they spoke, thrust it back into her hands. 'Off with you now. I'm sure we shall meet again.'

Tom heard the Voice reminding him of the good times. But even though he longed to answer, to tell the speaker that her words were indeed pulling him back to the real world, he could not do so. However, he was sure that the time would come when he could respond. Once, when she mentioned a bottomless pool, he felt convinced that if he let the memories wash around him at their own pace, the girl with the small and steady voice would rescue him from whatever gripped him in both mind and body.

He slept.

'Marigold? It's Maddy. Can you get leave and come home? It's important, or I wouldn't ask.'

'What? Who *is* that?' Marigold's voice was tiny with distance and the crackling of the bad line did not help, but Maddy, sighing with exasperation, thought she would have known it anywhere, even if her friend didn't recognise hers.

'Oh, don't be so daft, Marigold, pretending you don't know who I am,' she shouted into the receiver. 'It's Maddy – remember me? – and I'm ringing to tell you that Tom's in hospital. He was badly wounded some weeks ago and is still suffering from concussion. Matron said that if I could contact an old girlfriend, someone he really, really liked, then her voice might penetrate the sort of fog he's in. I know Tom was very fond of you – and of Alice, of course, but she's abroad still – so I'm asking you to come home.'

There was an appreciable pause before Marigold

answered. 'Well, I could ask for compassionate leave, I suppose,' she said slowly. 'But are you sure Tom still likes me? He hasn't written for ages, and to tell the truth, Maddy, that Spitfire pilot I told you about is getting serious. In fact—'

Maddy cut in impatiently. 'Are you telling me you like some Brylcreem boy more than you like our Tom? And letters go astray all the time, as you should know. Don't you want to help him? I should have thought . . .'

'Oh, of course, if it's a question of helping Tom, naturally I'll come like a shot,' Marigold said quickly. 'But are you sure he'll want me? As I said, I have a shrewd suspicion that he's forgotten about me. But if you honestly think I can help . . .'

'I do, I do,' Maddy said. 'Please come, Marigold. Let me know when and I'll arrange for a taxi to meet your train and you can be here in no time.'

Marigold heaved a sigh, and even over a bad line Maddy thought she could hear her friend's exasperation. 'Where are you ringing from?' she asked. 'I'll see my CO and get the necessary permission and all that, and I expect I'll be with you in a few days' time.'

'A few days?' Maddy squeaked. 'Can't you make it sooner than that? What about this Spitfire pilot of yours? I remember you telling me he had a little sports car. Couldn't you persuade him to bring you down?'

There was another noticeable pause before

Marigold spoke again. 'I'll have a word,' she said grudgingly. 'Where are you speaking from?'

'Didn't I say? I'm at Windhover Hall – I'm sure you know that it's now a military hospital,' Maddy said quickly. 'I'll be here all afternoon, but I have to go back to Larkspur at around six o'clock. Do you remember my gran and the O'Hallorans? There's been a bit of trouble, but I won't go into it now. If you can find out how you're travelling and what the arrangements will be, you can ring this number and even if I'm not here you can explain who you are and why you are telephoning, OK?'

'Yes that sounds pretty reasonable. I can find out in a couple of hours, maybe less, whether I can get leave,' Marigold said. 'It'd be grand to see you again after so long, Maddy, and grand to see Tom too, of course. Is he badly wounded? Poor Tom – I hate to think of him chained to a hospital bed.'

'He's getting better,' Maddy said quickly, for she had heard the dismay in Marigold's voice and was glad that her old friend, if no longer in love with Tom, at least still wanted to help him. 'Thank you ever so much, Marigold; I look forward to hearing your plans. T.t.f.n.'

Once Tom knew who he was and more or less where – not trapped in a chimney – the fear which had consumed him gradually faded and a vague curiosity awoke. He knew, now, that the Voice went away at certain times and came back at certain times, too. That was reassuring. He would not be abandoned to the dark, and quite possibly he would wake up one day and open his eyes and see the owner of the Voice, the one who came to his bedside and spoke so kindly.

Then the Voice came to him with excitement ringing in every word. 'I rang Marigold and she's coming!' the Voice said. 'Marigold's coming all the way from Scotland, just to see you. Are you glad, Tom? Will seeing Marigold make you well again? Only my leave is up in a couple of days – I'd love to stay with you, but it's impossible. But Marigold will be here, and I'm sure if you'll come back for anyone it will be Marigold.'

He forced his mind to remember. There *had* been a girl called Marigold, a brightly coloured girl with – with blonde hair and a loud voice! Yes, a girl just like the flower she had been named after . . . but why did the Voice so constantly repeat the name? He wished he could make sense of what the Voice said, but when he murmured 'Marigold?' the Voice began to talk about caves, and kisses; about books and pictures and water babies and other things which he could not now recall. It was all too difficult, and he was *so* tired. Tom slept.

Maddy did not hear back from Marigold, but she knew how good her friend had always been at getting her own way so was not surprised, two days after the telephone call, to hear someone coming along the corridor with swift, impatient steps. Then the door at the end of the ward was flung open by a careless hand, and she saw her old friend hesitating in the doorway.

Maddy had been reading aloud from *The Water Babies* but she put the book hastily aside as Marigold clattered noisily up the room and cast herself on the still figure in the bed. 'Tom, darling!' she squeaked, and Maddy reflected, only a little bitterly, that she might have known how it would be. Marigold had never been one to consider other people's feelings, and the fact that Tom was a sick man who needed rest and quiet had clearly not entered her beautiful blonde head. Maddy half expected Tom to shoot up into a sitting position, or at least to open his eyes, but he remained as still as a stone statue.

'Oh, Marigold, I knew you'd come,' Maddy said, vacating the stool so that her friend might sit down. 'I'm sure you'll do Tom a power of good, only we've been told to talk quietly and not to excite him, so if you don't mind . . .'

'Darling!' Marigold squeaked again. 'I'm so sorry!' she giggled. 'I'm afraid I don't always think . . . oh, poor darling Tom! Someone said he'd lost a leg – I do hope it wasn't true . . .'

'Hush!' Maddy said, giving the other girl a reproving glare. 'We're not sure if he knows himself, so we don't talk about it; it's best to talk about happy times, Matron says, and to make sure he isn't distressed.'

'Oh! Sorry,' Marigold said contritely. 'I didn't think. You know me, Maddy: I always have the best of intentions . . .'

She flung herself once more on the still figure in the bed and Maddy, stepping forward to prevent her, stopped in her tracks when she saw Tom's arms go gropingly round that slender body. 'Mar . . . Marigold?' he murmured: in a sleep-blurred voice.

Maddy, still standing at the head of the bed, delight and envy filling her in equal measure, could have kicked herself. She had been so careful, hardly daring to touch him in case she did harm, and now she had lost her chance. Tom's first conscious contact might have been with her, but she had not had the courage to do more than hold his hand. Marigold, with all her usual ebullience, had not hesitated to sweep him into her arms, and undoubtedly it would be this fond embrace which Tom would remember for the rest of his life.

It could have been me, Maddy thought regretfully as Marigold planted an impetuous kiss on Tom's pale forehead. Another thought occurred to her. Marigold had already admitted that her Spitfire pilot was serious, and serious, to Marigold, would undoubtedly mean marriage. Fond though she was of her friend, Maddy had known for ages that when Marigold married it would be to her own advantage; Marigold herself had said so many times in her letters. And if that were true, though she had come to Tom's bedside when he needed her, Marigold would not dream of marrying anyone other than her very rich young man.

Marigold had managed to get permission for ten days' leave, but she did not intend to remain in the Yorkshire Dales. When the girls had told Matron that Tom had shown signs of returning consciousness, Marigold had confided to Maddy that she would be leaving that very evening. 'Tom's better, so there's no need for me to stay. I might as well tell you – Ralph and I are engaged, and he's picking me up from my mother's tonight to take me to meet his parents. I know you think Tom's in love with me, but I expect he'll marry Alice – she's a funny girl Alice, but I'm sure she'll make him an adequate wife.'

'Adequate!' Maddy squeaked. 'What sort of a foundation is *adequate* for married life?'

Marigold laughed. 'Just a figure of speech,' she said airily. 'Tell Tom cheerio from me; sorry I can't stay longer.'

Maddy looked at her friend and knew it was no good even suggesting that Marigold might stay. Probably Marigold was right anyway; Tom did not need her. 'Give your mother my regards then,' Maddy said as they parted in the lane. 'And don't forget to invite Tom and me to your wedding!'

Maddy had told Marigold, truthfully, that her leave was almost at an end, but she had not admitted that she would be leaving herself the very next day. What was the point, after all? She knew it was her duty, as soon as Tom was well enough, to tell him that Marigold was going to marry her Spitfire pilot, but there was no point in doing so whilst he was still so muddled. Indeed, he did not even know, as yet, that his best friend had been killed by the explosion which had maimed Tom himself. And since Maddy did not intend to show any undue emotion when they parted, she had arranged with Matron that she would go to the hospital just before catching the train which would take her on the first stage of the journey back to her battery.

She had intended to make her leave-taking light-hearted but found, as she approached the small private room in which Tom now lay, that her heart was fluttering and she felt sick. Idiot woman, she scolded herself as she eased open the door; it's not as if Tom is going to be far away. As soon as she was free to come back to the dales, she and Tom could resume their old friendship. He did not know that Marigold had fallen out of love with him, and in her heart of hearts Maddy thought that he had never really intended to marry Alice. It has merely been that the rich and easy life she represented must have seemed, to one fighting for his life in the hostile desert, like a glimpse of paradise. So now she crossed the room quietly, sat down on the stool beside the bed and took his hand.

'Tom? Can you hear me?' She waited until she felt

a slight tightening of his fingers on hers and then continued, trying to keep her voice steady. 'Tom, I've come to say goodbye. My leave is up so I have to return to my battery, and I shan't be in the first batch to be demobbed because that privilege goes to married women with children. It's fair enough, since they have suffered the double deprivation of being without husbands and families whilst hostilities continued. Oh, Tom, you're on the road to recovery now and will soon be your old self. Why, I dare say you'll be demobbed before me, but I promise I'll come back to the dales to see you just as soon as I can. Can I give you a quick farewell kiss without you thinking I'm taking liberties?'

He mumbled something and his hand clutched hers convulsively. Maddy bent over the bed and kissed his cheek lightly, then gasped as his arms came round her, and gently pulled her close. It was a loving embrace, and to her astonishment he began to speak, his voice cracked from disuse. 'Always loved you,' he was saying, 'always loved you, Marigold. Come back to me. Oh, Marigold . . .'

Making her way down to the station Maddy let the tears fall down her cheeks unchecked, her mind in a whirl. He had spoken, had hugged her and even kissed her cheek, but he had done so believing her to be Marigold. The pain was tangible, and yet against all the odds happiness had flooded through her. She did not believe for one moment that Marigold loved Tom; nor, in her heart, did she believe that Tom loved Marigold. All she had to do was bide her time and do everything she could to aid her old friend's recovery. She realised that she and Tom might never share anything but friendship, but friendship could turn to love, she was sure of it, so she would not give up. As soon as she was able, she would return to the dales, and Tom.

Chapter Sixteen

Tom had been heartbroken when he learned that Ricky had been killed in the same incident which had maimed Tom himself. They had gone through the war together and he found it difficult to accept that the world could keep on turning when his oppo was no longer part of it. However, every time he thought of Marigold's warm and loving embrace on the day she left, he realised what a lucky bloke he was. She had clung to him and promised to return to the dales so that they might be together as soon as they were both demobbed. It meant a great deal to him to have something to look forward to, for though his father had talked of the pair of them going into partnership and buying a market garden he knew they lacked the means to do any such thing.

But what did it matter, Tom asked himself dreamily in the long watches of the night when he could not sleep. He was no longer alone. The girl he had loved, he now believed, ever since they had first met loved him back and together, he told himself, they could do anything.

When the matron told him that he was booked into

a rehabilitation centre in London, where he would be fitted with his new leg and taught how best to live with it, he was complaisant. He would agree to anything if, at the end of it, he would be reunited with Marigold.

It was a grey day and Maddy, waiting impatiently on the station platform for Alice's arrival, found herself wishing that she had something more cheerful to wear than a navy blue skirt and jacket, a cream-coloured blouse and stout walking shoes.

She had been demobbed for several weeks now, for the war had ended decisively when the Allies had bombed Hiroshima, and accepted Japan's surrender. Maddy had heard that Mr Churchill had wept when he had heard of the terrible damage inflicted by what they were calling the atom bomb, but Maddy accepted it had been the only way to finish the war. As far as she could see, if it had not been for that dreadful unleashing, it might have dragged on for months, or even for years.

And because of that dratted Deed of Gift, the O'Hallorans had made it pretty plain that whilst she might continue to live at Larkspur for the time being she was tolerated rather than welcomed. Since she was giving Declan O'Halloran a hand with the kitchen garden, they could scarcely refuse to feed her.

However, things would undoubtedly change now that the war was over. In theory Maddy herself could apply for jobs all over the country and take any which appealed to her, but she still hoped that the Deed of Gift could be overturned somehow and she could stay on at Larkspur with Gran. Perhaps they could employ an out-of-work ex-soldier to help with the kitchen garden . . .

At this point in her musings the train drew alongside the platform with a shriek of steam and the porter emerged from his cosy hideout waving his flag and shouting out the name of the station. The train was almost an hour late and Maddy hardly dared hope that Alice might really have arrived at last, but the crowds of people emerging from the carriages presently parted to reveal a slim figure in a bright blue matching coat and hat lugging a large suitcase, which she promptly dropped as Maddy ran towards her and the two girls fell into one another's arms.

'Alice! You look absolutely wonderful!' Maddy gasped, trying to tug the suitcase, which Alice had picked up as soon as their first greeting was over, out of her friend's hands. 'Let me carry that. I've done nothing for the past hour but walk up and down the platform and wait for your train. I couldn't book a taxi, not knowing exactly when you would arrive, but Mr Gray says if we go straight to his car he'll tell the queue it's a pre-order and they'll have to wait.'

Alice pushed Maddy off her suitcase. 'Darling Maddy, after six years of nothing but letters it's grand to see you again,' she said. 'And I've got a huge favour to ask: the army have given the Hall back to Aunt Ruby but apparently it's in the most God-awful mess. Do you think I might beg a bed from your gran at Larkspur? Just until we get ourselves sorted out, I mean.'

Maddy had anticipated this and had had an argument with Mrs O'Halloran, who had said indignantly that now the farm was hers she could refuse to put up anyone she didn't want, particularly someone who had no intention of paying for her keep. But Gran was growing craftier as she got older and had learned that the mere suspicion of a chesty cough, or an accusation that her rheumatics had been set off again because one of the family had left the back door open, immediately put the O'Hallorans in a flat spin.

They would have liked to hurry things up, to say that the meeting to verify the Deed of Gift could not be delayed any longer, but Gran had reminded them, quite sharply, that she was not yet in her dotage and could remember exactly what the Deed had said. 'You are to take care of me and continue to put my wishes first,' she had reminded them. 'My granddaughter has to be here to look after not only myself, but my interests, so don't you try and arrange things for your own convenience, Eileen, or I dare say you'll be breaking the Deed.'

Maddy, present at the time, had smiled to herself. Gran was no pushover, as the O'Hallorans were learning, and now, as she and Alice climbed into the waiting taxi, she said, 'The evacuees have gone home so there's enough room for both of us, and you're very welcome to stay at Larkspur until the Hall is habitable,' she said. 'Hand over your ration book whilst you're with us, and speak soft to Mrs O'Halloran, and we'll sail through your stay.' Curiosity getting the better of her, she added: 'What exactly do you want to do whilst you're here, Alice?'

'I'm looking for a smallholding, or a market garden, something not too expensive which two men could cope with,' Alice told her. 'Of course, we could farm anywhere in Britain, but we've both got a fancy for the dales. I'm afraid I shan't be much help at first, but I'm determined to learn. If only I'd realised, I'd have joined the Land Army, which would have given me lots of useful experience, but of course I didn't know then how my life was going to turn out. Do you know anything about the price of land, Maddy? We'd need a little cottage or something, and probably around half a dozen acres.'

'But surely your father will finance you, won't he?' Maddy said after a few moments had elapsed. 'Of course you'd be welcome to carry out your search from Larkspur, but surely, now the Hall has been returned to your family . . .'

Alice shrugged helplessly. 'Aunt Ruby intends to sell the Hall as soon as she can get it back into some sort of order, and of course I have no right at all to the land. It had to be handed over to farmers when my uncle went to London, and I'm jolly sure it's too precious to be given back willy-nilly to someone who might make a real mess of it.'

'We're in the same boat then,' Maddy observed. 'Gran's gone and made an arrangement with the O'Hallorans.'

Alice raised her brows. 'An arrangement? What do you mean?'

As succinctly as she could, Maddy explained about the Deed of Gift and her own position, and Alice whistled softly beneath her breath. 'We *are* in the same boat,' she said in a low tone. 'If only my father would listen to reason. But he doesn't approve of my choice of husband, says things like "you're too young to know your own mind" and "I don't approve of the age difference . . . the fellow sounds like a bounder, taking advantage of my daughter."'

'But how can he object, when I'm perfectly certain they've never met?' Maddy cried. 'And as for the age difference, what does that matter?' She seized her friend's arm and gave it a sharp nip. 'I know you have to get your father's permission before you can marry Tom, but . . .'

It was Alice's turn to exclaim. 'Marry *Tom*?' she said incredulously. 'Whatever are you talking about? I'm not going to marry Tom; I'm marrying his father!'

That night, as Maddy lay in bed, she allowed herself to imagine her first meeting with Tom as, so to speak, an unattached male.

She had gone to Windhover Hall as soon as she could when she returned to Larkspur after her demob, and knew that the nursing staff had had to tell Tom, in response to a straight question, that there had been no sign of Ricky after the landmine and it was assumed that his old friend had been blown to bits.

'No one knows for certain what happened to him, but if he is dead, he could have known nothing about it,' a nurse had reassured him. 'Of course I never met him, but I'm sure everyone would prefer a quick, clean end to dragging out an existence terribly crippled and unable to help oneself.'

Maddy turned restlessly in bed, seeking for a cool spot on the pillow. What should she do? Oh, what *should* she do? Now that Tom was free no one would blame her for doing her best to comfort him in his loss, but if she went to the rehabilitation centre Matron had told her about and perhaps tried to find out how he felt about losing both Marigold and Alice, it would look as though she was chasing him, and that was the last thing she wanted. On the other hand, if she did not make a push to gain his interest, he might well turn to some girl more generous and experienced than she could possibly be. She was certain that a kiss was not all that happened between an engaged couple, but try though she might, she could not imagine hurling herself into Tom's arms as Marigold had done that time. What if he met some beautiful nurse at the rehabilitation centre and fell for her, never dreaming that Maddy loved him? After all, she had given him no indication that she was anything but his friend.

Maddy crunched up her knees close under her chin and then shot her legs out straight. What *should* she do? A dozen possibilities raised their heads and suddenly, just as she was on the very verge of sleep, she made up her mind. She would telephone Tom at the rehabilitation centre, ostensibly to congratulate him on his father's forthcoming marriage, and tell him at the same time that Marigold, too, was about to become riveted to her Spitfire pilot. She would tell him that they must go to Marigold's wedding together, for Marigold had promised to invite them both, and then, during the journey, or perhaps even at the wedding itself, she would find out whether Tom was carrying a broken heart in his breast. If only she was more experienced! She had no idea whether it was the done thing to tell a man she loved him; she rather thought not. But she could not afford to waste time in pretence of indifference when her whole being yearned to feel his arms about her, and hear his voice assuring her that she was the one he loved.

Having made up her mind to act, whether for better or worse, she felt as though a great weight had been lifted from her shoulders. So folk would say she was chasing Tom Browning; so what? She jolly well would pursue him, tell him she had always loved him, just hadn't recognised her feelings for what they were, and if he repulsed her, go away from the dales and never come back. Alice and Jim Browning wanted to buy property in the dales and Maddy remembered that, long ago, Tom had talked of going into partnership with his father in a market garden or smallholding. If that happened, and especially if Tom was in love with someone other than herself, Maddy wanted to be far away.

As for me, she told herself defiantly, if only Gran and I could find a way round the Deed of Gift, then I could seriously start work on getting Larkspur back into profitability. I'd get the two older evacuees to come back; Miss Evans told me that despite being boys and pretending indifference, when she saw them off on the train there were tears running down their cheeks, and Herbert leaned out of the window shouting, 'We'll come back, Miss E, we'll come back if we have to walk every mile of the way.'

But of course she couldn't do anything if the place belonged to the O'Hallorans. Maddy sighed, and sat up to turn her pillow over, telling herself that if she did not go to sleep in the next five minutes she would go downstairs, make herself a hot drink and read a book until morning arrived.

But she had scarcely pulled the blankets over her shoulders before the door creaked open and Gran came quietly into the room, carrying a candle whose flame dipped and swayed in the draught of her progress. 'I can't sleep. I don't know why, 'cos I usually drop off the moment my head touches the pillow,' she said peevishly. 'But tonight's different.' She glared across at Maddy, who was trying to feign sleep herself by giving gentle snores. 'And don't you mess with me, young woman, because I know very well you're awake. Just answer me this. If I'd not signed the Deed of Gift, would you and young Tom have got riveted and worked to get Larkspur back to what it used to be? Answer me that!'

Seeing that pretence was useless, Maddy sat up, rearranged her pillow and pointed to the bedside chair. 'Hush, Gran, and sit down,' she said in a low voice. 'That wall is only a wooden partition and for all I know Alice might be a light sleeper. I can't answer for Tom, of course, but I've already told you I would put all my effort into bringing the old place back to what it was in Grandpa's day, if I got the chance. Only there's no use talking, because you gave it to the O'Hallorans, and if they mean to sell it they'll be asking a much higher price than all of us together could afford.'

Gran sniffed. 'Until quite recently I thought Tom was going to marry that flighty blonde piece, or go for the money and take on the Thwaite girl,' she said. 'But remember, Eileen and Declan can't sell Larkspur and go because the Deed says they must look after me.'

'Huh!' Maddy said explosively. 'They could disappear like a teardrop in a puddle, and you with them. They could take you away from here and then

370

abandon you. All they'd have to do is swear you left them. Has it never occurred to you that that might happen? They'd make sure the money had been handed over and just go, and if you think we could get the place back you're completely wrong; it would legally belong to whoever had paid them for it. Oh, Gran, didn't you think of that?'

'Eileen wouldn't . . .' Gran began, but looking at her across the candlelit bedroom Maddy saw the doubt on her face. It was all very well to assume that Eileen would keep her word, but now Maddy could see that Gran was beginning to realise the Deed was a double-edged sword. There was nothing to stop the O'Hallorans leaving provided they took Gran with them.

Gran tightened her lips and got to her feet. 'I've a good mind to tackle Eileen right away,' she said crossly. 'If I could lay my hands on that Deed it'd be confetti two minutes later. So you think they mean to cheat me? Well, I'll see they regret it. But aren't we rather jumping to conclusions? I signed that Deed so long ago that I might have forgotten bits of it. Let's have this meeting with the O'Hallorans and anyone else concerned. Your Tom's a sharp young feller; do you think he ought to be included just in case the Deed isn't as waterproof as they think?'

'He's not my Tom,' Maddy said automatically. 'But you're right; I'd like him to come to the meeting with the O'Hallorans. We'll have to wait until he's

discharged from the rehabilitation place, of course –
Matron said it should be quite soon – but I'm sure the
O'Hallorans won't run until they've got the money
for the property. It's not even on the market yet, so
we're safe for a bit.'

Gran nodded grimly. 'Tell Tom to give us a date
and we'll make sure the O'Hallorans agree to it.'

Maddy nodded also. 'Then we'll have to get the
Deed of Gift from the solicitors . . .'

'It's not at the solicitors,' Gran cut in. 'I remember
now, the O'Hallorans rented a deed box at the bank,
the one on the corner of Skellgate and Westgate; they
said it would be safer.'

Maddy's brow furrowed. 'I wonder why they
thought it would be safer in a bank rather than in a
solicitor's office?' she murmured. 'Well, never mind;
I'll telephone Tom tomorrow and find out when he'll
be free.'

Gran grinned and headed for the bedroom door.
'I feel much better now that we've sorted everything
out. I'll probably sleep like a log,' she said cheerfully.
'I'll tell Eileen what we've decided, and let her know
that if she tries any funny business we'll have the
authorities on her before she can say knife. Not that
she would; she's an honest woman is Eileen, though
Declan may be a little quick off the mark.'

Snuggling down again once Gran had left, Maddy
thought how strange it was that two people could
have entirely different opinions of another. She

thought Declan reasonably truthful and reasonably trustworthy, but she would not have trusted Mrs O'Halloran further than she could throw her – which was not far. Yet Gran, who knew both husband and wife a good deal better than she did, had complete trust in the woman and openly avowed that she thought Declan a slippery customer.

Well, they would soon find out who was right, and with a lovely warm glow inside at the thought of seeing Tom quite soon, Maddy slipped into sleep.

Maddy and Tom had agreed to meet at the Hall, and the previous day she had received a letter from him saying that he would be arriving this very afternoon. Now, as she waited impatiently for his arrival, Alice was explaining how Mr Thwaite still did not approve of her marriage to Jim Browning. 'My father's still being very silly about my marriage,' she told Maddy. 'But he's coming to England some time in the next two or three months, and I'm sure once he meets Jim his whole attitude will change. Not that it really matters, because when you love someone all you want is to be with them, and my father can't prevent our marriage once I'm of age, which is only a few months now.'

'I'm sure when he meets Mr Browning he'll change his mind . . .' Maddy was beginning, then stopped short as the front door was flung open to reveal Tom, in a rather uncomfortable-looking suit.

He came across the hall, his eyes fixed on Maddy,

with a slow, delighted grin spreading across his face. Maddy barely had time to notice that he was walking with scarcely a limp before she found herself in his arms. 'Oh, Marigold, I've missed you dreadfully,' he said. 'I've thought of nothing but your voice, telling me that I'd be all right. You gave me hope, which I thought had gone for ever. I wanted to write, but I didn't dare, in case you had changed your mind and didn't mean to come back to the dales.' He held her away from him, smiling. 'When you left you said you'd come back for *me*. Oh, Marigold, does that mean that you love me as much as I love you?'

Madeleine felt that with almost no encouragement at all she could have climbed Everest, or jumped clear over the tallest tree in the woods. Ignoring the interested gaze of Alice and various helpers, she snuggled, purring with pleasure, into Tom's embrace. 'It means whatever you want it to mean,' she said huskily, 'as long as you remember I'm not Marigold, I'm Madeleine! Oh, Tom, when you called me Marigold in hospital I was so unhappy because I thought it meant you really did love her, and would be heartbroken when you found she was engaged to someone else. What on earth made you think I was her?'

'Oh, darling Maddy, I'm so sorry! When I was just coming out of the concussion, and I was falling in love with your voice you kept saying Marigold, and I thought you were talking about yourself,' Tom said.

'But it was you I was thinking of – I never muddled you up with – well, with Marigold. I love you, Maddy.' He pulled a rueful face. 'And I've so little to offer you!'

'Don't care,' Maddy mumbled against his neck. 'Oh, Tom, this is the happiest day of my life!'

Chapter Seventeen

Once the euphoria of their first meeting as civilians was over, practical things came to the fore. Maddy and Tom left Alice at the Hall and went, with their arms about each other's waists, to the summer house where they sat on the old rustic bench, Maddy cuddling as close to Tom as she could get. Their conversation began with 'Do you remember . . .' but eventually, after they had reminisced and also done a good deal of kissing and cuddling, it occurred to Maddy that she was supposed to be telling Tom all about the Deed of Gift which had stripped her of her rights to Larkspur.

'I need to know the terms of the Deed and Gran's forgotten some of the details,' she explained, 'but we can only look at it when the O'Hallorans are present too, as the other interested party. Gran suggested we might ask you to come with us to check that everything's above board.'

Tom nodded seriously. 'She was right, because I've a good deal of common sense, even if I'm not a legal buff,' he said. 'Are you hoping that the Deed is somehow invalid? Or have you some other scheme in mind to cheat the cheats, so to speak?'

He looked at her hopefully but Maddy was forced to shake her head. 'I've thought and thought, but I've not had any bright ideas,' she admitted ruefully. 'I've begged Gran to try to remember if there were any peculiarities in the document and though I'm sure she's done her best, she's not thought of one single thing. Do you want more time, Tom, before we have the meeting? Only I can't see the O'Hallorans taking kindly to much more waiting about. You see, I'm convinced they'll want to sell Larkspur as soon as they can – it's bursting at the seams already and Mrs O'Halloran seems to have an inexhaustible supply of relatives looking for somewhere to live. If the land is theirs to sell as well they'll be able to afford a much bigger place.'

'I see,' Tom said thoughtfully. 'I suppose we couldn't buy it back? All of us, I mean – you, me, Dad, and my new stepmother? We've all saved like billy-o . . .' He stopped, for Maddy was regretfully shaking her head.

'No, I'm afraid not,' she said. 'It'll be far above our touch, so we might as well arrange to see the document tomorrow and get it over with. It's been kept in the bank, though I'm not sure why.'

Tom frowned thoughtfully. 'If you were to say you thought the Deed had been signed by your gran under duress, might it become null and void?'

Maddy grinned at him, but shook her head. 'If only it were that simple! But Gran signed the Deed in front of a solicitor, so there's no get-out there.'

'Right. Then let's have a look at it as soon as possible,' Tom said. 'We might as well know the worst.'

'Are you all right, Gran? We can easily push the bath chair inside and round to the room where they will have the O'Hallorans' deed box,' Maddy said next morning as they approached the bank.

Gran, however, shook her head. 'Park the damned thing on the pavement; I don't mean anyone to believe I can't walk twenty yards,' she said brusquely. She got slowly out of the bath chair and clicked her fingers at Tom, much as though, Maddy thought, he were some sort of servant. 'Come along, young man, and lend me your arm. I want to get this over as soon as possible.'

Tom winked at Maddy but gave Gran his arm as requested, and the three of them progressed in a stately fashion into the echoing hall of the bank, where the O'Hallorans awaited them. 'Shall I be taking your other arm, Mrs Hebditch?' Declan asked in a conciliatory tone. 'We's promised to look after you for the rest of your natural life, same as we always have done.' He beckoned to his wife. 'You tek one arm and I'll tek the other. Might as well continue as we mean to go on . . .'

'You can leave my grandmother in my charge,' Maddy said frostily. She bent to whisper in her grandmother's ear. 'Keep your pecker up, Gran, and as soon as this is over we'll go to the café in the square and have coffee and biscuits, maybe even scones; you'd like that, wouldn't you?'

Gran sniffed. 'Wait and see,' she said gruffly. 'There's many a slip twixt the whatsit and the doodah.'

The bank manager went ahead of them to open the door into an office, and was only just in time to escape being dug in the back by Gran's walking cane. He had already introduced himself as Mr Rankin, and on the large desk in front of the window stood a deed box with the name *O'Halloran* written on it. Mr O'Halloran lifted the lid with as much care as though it contained gunpowder, and withdrew a most impressive-looking document. It was written on some sort of parchment and bore a number of seals of scarlet wax.

Eileen O'Halloran looked at Gran. 'Is this the document you saw drawed up and signed?' she said. 'Would you care to read them words aloud so that everyone can hear that you weren't tricked or bullied into it?'

Gran sighed. 'All right, all right; I admit I made a dreadful mistake and signed the wretched thing without thinking first,' she admitted. 'Here, Maddy – and you, Tom – you'd best just check that your grandmother is a silly old fool and handed her inheritance to a pair of fair weather friends in exchange for that there mess of porridge, like what it says in the Bible.'

Everyone leaned forward and Maddy, remembering the number of times that in the early days Declan had addressed her grandmother as Mrs Hebdyke, went eagerly to the name at the bottom of the page, only to be disappointed. Declan, aware of his weakness so far as writing was concerned, had got someone else, presumably the lawyer, to fill in the space and there it was, plain as a pikestaff, *Eleanor Mary Hebditch*, printed neatly beneath Gran's own copperplate signature.

There was perhaps two minutes' silence before Gran broke it. 'Well, that's that,' she said resignedly. 'Larkspur is yours, and provided you keep me in good health . . .'

But Tom was clearing his throat loudly, and Maddy looked at him curiously. His cheeks were very flushed and he was grinning broadly. The bank manager had been asked to stay in the room to act as witness to the proceedings, and now he looked from Tom to the Deed of Gift, and then from the Deed of Gift to Tom. 'If there's an irregularity . . .' he started, and Tom put his finger on the first sentence of that noble document and read it aloud.

'*I, Declan O'Halloran, hereby make a Deed of Gift of Larkspur Farm and all its land to Eleanor Mary Hebditch. I shall keep her in good health . . .*' He stopped speaking as Maddy gave a crow of triumph, closely followed by a shout from Gran, whilst Declan O'Halloran stared in complete bewilderment at the words he could not read.

Mrs O'Halloran looked from face to face and then stared at the Deed of Gift as though, if she stared hard enough, it might speak to her, tell her what, if anything, had gone awry. Then she turned to the bank manager. 'What have we been and gone and done wrong?' she said aggressively. 'We had it drawed up and checked over by my brother-in-law what knew a lawyer before it were copied all legal-like by that there Mr Tebbit. Eoin swore there was no mistakes, so why's them Hebditches lookin' so bleedin' pleased with theirselves?'

Tom explained to Eileen that her brother-in-law must have been too intent upon getting the legal wording right to check that he'd got the names in the intended order. 'The Deed should have read *I, Eleanor Mary Hebditch, hereby make a Deed of Gift of Larkspur Farm and all its land to Declan O'Halloran*, whereas your brother-in-law muddled the names so that Declan is making a Deed of Gift to Mrs Hebditch.'

Maddy suddenly clapped her hands. 'That explains why the Deed had to be kept here and not at the solicitors,' she said joyfully. 'Mr Tebbit didn't draw up the document, he just had it copied, so of course it wouldn't be kept in his files. And his clerk didn't spot the mistake because he didn't know what it *should* say. It's a perfectly legal document as it is – or it would be if Declan O'Halloran had ever owned Larkspur Farm!'

There was a long frowning pause before Mr O'Halloran rounded on his wife, his face sharp with annoyance and disappointment. 'That ignorant little

... just wait till I get me hands on him,' he said wrathfully. 'It's all his fault. And if you, Mrs Hebdyke, weren't old enough to be me own sainted mammy ... Well, you won't be seein' us again, so I wonder how long you and your precious granddaughter will be able to stay in the house you've stolen from us. Come on, Eileen – we're away from here.'

The Hebditches and Tom left the bank and went straight to the Splendid Café, ordered coffee and cakes and sat at a small window table to celebrate. 'I feel ten years younger, and not at all sorry for all those horrible O'Hallorans,' Gran said smugly. 'And don't you, Madeleine Hebditch, because they'd have done you out of your inheritance without a second thought. It ain't as if we haven't paid them, because they've not only had my pension but also a weekly wage, and when I've had my coffee and cake I mean to celebrate by having a nice long look at the shops.' She grinned at Tom. 'You can push my bath chair. How about seeing a fillum later, and then getting ourselves a bite before we go home? Oh, I'm that excited! Do you know, I've blamed myself, but of course I always knew that that their Deed wouldn't hold water.'

Maddy was about to say, severely, that they had come mighty close to losing everything when she reminded herself that Gran could never bear to be in the wrong, so she let the comment pass. Instead, she agreed with all Gran's suggestions as to how they should celebrate their lucky escape, for she believed Gran had a very good reason for not wanting to return to Larkspur at once. She would want to give her one-time employees plenty of time to pack up and go.

When Gran pushed open the kitchen door she was not surprised to find the room stripped bare of anything portable. She took a seat by the empty grate, and, looking across the room at the open door which led to the pantry, saw that not so much as a crust of bread remained on the shelves. When Maddy came downstairs from her exploration of the bedrooms, she merely nodded grimly at the news that all the wardrobes had been stripped of their contents, and the little box in which Gran kept her small treasures was empty.

'They only took what they felt was owed,' she pointed out rather guiltily. 'I don't grudge 'em any of it so long as it means they'll never come back. Oh, I know you had a soft spot for Declan, Maddy my girl, and I had many a laugh with Eileen when I was teaching her to cook, but that's all in the past, and best forgotten as soon as possible.' She stared hard at Tom. 'I take it you're going to make an honest woman of my granddaughter? Of course folk will say you only took up with her once you were sure she would inherit Larkspur one of these fine days.'

'Gran, what a thing to say!' Maddy interjected, turning pink. 'It's going to be many a long day before Larkspur is its old self again.'

'I'll speak to the vicar in the morning,' Tom said, grinning. 'No point in waiting, because you know what villagers are like; if I moved into Larkspur without marrying you first, locals would say we were living "ower t'brush". We'll get him to read the banns next Sunday for the first time, and then we'll be able to marry two weeks later. In the meantime I'll see if I can move into our old flat at the Hall. It'll be weeks before Alice and her aunt get Windhover put to rights, so they'll be glad enough if I do some of it for them.'

When Gran finally took herself off to bed after what she called their 'council of war', Maddy and Tom laid their plans for the next few weeks. 'We'll buy geese, for a start,' Maddy said decidedly. 'The O'Hallorans were frightened of them, which I think is why they got rid of them, because they must have known that goose eggs bring in a tidy sum.'

Tom had been scribbling busily on the back of an envelope and now he raised his eyebrows. 'I thought we'd decided to start clearing up at Larkspur before buying stock.'

Maddy shook her head. 'We need the geese to keep strangers at bay,' she said. 'Tomorrow's market day, and there's no point in waiting. I think we ought to have at least one milch cow too, but apart from that I agree with you completely; tomorrow we must start clearing up. Now, it's getting late, so I'll walk back to the Hall with you. I could do with the exercise.' She opened the back door and gazed up at the great silver moon which illumined the scene. 'Oh, Tom, what a night. By the way, can you still ride a bike?'

'Of course I can; it isn't as if I'd lost my whole leg, only from below the knee down, and my peg is pretty efficient,' Tom told her rather indignantly. 'Why? Don't tell me that it's still around?'

'It is. When the military took over the Hall I was still working at the factory, and Mr Thwaite gave me your bike to look after. We kept it round the back, in one of the sheds; the O'Hallorans can't have known it was there,' Maddy said. 'Tell you what, if it still is there you can give me a seater as far as your old flat, and then I can ride home. Oh, Tom, I'm so happy I don't care how long we have to wait, as long as we're together.'

The bike was still there and their plan was carried out, but when they reached the part of the track which ran alongside the beck Tom stopped his smooth pedalling and lifted Maddy from her perch. 'Let's have a look at the bottomless pool,' he murmured. 'When we were fighting in the desert I used to dream of it; in my mind's eye I saw it as it will be tonight, with the reeds silvered by moonlight and the water deep and cool and full of magic. Can you spare five minutes to walk down there so I can relive my dreams?' He leaned the bicycle against a willow's bole as he spoke, then put his arm round Maddy and led her to where the bottomless pool gleamed in the moonlight. They settled themselves in the very spot where Maddy used to sit so long ago, and watched the reflection of the great silver moon in the dark waters.

Tom sighed. 'We never found Charles Kingsley's Vendale,' he said regretfully. 'I suppose we're going to be far too busy putting Larkspur to rights to go searching for it again, though.'

'Oh well, it'll be something for our children to do,' Maddy said dreamily. 'But on a magic night like this, anything could happen.'

They sat on for another ten minutes and then a fish jumped and they saw the silver rings spread outwards and heard the gurgle of the beck as it gradually calmed once more. Tom stood up and gestured to Maddy to do the same. 'We'd best be off before we get moon madness,' he said softly. 'No need for you to come further. If we turn round at this point it's all easy cycling back to Larkspur.' He gave her a hug and then helped her on to the saddle. 'Good night, sweetheart; see you in the morning,' he said. 'I'll be with you bright and early, probably before you've had your breakfast. Sleep well, my darling.'

Tom watched Maddy until she was out of sight but even then he lingered, sure that he could hear the rattling progress of the old bicycle as Maddy navigated her way through the gate and across the Larkspur farmyard. Faint and far distant, he fancied he heard the back door open and close, and only then did he turn his footsteps towards the Hall and the flat above the stables. As he walked he remembered the ripples spreading across the entire surface of the bottomless pool in that magical moonlight. Could it be, he wondered, that the bottomless pool itself was Vendale? And if so, had it been a fish jumping, or . . . but of course it must have been a fish.

Maddy rode the bicycle sedately along the rough and rutted lane, then dismounted to open the mossy five-bar gate. Tomorrow she would ask Tom whether he thought it *was* a fish they had seen leaping from the bottomless pool tonight.

But tomorrow there would be no magical moonlight, and their work would keep them far from the bottomless pool. She had been right when she said that they should leave the search for Vendale and its occupants to their children. After all, the really big adventure would be the one which she and Tom were going to embark on in less than three weeks' time.

Maddy let herself into the farmhouse and crept slowly up the stairs. Despite all her worries, everything had turned out right. She and Tom loved one another and were going to get married. She would leave the mysteries and the magic for their children to discover.

Silent as a mouse, she checked that her grandmother slept, then went to her own room. Tomorrow, she told herself, tomorrow would come soon enough.

Presently, Maddy smiled as she slept.

ALSO AVAILABLE BY KATIE FLYNN

Time to Say Goodbye

Katie Flynn

It's 1939, and three girls meet on a station platform

Imogen, Rita and Debbie missed the original evacuation,
and the village is full, but to their relief Auntie, who runs the
Canary and Linnet pub offers to take them in.

Then they meet Woody and Josh, also evacuees, and find
that by climbing the tallest tree they have a bird's eye view
of the nearest RAF station. They watch the young fighter
pilots as the Battle of Britain rages, though after they find
an injured flier, war becomes a stark reality.

Then, twenty years on, the girls decide on a reunion, and
many surprises come to light . . .

arrow books

The Forget-Me-Not Summer

Katie Flynn

Liverpool 1936

Miranda and her mother, Arabella, live comfortably in a nice area. But when her mother tells her she can no longer afford their present lifestyle, they have a blazing row, and Miranda goes to bed angry and upset. When she wakes the next morning, however, her mother has disappeared.

She raises the alarm but everyone is baffled, and when searches fail to discover Arabella's whereabouts, Miranda is forced to live with her Aunt Vi and cousin Beth, who resent her presence and treat her badly.

Miranda is miserable, but when she meets a neighbour, Steve, things begin to look up and Steve promises to help his new friend in her search, and does so until war intervenes...

arrow books

ALSO AVAILABLE IN ARROW

The Lost Days of Summer

Katie Flynn

Nell Whitaker is fifteen when war breaks out and, despite her protests, her mother sends her to live with her Auntie Kath on a remote farm in Anglesey. Life on the farm is hard, and Nell is lonely after living in the busy heart of Liverpool all her life. Only her friendship with young farmhand Bryn makes life bearable. But when he leaves to join the merchant navy, Nell is alone again, with only the promise of his return to keep her spirits up.

But Bryn's ship is sunk, and Bryn is reported drowned, leaving Nell heartbroken. Determined to bury her grief in hard work, Nell finds herself growing closer to Auntie Kath, whose harsh attitude hides a kind heart. Despite their new closeness, however, she dare not question her aunt about the mysterious photograph of a young soldier she discovers in the attic.

As time passes, the women learn to help each other through the rigours of war. And when Nell meets Bryn's friend Hywel, she begins to believe that she, too, may find love . . .

arrow books